SHATTERED

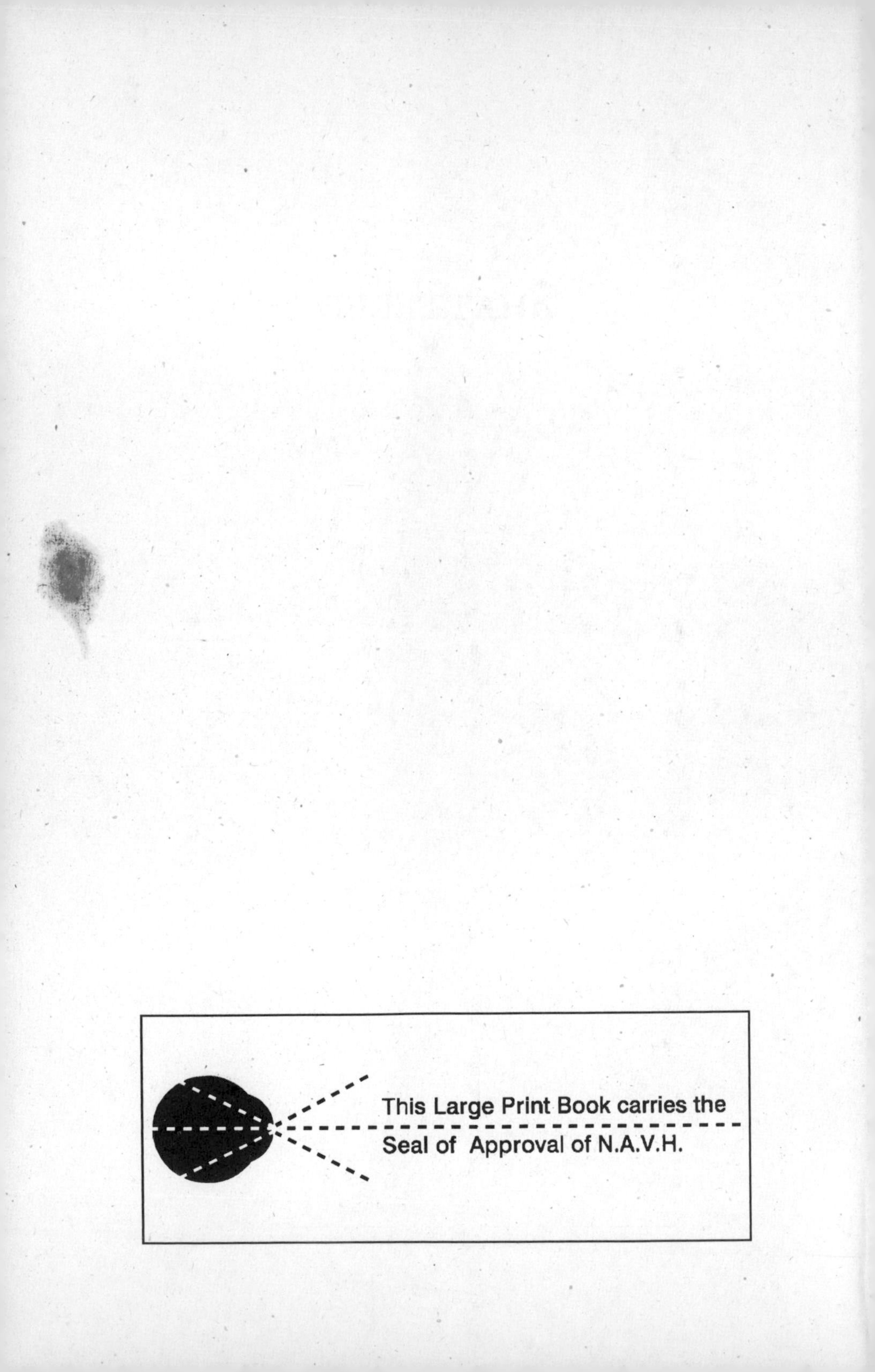
This Large Print Book carries the
Seal of Approval of N.A.V.H.

Shattered

Karen Robards

WHEELER PUBLISHING
A part of Gale, Cengage Learning

Detroit • New York • San Francisco • New Haven, Conn • Waterville, Maine • London

Wheeler Publishing Large Print Hardcover.
The text of this Large Print edition is unabridged.
Other aspects of the book may vary from the original edition.
Set in 16 pt. Plantin.

LIBRARY OF CONGRESS CATALOGING-IN-PUBLICATION DATA

Robards, Karen.
Shattered / by Karen Robards.
p. cm.
ISBN-13: 978-1-4104-2369-6 (alk. paper)
ISBN-10: 1-4104-2369-7 (alk. paper)
1. Young women—Fiction. 2. Cold cases (Criminal investigation)—Fiction. 3. Family secrets—Fiction. 4. Large type books. I. Title.
PS3568.O196S53 2010b
813'.54—dc22 2010001908

Published in 2010 by arrangement with G. P. Putnam's Sons, a member of Penguin Group (USA) Inc.

Printed in the United States of America
1 2 3 4 5 6 7 14 13 12 11 10

To Doug, Peter, Christopher,
and Jack, with love

ACKNOWLEDGMENTS

Thanks go to my wonderful editor, Christine Pepe, who has been a great source of support. I also want to thank my hardworking agent, Robert Gottlieb, and his staff. More thanks to Ivan Held, Leslie Gelbman, Kara Welsh, Stephanie Sorensen, and the entire Putnam family. You've been fantastic as always.

Prologue

May 1, 1981

"Mommy, somebody's watching us from the woods again."

Five-year-old Marisa Garcia grabbed a handful of her mother's pale yellow cardigan sweater as she whispered the warning. The angora knit was fuzzy and soft, and she hung on for dear life, bobbing along behind twenty-nine-year-old Angela Garcia like the tail on a kite as she stared fearfully at the dark shape she was sure she could see hiding in the undergrowth beneath the trees that crowded close to the gravel driveway.

A wind blew through the branches, making them whisper and creak. Marisa looked away, shivering, and tightened her grip on the sweater. There were no lights on in the house yet, no lights visible anywhere because the car headlights were off and they lived out in the country now, with no other houses nearby. Only the moon peeped at them over the swaying treetops, a pale sliver of light that looked as thin as white tissue paper pasted against a dark purple sky.

"There's nobody in the woods, baby." Her mother's tone was of patience stretched thin. Her arms were full of groceries, and she was walking quickly through the grass that was wet from the rain earlier in the day, toward the back door of their small brick house without even bothering to look around at the woods. She thought Marisa was making things up. She always did, because Marisa did make things up. Sometimes.

But not now.

"Yes, there is." But Marisa said it hopelessly, because she already knew nobody was going to listen.

"Marisa's a baby, Marisa's a baby. . . ." That was her brother, Tony, who was almost seven. Swinging the grocery bag he was carrying over his head so that the Cheerios and hamburger buns and bag of potato chips inside threatened to fall out, he danced around, making faces at her.

"*Stop,* Tony." Their mother was grumpy tonight, because they were late getting home. It was already full dark out, which meant it had to be getting pretty close to seven, and her dad got home at seven, and if supper wasn't on the table when he walked in the door, he got mad.

When her dad was mad, he scared her.

Sometimes — she knew it was bad to think it, but sometimes — she didn't really like her dad.

"Here, Marisa, take this." Her mother thrust a grocery bag at her. Her mother didn't like her hanging on to her clothes. Angela was always telling her that, so Marisa knew that her mother's giving her the grocery bag was the signal for Marisa to let go. She did, letting go of the soft knit and taking the bag because her mother wanted her to and she always tried to be good, even if she didn't always succeed.

"I got put in time-out today." Tony said it as though he didn't care. He'd been getting in trouble at school and it worried Mommy. In fact, a lot of things seemed to be worrying Mommy lately. She didn't smile much anymore. Not like she used to.

"Oh, Tony. What did you do?"

Marisa tuned out her mother and Tony and concentrated on carrying her grocery bag, which had the eggs in it, which were important because her mother was trusting her not to drop them. Marisa's other arm was wrapped protectively around Gina, the nearly life-size doll she had gotten for her birthday last week. Gina was so great, a My Best Friend doll that all the girls at home had and she'd been wanting so much but never expected to get because they cost *a lot.* Gina even looked like her, with the same black hair and clothes and everything, and getting her would have made it the best birthday ever, if they hadn't been living *here.* She hated this new house, hated her new school, hated the kids who called her fat even though she wasn't — she was *healthy,* Mommy said — hated that Daddy was living with them all the time now instead of usually being away. But most of all she hated the woods that rose up on either side of the house, looking like big, black chicken-claw hands all winter, and now that the trees had turned green they cast a shadow over the house and yard so that even in the middle of the day it always seemed dark and scary. There were *things* in the woods, creatures with glowing eyes that she could see from her bedroom window at night, and lately there'd been people. She had never actually really *seen* them, not as anything more than dark shadows hiding in among the trees, but she knew they were there. She knew they were mean. She'd tried to tell her mother and brother before, but they wouldn't listen. Now one of the shadow people was back again. She could feel the weight of eyes on her, feel the person's dislike even across the distance that separated them, and she scrunched up her shoulders protectively as she hurried up the back stairs in her mother's wake.

As soon as the door opened, Lucy came bounding out, barking her head off and jumping on them all and then running around in circles because she was so glad to see them. Lucy was their dog. She was big and black and furry — a mutt, Tony said — and they'd had her for as long as Marisa could remember. They'd brought Lucy with them when they'd moved to Kentucky from Virginia last fall. Lucy didn't like Kentucky, either, Marisa knew. They had to keep her locked up in the house all day because this new house didn't have a fence and they didn't have enough money to put one up, and Lucy liked to chase the neighbor's cows. What kind of place had *cows* living practically next door, anyway?

I want to go home, she thought, as they all, Lucy included, piled into the small, ugly kitchen and the light was turned on and the door was safely shut and locked behind them, closing out the night and the woods.

Home was Virginia, a nice white house with lots of other houses around it and only one big tree in the yard. She missed it so much that whenever she thought about it she felt like crying, so she tried not to. But tonight, because it was dark outside and they were late and her dad was probably going to be mad and there was someone in the woods, she thought about home again.

Her chest started to feel all tight, like it did sometimes when she remembered.

"Here, quick, let's get dinner going. Marisa, you can set the table. Tony, get Lucy's leash and take her out in the yard and put her on her chain." Her mother was already ripping the plastic off a package of hamburger meat and dumping it into the big silver frying pan on the stove. From that, and the box sitting on the counter beside the burner, Marisa knew what they were having: Hamburger Helper.

It was okay, not her favorite.

"Be careful. There's somebody out there in the woods," she told Tony as she started to get some clean plates out of the dishwasher, and he took Lucy, clipped to a leash now, so she wouldn't go running off after any old cows, back out into the dark. She'd propped Gina in a corner so the doll could watch. She would have liked to have her sit at the table, but Tony would have made fun of her, and Daddy wouldn't have allowed it. Only her mother understood about Gina.

"There is not, turd brain," Tony said, and her mother sighed.

"I got an award today," Marisa told her mother when they were alone. She didn't like to tell things like that in front of Tony; he would feel bad because he never got any awards, and that would make him *be* bad, and then he would get in trouble, and that made *her* feel bad, so she just didn't do it. The award was a big silver medal that hung from a blue ribbon around her neck, and she lifted the metal disk for her mother's inspection. "For being a blue-ribbon reader. See, it has my name on it."

Her mother stopped stirring the hamburger stuff to look at the medal and then smiled at her. "Wow, Marisa. Good job. I'm really proud of you, baby."

Marisa smiled back. Sometimes, when she was alone like this with Mommy, it was almost as if they were at home again. As if nothing had changed.

"Dad's home." Dragging a trail of mud in with him, Tony stomped into the kitchen, letting in a cool, damp-smelling breeze that fluttered the blue-checked curtains over the sink before he slammed the door. The kitchen was already smelling like cooking hamburger stuff with a whiff of gas from the leaky burner, so the outdoor scent just kind of mixed in.

"Oh." Looking harried, her mother grabbed a can of green beans and a can of corn from the bags that hadn't yet been emptied and jammed the can opener into the top of the beans. The sound of it creaking around the lid joined the sizzle of meat and the thud of Tony's muddy shoes as he kicked them off and, from outside, Lucy's barking. "Go put your pajamas on, Tony, you've got mud all over your jeans. And wash your face and hands while you're at it."

"Lucy kept jumping on me. She got me muddy."

Lucy didn't like being left outside all alone in the dark. She didn't like being fastened to a chain, either. Like Tony and herself and Mommy, too, Marisa suspected, Lucy just wanted to go home.

The beans and corn were in pans, the pans were on the stove, Tony was nowhere in sight, and Marisa had just picked up Gina when Michael Garcia came in through the back door. He was wiry, and he wasn't all that tall, but in his jeans and flannel shirt and boots he looked enormous to Marisa. A baseball cap was jammed on his head and, beneath the brim, his mouth and eyes were tight.

Daddy's mad.

She could tell as soon as she saw him. Clutching Gina tight, sticking her thumb in her mouth, she sidled closer to her mother, and never mind that she'd been told time and time again not to get too close to the stove.

"God, I've had a hell of a day." Looking from Tony's muddy tracks to the grocery bags crowding the counter, and shaking his head at what he saw, he shut the door, then walked into the middle of the kitchen to dump something on the table. Pressing back against the cabinet by the stove, close enough to her mother now so that she could smell the nice scent Mommy always wore to work, Marisa clutched Gina closer and sucked harder on her thumb. "Supper isn't ready yet? You've got to be kidding me."

"I just got home myself." Her mother never acted mad at her dad, never yelled. She simply got quieter when he was around, as if she was trying to stay very calm. Marisa guessed that sometimes her mother was afraid of him, too. "It'll be just a minute."

"What's that you're making?" He looked at the pans on the stove and frowned. "That crap again?"

"Money's tight, Mike."

"You blaming *me* for that?" He sounded so angry that Marisa's throat went dry. She would have clutched at her mother's skirt if she'd had a hand free. But she didn't, so she could only stand there and try to be invisible. "We moved down here to hicksville because of *you.*"

"I know."

Trying to be invisible didn't work, Marisa discovered. All of a sudden her dad's eyes focused on her. Marisa's stomach lurched. When he was in a bad mood, he had to take it out on somebody. Usually it was Tony, because Tony was so much noisier and bigger and harder to miss. But Tony hadn't come back from putting on his pajamas yet, probably on purpose. So that left Mommy and her.

"Get your thumb out of your mouth," he barked, so loudly that Marisa jumped, and he drew back his hand as if he was going to smack her. It scared her so much that she almost wet her pants. She pulled her thumb out of her mouth, then stuck the hand with the wet, glistening, telltale thumb behind her back. She knew sucking her thumb was bad. He'd told her before.

"Supper's ready." Frying pan in hand, her mother turned away from the stove to start dishing the food out on the plates. "Marisa, go get Tony, would you, please?"

Marisa nodded, edged around her mother, and, with a last big-eyed look at her dad, fled the kitchen. Only she walked, because she knew seeing her run away from him would make him madder.

"Don't you start on her, Mike. I'm not going to stand for that."

She could just hear her mother's low voice as she went into the hall that connected the three small bedrooms and bathroom to the living room.

"You're going to stand for any damn thing I tell you to stand for, got that? After what you did, you owe me, and don't you forget it."

"I'm making up for it, aren't I? I'm here."

"You're here, all right. And we both know why."

None of that made any sense to Marisa, and she didn't hear any more, because she found Tony. He was in the living room, curled up in a corner of the couch, wearing his pajamas and watching TV with the volume turned down low, because he didn't want to do anything that might attract their dad's attention unnecessarily.

"Supper," Marisa announced, then added in a confidential whisper, "He's mad."

"He's a dick," Tony said bitterly, and Marisa's mouth dropped open in horror. They weren't allowed to say bad words. But then, Tony never seemed to care about what they weren't allowed to do.

"Tony! Marisa!" their mother called.

Tony got off the couch. "You better leave the doll in here. You know he doesn't like you to carry it around everywhere you go."

"Thanks, Tony," Marisa said humbly, because it was true. Daddy had already yelled at her about it, and he got really mad if he had to yell about the same thing too much. She carried Gina to her bedroom, propped her carefully against the wall by the door, and went in to supper.

Nobody said anything much while they ate, and Marisa finished as fast as she could. When it was over, Daddy said he was going out and left, and the rest of them gave a big sigh of relief.

She helped her mother clear the table while Tony did his homework with them in the kitchen, and then her mother fixed her a bath. She was just getting out of the tub and her mother was just wrapping her in a towel when they heard Lucy barking outside.

"Your daddy must be home," Mommy said with a sigh.

Marisa's stomach got a knot in it.

A moment later came the sound of the kitchen door opening and slamming shut.

"Angie! Angie, you get your ass in here!"

Her mother was still crouched down beside her, still rubbing her with the towel. Her hands stopped moving and she went really still as she looked toward the kitchen. Then she stood up fast, but not before Marisa saw fear flash into her eyes.

"Get your nightgown on and get into bed. Tell Tony I said go to bed, too." Her mother's voice was quiet.

"Mommy." Marisa wanted to hold on to her mother, but she was already gone, her skirt swishing as she moved fast down the hall. By the time Marisa had her nightgown pulled on over her head she could hear her dad shouting, yelling loud, nasty things. Her heart started beating really fast. Goose bumps rose up on her skin with a prickle. Trying not to listen, she picked up her medal and hung it around her neck, then went to get Gina. Hugging the doll close, she started for Tony's room to tell him to go to bed. His door was closed. She thought he probably had it locked, which meant she was going to have to knock, which meant Daddy might hear and come into the hall and see her.

She felt all shivery inside at the thought.

A giant crash from the kitchen made her jump. Then her mother screamed, the sound so loud and shrill it hurt her ears, and her dad shouted. Marisa's heart lurched as a terrible fear gripped her. There was a sharp bang, then another, like firecrackers going off in the house. An icy premonition raced down her spine.

"Mommy!"

She ran for her mother. A second later, Marisa found herself standing in the kitchen doorway, her eyes huge and her mouth hanging open as she looked at the most terrible sight she had ever seen. Her heart pounded so hard she could barely hear over it, and she had to fight to breathe. With one disbelieving glance she saw her dad lying facedown on the floor in what looked like a big puddle of bright red paint and her mother turning to face her with the front of her yellow sweater turning bright red, too, as though something was blossoming on it, some awful flower that was getting bigger by the second as it gobbled her up from the inside out.

Mommy. But Marisa was so terrified now that although her mouth opened and her throat worked, no sound came out.

"Run, Marisa," her mother shrieked, her

face white and terrible. "Run, run, *run!*"

There was another person in the room, Marisa saw, as beyond her mother something moved. Instantly she knew in her heart that it was one of the shadow people from the woods. Seized by mortal fear, she whirled around and ran like a jackrabbit with her mother's screams echoing in her ears, darting through the living room, bursting out through the front door as the cool night air whooshed past her into the house, leaping across the wet grass that felt cold and slippery beneath her bare feet, flying into the darkness as the shadow person gave chase.

There was nowhere else to go: Sobbing with fear, she ran into the woods.

1

"You missed court! The judge chewed Kane out for being unprepared. She ain't happy, and let me tell you, neither am I." Scott Buchanan let fly before the door to his office, which Lisa Grant was, at his direction, closing behind her, was even all the way shut. Knowing she was at fault, Lisa still winced inwardly at the idea that their colleagues — no, her colleagues, because he was the boss — could hear every word.

"I had car trouble." She should have been apologizing abjectly, she knew. She would have been, if her boss had been anyone other than him. Stomach tight, she stopped in the center of the spacious corner office to meet his gaze.

"Bullshit." He stood behind his battered metal desk — no expensive mahogany for this district attorney, the blue-collar man's friend! — glaring at her out of light blue eyes that were, on this Tuesday morning, slightly bloodshot, as though he'd tied one on the night before or, more probably, though she hated to admit it, been working until the wee hours. His short, thick tobacco-brown hair looked as if he'd recently run his hands through it from sheer aggravation. His thick brows beetled over his meaty nose. His square jaw looked even more pugnacious than usual. He had his suit coat off — it was draped over the back of his chair — and the contrast between his white dress shirt and pale blue tie and the tanned skin of his face and neck was marked. He was a wide-shouldered, muscular man of thirty-two who looked like what he was: the son of a no-account, chronically unemployed sometime mechanic, who'd done physical labor all his life until he'd managed to claw his way through law school.

"It's the truth."

His face tightened. "Come here."

From the way he was looking at her she knew he meant it, so she complied, holding her head high as his eyes ran derisively over her, aware that her cool elegance in the face of his wrath and the already sultry late-June heat was maddening to him and taking at least a small degree of pleasure in the fact that this was so. At age twenty-eight, she'd been told often enough that she was beautiful to have a healthy sense of her own attractiveness, and she was perfectly sure he was aware of it, too. Her face was oval and fine-featured. Her eyes were large and caramel-brown, with a slight tilt to them. Her complexion had a naturally tawny tint that meant she only rarely had to resort to fake tans, and her hair, currently twisted into a chignon at her nape, was long, thick, and black as a crow's wing. Her black linen pantsuit looked as though it had cost the earth, and never mind that it was two years old. It fit her tall, willowy form like it had been tailored to it, which it had. The sleeveless white shell beneath was silk. Wearing her expensive Louboutin heels, unmistakable because of their red soles, she still lacked a few inches of reaching his height of six-foot-one, but not many, which she devoutly hoped he found maddening, too.

"Look out that window." As she reached him, he slid a hand around her arm just above her elbow, pulled her a few inches to her right, and yanked the cord of the dusty mini-blinds that covered the big window behind his desk. The blinds shot up with a rattle. Blinking at the sudden onslaught of bright sunlight, Lisa found herself looking out on busy Main Street, the building's front entrance, and the nearly full parking lot. "That's what I was doing about, oh, let's say ten minutes ago, because I got a call from Kane saying you hadn't shown up for court and I was checking to see if your car was out there in the parking lot. Know what I saw instead?"

It was a rhetorical question, and Lisa knew the answer even before he told her. Knowing he was looking at her, she had to suppress the urge to grimace.

"Loverboy in his red Porsche, dropping pampered Princess off at the door. Oh, and let's not forget the five-minute-long goodbye smooch. Pretty steamy, especially when you're a fricking hour and twenty minutes late. What, did the morning quickie run long?"

He let go of her arm. Head high, she moved away from him, walking back around his unbelievably messy desk to stand facing him across it.

"Go to hell." Her voice was perfectly pleasant.

"You're fucking fired." His wasn't.

"I'm sorry, okay? My car really did break down." She desperately needed the job, or she wouldn't have said it. "I had to call Joel" — the man she was currently dating, Joel Peyton, aka Loverboy — "to come and pick me up."

"How about calling in to the office at the same time? Just to say, oh, I don't know, you might be running late." His voice dripped sarcasm.

In point of fact, she had called in and spoken to one of her fellow research assistants, Emily Jantzen, who had promised to grab the needed material from her desk and hurry over to courtroom twelve to cover for her. She wondered what had happened to Jantzen. Something clearly had.

Whatever, there was no way she was getting Jantzen into trouble on her behalf.

"I'm sorry," she said again.

Scott snorted. "You missed court. We don't do that here in the DA's office. That's a big no-no with us." He said it as if he were talking to a slightly stupid two-year-old. "Judges don't like it when we look unprepared. I don't like it. It's un-*pro*-fessional. You ever heard that word before?"

God, she hated to grovel to him. "It won't happen again."

He gave her a level look, and she knew she was safe. From being fired, at least. Well, she hadn't really thought he meant it.

"It better not. You probably don't know it, having just come down from Mount Olympus like you have, but this here is called a job because we work. From eight a.m. on the dot until whatever time the work is finished. Pretty much six days a week. No excuses accepted. Got that?"

"Yes."

"We have to have this talk again, and you'll be out on your ass before the first wheedling little apology gets all the way out of your mouth. Am I making myself clear?"

It was all she could do not to shoot him the bird and turn on her heel. "Yes."

"Great." The phone on his desk began to ring. He picked it up, said, "Yeah. On my way," into it, and hung up again, all without taking his eyes off her. "I don't have the time or the patience to follow you around and make sure you're doing what you're supposed to be doing when you're supposed to be doing it, and I can't spare anyone else to babysit you, either. Until further notice, you're down in the basement sorting through the cold cases. When you get down there, you can send Gemmel up here to take your place. She at least has some kind of work ethic."

That stung. "Scott . . ."

He was already shrugging into his light gray jacket and coming around his desk, heading for the door. Since everyone in the office called one another by their last names, that slip of the tongue had his eyes colliding with hers and holding them for a pregnant instant.

"Baby, you're that close" — he pinched together his thumb and forefinger so that there was maybe half an inch of air between them — "to being out of a job, so I'd watch myself if I were you. I didn't want to hire you in the first place. The only reason I did was because of your mom."

The thought of mentioning that she probably liked being called *baby,* especially at work, even less than he enjoyed hearing her say *Scott* occurred, only to be instantly dismissed. To begin with, the first time he'd called her that had been roughly a dozen years ago, so despite the fact that he was a male DA speaking to a newly hired female attorney currently working for him as a research assistant, it wasn't as demeaning as it might seem. Second, ticking him off any more probably wasn't something she wanted to do right now. No, correction, something she *should* do. Because she wanted to. She definitely wanted to.

"She loves you, too." As annoying as it was to admit, it was the truth. Her beautiful, kindhearted, gentle-souled mother, the owner of Grayson Springs, the storied, thousand-acre horse farm she had inherited

from her wealthy pa
interest in the young s
from the time he'd fi
jobs for them for a c
he was about twelve
time on, as he grew u
spent his summers a
working on their far
invited him into th
meals were prepared
a teenage farm work
been allowed inside t
Martha's say-so) an
was always work fo
looking for it, and ha
things on his behal
knew nothing about
making calls that g
money he'd neede
beyond. That was
when the prestigi
worked for had go
economy and there
in the area to be h
her pride and co
former farmhand r
her girlfriends from
School, the priciest
ton, Kentucky, had
ago wiled away m

s he went about his
xactly been gracious,
job. As a research as-
e more than half her
he'd said, the only
e it or leave it.
she'd been doing a
it, too. The material
in court this morning
nation on the defen-
results, the impact
n — had been com-
ready and waiting in
er to take with her to

n of the six-year-old
had intervened, and
e side of a narrow,
odford County until
hen Joel had arrived.
get out there to see
?" he asked as he

doesn't complain."
She's a fine lady.
ur dad, isn't it?"
opened it, then held
for her to preced
at the low blow –
d, and her relation

e
at
h-
ish
m-
se.

Gaylin, Lisa knew, was the crack-addled suspect who'd been taken into custody the day before, charged with murdering his own grandmother with a hammer when she wouldn't give him any money for dope. The whole office was taking an interest in that one, herself included.

"Let's go." Joining them, Scott strode away without a backward glance. Sally dared to look up then, and gave Lisa a commiserating look.

"You okay? Whatever he said, don't take it personal. He's been in a really bad mood lately." The fact that Sally was almost whispering said volumes, in Lisa's opinion.

"I'm fine."

"A little shaky" would have been a truer answer, but she wasn't about to let it show. Returning Sally's sympathetic smile with a quick, resolute one of her own, Lisa headed for the ladies' room to give them time to get clear. The last thing she wanted to do right now was ride down in the elevator with Scott Buchanan.

It proved to be a mistake. Instead of riding down in the elevator with Scott, she was standing there in front of the elevator bank when a car going up arrived and opened to disgorge, along with half a dozen others, Kane and Jantzen. Assistant DA Amanda

Kane, a hard-charging, pretty platinum blonde of maybe thirty who was wearing a sleeveless navy dress and carrying her jacket along with her briefcase and purse, looked tense. Research assistant Jantzen, an equally pretty but much softer sandy blonde just a couple of years out of college, who was clad in a bright print skirt and pink tee, looked miserable. Both of them spotted Lisa at the same time.

Jantzen's eyes widened. Kane's narrowed.

"Oversleep, Grant?" Kane glared at her. "I guess eight a.m. *is* a little early."

"I'm sorry." Lisa knew the apology was owed, and Kane's annoyance was justified. It didn't make her feel any better about it. Her stomach was still tight from her meeting with Scott, and this was just rubbing salt in the wound. "My car broke down."

"Tell it to Buchanan."

With that she swept on by. Trying not to let her chagrin show on her face, Lisa looked a question at Jantzen.

"As soon as you called, I rushed the folder over there just as fast as I could." Jantzen spoke in a hurried, hushed voice. "I got there maybe ten minutes after court started. She wouldn't take it! Said she'd already told the judge she was unprepared. If you ask me, I think she was just being as difficult as possible to get you in trouble. She is such a *bitch.*"

"You've got to be kidding me." Lisa looked after Kane. She'd thought before that the other woman didn't like her, but this was the first overt indication that she was right. Laying the whole sequence of events out before Scott in an attempt to point out that she was not the only one at fault here instantly occurred to her, only to be as quickly dismissed. It might get Kane yelled at, but it wouldn't make her any friends, or even change Scott's feelings about the screwup, which was, in the final analysis, still her fault. Besides, she wasn't one to carry tales out of school. Her attention shifted back to Jantzen. "Thanks for trying, anyway. I owe you."

An elevator *ping*ed. This one, she saw at a glance, was heading down.

"No problem." Jantzen smiled at her. The doors opened, revealing a couple of people already inside. Jantzen looked a little puzzled as Lisa moved to join them. "Where are you going?"

"The basement. To sort through the cold-case files." Having stepped into the elevator, Lisa turned and made a wry face at Jantzen.

"Oh my God, he's sending you to Siberia!" She gave a nervous giggle. "He does that when he's really —"

Whatever Jantzen had been going to say was lost as the elevator door closed and Lisa was carried ten floors below to the basement, where, in one of the rooms, boxes upon boxes of old files waited to be sorted through. Originally housed in the basement of the venerable county courthouse, the files had been transferred when the prosecutor's office had moved into this building, which was new. Instead of just putting them in storage and forgetting about them, which, among the staff, was felt to be pretty much the consensus of the best thing to do, the files were being reread, checked for any forensic evidence that had been collected at the time for which tests that had not been available then were now available, quickly evaluated to see if anything in them seemed in any way to be linked to any case the county was currently working on, and entered into the computer system for possible future reference.

It was a thankless, seemingly endless job that nobody wanted to do.

The basement was a windowless warren of storage rooms that seemed airless and already felt a little dank, despite the building's newness. The lighting was of the overhead fluorescent variety, and dim. The walls were yellow, the floor a shiny, hard gray. Realizing that she was still on edge from her recent unpleasant encounters, Lisa took a deep breath as she reached the room where the files were stored, then opened the door. When she did, the musty smell of decades-old paper made her nose wrinkle. Brown cardboard boxes were stacked everywhere, rising almost to ceiling height against the walls, piled layers deep so that the only clear space in the room was a path leading from the door to an area around a table near the far wall.

At the sound of the opening door, both Alan Rinko and Tamara Gemmel looked up in surprise. In his early twenties, pale and plump, with short, frizzy brown hair and wire-rimmed glasses, wearing rumpled khakis and a short-sleeved white shirt and red tie, Rinko was a rising 2L spending the summer before his second year of law school interning in the prosecutor's office. A research assistant, Gemmel was maybe thirty-five, tall and wiry, with shoulder-length black hair and a predilection for the color red, which she was wearing today in the form of a short-sleeved blouse with a pair of black pants. In the brief time Lisa had been in the prosecutor's office, she'd developed a liking for Gemmel, who'd done her best to try to make the newcomer feel at home.

"Yo, Grant. What are you doing down here?" Rinko asked. He was sitting cross-legged on the floor with an open box next to him and manila folders piled in his lap. The top folder was open.

"I've been banished." Closing the door behind her, Lisa made a comical face as she advanced toward the table where Gemmel sat behind a computer. With Rinko on the floor to her right and a stack of folders on the table beside her, Gemmel clearly had the job of entering the information into the system after Rinko had first gone through the files.

Gemmel grinned at her. "What'd *you* do to get on the shit list?"

"Was late, among other things. I'm sure you'll hear all about it." She motioned for Gemmel to rise. "I'm supposed to take your place."

"Restored to the land of the living at last!" Gemmel stood up with alacrity. "I've been down here for a week. I was beginning to think nobody else was ever going to screw up."

"Yeah, well, that would be me." Lisa took Gemmel's vacated seat, looked at the screen in front of her, glanced at the open file from which information was obviously being transferred, and stifled a sigh. "What do I do?"

"You don't have to type in everything." Gemmel stood beside her while they both looked at the screen. "Just fill out a form for each file, and give each file a number. Once you do that, you can just scan the rest of the documents in. If anything jumps out at you — you know, something like available DNA that we can do something with — set that file aside. Actually, Rinko is supposed to look out for that. You're just backup, in case he misses something."

"The Rink don't miss nuthin'," Rinko said. "Guaranteed."

Lisa looked at the stack of manila folders beside the computer. "After the information's entered, what do we do with the files?"

"It depends. Tell her, Rinko."

"Most of 'em, the ones we can't do anything with, they go back in the boxes," Rinko said. "Stuff that is still relevant, like a rape case or a murder where we got DNA to test, goes in this blue tub." He jerked his thumb toward a blue plastic tub with a few files in it that sat near the table. "Urgent stuff, like a prior on somebody currently in the can, we're supposed to call up to whichever prosecutor can use it. We've had only one of those since I've been here. Orders are not to destroy anything, or let anything leave this room without permission from above."

"Not God, Buchanan," Gemmel clarified.

"You're impressing me, Rinko," Lisa told him.

"Hey, I've been down here for weeks, so I know this stuff cold."

"That reminds me." Gemmel reached around Lisa for a file that had obviously been set aside at the far edge of the table, plopped it down where Lisa could see it, and flipped it open. "I was gonna call you to come down here and take a look at this anyway. What do you think of that?"

She tapped the open page with a forefinger.

Lisa obediently looked. She frowned at what she saw. Secured with yellowing Scotch tape to the inside cover of the grungy manila folder was a Polaroid snapshot of what appeared to be a family: a young couple, two small children, and a dog. They sat close together on the front steps of a nondescript one-story ranch house, with the adults on the top step and the children, a boy and a girl, maybe six and four years old, respectively, on the bottom. The boy had his arm draped around a big black dog that sat, tongue lolling, beside him. The date, September 2, 1980, was scrawled in fading ink on the white strip at the bottom of the snapshot.

There was a darkness to the picture, a sense of ineffable sadness of the type that often clings to images of people and things long past. Or maybe she just felt that way because, if the picture was taped to a manila folder stored in the prosecutor's office, clearly something bad had happened to somebody in it. But it was not that which made Lisa's eyes sharpen, or caused her to suddenly lean closer.

It was the woman, the mother, who caught her eye.

Clad in jeans and an oversized white sweater, she faced the camera unsmiling, her long, thick black hair blowing a little in what was obviously a breeze, her arms wrapped around her knees.

Lisa's first shocked thought was that she was looking at a picture of herself, as she was right now, taken, impossibly, almost thirty years in the past. Before she had been born, in fact.

2

"What'd you do, time-travel?" Gemmel's tone said she was joking.

"Looks like it, doesn't it?" Lisa was still studying the picture. As near as she could make out — the image was small, old, and grainy — the woman in the picture looked enough like her to be her twin.

"Woo-ooo-ooo-ooo." The eerie bit of tune came from Rinko. Then he added prosaically, "She wouldn't happen to be a relative, would she?"

"The family name is Garcia. The parents are Michael and Angela, the kids Tony and Marisa," Gemmel added.

Her eyes on the picture, Lisa shook her head. "Doesn't ring a bell."

She glanced over at the sheet of paper on top of the nearly inch-thick file. Handwritten, raggedly torn from a yellow legal pad, it appeared to be notes of some sort. What she could understand of it — the handwriting was hard to decipher — didn't tell her much. It looked like a detective's contemporaneous account of an interview with someone who basically stated that the Garcias were a nice family. She lifted it aside. A typewritten list of names, none of which meant anything to her, was next. She suspected it was a list of people the police had either interviewed or meant to interview, but she had no way of knowing for sure.

"So, what happened?" she asked, glancing up. If she knew anything about Gemmel, she'd read everything in the file.

"They disappeared. The whole family, including the dog. Vanished without a trace. One day the husband doesn't show up for work. Neither does the wife. The kids are absent from school. No answer when people try to get them on the phone. Finally somebody goes out to the house to check. They're gone."

Lisa frowned. "So, maybe they just took off."

"That's what the police originally thought. The husband's car was missing, although the wife's car was still there. They could all have piled in and headed out. But they hadn't told anyone they were leaving, and the house was ransacked. Dirty dishes from that night's supper were in the dishwasher, which hadn't yet been turned on. There was water in the bathtub, and a couple of floaty toys, too, and the dirty clothes the girl had been wearing that day were crumpled on the floor beside the tub, which made police think the mother might have been giving the daughter a bath. In other words, if they just took off on their own, all indications were that something occurred to make them leave in a hurry."

"Like what?"

"No clue," Gemmel said. "Unless maybe they were hiding from something or somebody and were afraid they'd been found. The police did follow a couple of leads that the husband was involved in criminal activity, but nothing seemed to ever really pan out."

"Tell her about the blood," Rinko said.

Lisa looked a question at Gemmel.

"There were indications that some blood had been spilled in the kitchen and cleaned up. Actually, a lot of blood. As in somebody bit the big one."

"Whose was it?"

Gemmel shrugged. "If they ever determined that, it's not in the file. Or at least if it is, I missed it."

"Hmm." Conscious of a vague feeling of unease, Lisa glanced down at the file again.

The tiny faces in the picture stared back at her solemnly. The man and boy were, like the woman, wearing jeans. The man had on a navy windbreaker with a baseball cap pulled down low over his eyes so that his hair was hidden and his features were in shadow. The boy was black-haired and handsome in a white sweater like the mom's. The little girl was chubby-cheeked and adorable in a long-sleeved blue dress that might have been velvet, with a lace collar, smocking on the bodice, and white tights and Mary Janes. Her hair was black, too, cut so that it just brushed her shoulders, with bangs almost reaching her eyes. There was something about the picture that Lisa found disturbing, which probably had a great deal to do with the way the woman looked. It was impossible that these people had anything to do with her, of course. Even the close degree of resemblance between herself and the woman might be the result of the small size and slightly out-of-focus quality of the images. If she had a good, clear photo, probably the similarities would come down to coloring and build, and that would be it.

"Weird," she said, closing the file and setting it aside.

"Yeah," Rinko agreed, adding another file

for scanning to the small pile beside the computer, while Gemmel demanded with a trace of indignation, "Is that all you have to say about it?"

Lisa shrugged. "Don't they say that everybody has a doppelgänger somewhere? Maybe this is mine."

"Well, if it were me, I'd sure want to know more, but whatever." Gemmel sounded disappointed. A few minutes later, she left the room, and Lisa got down to the truly stultifying work of computerizing the files.

By the time five o'clock — quitting time in her previous, much lamented position as a rising associate for Todd, Larchman, and Springer — rolled around, her back ached. Her arms felt as if they were ready to fall off. She was seeing purple spots in front of her eyes from staring too long at the computer screen. Conscious that she had been, as Scott had so kindly pointed out to her that morning, an hour and twenty minutes late, she kept doggedly working even after Rinko, groaning and complaining that his butt was numb, got up from the floor and gave every indication that he was ready to call it a night.

"Go on, I'll be fine," she urged him. It was, she saw with a glance at her watch, about ten minutes after six o'clock. By six-thirty, she would have made up the missed time and then some, and Scott could go take a flying leap.

"Yeah, I go off and leave you down here all alone and some psycho comes in and pulls a Jason." Rinko shook his head. "This place was made to be an abattoir. Come on, Grant, use your imagination. Get out while you can."

Looking up from the screen, Lisa had to laugh. "I'd rather not use my imagination if that's where it's going to take me."

"These files aren't going anywhere, you know. I've been down here since the middle of May and haven't even made a dent. I think they reproduce in the dark."

The bit about the files not going anywhere was so true that Lisa was persuaded. Pushing the chair back, she got up and stretched. God, her back was stiff! Her eyes fell on the Garcia family file. She knew that it was ridiculous to imagine that it had anything to do with her, but still she was intrigued by it, by the thought of the family that had so mysteriously vanished, by the resemblance. Maybe they *were* relatives, some sort of distant cousins. Somebody at home might know. At the very least they might remember when the family had gone missing, because it was bound to have caused an uproar in the local media.

"You're supposed to lock up, aren't you?" A lightbulb having suddenly come on in her mind, she grinned at Rinko as she retrieved her purse and briefcase from the floor. The keys he jangled impatiently while he waited for her gave it away. "That's why you want me out of here. You can't lock up until I'm gone."

"Maybe." His answering grin told the tale. "Maybe there's a concert I got tickets to, and it starts at seven. Just maybe, that's all I'm saying."

"What concert?" With a guilty glance at Rinko, who was returning the unread files from the floor to the box from which they had been taken, she picked up the Garcia file and slid it into her briefcase. She would read it tonight on her own time and bring it back tomorrow with no one the wiser and no harm done. She wouldn't even have concealed what she was doing from Rinko — who couldn't have stopped her, in any case — except she didn't want him to get in trouble if anyone found out she'd borrowed the file.

"Dead Vampires. They're playing with Scooter Boys and La Gordita."

Those were, as Lisa kind of vaguely thought she knew, local bands.

"Sounds lovely." She led the way out of the room, waited while he turned off the lights and locked up behind her, then walked with him to the elevators.

"Should be great," he agreed.

"Rupp Arena?" she asked as they stepped into an elevator, thinking of the traffic that would clog downtown if this main venue for the performing arts and every other big event, including, and most important, University of Kentucky basketball, was involved.

"They wish." He shook his head. "It's outdoors, at Frawley Park."

"Do you have a date?"

"Just hangin' with friends."

The elevator stopped, and they, the only two in it, stepped out into the building's vast, echoing, marble-floored entry court and joined the stream of stragglers exiting the building. The warm, mellow sunshine of a late-June evening spilled over them as they pushed through one of the many tinted doors that formed part of the long front wall of amber glass. The textured concrete beneath their feet still retained enough heat to fry an egg, the sun still hung like a blaze-orange tennis ball a few feet above the horizon, and the inside of the Jaguar, which had been repaired and delivered to the parking lot while she worked, would be hot as an oven. But these soft, golden evening hours were what made summer magical in Kentucky's bluegrass region. They were what Lisa had missed most when she had gone away to Wellesley College in Massachusetts and from there to Boston University School of Law, then to a fast-track job as an associate in one of Boston's premier law firms. She had come home last October because of her mother, but this, her first summer spent in the South in years, reminded her why, when the time had first come for her to go away, she hadn't wanted to leave.

"It's a beautiful night for it," Lisa said.

"Yeah."

" 'Night, Grant, Rinko." Jantzen spoke over her shoulder as, juggling an armful of books and files as well as a briefcase and her purse, she hurried past them and toward the parking lot.

" 'Night," she and Rinko called back in unison.

A glimpse at the wistful expression on Rinko's face as he looked after Jantzen's swinging blond hair and swaying skirt provided Lisa with a surprising revelation: He had a thing for Jantzen.

"Go offer to help her carry some of that

stuff," she urged Rinko in an undertone.

Glancing at her in some surprise, as though he was suspicious that she might somehow, mysteriously, have divined his secret, he shook his head.

"Nah. She's got it under control, and anyway, I got to get to my concert." They had reached the parking lot by that time, and Rinko, lifting a hand in farewell, turned right toward his ancient Dodge Caravan while Lisa proceeded straight ahead to where the man from the dealership had told her he'd parked the Jaguar. "See ya tomorrow."

"Enjoy your concert."

Fifteen minutes later, Lisa had left the small but vibrant city that was Lexington behind. Once across the old two-lane bridge that arched over the Kentucky River, a sleepy expanse of muddy green water that was a favorite of local fishermen, she was in Woodford County. The leafy back roads that led to Grayson Springs were narrow and winding, distinguished by a series of picturesque bridges that arched over meandering streams and lined with mortarless stone walls that had been constructed by itinerant Irish masons some two hundred years before. Farms, small and large, dotted the landscape, ranging in type from the hardscrabble six-chickens-and-a-cow ones that could no longer eke out a living for their owners to the mansions and climate-controlled stables and vast acreage of the premier Thoroughbred operations, of which Grayson Springs had once been a crown jewel. On all sides, lush fields of Kentucky's fabled bluegrass rolled away for as far as the eye could see. As Lisa had several times had to explain to disappointed friends visiting from college, the bluegrass wasn't really blue. It was as green as the grass anywhere, except on certain days when the wind blew in the right direction and the light was just right and . . . well, suffice it to say that ninety-nine percent of the time, the bluegrass was green. But whatever color it was, it was absolutely ideal for raising the best racehorses in the world, and for generations now that was the use to which it had been put.

This place was, Lisa had often thought, one of the last refuges of aristocracy in America. People here knew one another's lineage, and who you were mattered. If you weren't the son or daughter of one of the upper-crust families, then you were to all intents and purposes invisible, just a worker bee toiling in the hive of ordinary life. Some of the wealthiest people in the world lived here, or had second homes here, or visited often. The Queen of England spent a nearly annual vacation at Lane's End, another of the top-flight Thoroughbred farms, whose owners were among Her Majesty's closest friends. The rulers of Saudi Arabia were regulars at the local horse sales, and they snapped up prime breeding stock for prices that brought smiles to the faces of the consignors. Hollywood icons, famous European fashion designers, and billionaire businessmen alike lived in quiet splendor on vast properties that no one outside this little enclosed world knew they owned. So many top-of-the-line private jets flew in to Blue Grass Airport that its commercial operations were secondary to its real function, which was catering to the elite. Lexington's fabled Keeneland Race Course catered to the moneyed few and was far too swanky to allow itself to be referred to as Keeneland Race Track.

It was beautiful, anachronistic, and home sweet home. She'd been back for only eight months, and she was ready to swear she could feel her bred-in-the-bone southern gentility rising in her veins like sap.

Sometimes she longed for Boston like she longed for a cool breeze in the midst of all this cloying heat. One day, when everything here was settled, she meant to go back and pick up the pieces of the life she had made for herself there.

Lisa was jolted back to the present by the sounds of Beethoven's Fifth Symphony emanating from her purse. It was her ringtone, and as she fished her cell phone out she saw that the caller was Joel. A junior partner in his wealthy father's real estate development company, he'd flown with his father to Chicago, where they had business that would occupy them overnight, after dropping her off at work.

"Just calling to check in," he said when she answered, and she guessed that he had only just arrived. Bronzed, blond, and handsome enough to star in a Ralph Lauren ad, Joel was another offspring of the elite. His father was a close friend of her father's, which meant she'd known Joel forever. They were the same age, he'd been part of the wild crowd of rich kids she'd run with in high school, and back then they'd dated for just long enough so that he'd been the one to take her to her senior prom. When he'd asked her out not long after she'd gotten back to town, she'd seen no reason not to say yes. Since then, she'd been seeing more and more of him. He'd made it pretty clear lately that he wanted to take things to the next level — i.e., he wanted them to have sex — but she wasn't quite ready for that. In her experience, sex plus guys added up to big, messy drama sooner or later, and she had too much on her plate right at the moment to indulge in what — unless she meant to stay in Lexington permanently, which she didn't — couldn't ever be more than a fling.

"How was your flight?" she asked.

"Fine. Did you get your car fixed?"

"I'm driving it home right now."

"That's good. Anything interesting happen at work?"

Lisa thought about telling him that she'd nearly been fired, but that would mean bringing Scott into it and, given that the two had never liked each other, that would involve a more intense conversation than she wanted to have. Instead, she told him about the Garcia file and how much she resembled Angela Garcia.

"Before you start reading all kinds of things into it, you probably ought to take a closer look at that picture." Joel's voice was dry. "A blurry Polaroid doesn't sound too reliable."

"I brought the file home with me. I could drop the picture off at Walgreens on the way into work tomorrow and have it copied and enlarged." The idea had just occurred, but it was a good one.

"Sounds like a plan," Joel said. Then Lisa heard someone say something in the background, and he added, "Dad says hi."

"Tell him I say hi back," Lisa responded. Sanford Peyton had never been one of her favorite people — besides being a friend and business associate of her father's, he tended to treat Joel as if he were ten years old and incompetent, and had always seemed to disapprove of her — but she could be polite.

"Listen, I've got to go. I'll be back late tomorrow. Don't forget we're going to the country club on Saturday if I don't see you before then. I'll pick you up at seven."

"I'll be ready." Lisa said good-bye and disconnected. The coming Saturday was the Fourth of July, and the club sponsored an annual buffet, dance, and fireworks display in honor of the holiday. It was a popular event, always crowded and always fun. Most of her friends who were still in town would be there. She only hoped nothing came up at work to keep her from going. Weekends, particularly Saturdays, seemed like something of a theoretical concept to nearly everybody in the prosecutor's office.

The Fourth of July was a national holiday, however, which should mean something. If not, she would just plan to lie through her teeth about the reason she couldn't work if she was asked to.

Turning over possible foolproof excuses, she was absentmindedly watching the antics of a field full of frisky yearlings when the Jaguar hit a pothole and died. Just like that. Bump and out.

"Oh, no," she moaned, listening to the complete cessation of engine noise with dismay.

She barely had time to steer the car to the side of the road before it stopped dead.

"Piece of junk," she muttered.

Shifting into park just because she thought she should, she looked despairingly at the fuel gauge in hopes that the fix could be as simple as that. No such luck: The thing read full, so unless the gauge was as faulty as nearly everything else on the car, the cause lay elsewhere. Probably, Lisa thought, in the transmission the dealership had supposedly just fixed. The car wasn't even hers. It was her mother's. Martha Grant had always driven a Jaguar, time without end, and this was the last one she had bought before she had started to exhibit the symptoms that eventually led to her being diagnosed with ALS four years before. It was, unfortunately, not suited for transporting a woman in a wheelchair, which her mother now was, so Lisa had traded in her own reliable Honda for a van roomy enough to serve the purpose. With the farm's finances in the state they were in, they couldn't afford another car, and she wouldn't dream of distressing her mother by getting rid of one more symbol of the way things used to be.

Which meant she got stuck with the Jag.

Lisa was fumbling in her purse for her cell phone when the sudden opening of the driver's-side door made her jump and squeak with alarm.

3

Even as Lisa's heart shot into her throat and her gaze darted around to discover who was accosting her on this lightly traveled country lane, she recognized Scott with a rush of relief.

"Problems, Princess?" His voice was dry. With one arm resting on the roof, he leaned down to look at her sardonically through the open door.

The annoying part was, she was actually glad to see him.

"The damned thing just stopped. I told you this morning I was having car trouble, so maybe now you'll believe me. And don't call me Princess."

His lips thinned. "Want to turn off the ignition?"

As she complied, he moved away from the door and rounded the fender to stand in front of the car.

"Pop the hood," he called, looking at her

through the windshield.

She did; then, as he lifted the hood and disappeared behind it, she got out, closing the door and walking around to join him. A distant droning told her that although she couldn't see it, somewhere in the vicinity farm machinery was at work. The faint, sweet smell of just-cut hay provided a soft undertone to the more acrid scent of something burning. That something being, she very much feared, a vital part of her engine.

Damn it, anyway.

Having shed her jacket when she'd gotten into the car, she welcomed the evening's heat as it caressed her air conditioner–chilled bare arms. Scott, too, had shed his jacket, she saw. His shirtsleeves were rolled up to his elbows, and he'd lost the tie and unbuttoned his shirt at the throat. A narrow black belt circled his trim waist, anchoring his gray suit pants just above the hipbones. Bent over the engine, he was jiggling wires and loosening caps. Reluctantly, she noticed, as she had countless times many years before, that he had a nice butt, small and tight and as toned as an athlete's.

She believed that she just might have told him so, on one memorable occasion when she'd been an arrogant and hormone-fueled teenager. In fact, she knew she had. Her exact words had been "Nice ass" when she'd come across him, clad in shorts and a sweaty T-shirt, bent over a recalcitrant lawn mower. His reply? A scornful "Go play with your dollies, little girl."

The memory was embarrassing, and she immediately did her best to banish it.

"You got a loose battery wire. That's what made the car stop," Scott said from under the hood. "I fixed it."

"So, I'm good to go?" she asked hopefully. He was handy with engines of all types, so she wasn't really surprised. Being the son of a mechanic, though in the case of this particular mechanic it definitely came with its own set of issues, had an upside to it. From the time he first got his license at sixteen until, as far as she knew, just about now, he'd driven a series of junkers, but he'd always managed to keep them running. She'd known him to fix kitchen appliances, the occasional broken air conditioner, and farm machinery of all types.

"Nope." Tightening a cap he'd loosened, he straightened to look at her. "The big problem is you're out of transmission fluid. Lucky you didn't burn the thing up."

"They just worked on the transmission today!"

Disengaging the support, he shut the hood

with a *thunk.* "Well, either they forgot to put the fluid back in or you've got a leak. You're lucky the battery wire came loose when it did or you'd need a new transmission. Come on, I'll give you a ride home. Unless you want to wait here for Loverboy?"

Annoyed by this reference to Joel — which was, she knew, his intent — Lisa trailed him back around to the driver's-side door. By the time she got there, he had already opened it for her.

"Joel's out of town. And by the way, FYI, a word to the wise, Mr. District Attorney: Calling people names like Loverboy and Princess comes across as just a little bit juvenile," she said. He was leaning against the rear door with his arms folded over his chest, watching her approach. "Maybe it's time you outgrew it."

He laughed as she ducked inside to collect her things.

"You bring it out in me. Probably because having you around dredges up all those old juvenile memories. Hey, remember the night when your mom called me over to fix the air conditioner, and you and your girlfriends — there were five of them, weren't there? You must have been having a slumber party — decided to beat the heat by stripping off and going skinny dipping in the pool right where I could see? Wasn't it you who yelled out, 'Hey, stud muffin, quit looking and come and join us?' "

Removing her keys from the ignition, juggling her belongings, Lisa felt her cheeks heat even as she emerged from the car to glare at him.

"It was Nola, and you know it." Nola Hampton had been her best friend for as long as she could remember. "We were *sixteen.*"

"Believe me, I was aware. Only the word that kept popping into my mind at the time was *jailbait.*"

"Is that why you didn't come swimming?" Forced mockery infused her tone as she shut the door with a swing of her hips. Another embarrassing memory with the power to make her squirm, but she'd be boiled alive before she'd let him know it.

"Absolutely." His grin broadened as their eyes collided. "Try me now."

For a moment her heart beat faster at the thought, even though she was pretty sure he didn't mean it.

"Not gonna happen."

Glad of the excuse to drop her eyes, she pushed the button on the key ring, locking the door with a beep. As she did, she lost her grip on her briefcase. It hit the pavement with a thud that popped the lock and then tipped it on its side, with about half the contents fanning out through the opening.

"Oops," he said.

"Damn it!" Juggling purse, jacket, and keys, she crouched to shove the contents back inside and retrieve her briefcase. Scott was before her. Lisa took one look at his big, tanned hands on the partially disgorged items, remembered the Garcia file that was on top and impossible to mistake because of the red label on the tab, which all the prosecutor's files bore, spotted it, and felt her heart start to beat faster as she waited for the inevitable explosion.

It didn't come. Instead he pushed the files and papers back inside the briefcase, clicked the lock shut, and stood up with it. If he'd noticed the file, he gave no sign.

Lisa let out a breath she hadn't realized she'd been holding. She didn't think he would actually fire her, but she wasn't positive. Getting caught taking a file from the prosecutor's office without permission was a good way to find out.

"I hate to hurry you up, but I need to be getting a move on."

He headed back toward his black Jeep, which was parked behind the Jaguar, as he spoke. Putting her briefcase in the backseat, he opened the passenger door for her before walking around and sliding behind the wheel.

"What are you doing out this way, anyway?" she asked as they got going. She'd forgotten, briefly, that he no longer lived in the farmhouse next door to Grayson Springs, where he'd grown up.

"My dad called about an hour ago." He didn't have to say anything else for her to instantly get the picture. The thing about embarrassing memories was that they went both ways. Most of his probably centered on his father, a raging alcoholic who'd thought nothing of beating his sons — Scott had an older brother, Ryan — when they were growing up, or firing off shotguns for no reason, or driving around drunk in their old pickup, screaming obscenities out the window. "He wasn't making a whole lot of sense, but I thought I'd better come check things out."

"Oh." The syllable acknowledged the fact that Bud Buchanan — *Mr. Buchanan* was how Lisa still thought of him — was probably out-of-his-mind drunk when he'd made the call. Given the way Mr. Buchanan had treated Scott — she could remember him sporting countless black eyes and fat lips, which gossip had laid at his father's door — she thought it said a lot for him that he was still taking his father's calls, much less driving all the way out to Woodford County after work to check on him.

"How's it going living at home again?" Scott asked. Clearly he had no wish to talk about his father or whatever problem he was having that might have precipitated the call, and she respected that.

"It's okay. A little claustrophobic, but I'm glad to have the time with my mother." Her mother's diagnosis was terminal. The only question was, how long did she have? Lisa hoped years, but she feared it might be much less. "Given the circumstances, there's nowhere else on earth I'd rather be."

"Yeah." Scott's answer, too, acknowledged a truth that they both knew. Martha Grant had been a wonderful, loving mother to her sometimes undeserving daughter, just as she had been a staunch friend to him.

Lisa remembered something. "So, did Gaylin confess?"

There was a pause as he shot her a quick surprised look. Then his mouth curved wryly. "For a second there, believe it or not, I had no earthly idea how you could have known that."

"Jungle drums." Her tone was light.

"No, I mean, I clean forgot you're an honest-to-God lawyer now. Who would have thunk it? I look at you, and I automatically think of that spoiled-as-hell teenager who followed me around for a couple of summers, practically begging me to do something illegal to her."

"I've grown up," she said shortly. "It'd be nice if we could move past our shared memories. I'll make you a deal: I'll forget them if you will."

His gaze flicked toward her, and then he smiled, a slow, lazy smile that had her narrowing her eyes at him.

"Nah, remembering's too much fun."

Lisa refused to lose her temper. "Did Gaylin confess or not?"

"Yeah, he confessed. Even told us where he hid the murder weapon. After we cut him a deal. No death penalty."

"He wouldn't have gotten it, anyway. Any good defense lawyer would have argued diminished capacity and then put half a dozen weeping relatives on the stand to testify about what a good boy he was really, and how Granny wouldn't have wanted to see her grandson executed."

"That's what I figured. Plus, he's nineteen. Eighteen when he committed the crime, which would have given the defense another angle. And he agreed to life."

"He'll be out in fifteen."

Scott shrugged. "The legal system's —"

He broke off as they reached the fork in the road where the lane joined the larger Mount Olympus Road. His face changed, and his hands tightened on the wheel. Glancing around to see what he was looking at, Lisa was able to see, down the way, the Buchanan farmhouse, which was at the top of the long drive leading down to Grayson Springs. A quartet of police cars was parked in the scrub-grass yard, strobe lights flashing. A uniformed cop could be seen hurrying up the steps to the house.

"Uh-oh," she said.

"Shit." Scott turned toward home and sped up.

4

"Do me a favor, would you? Drive yourself the rest of the way home, and I'll come by and collect my car later."

Mouth tight, Scott glanced at Lisa as he braked, then slid the transmission into park at the top of the paved drive that led down to her home. To his right, three police officers were now dragging his struggling, handcuffed father, clad in a wife-beater and baggy black pants and cursing at the top of his lungs, out of the run-down white farmhouse where Scott had grown up.

Lisa barely had time to say "Sure" before he got out of the car, leaving the door open for her, presumably, to take his spot behind the wheel.

"Settle down, Dad," he called sharply, striding toward the scene of the fracas as she got out, too.

"You no-good piece of shit, where the hell have you been?" The cops were force-marching Mr. Buchanan down the steps as he turned his vitriol on Scott. Lisa, trying not to hear, walked around the front of the car. "Think you're too important now to come over here and help me out when I call you? If it'd been you who'd come through that door, I'd have taken a shot at you, too. And I would have been pissed as hell that I missed."

Lisa winced.

"Shut up, Dad."

Scott's voice was hard, his body tense, his hands curled into near fists at his sides. If he remembered her existence as he crossed the yard toward where the little group had stopped to wait for him at the foot of the steps, he gave no sign of it. She understood. With herself and the cops as witnesses, this was embarrassment on a far higher order than any she had ever experienced, and she had little doubt that there was pain connected to his father's nonstop boozing mixed in there somewhere, too. This was trouble, but it was Scott's trouble to deal with, an ongoing burden he'd been carrying for his entire life.

"What's up, guys?"

This question Scott addressed to the cops, who were clearly doing their best to control their belligerent prisoner without resorting to violence. Beth didn't wait to hear the reply. Instead of lingering to add to Scott's problems, she got into the Jeep and drove away. But not before she saw the whole group talking at once as Scott reached them.

He was the Lexington-Fayette County DA, but this was Woodford County. He had influence but no authority here. As she drove on down the lane, she wondered if he would be able to convince the cops to let Mr. Buchanan go. Then she wondered what the mean old man had done to get the cops called on him. With no kids left at home to beat up and his wife long dead, there wasn't a lot he could do to attract police attention at home. He'd said something about shooting at Scott. Since that hadn't happened, he'd probably taken a shot at somebody else.

Whatever, she had little doubt that Scott would deal with it, just as he'd dealt with all kinds of problems having to do with his father over the years. In the meantime, she had problems of her own, first and foremost of which was a broken-down Jaguar. Fishing her cell phone out of her purse, she called Triple A and arranged to have it towed back to the dealership that was supposed to have fixed it. For tomorrow, she supposed she could take the farm truck. Or, well, she'd work something out. The key was not to be late for a second day in a row. At the idea of facing Scott again under those circumstances, she grimaced.

Grayson Springs was maybe half a mile in distance but light-years in every other respect away from the five-room, two-story farmhouse with the saggy front porch and leaky tin roof where Scott had grown up. Her own home, she thought, as it came into view at the bottom of the oak-canopied lane, was the very picture of an antebellum southern mansion. Surrounded by undulating acres of grassy fields crisscrossed with miles of four-board white fences, Grayson Springs was a white-painted stone house with front double porticos supported by soaring Grecian columns that stretched up more than forty feet to the slate roof. It looked like something that belonged in *Gone With the Wind.* The original part of the structure, the main house, had been built before the Civil War and was three stories tall. The two-story wings, one on either side, had been added later. There were more than twenty rooms, not counting bathrooms and pantries and connecting hallways as large as rooms and the odd little nooks and crannies common to old houses. Most of them were unused now. The size of the place meant that the utility bills were outrageous, as Lisa knew only too well because she now paid them. Another half-mile or so behind the house were the barns, four of them, once the heart of the operation that had made the name Grayson Springs revered in horse-racing circles and now empty of Grayson Springs–owned horses except for her mother's twenty-eight-year-old mare, Firefly. A host of factors, from the crashing economy in general to the savage downturn in the Thoroughbred industry in particular and including the long decline in its owner's health, had led to the present sorry state of affairs. Its horses sold off, mortgaged to the hilt, its glory days no more than a memory, Grayson Springs teetered on the edge of bankruptcy. Lisa had little hope of saving it beyond her mother's lifetime. But as long as Martha Grant breathed, Lisa would do everything in her power to keep them all in the house, the bank at bay, and the property unsold. Lisa was determined that her mother's last days, however many she had left, would be spent in the home she loved, unclouded by the knowledge that the trust funds set up to secure their futures were all but gone, casualties of bad management and the tsunami known as the Great Recession that had so recently rocked the financial world. She was fairly confident that when the farm was eventually sold, as it would have to be, it would bring enough to pay off the mortgage that had most ill-advisedly been taken out when the income had started to drop, and the other debts as well, but there would be precious little, if anything, left over. What she was going to have once her mother was gone was what she could earn for herself, and no more, which wasn't the greatest news she had ever heard but was something she could deal with. Most likely she would move back to Boston, where a lot of her law school classmates had settled and where she could reasonably hope to find work as a full-fledged attorney again rather than being stuck earning a less than adequate living as a research assistant due to the lack of jobs. In any case, until that happened she meant to do what she could to keep things going here until there was no longer any need to pretend that life was the same as it had always been. She had leased the barns and fields to a nearby Thoroughbred operation so that, from her windows, her mother saw as many horses about the place as she always had. She did her best to keep up the gardens, with their winding brick paths, where Robin Baker, the family's longtime employee, pushed

Martha every pretty day in her wheelchair, and the yard and the house. If they no longer entertained lavishly, well, as far as anyone knew, that was because of her mother's health and Lisa's own disinclination. If the full-time staff had dwindled to two, they were the two Martha most counted on. Robin and her brother, their erstwhile farm manager Andy Frye, who, at sixty-six, stayed on with them as kind of a groundskeeper cum jack-of-all-trades because he had worked for Grayson Springs for most of his adult life and was, as he said, too old now to make a change, had over the years become almost family. Keeping Martha's world intact until she no longer needed it was, Lisa felt, the least she could do for the mother who had adored her all her life, and whom she adored in turn.

I'll be sad when all this is gone. When Mother's gone . . .

Even the thought made her throat tighten, and resolutely she pushed it away. She wasn't going to think about that. Not now. Not until she had to.

As she pulled the Jeep up under the porte cochere and got out, a glance at the asphalt parking area just a little farther on told her that the workers were still there, repairing the damage from the tree that had come crashing into the roof of the north wing during a violent thunderstorm the previous month. They'd finished fixing the roof last week and had moved on to repairing and painting the ceiling of the bedroom the tree had lodged in. It wasn't too far from her own room, so she supposed she ought to consider herself lucky that it hadn't been hers that had been hit. The thing was, though, their homeowner's policy had a big deductible, and she was going to have to figure out some way to come up with the funds to pay that part of the bill.

Chalk up one more headache.

"Whose car you got there?"

Andy's voice had her head turning to find him. Tall and spare, his military-cut hair a reminder of a youthful stint in the army, his face deeply lined from years spent working in the sun, he was on the back porch, which was connected to the porte cochere by a set of steps and ran the full length of the back of the house. His arms were full of flowers. The vibrant oranges and whites and purples of the mixed lilies and hydrangeas and butterfly bush blossoms were one of the signs of summer she loved the most. As determined to keep Martha from finding out the truth about the farm's precarious state as Lisa was herself, Andy had been working in the garden, she knew, and was bringing the flowers in for her mother. Like everyone else, Andy had benefited from Martha's kindness over the years. He was another of those who loved her dearly.

"Scott Buchanan's. The Jag broke down again, and he gave me a ride home."

Andy glanced past her, toward the car, then lifted his eyebrows at her questioningly as, heading for the kitchen door, she joined him on the porch.

"So, where is he?"

"At his house. Scott got out there. There was some problem with his father." No need to tell anyone about the police being at the house. That was Scott's business, to disclose or not as he chose. "He'll walk down to pick up his car later."

"What's the old bastard up to now?"

He was referring to Mr. Buchanan, whose proclivities were common knowledge.

"The usual. Drunk and mean."

"Cracker." Uttered in a contemptuous undertone, the term was beyond derogatory. Lisa didn't reply but instead turned the conversation in another direction.

"Andy, do you remember hearing about a family that disappeared around here about, oh, thirty years ago? Their name was Garcia. A couple and two children."

He frowned, then slowly shook his head. "Can't say that I do. Why?"

"Oh, nothing. Just a case I came across at work. I was curious, that's all. Listen, I'm probably going to have to take the truck into work tomorrow. Can you manage without it?"

"Sure. You know where the keys are kept." On the hook in the kitchen beside the refrigerator, which was where all the keys to all the vehicles were always kept. Andy's face creased in a smile. "That's going to be something to see, you in your fancy clothes driving into your fancy office in that old truck."

"Hey, a girl's gotta do what a girl's gotta do." Lisa smiled in turn, though the idea of driving the mud-spattered farm truck to work was a little ego-deflating. She only hoped that no one would be around to see her park and get out.

With Lisa in front, they'd reached the kitchen door by this time. Opening the creaky screen door and then pushing the wooden door open, she gestured for him to precede her inside, enjoying the spicy fragrance as he carried the flowers past her into the kitchen. It was a large, old-fashioned, sunny room with white cabinets, white tile countertops, and a well-worn hardwood floor. A large oak table occupied the center of the room. Except for the color of the paint on the walls, which were currently a soft blue, and the appliances, nothing had changed in it for as long as Lisa could remember.

"Those for me?"

Having acknowledged Lisa's arrival with a quick smile, Robin addressed the question to Andy. Square-faced and stocky at sixty-four, with chin-length hair dyed a defiant red, clad in a flowered smock and bright pink polyester pants, Robin was now her mother's near-constant companion. She was still nominally the housekeeper, a position she had held for longer than Lisa was old. As Martha's health had declined, Robin's primary task had become taking care of her, although she still did some housekeeping and cooking as well. A nurse had started coming in to relieve her and Lisa, who'd been trading off sleeping in Martha's room until her breathing had gotten so bad six weeks ago. At the moment, Robin was stirring something in a tall stockpot on the stove. From the smell, Lisa guessed a significant ingredient was chicken.

"That for me?" he countered, glancing significantly at the pot as he carried the flowers over to the counter beside the sink.

Robin made a face at him.

"Who'd want your ugly mug at their supper table? Not me, that's for sure," Robin retorted, then smiled at Lisa. "Miss Martha's in the TV room. Mrs. Thompson and Mrs. Painter are with her."

They were two of her mother's legion of friends. Lisa nodded and headed upstairs to change clothes without interrupting. Martha had so few diversions now that visits from friends were highly prized. Lisa was only glad that they hadn't forgotten her mother.

By the time she had discarded her suit in favor of conservative, mid-thigh-length khaki shorts, a white tee, and slip-on Keds — now that she was home again, she eschewed anything too short, too tight, or too trendy out of deference to her mother's sensibilities — most of the day's tension had left her. This beloved house where she had grown up always had a calming effect on her, and even the muffled hammering that accompanied the ongoing repairs — and the worry of paying for them later — couldn't change that. Everything about the house, from the rich wood paneling in the reception rooms on the first floor, to the beautiful stained-glass windows that shed prisms of colored light into the most unexpected places, to the hand-carved, winding main staircase that curved up from the center hall, to the leaded glass dome that was a central feature of the roof, was a reminder of a bygone age. She felt almost as though she were a part of the house, as if living there was something that had been bred in her bones, which she supposed, since it had been in her mother's family for generations, it had been. Her own large bedroom was located at the back of the newer (having been constructed in 1894) north wing, not far from her mother's. Or at least not far from her mother's old room. Since her illness had progressed to the point that she had to be carried up the stairs, Martha had had the library, which was on the ground floor of the main wing, converted into a bedroom for her use, both for ease of access and because the halls in that section of the house were consistently wide enough to accommodate a wheelchair. That meant Lisa was all alone in the north wing. Not that she minded. To tell the truth, she relished the privacy, which had been in short supply since she moved back home. Plus, she loved her bedroom. The walls were real plaster, painted a creamy yellow, and a cheerful and ruinously expensive floral chintz in yellow and pink and green that she had chosen herself at age sixteen had been custom-made into draperies and a matching bedspread. A Tabriz carpet in faded shades of rose and blue covered the floor. The room had twelve-foot ceilings, a rarely used fireplace with an elegant Adam mantle, and tall windows overlooking the swimming pool and the Baby's Garden, which was a brick-walled explosion of roses in gorgeous peaches and pinks and reds surrounding a small bronze fountain in the shape of a winged baby-boy cherub, from which the garden took its name. Her furniture was antique except for the bed, a queen-size four-poster, and the soft-green easy chair and ottoman in one corner. An en suite bathroom and a room-size closet had been fashioned out of the bedroom next door at about the same time she had chosen the chintz. The bathroom stood between the bedroom and the closet, with a door opening into each. Walking into the bathroom, Lisa washed her hands and face and touched up her makeup. As she stood in front of the bathroom mirror brushing her hair back into a ponytail in a concession to the heat, she realized she'd left the door to her closet open. She was able to see, through the mirror, both the rack where she had hung her discarded suit among her other clothes and the collection of dolls that lined the shelves. Growing up, she hadn't exactly been a girly girl, but she had loved her dozens of dolls, and even when she'd stopped playing with them she'd carefully kept her favorites.

Now, as she secured the elastic around her hair, her gaze ran over them absently, only to stop with an arrested expression on Katrina, as she had named the nearly life-size toddler girl doll that now stood all but forgotten in a corner. Katrina had shoulder-length black hair, deep bangs, and was dressed in a blue velvet dress. With a lace collar and smocking on the bodice.

Looking at her, Lisa drew in her breath.

The little girl. The missing family.

The doll's coloring. Her hairstyle. Her dress. It all made her look eerily similar to the picture of the young daughter of the Garcia family. What was her name?

Marisa.

The name seemed to whisper through her mind.

Arrested, her gaze still fixed on the doll, Lisa felt her heartbeat quicken and her pulse kick up a notch.

"Don't be stupid. Of course it's a coincidence," she scolded herself aloud, just to break the tension that had held her momentarily spellbound. Making a face at herself, she turned away from the mirror and stepped into the closet, which despite having had the bathroom carved out of it was as large as most bedrooms. The windows that still remained were covered with heavy closed curtains. As ridiculous as she knew it was, the deep gloom made her uneasy. Quickly she snapped on the overhead light, then knelt in front of the doll that she'd happily played with for years and was now, suddenly, embarrassingly, just the tiniest bit afraid of.

You're being a complete idiot here.

She knew that, of course, but knowing it didn't help. She'd had Katrina for as long as she could remember, for so long that she couldn't even remember getting her. Katrina had just always existed in the background of her life. Lisa's mouth went dry and her pulse began to race as she looked the doll over. Designed to depict a child of perhaps four or five, Katrina was pink-cheeked and sturdy, with wide blue eyes that stared sightlessly forward beneath a sweep of bristly black lashes. Warily, with what she knew were ridiculous visions of the evil doll Chucky dancing in her head, Lisa touched Katrina's face. The reassuring smoothness of cool, hard plastic eliminated the wildest flight of her imagination; this was not little Marisa Garcia's somehow amazingly well-preserved body, hidden all these years in plain sight in her closet. It was, instead, simply her own familiar, well-loved doll.

Whew.

Lisa let out a breath she hadn't realized she'd been holding. She didn't even know what she'd been thinking precisely, but it was a relief to discover that whatever it was was wrong.

But if her memory served her correctly, the outfit at least was, indeed, strikingly similar to the one worn by the little girl in the picture.

Trying not to be unnerved by the blank stare of the china eyes, Lisa slid a questing finger along one blue velvet sleeve, rubbed the skirt between her thumb and forefinger, then touched the smocking on the bodice. The velvet was smooth and thick, obviously of good quality. The smocking seemed to have been done by hand and was adorned with real embroidery. Glad now that she had brought the Garcia file home with her, Lisa quickly got to her feet and went into her bedroom to retrieve it from her briefcase, which she had dropped on the floor beside her bed. Opening the folder even as she returned to crouch in front of Katrina,

Lisa looked from the little girl in the picture to the doll with widening eyes.

5

Wow, Lisa thought. The dresses each wore were so similar as to appear identical. In fact, the child and the doll looked so much alike that it was eerie.

It was, of course, impossible to tell much from the small, slightly blurry photograph, but the resemblance couldn't be as uncanny as it seemed. There was no way to know, for example, if Marisa's eyes were blue or if the embroidery on the child's dress depicted tiny pale blue and white flowers with green leaves, as the doll's did, but it seemed unlikely. Marisa's skin tone was certainly darker than the doll's creamy complexion, and the exact shade of blue of her dress also seemed darker in the picture. But both the child's dress and the doll's dress were long-sleeved and full beneath the smocking, were of approximately the same length, and had white-lace Peter Pan collars edged in a tiny ruffle.

Lisa realized her heart was thumping.

Get a grip, she told herself. *There is no way that this is anything but a coincidence.*

Obviously, the doll had been dressed like a real little girl. Blue velvet smocked dresses must have been popular among the preschool set back about the time she'd acquired Katrina. Which, since she didn't remember getting her, must have been when she herself was of preschool age. The doll was supposed to mimic a real child. Therefore, it made sense that she would be dressed like one. There were probably thousands of dolls that were dressed just like this, that looked just like this, scattered all across the country.

As logical as that argument was, Lisa still picked up Katrina and was turning her over to check for a label on the dress or some identifying mark on the doll itself when her cell phone rang. The unexpected burst of Beethoven's Fifth made her jump.

Her phone was in her purse, which was in the bedroom. Putting Katrina down, Lisa got to her feet and hurried to answer it.

"I'm going to have to cancel our lunch on Friday."

The voice was her father's. C. Bartlett Grant was an esteemed federal judge who now lived some seventy miles away in the exclusive Glenview section of Kentucky's largest city, Louisville. Tall, fit, and still strikingly handsome at sixty-eight, he was a former congressman who had once had far loftier political aspirations. But a losing Senate bid had soured him on personally pursuing public office, and he'd embraced the role of party elder instead. Still a local mover and shaker and, thanks to his two wives, both of whom were or (in her mother's case) had been heiresses, a wealthy man, he was highly thought of by almost everyone, his daughter and former wife excepted. Though Lisa was his only natural child — he had acquired three stepsons upon his second marriage — their relationship had been rocky since the extremely contentious divorce from her mother, which had taken place when Lisa was six. In fact, they'd had practically no relationship until Lisa had returned home to Grayson Springs the previous autumn. Since then, always at Barty's (he hated it when she called him that, so Lisa invariably did) instigation, they'd met occasionally for a meal. She figured that since she was now a lawyer like himself, he was afraid that their circles might start to overlap and wanted to do what he could to head off anything unflattering she might say about him.

Barty had always hated being made to look like the bad guy. And of course he didn't know her well enough to know that she had enough family loyalty to keep her unflattering opinion of him to herself.

"Family obligations?" Lisa asked sweetly, knowing that he put on a great show of being a devoted husband and father.

"As a matter of fact, the trial I'm presiding over looks like it's going to run long. I won't be able to get away."

"I saw in the paper that Todd" — his youngest stepson, who was a seventeen-year-old senior in high school — "was competing in a track meet on Friday." Her tone was carefully neutral.

He let out a sigh.

"Okay, you got me. Yes, I'm going to watch Todd run. Jill" — his wife — "doesn't want to go alone."

"You don't have to make excuses, you know. I'm perfectly fine with you canceling our lunch to go watch Todd's meet. I only wish you'd been that good a father to me."

"Lisa . . ."

"I know, Barty, I know. Age brings perspective." During one of their earlier lunches, her father had made sure to tell her that he regretted not having been around much when she was growing up, or at all since the divorce. Advancing years, he'd said, had imparted wisdom and caused him to reshape his priorities, with family now being number one. Maybe he even meant it; certainly, with his second family, he acted as though he did.

"I've asked you before not to call me Barty."

"I'll try to remember." Lisa's brow knit as a thought occurred. "I wasn't adopted by any chance, was I?"

She knew the answer, of course. Or at least, she was as sure as it was possible to be that she did. But something — his lifelong relative indifference to her as compared with his attentiveness to his stepsons, who were not, after all, even related to him by blood; her resemblance to Angela Garcia; the damned doll — caused the question to spring into her mind out of nowhere.

There was the briefest of pauses.

"Why on earth would you ask me something like that?"

"Because I came across a cold-case file today at work concerning the disappearance of a family from this area in the 1980s. The thing is, I look like the dead mother — Angela Garcia. A woman I work with thought so, too. She gave me the file, I brought it home, and I was just looking at the picture again when you called. The resemblance is unreal. And I thought if I was adopted, that would explain so much."

Like why you've never loved me, she thought, but didn't say it aloud.

She could hear him spluttering on the other end of the phone.

"That's the stupidest thing I ever heard! Of course you're not adopted. Your mother gave birth to you on April seventh, 1981, around seven in the morning, in some hospital or another — I've forgotten its name — in Silver Spring, Maryland. I was there, she was there, you came out the natural way. There's probably even a videotape of it around somewhere. Listen here, Lisa, if you want to succeed as a lawyer, you've got to put that over-the-top imagination of yours to rest."

The fact that she'd had an imaginary friend when she was a little girl, and then, as a preteen and beyond, been sure enough that the house was haunted that she'd had to sleep with a light on, was, no doubt, the basis of his "crazy imagination" crack. It didn't make her feel any fonder of him.

"Lisa! Supper!" Robin's voice floated up the stairs.

"Look, Barty, I've got to go. Tell Todd

good luck from me when you see him Friday."

"Lisa —"

But whatever else he had been going to say was lost as she disconnected.

"Lisa!" Robin yelled again. Knowing that such volume meant that her mother was already making her way toward the table, Lisa stuck her phone in her pocket and hurried from the room.

"Coming!" she called back.

When she got downstairs the visitors were gone and her mother was sitting in her state-of-the-art wheelchair at the head of the highly polished mahogany table in the dining room, where they still ate simply because they had always done so, despite the fact that the kitchen would have been much more practical. Hand-painted Chinese wallpaper, a thick Aubusson carpet, and heavy gold silk draperies gave the room a formal feel. Pretty place mats had been topped with her mother's favorite Herend china, and Robin was in the process of ladling delicious-smelling soup into bowls.

"Annalisa." Her mother's still beautiful blue eyes brightened as Lisa entered the room, and a warm smile curved her mouth. Annalisa Seraphina was her full given name, chosen, Martha had often told her, because

"I hear there's trouble up at the Buchanan house," Robin announced as Lisa took her seat. Lisa made a wry face. There were no secrets in Woodford County. No doubt Andy or perhaps some passing neighbor had seen the police cars or heard something and had immediately called Robin to pass on the news or ask if she knew what was going on. "Bud Buchanan got carted off to jail."

"What — did he do?" Martha asked with interest. Lisa held a spoonful of chicken soup to her mother's lips, and Martha opened her mouth and swallowed without ever taking her eyes off Robin. Robin had offered many times to sit with them while they ate and feed Martha so that Lisa and her mother could simply talk without Lisa having the bother of trying to get her mother to eat while she consumed her own meal, but Lisa refused, reserving this bit of her mother's care for herself. She was ever, achingly, conscious that they were running out of time.

"Took a shot at a deputy who came to question him about a hit-and-run out on Travis Road. Drunk, of course. The police came, and they locked him up."

"It's a wonder they didn't shoot him," Lisa exclaimed, feeding her mother another spoonful of soup. If he'd actually taken a shot at a deputy, the mean old man was in a world of trouble, and deservedly so. She wondered what Scott was doing about it. Something, she was sure.

"The world couldn't get that lucky," Robin said darkly. Robin's take-no-prisoners personality, coupled with Bud Buchanan's obnoxiousness and proximity, meant they had warred for years.

"Poor — Scott." Her mother shook her head when Lisa tried to get her to swallow another spoonful of soup. "You — eat. Have you seen him much — at work?"

"I saw him today." Lisa obediently downed some of her own soup, then offered more to her mother, which this time was accepted. Keeping her mother's thoughts focused on events beyond the household and her illness was an object with Lisa. As long as Martha was interested in the outside world, Lisa felt, she would hang on. But she didn't want to burden her mother with anything that might distress her, so she was careful to paint everything that happened in the rosiest possible light. "He sends you his love."

"Such a — smart boy. I always knew — he'd be a success."

Robin snorted expressively. Neither she nor Andy was a big fan of Scott's. Of course, he'd had the stigma of his background to overcome as a youth, and they'd rarely seen him as an adult. But years ago, when he'd been a favorite of her mother's, Lisa suspected they'd also been jealous.

"Now, Robin. You know he's — really made something of himself," Martha reproved. Robin grimaced, but at least she did it so Martha couldn't see.

"He certainly has," Lisa agreed cheerfully, forbearing to add that he was also, more often than not, an overbearing jerk, which was beside the point anyway. No one could deny that Scott had done good.

"District attorney," Martha marveled. "Whoever would have — thought it."

"Once poor white trash, always poor white trash," Robin muttered.

"I think we're finished with the soup now, Robin." Lisa shot her favorite old family retainer a quelling look. Rolling her eyes, again out of Martha's view, Robin took away the soup bowls and returned with plates of baked fish and salad. Her mother's had been chopped so finely that it was almost unrecognizable. Lisa fed her a bite of the near mush, then made sure to eat some of her own supper. If she didn't, her mother would notice and refuse to eat until she did.

"Did you — have a good day?" Her

mother was focused on Lisa now.

Knowing that Martha genuinely wanted to know, Lisa smiled and nodded and related a highly edited version of her day — no need to report that the Jag had broken down, or that her mother's golden boy had threatened to fire her, or that she was in the proverbial doghouse at work — as she got Martha to eat her meal. As they talked and ate, Lisa found herself watching her mother. Not for the first time, she noted how little they physically resembled each other. This was, however, the first time it bothered her. But, she told herself, though their features and coloring were not similar, she shared many of her mother's mannerisms and facial expressions. Leaving aside the effects of her mother's illness, their voices even sounded much the same, and everyone said they had the exact same laugh. Still, the image of Angela Garcia would not leave her. It was ridiculous to think that the fact that a figure in a grainy, thirty-year-old photograph looked so much like her meant anything — what could it possibly mean? At most, that they were distantly related. What other alternatives were there? That she was Angela Garcia reincarnated? That she was little Marisa Garcia, having been secretly adopted and then somehow age-regressed?

How idiotic was that? But the resemblance nagged at her enough so that at the end of her recitation she added, pseudo-carelessly, "Oh, I have to ask you something: What was the name of the hospital where I was born?"

"Saints Mary and Elizabeth's." Martha's reply was prompt. Her face softened as she smiled reminiscently. "It was the happiest day — of my life. I got — my own precious — angel baby. When they handed you to me, I — cried." Her eyes sharpened fractionally on Lisa's face. "Why — do you ask?"

"I had to fill out a form at work today," Lisa answered evasively. "Mother, eat another bite of this."

Her mother shook her head. "I'm — full." She smiled hopefully at Lisa. "I have pictures of the hospital — in your baby book. Would you like to see them?"

Martha liked nothing better than to look through the numerous photo albums she'd compiled of Lisa's life, and as a result, Lisa had seen enough pictures of herself growing up to last through several lifetimes. Before her mother had gotten sick, Martha had only to pull out a photo album for Lisa to find that she had somewhere else she needed to be. Since she'd returned home, though, she'd been much more patient, and thus she'd been treated to numerous photographic trips down memory lane, which she'd endured with good grace, knowing that they gave her mother pleasure. She had not, however, paid any real attention. Now, suddenly, she was not only interested, she was eager.

"I'd love to."

Beaming with surprised gratification, Martha looked at Robin. "You know where I keep — Lisa's baby book. Would you bring it to us — in the TV room, please?"

"You want I should bring some ice cream, too? We've got peach." Like Lisa, Robin was always trying to tempt Martha to eat, and peach ice cream was one of her favorite sweets.

"I don't — want any, thanks. Lisa?" She looked at her daughter, who shook her head.

Ten minutes later, they were in the TV room with their heads together over Lisa's baby book. The TV, which had become Martha's chief distraction as her world continued to shrink around her, was on, but the volume was muted. Tall windows looked to the east, where shadows were just starting to purple the distant rolling hills and creep across fields full of grazing horses. The hand-carved paneling and book- and memento-laden shelves should have made the room feel dark and closed-in, but the bamboo blinds were raised to the tops of the windows to admit the full complement of golden evening light, and that plus the sheer size of the space made it feel surprisingly cheery.

"Look — how big I was." Martha pointed to a picture of her pregnant self standing in front of a glass door leading through a concrete wall, which Lisa knew from the sign above it was in fact the hospital. Her knowledge of her parents' lives up until her birth was a little hazy — mostly from lack of interest on her part, she had to admit — but she knew she'd been born in Maryland, right on the outskirts of Washington, D.C. The photographer, she presumed, had been Barty. Back when he and Martha had still been a couple. Lisa wondered briefly if they'd been happy, then dismissed the thought from her mind. "I had — such a hard time getting pregnant. I was so — excited. I wanted you — very, very much."

"If you'd known how much trouble I was going to be, you would have run away screaming right there and then, right?" Lisa gave her mother a teasing grin. She'd been a wild teenager, sneaking out, partying, running with an out-of-control crowd of other privileged kids who'd had, basically, three thoughts in their collective heads: getting drunk, getting high, and getting laid. She hadn't been as bad as some of them, but she'd been plenty bad enough to provoke innumerable screaming fights with her worried mother.

"Are you — kidding? I wouldn't have — missed a minute of it. Raising you — has been the joy of my life."

An unexpected lump rose in Lisa's throat. She had no doubt that her mother meant it, and equally no doubt that she didn't deserve all that unconditional love. After her wild teenage years, she'd gone away to college, and then law school, with scarcely a backward look. After the first summer, she'd rarely even come home. She'd taken everything — her mother's love, the slightly anachronistic world she'd left behind, the constant security of having plenty of money — for granted. If she'd ever bothered to think about it at all, which she hadn't, she would have been sure that all of it, everything, would always be there waiting for her. It had been bewildering — shocking, even — when she'd first begun to realize that that was not so.

"A glutton for punishment, aren't you?" Lisa asked lightly, determined not to let her own maudlin reflections dampen her mother's mood. Martha laughed, and Lisa smiled, too. Depression was an understandable side effect of the illness, and Lisa made every attempt to keep her mother upbeat.

At Martha's direction, Lisa slowly turned the pages, looking at pictures of her mother in the hospital bed with Barty standing beside her, of her naked baby self, blood, umbilical, and all, clearly having just been delivered, being carried by a nurse toward what looked like a scale in the corner of the room, then cleaned up and wrapped now in a pink blanket with a tiny pink cap on her head, being handed to her mother, of the three of them, Martha in the hospital bed, Barty standing beside it, and her baby self in her mother's arms. She was convinced. It was all there, from the carefully saved bracelets she and her mother had worn in the hospital, to her own tiny footprint, to the date, time, and place of her birth, along with her height in inches and her weight. There had been, as her father had assured her, no adoption. She was indeed Annalisa Seraphina Grant, her parents' natural child, and the resemblance to Angela Garcia could be only a trick of distant-relative-type genetics or sheer chance.

Which was a surprisingly big relief.

Promptly at nine, Lynn Carter, the nurse

who came in to get Martha ready for bed and then stayed with her during the night, appeared in the TV room's doorway. She knocked lightly to get their attention, and Lisa looked around from her seat on the couch and smiled at her. Martha couldn't turn her head to that extent, but she knew who it was, because this had become the familiar routine.

"Ready to go, Miss Martha?" Lynn asked. A tall, thin, black-haired woman in her fifties, with steel-rimmed glasses and, when needed, an equally steely manner, Lynn took her job seriously. Case in point, her nurse's uniform, which today was a short-sleeved white pantsuit. Lisa had told her that wearing a uniform wasn't necessary. Lynn had insisted. It gave her authority, she said. Besides, she never had to worry about what to wear.

"Do I — have a choice?" Martha's voice was gently humorous.

"No, ma'am," Lynn said.

"Well, then — let's go."

Lynn smiled at Lisa as Martha pushed the button that turned her wheelchair away from the TV and toward the door. The gentle whirr of the chair's motor had become so familiar to Lisa that now she scarcely heard it.

Lisa said good night, and then her mother was gone. Left alone, Lisa hit a button on the remote and turned off the TV. Since coming home, she thought, as she stood up and stretched wearily, she'd watched more TV than she ever had in her life — and the sad thing was, she found she was actually beginning to care what was in those briefcases on *Deal or No Deal,* or who could lose the most weight on *The Biggest Loser* — but she couldn't regret it. Watching TV with her mother was time shared with her, and time, she was becoming convinced, was an increasingly precious commodity for the two of them.

She shied away from the thought. The feeling she had that Martha had months rather than years remaining to live was far too depressing to dwell on tonight.

The good news about being banished to Siberia was that for the first time since she'd started working at the prosecutor's office, she'd had no work to bring home. Somebody else was responsible for making sure that all the paperwork needed for tomorrow's cases was done, which gave her some much-appreciated free time. She called Triple A to make sure her car had been picked up — it had — and then called Nola to arrange to go to lunch with her on

Friday, now that her father had bailed. After that, she headed outside, hungry for fresh air. She'd never been one for staying home, or staying inside, but since she'd come back to Grayson Springs she'd pretty much done just that.

Neither Robin nor Andy was anywhere in sight as she went out through the kitchen and across the porch, although the flowers Andy had brought in now took pride of place on the kitchen table. The workers' vans were gone, too, she saw, so for once she had the five acres of gardens and lawn that made up the backyard completely to herself. The fading light had mellowed still more, so that everything was awash in the soft pinkish glow of the approaching sunset. Beyond the manicured grounds around the house, just visible through the trees, the distinctive red roofs of the farm's horse barns seemed to shimmer as the sun's last rays danced over them. A leggy foal frisked along a white fence while its mother and companions grazed nearby, paying it no heed. Closer at hand, insects chirped, tree frogs sang, and leaves rustled faintly in the welcome breeze. She had some thought of deadheading the geraniums or maybe weeding the tomato patch, but for the moment that was all they were: thoughts. Instead she headed for her favorite spot. Long shadows from the giant oaks and walnuts and tulip poplars that vied with one another to shade the back lawn striped grass that was thick and lush as an emerald carpet beneath her feet. Bypassing the formal flower gardens with their low brick walls and paved paths, Lisa walked until she came to the huge, old mulberry tree that she'd loved to climb as a child. Her rope swing still hung from a sturdy branch. There was a hammock on a stand nearby, flanked by a pair of white-painted Adirondack chairs. Plopping down in the swing, lost in thought, she pushed a foot absently against the ground so that she was rocking gently back and forth.

When someone caught the ropes from behind, stopping her in mid-motion, she glanced up, shocked.

Scott was looking down at her. She hadn't heard him approach.

"Want a push?" he asked.

6

Before Lisa could answer, Scott's hands slid down the ropes, and he started pulling the swing backward until she had to cling to the ropes to keep from sliding off the seat and her feet dangled inches off the ground.

"Hey . . ." she protested, half laughing. He was still wearing his white shirt and gray pants, and she realized he must have walked down from his house to pick up his car.

"Hang on."

Having dragged her high, he let go, and away she sailed, only to fall back toward him a moment later. He pushed her again, catching the edge of the wooden seat and heaving so that she would go high. In that instant, as she flew upward and her feet stretched out toward the curving, berry-laden branches, she was maybe eleven years old again and he was the too-cool-for-words older boy who would push her in the swing if he was the only one around and she begged hard enough.

"You keep away from that Buchanan boy," she could almost hear Robin and the rest of the household staff scolding her, as they had all those years ago every time they had chanced to see them together. "That whole family's no good."

She hadn't listened, of course. When had she ever listened to anyone? Back then, before any hint of sexuality had entered her head, she had simply thought of him as a magnificent older potential playmate who would only rarely condescend to so much as speak to her. She'd been too young to realize that in this small, closed society with its strict social stratifications that remained only slightly diluted to this day, he wasn't considered a fit friend for Miss Lisa Grant of Grayson Springs. Now she saw it and realized how snobbish and stupid that was, and how hurtful — for him — growing up around here must have been. At the time, she had accepted as "just the way things were" the warnings to her that no one had cared enough about his feelings to bother to whisper, the fact that he wasn't allowed to use the swimming pool or the tennis court or even come into the house for a drink of water without Miss Martha, his champion, being right there to expressly say so, or to so much as talk to her and her friends any more than necessity dictated.

She was glad, she realized with some surprise when he pushed her again, that he had, in her mother's words, made something of himself. The boy who'd been looked down on for all those years deserved that much revenge.

When the swing flew back toward him once more, there were no hands to catch her and send her soaring again. Glancing over her shoulder in surprise, she saw that he was gone, walking away toward the house.

Jumping lightly off the swing, Lisa hurried after him.

"Your keys are on the hook in the kitchen," she told him when she caught up and fell in step beside him.

"I know. I already got them. I just walked out to let you know, because I didn't want you to think someone had stolen my car. I meant to say hello to your mother, but Mrs. Baker" — Scott had always called Robin Mrs. Baker, with the utmost respect — "said she'd already gone to bed."

"She goes early now." Lisa hesitated, not sure whether she should even mention the subject. "Is everything okay with your dad?"

Scott shrugged. "He's in jail. Apparently

he sideswiped a car at an intersection, then just kept on going until he got home. That's when he called me, but by then they'd tracked him down and sent somebody out to question him. He took a shot at a deputy who stepped through the door. He's probably looking at three to six months at a minimum. It'd be a hell of a lot more if everybody didn't know him around here, and the deputy wasn't Carl Wright."

Carl Wright was another longtime neighbor. "You could pull some strings."

"I don't want to pull any strings. Not tonight, anyway. Ask me tomorrow."

From that she gathered he'd had it up to his eyeballs with his father, for which she didn't blame him a bit.

"Have you had supper?" she asked.

"Not yet."

"There's some chicken soup left. And some fish. I could heat it up."

"Are you offering to fix me a meal?"

"More like zap it in the microwave."

He smiled, apparently deriving considerable amusement from the image her words conjured up. "Mrs. Baker would love that. She did everything but give me the evil eye when I stepped into the kitchen to get my keys."

"She's that way with everybody. Robin is

not what you'd call a people person." It wasn't exactly true — Robin was graciousness personified with those she deemed worthy of it — but it was close enough.

"Yeah, well, not that I mean to denigrate your zapping skills or anything, but I think I'll take my chances with a burger at McDonald's."

Lisa grimaced. "We could go to Jimmy's."

Jimmy's was a little diner about five miles down the road toward Versailles, which, in the local pronunciation, was "Vir-sails." Besides decent food, it had music and, at almost any hour of the day or night, a lively crowd. What she needed, Lisa had just decided, was to get out of the house. With her mother in bed, the night yawned before her, as empty as a black hole. Even Scott's company was preferable.

His brows lifted. " 'We'?"

"Why not? I'm bored. And I don't have a car, so I can't go anywhere on my own. And I am sick to death of watching TV."

A beat passed.

"Just so you know, Princess, I got a rule about dating people who work for me. Therein lies a whole host of problems I don't need. You want to go out, I suggest you call Loverboy."

Lisa stopped dead. "I wasn't asking you

out. Not like on a date. God forbid."

"Good to know we agree on something." He kept walking, heading toward the porte cochere and his car.

"I was just trying to be nice to you," she called after him, feeling her blood pressure start to rise.

"Do me a favor: Be nice to somebody else."

"In future, don't worry, I will."

He reached his car, opened the door, and lifted a hand in farewell. "Don't be late to work tomorrow."

The warning about being late was downright infuriating.

"Jerk," Lisa muttered as he got into the car and shut the door. He couldn't hear, and she tried to be glad, because calling her boss a jerk was a really dumb career move. But as far as she was concerned, he was Scott first and her boss second. At least when they weren't at work. And it had been Scott she'd been calling a jerk. Because he was, and always had been, world without end.

"Kinda late for visitors, isn't it?" was how Robin greeted her when she stalked into the kitchen and shut the door with what, had she not mitigated it by grabbing the knob at the last minute, would have been a slam.

"Course, you can't expect that Buchanan boy to have any manners."

As annoyed as she was at Scott, that set Lisa's teeth on edge.

"First, he is not a boy. He's thirty-two years old, which makes him a grown man." Lisa paused long enough to jerk open the refrigerator, grab a Diet Mountain Dew, close the door, then glare at Robin. "Second, having been nice enough to give me a ride home when the Jaguar broke down, he had to come by and pick up his car. Third, he's the Lexington-Fayette County district attorney, which means he's a very successful, powerful lawyer. He's also my boss, and I'd appreciate it if you would be polite to him when you see him."

"I'm polite to him," Robin protested, eyeing her with surprise. "I'm polite to *everybody.* But there's no getting around the fact that he's trouble and always has been. All them Buchanans are."

"Polite," Lisa insisted through her teeth, popping open the soda as she headed out of the kitchen. "I mean it, Robin."

What Robin said in answer she didn't know, because she banged the door behind her as she headed for the workout room in the south wing. If she couldn't go out, she could always run on the treadmill until she tired herself into a near stupor. Physical exhaustion was what she needed if she was to have any hope of banishing the edginess that had bothered her all day.

It was really kind of pathetic, Scott reflected sourly as he drove up the lane toward the main road that would eventually take him to Lexington and the apartment he called home there. Here he was, at age thirty-two, still dealing with the exact same set of problems that had bedeviled him as a teenager. First there was his father, whom he was pretty sure he didn't give a shit about but was damned well sure he was stuck with. In a community this size, where everyone knew him as Bud Buchanan's boy, there wasn't any way of distancing himself from his father even if he wanted to, which ninety-nine percent of the time he absolutely did. The same mean, violent drunk he'd always been, the old man had done his best to run off anyone who had ever cared for him, Scott included. Only sheer dogged determination not to let the old bastard win kept Scott coming back. That and the knowledge that the crazy SOB needed him, though the last thing on earth he'd ever do was either face it or admit it.

The other problem that had boomeranged

right back at him was Lisa.

He'd been wanting to get inside her panties for so long now that it felt like a given of his life. From the time she'd first started coming on to him when she was about fourteen to this day, he'd been fighting the urge to jump her bones. At first she'd been too young; he'd been ashamed of himself for even thinking about it, no matter how many times she had deliberately jiggled past him in a bikini or needed his "help" to reach something or carry something or fix something, all of which required a lot of brushing up against him, or said or did something so outrageously suggestive that she might as well have just begged him to screw her and have done. When she'd reached the age of consent, he'd still been too cautious, too aware of their relative positions in life and how easy it would be for her and her family to annihilate him if something went wrong, and too conscious of what he owed Miss Martha to fool around with the daughter she adored. But all the way up until Lisa had graduated from college and quit coming home in the summers, he'd had it in his mind that one day he was going to say to hell with all the reasons why he shouldn't and give her what they both wanted. By then, having graduated at the top of his class at the University of Kentucky law school, he was a fast-rising star in the prosecutor's office and dating her was no longer out of his reach. All those old prejudices about the rich society girl and the dirt-poor local drunk's son no longer applied.

Only it seemed that maybe they still did.

Back then she was in the society pages a couple of times a month, going to this charity ball and that fund-raising luncheon, wearing the latest designer fashions and with what he'd come to think of as her boyfriend of the month in tow. He'd known the posse of girls she hung out with for about as long as he'd known her, but they, and he, existed in different milieus. Theirs was the country-club set, his the working-stiff set, and the two rarely mingled. Pulling himself up by the bootstraps by dint of sheer hard work, hobnobbing with wealthy Lexington power players on a somewhat equal basis for the first time in his life, he watched his boss and his boss's boss kowtow to moneyed families like the Grants and realized just how wide the gulf between him and Lisa still was.

Then, while he was still feeling his way into his career, she was gone.

After that he saw her around only occasionally, when she came home to visit.

She was as sexy and beautiful and sure of herself as she had always been, but by then he'd grown up and wised up and learned that it was best to leave trouble the hell alone whenever possible. He still wanted to get in her pants, and he was as sure as it was possible to be that she wouldn't exactly run shrieking in the opposite direction if he made the attempt, but he didn't. Exactly why he didn't he couldn't have said, because as her party-girl reputation made far too clear, he almost certainly wouldn't have been taking anything that wasn't widely available. Except maybe that was it. Maybe he had a burning aversion to becoming just one more choo-choo in the train. Or maybe he just had too much respect for Miss Martha, who had done more for him, growing up, than anybody he could think of — certainly more than his own kith and kin — than to bed her wayward daughter. Yeah, he liked to think that was it.

When Miss Martha's health had brought Lisa home in October, he'd been aware that she was back, even caught a few glimpses of her, but he'd been content to keep his distance. His career was taking off; he was making plenty of money; he had ambitions that included the governorship someday. He was working hard, focused, getting the job done for the county and for himself. The last thing he needed in his life was to find himself jonesing for Lisa Grant again. A fling with a socialite who was in town only until her mother died and she could hightail it back to Boston didn't fit into his plans. Then she'd come to him and asked for a job.

Hell, he'd known better. He'd almost said no. But she'd looked at him out of those big caramel-colored eyes and explained her situation, said that she'd take anything, that she was asking for her mother's sake, as a favor, and he'd caved. He hadn't really thought she'd take the research assistant position that he'd offered her, but she had accepted on the spot.

Since then, since he'd boneheadedly allowed her back into his life on a near-daily basis, she'd bugged the hell out of him. Oh, not by coming on to him. Thank God she'd grown up enough to have cut that out. She wasn't even doing it on purpose, he knew. But just having her around bugged him. Knowing she was there in the same building bugged him. Hearing her voice, seeing her frown over a brief as she worked in her cubicle, watching her walk past his office with that inimitable sway of hers, getting a glimpse of her standing in line for the copy machine, even having to listen to other people talk about her, bugged him.

Watching her kiss Joel Peyton from his window that morning had bugged him most of all.

Tonight, when she'd suggested they go to Jimmy's together, he'd still been bugged enough that he had *almost* taken her up on it.

Then he'd regained enough judgment to turn her down. The plain truth was that he was hot for her and she was almost certainly willing, and given those facts, that meal at Jimmy's could very well have wound up with them in bed. Though he'd fantasized about sleeping with her for most of his life, he had just enough sense left to know that actually doing it would be a mistake. The kind of gigantic, catastrophic mistake that could derail him, personally and professionally.

He wasn't going to let it happen. He'd worked too hard, and too long, to get where he was.

The thing was, seeing her on the swing had taken him back. He'd grabbed the ropes, just as he had many times many years before, and she'd tilted her head back and laughed at him. Even as he pushed her, it had hit him: They were all grown up now.

He could have her if he wanted.

Heat had blown through him at the thought. He'd been just smart enough to turn around and walk away.

Congratulating himself for using the intelligence God gave him was what he ought to be doing about now. Instead he felt more like punching a wall.

The ringing of his cell phone distracted him. Glancing down, he saw the number scrolling across his caller ID and grimaced: Janie.

He didn't pick up.

Janie Ungar was a twenty-six-year-old loan officer at his bank. She was a college graduate from a middle-class family in Lexington. Bright and pretty, with short brown hair and a petite but curvaceous figure, she was exactly the kind of nice, wholesome girl he ought to be seeing. He'd taken her out regularly throughout the spring, enough so that she had started to think of them as a couple. Only they weren't, not in his mind, at least. He'd realized she was getting too serious and he'd started backing away, and then when that hadn't worked he'd spelled it out for her, although as gently as he could. All that had happened about three weeks ago.

Ask yourself why.

All right, so the timing coincided loosely with Lisa's arrival in his office. He didn't like to think that the two events had any bearing on each other. But probably they did.

I was just trying to be nice to you.

Lisa's parting shot still rankled. If he let her, he had no doubt she would be nice to him, all right, just like she'd been nice to no telling how many guys before him. Then she would move on to the next poor fool with as little remorse as a butterfly flitting from flower to flower, and he would be left to deal with the wreckage she left behind.

Put your hand in the fire and it's gonna get burned.

Appropriate as it was, the warning that popped into his head had been issued in another context, and Scott found himself frowning at the memory it evoked. They'd burned a lot of trash in the yard when he was growing up, and his father's method of teaching him to keep away from the fire had been rough and ready: a warning, delivered in a drunken taunt and accompanied by grabbing his wrist and thrusting his hand out over leaping flames that were just high enough to singe his fingers and palm. It had been right after his mother's death, so he'd been about six years old, but he could still remember the searing pain and the cry he gave as he snatched his hand to safety while his father laughed.

Bastard, he thought dispassionately of the old man as the Jeep reached the end of the lane.

Braking, he glanced over at his father's house, which should have been dark and deserted, and was surprised to find that it was not. Lights were on in the living room and kitchen, and a car and a pickup truck were in the driveway. The white Ford F-150 he thought he recognized: Unless he was mistaken, the pickup belonged to his brother. The green Lawn-Pro logo painted on the driver's door clinched it. Lawn-Pro was the yard-cutting service that his brother owned.

As far as he knew, Ryan hadn't spoken to their dad in more than a year. What was he doing at the house? And who did he have with him?

Whatever was going on, if it involved Ryan, it probably wasn't anything good.

Blowing out a sigh, wishing that he was anywhere else, knowing that the problem was his to deal with, Scott turned left, bumped up onto the lawn, stopped the Jeep, and got out.

clear. This wasn't his brother but his brother's only kid, who was, if his memory served him correctly, a fifteen-year-old sophomore in high school. Ryan, who lived in Lexington, shared custody of Chase with his former wife, Gayle, who lived in Versailles. Given that Ryan's truck was parked in the yard, Scott was pretty sure that the kid had come from Ryan's. One thing he knew for sure: Chase wasn't yet old enough to drive.

"I thought you said your grandpa was in jail," one of the boys said in an accusing tone. "I thought you said the house would be empty."

"My grandpa is in jail." Chase recovered his aplomb. "My bad about the house being empty. This is my uncle. Hey, Scott."

With an elaborately casual nod at him, Chase resumed his walk into the living room, taking a swig from the beer in his hand for good measure. The purpose, Scott knew, was to prove to his friends just how cool he was.

Shit.

He didn't want to embarrass the kid, but ere was no way he could let this pass. He rely knew his nephew, just like he barely ew his brother anymore. Just as he himself d, Ryan had done his own thing since aping from this hellhole, and if they

7

Thumping, bass-heavy music greeted Scott's ears, barely muffled because it was blasting away inside the house. He and Ryan were the opposite of close, but it wasn't the kind of music he would have expected his brother to listen to. Of course, Ryan was clearly not alone.

Knowing his brother, that left open all sorts of unsavory possibilities.

There was no way Ryan could have managed to get their dad out of jail. Bail hadn't even been set yet, and unless Ryan's finances had changed considerably, Ryan wouldn't have had the money to bail him out in any event. So the possibility that their dad was one of the people in his house seemed remote.

Surely Ryan hadn't brought some friends — he didn't even want to think about what kind — to party in the empty house.

It was full twilight now. The purple of

encroaching night should have softened the worn steps, the dusty porch that retained only a few slivers of its original gray paint, the scarred black front door. But nothing had changed since he'd lived there, and Scott's memories of the place he'd used to dread coming home to were too entrenched to allow for any softening. The curtains were drawn over the front window as they had always been, so that from the porch you saw the stained, once white linings of the puke-green dollar-store specials that had been hanging in the living room for as long as he could remember. Bud Buchanan watched a lot of TV, hated glare, and was obsessed with the idea that people were looking in at him at all hours of the day and night, and never mind that only a few people ever drove past and the nearest neighbor, Grayson Springs, was too far away for anyone to see in even if they were interested, which they weren't.

Music pulsed through the door, and he could hear a number of voices. He tried the knob and wasn't surprised to find that the door was unlocked. People rarely locked their doors around there. Although he had locked this particular door himself not more than an hour previously, the new arrivals clearly hadn't felt the need. Pushing it open,

he stepped into the lamp-lit living ro
took in the scene at a glance, and stop
dead.

For a moment everyone else in the ro
stopped in mid-motion, too, while they
stared at one another with roughly the san
degree of shock.

The kids — he'd walked into a roomful o
teenagers — recovered first.

"Oh, shit," one of the boys said. Then they all started to scramble, off the couch, off the floor, out of the chair, pinching out joints, putting beer cans on the ground. The sickly-sweet smell of pot wafted beneath his nose.

"What the hell?" Scott broke off as a slight blond kid with shaggy hair, saggy jeans, and a skull and crossbones on his black T-shirt sauntered out of the kitchen, chugging a can of beer. Spotting him, the kid choke
on the mouthful of brew he was swallowi
and froze in his tracks, the can now clutc
in a death grip, his blue eyes going w
while Scott's eyes narrowed on his fac
their feet now, banding together at t
side of the room, the rest of the kids
all, three guys and two girls, eyed h
alarm.

"Chase." Scott's tone turned
that moment, the scenario bec

spoke once every three or four months they were doing something. But here he was, a presumably responsible adult, faced with a roomful of kids breaking the law in so many ways he didn't know where to start. That one of them was his own nephew was simply the icing on the cake.

So handle it.

"Go pour the beer down the sink in the kitchen," he said in a level tone as Chase, chugging from the can again, high-fived one of his relieved-looking friends. Another of the boys — older-looking, taller than Chase but still spindly in the way of teenage boys, with spiky black hair and a single earring — was already leaning down to retrieve his beer from the floor. Straightening with it in his hand, he met Scott's gaze. There was defiance in his eyes, but Scott thought that beneath it he detected a trace of uncertainty, too.

"All of you," Scott added firmly. "Go pour it out."

"Man, that's a waste of good brew," the kid protested.

"Do it."

Chase shot him a challenging look. "Just because you're my uncle don't give you the right to tell me or my friends what to do."

"Then how 'bout just because I'm the

Fayette County prosecutor with the power to throw all of you into juvie hall?" The smile he gave Chase was grim. Pulling his cell phone from his pocket, he held it up for them to see. "I'm giving you all to the count of ten to go pour out the beer and get back in here or I call the cops. Oh, and you can put any pot or anything else illegal you have on you down there on that coffee table when you get back. You don't take this chance to come clean and I find it on you later, you're in big trouble. And anybody getting the bright idea of running for it, forget it. I took down your license-plate number before I came in."

The lie came easily to his lips.

"Is he for real?" the kid holding the beer asked Chase.

Chase shrugged, looking sullen. "Maybe."

"Yeah, I'm for real. Believe it. *One.*" Scott started to count, while his nephew cast him a look of loathing. "Two."

"Come on," Chase said in a sulky tone to his friends. Gathering up beers, shooting him angry looks, they trooped to the kitchen. Scott moved so that he could keep them in view. When they trudged back into the living room, Scott was on *seven.*

"Pot." He indicated the rickety faux-maple table that had occupied pride of place in front of the ancient green tweed couch for as long as he could remember. In a nice counterbalance to the differing shades of green offered by the couch and the curtains, the walls were a faded mustard and the only chair was a brown vinyl recliner. His dad's pride and joy, an aging, console-type big-screen TV, stood in front of the closed curtains. A cheap landscape hung over the couch, and a rectangle of carpet remnant in a never-show-dirt shade of brown covered most of the floor.

"Satisfied?" Chase glared at him as his friends dropped a few joints on the coffee table.

"*Nine.* I'm telling you, this is your last chance." Scott glanced sternly around the group. One girl was plump, with long, dyed blond hair and too much eyeliner. The other was thin, with short, black hair and a ring through her nose. Both were about five-foot-five and wore tight tees — pink for the blonde, green for the brunette — over tiny little shorts. One of the boys had glasses and a blond buzz cut. Another had a sweep of brown hair carefully styled to cover one eye. All wore saggy jeans and tees. The kid with the sweeping hair grimaced and dug into a pocket of his jeans. He came up with a baggie, which he dropped on the table. In the baggie was a whole lot of what looked like crumbled grass. Pot, enough for maybe a dozen or more joints. Enough so that the idiot kid was looking at possession with intent to sell.

"What's your name?" he asked the kid.

"Austin."

"Austin what?"

"Spicer."

"How old are you?"

"Sixteen."

"You dealing?" The amount of pot prompted the question.

"No! It's just for us."

The indignation on his face convinced Scott he was telling the truth. Which made the situation better but not a whole hell of a lot better.

Shit again. This I do not need.

"Please don't call the police." The plump blonde was visibly shaking. Her eyes, which were ringed by enough black eyeliner to do a raccoon proud, beseeched him. "I've got a three-point-eight grade point average. My mom says if I keep it up I can get a scholarship to maybe an Ivy League college. But if I get arrested, I probably won't even be able to get into college. *Any* college. My mom'll die."

"Juvenile records are sealed," the guy with

the spiky black hair said scornfully. "You get arrested when you're under eighteen, nobody ever knows."

"You been arrested?" Scott asked him. If this kid had priors, it would make a difference.

"No."

"Then where you getting your information?"

"I heard it around."

"Any of you been arrested before?"

He was answered by a chorus of scared noes.

"Who drove?"

The kid with the spiky black hair held up a hand. Scott's lips thinned.

"Besides the whole being underage thing, you ever hear of the law against drinking and driving?"

"I wasn't drinking and driving! I just opened up this one beer after I got here. I didn't even get a chance to take a sip."

Scott had already concluded that he'd interrupted the group almost immediately after they'd arrived. Nobody'd had time to get so much as a buzz going.

"Who else drove?"

Silence greeted that. Between the guilty expressions and the scared ones, and adding in his brother's truck, Scott was pretty sure he knew the answer even before Chase gave him a truculent look and said, "Me."

Scott held his nephew's gaze. The blue eyes that ran in the family stared back at him defiantly.

"Any of you working? In summer school?"

"Nobody's hiring. Not even Walmart," Austin said. "Sometimes Matt and I cut grass."

"I babysit sometimes," the black-haired girl said.

"That it?" Scott looked around. Nobody said anything.

"What are you going to do?" The blonde's voice shook.

Scott made up his mind. Hell, he'd known enough wild kids in his life to fill up a stadium. The majority of them had even turned out okay. Luckily, stupid was something most people grew out of.

"First, I want everybody's name, address, and phone number. And I want to see some ID."

Two driver's licenses were produced. The others were too young to possess them. Improvising, he used his cell phone's camera to record them giving the information he'd asked for. The object, besides the obvious, was to scare them into realizing how much trouble they were in.

"Ashley Brookings. I'm fifteen." That was the blonde girl. She brushed away a tear, and he saw that she had black nail polish to match the mess around her eyes. She gave her address and phone number, adding, "Oh, please don't call my mom."

"Matt Lutz. Sixteen," the kid with the spiky black hair said as Scott next pointed his phone at him. He, too, gave his address and phone number. "Hey, Ashley, the worst your mom'll do is ground you. Big deal. If my coach finds out, I'll get kicked off the basketball team."

"My mom will *cry.*" Ashley's lips trembled. Jesus, he was starting to feel like an asshole. Next thing on his list should be kicking puppies. But what else could he do? "She'll think she's done a bad job raising me. Because she's a s-single mother."

"You only ever sit on the bench, Matt. It's not like you getting kicked off the team would be some big loss," Austin said.

"At least I made the team," Matt retorted, and the two glared at each other.

"That's enough," Scott intervened, and pointed his phone at the black-haired girl. "You. Go."

"Sarah Gibbons. I'm fifteen." The black-haired girl looked at him instead of at the camera as she provided the rest of the required information. "I live with my grandparents. Me and my brother. If they find out about this, they're going to be so pissed at me."

"They're always pissed at you," Austin said. "It's 'cause they didn't want to get stuck with you in the first place."

"That's not true, Sarah." Ashley turned reproachful eyes on Austin, who shrugged.

Scott gritted his teeth and aimed his phone at the next kid. If he had it to do over again, he would have just kept on driving when he'd seen the lights on in the house and the vehicles in the driveway. But having stopped, now he was stuck. The kids had broken the law and deserved punishment, but he couldn't bring himself to call the cops. Getting these kids involved in the juvenile system wasn't the answer, at least not at this point. Probably calling the parents, grandparents, whoever, was the right thing to do, but he already knew he wasn't going to do that, either. The thought of the kind of punishment his own father would have meted out to him under such circumstances stopped him cold. His old man would have beaten the hell out of him, not because he'd been caught with illegal substances but because he would have been infuriated at receiving the phone call.

Right or wrong, he wasn't taking the chance of bringing something like that down on the heads of one of these kids. Call it a phobia of his.

"Noah Chapman. Fifteen." The kid with the blond buzz cut and glasses looked scared as he recited his contact information.

"I already told you my name and how old I am." Austin folded his arms over his chest when Scott pointed the cell phone at him. He provided his address and phone number with a shrug. "Go ahead and call my parents. They won't give a shit."

In Scott's opinion, the kid's bravado said volumes about his life, and none of it was good.

"Shut up, Austin," the girls and Matt snapped at the same time.

"You understand I got to take some action here." Scott tucked the phone away when he had them all on camera. "Smoking pot is against the law at any age. Drinking alcohol when you're under twenty-one is also against the law. Besides that, doing either is stupid. It messes up your brain. It screws up your life."

"Look, we're sorry, and we won't do it again, okay?" Chase glared at him, his expression the opposite of penitent. "So, how about you give us a break?"

"Yeah." The rest of the group nodded and threw in variations on the theme of *We've learned our lesson; we won't do it again.* All of it sounded about as believable as Chase's apology.

"Please," Ashley added in a small voice.

Scott looked at them meditatively.

"I am giving you a break. I haven't called the cops. And I'm not calling your parents, grandparents, guardians, whatever. Unless you make me." He paused, watching wryly as they, some more discreetly than others, slumped with relief. "But there are going to be consequences. First of all, we're all going to get together again tomorrow. In my office. Chase will tell you where that is. When's a good time?" He did a quick mental review of his schedule. It was hectic and unpredictable. There wasn't an ounce of free time in it anywhere to begin with, then add in the fact that he was going to have to deal with the ongoing problem that was his dad and it became impossible. But still he was going to fit them in. Hell, if he couldn't be there, he'd deputize someone else.

"Before noon," he added.

After that he had to be in court.

"Why?" Chase regarded him suspiciously.

"Because I think it's time you gave back to the community," Scott said. "We're going to find you something productive to do. Think of it as your own private pretrial diversionary program."

"You can't make us do anything," Matt said. "Only a judge can do that, and you've got to go to court first."

"I guess we can do it that way, if you want." Scott's tone was falsely amiable.

"Matt." Ashley glared at him.

He visibly wilted. "Just sayin'."

"I don't think I can . . ." Sarah began.

"You got here, you can get there." Scott gave them a grim smile. "Or we can deal with this some other way. Your call."

"Ten o'clock. We can make it." Ashley's tone verged on the desperate. "Can't we, guys?"

"But my grandma might not . . ." Sarah objected in an urgent undertone.

"You're supposed to be spending the night at my house. I mean, you *are* spending the night at my house. We can go by his office before you go home," Ashley hissed.

"Oh, okay."

"What about the rest of you?" Scott looked at the boys, who nodded morosely.

"Ten a.m. tomorrow in my office it is,

then. You're not there, I call your folks. Got it?"

"Yes," Ashley agreed, to the accompaniment of another round of less than enthusiastic nods.

"Good. Now get the hell out of here. Go home. All except you." He pointed at Chase. "You I want to talk to."

8

"No way," Chase protested as his friends, giving one another sidelong glances, headed in a relieved shuffle toward the door. He looked after them in alarm. "Hey, don't leave me."

Ashley sent him an apologetic look, and Noah muttered, "Sorry, man," but still they went. Chase would have followed, but Scott blocked his path.

"You can't make me stay here."

"Sure I can."

"Oh, what are you going to do, beat me up? Like I'm scared of you."

"You give me any more trouble, and I'm going to call your dad. And that's just for starters."

Chase sneered. "Good luck with that. Last time I saw him he was passed out on the kitchen floor."

"That how you were able to steal his truck?"

Chase glared at him. "I didn't steal it."

"No way in hell he gave you permission to take it. You don't even have your license yet."

"I needed to get something to eat, okay? There wasn't any food in the house, and he was passed out drunk. I went to Dairy Queen. What was I supposed to do, starve?"

"This place doesn't look like Dairy Queen to me."

"Matt and Austin were at Dairy Queen. We called the girls, then picked up Noah."

"Where'd Austin get the pot?"

Chase shrugged. Scott let it go. "Who got the beer?"

Chase shrugged again. Scott let it go again. He really didn't want to get into the business of busting half the high school kids in the county.

"How'd you know this house was empty?"

"Grandpa called Dad to come get him out of jail. He said you were a pissant bastard" — Chase reported this with relish — "who wouldn't do anything to help him. Dad was drunk off his ass, so he couldn't do anything, either. I don't think he would've anyway, but Grandpa was *mad.*"

"What'd you do, listen on the extension?"

"I had to hold the phone to Dad's ear. I told you, he was drunk off his ass, and he kept dropping it."

Scott let out a sigh. The reason he didn't have kids was that he had no desire at all to be a parent. The very thought of it made him go cold all over. But here was his nephew, already dabbling in trouble, looking at him like he was public enemy number one while living with his near-alcoholic-if-he-wasn't-there-already dad with his grandfather's indisputably alcoholic genes predisposing him to more of the same.

Clearly some attempt at guidance was called for.

"The bottom line is, pot's illegal. Stay away from it, period. And you know alcoholism runs in the family, right?"

Chase snorted. "Duh."

"That means you could get it, and the way to get it is just start drinking. A few beers here and there. Doesn't sound like it could lead to anything bad, does it? But it does. It makes people like us crave more, until we wind up being a pathetic old drunk like my dad or passed out on the floor like yours."

"What, you never have a beer?"

"Nope." He and Ryan had followed the classic paths of an alcoholic's children. Scott, having seen the misery alcohol caused, never touched the stuff. Ryan was the opposite: He'd started drinking as a kid even younger than his son was now, had been a hard-partying hell-raiser for years, and was well on his way, in his younger brother's humble opinion, to winding up just like their dad. Only maybe not as mean. Scott hoped. "Look, your dad's a good guy, but he's made some bad choices, as he'd be the first to tell you, and nearly every one of them that I'm aware of happened because he was drinking."

"Like losing his job."

Until three years ago, Ryan had been a manager of a chain of local Jiffy Lubes. Decent pay, good benefits, nine to five, five days a week. Steady. When his marriage had started going south, he'd started drinking heavily, which had eventually led to his getting fired. Undoubtedly it had been traumatic for the kid.

"Yep."

"Like my mom's divorcing him."

Okay, Scott didn't want to go there. He didn't really know all the ins and outs of that, and he didn't want to. But he had little doubt that Ryan's drinking had something to do with it.

"I'd say it was a contributing factor."

"Like them having me."

Ah, shit. He could see from Chase's face

that this was sensitive psychologica
that he didn't have a clue how to dea

"I don't know about that." Okay,
that was a little bit of a cop-out. H
again. "But I do know both your p
love you a whole lot."

Chase looked revolted. Scott didn't
him. The uncle he barely knew talkin
the parents who were pretty much
in action loving him had to sound
the very least.

"Look, I promise I'll never drink
beer or smoke another joint as long a
okay? So, can I go now?"

Scott believed Chase's promise ju
as much as he believed there would
on the ground in the morning, bu
didn't seem to be much point in bea
subject to death. This was somethin
going to have to take up with Ryan
he was sober. Which brought up
problem. Actually, a slew of other p
Starting with, where to take the kid

"We've established your dad's pa
on the floor, so I can't take you to h
ment. Where's your mother?"

"Oh, didn't you know? She got
last week. She's off on her honeymo
way Chase said that last word was d
savage. "They're going to be m

Cincinnati, where Don — that's her new husband — has a job. I already told her I'm staying with my dad."

Well, that explained Ryan's bender. He'd always hoped to get back with Gayle. *Way to go, brother.*

"Hmm," Scott said, temporarily at a standstill.

Chase scowled at him. "Anyway, what do you mean 'take me'? I drove myself here. I can drive myself home."

"Yeah. No. No more driving without a driver's license, you hear me? Number one, you get caught and you'll bc in a whole heap of trouble you'd rather not be in. Plus, you won't be able to get your license until you're eighteen. Wait a few months, and you can drive as legally as anyone else." Scott didn't bother to try to determine if that was making a dent. "You can spend the night with me tonight, and I'll take you home in the morning."

"I have to get the truck home before my dad wakes up."

The look that accompanied that said volumes. First, Ryan had no idea that his son drove his truck — good to know — and second, Chase, under certain conditions, was afraid of his father.

Something else to take up with Ryan.

Christ in heaven, why didn't I just keep driving?

"Here's the situation: We've got two vehicles here and only one of us has a driver's license. That would be me."

He supposed he could drive Chase, in the truck, to his apartment, where the kid could spend the night, then take him, again in the truck, over to Ryan's early in the morning. Which meant he'd have to get a taxi or some other ride to work — problematic but doable. Which also left his car here at his father's house, which left him without wheels until he could get back out here to pick it up. Scott thought of his upcoming day again. Not so doable.

"I can't go home without that truck." For the first time, panic was there in Chase's voice.

Scott frowned. This was something he wasn't going to be able to avoid, he could see. "You afraid of your dad?"

"If he finds out I took his truck? Hell, yeah."

"What will he do to you?"

Chase folded his arms over his chest. "Kick my ass. What do you think?"

Another conversation he needed to have with Ryan. At this rate, he and his brother were going to be talking more in the next twenty-four hours than they had in years.

Something to look forward to.

"How about if I come in with you and explain the situation to him?" Scott asked.

Chase looked at him in undisguised horror. "You're not going to tell him about this, are you? You said you weren't going to tell any parents."

Yeah, but your parent is my brother, he thought, but didn't say it.

A workable solution to the transportation difficulty had just presented itself to Scott. Lisa was without a car. He and Chase could spend the night in the farmhouse, and Lisa, driving his car, could follow them into town in the morning. He could drop Chase and the truck off at Ryan's and then drive Lisa on to work. It involved more contact with her than was probably good for him, but it solved everybody's immediate problem. Of course, if Ryan happened to wake up before morning and realized that his truck and son were missing, Chase was basically toast. But Scott wasn't too worried about that. From long experience with their dad, he figured that Ryan, drunk, would sleep like the dead for hours.

"Okay, I've got it figured out. You and I are going to spend the night here. In the morning, a friend of mine who lives nearby will follow us into town, driving my car. I drop you and the truck off at your apartment, then go on to work in my car." A glance at his watch told him that it was almost eleven-thirty, too late to call Lisa and apprise her of this change in plans. Well, he'd tell her when he drove the car down in the morning. He couldn't see any reason she'd object to it. Not even to piss him off.

"And you won't tell my dad about any of this, right?" Chase gave him a hard stare. Only if Scott looked closely could he see the anxiety beneath it.

Scott sighed.

"I'm thinking about it," he said. He was dog-tired and hungry enough to eat just about anything the old man had in the refrigerator. He headed toward the kitchen, which was dark except for the faint light from the rising moon that poured in through the window over the sink. One of the kids must have turned the light off after disposing of the beer. Scott flipped it on again, and the overhead fluorescent fixture gave a buzz like an angry wasp as it blinked its way toward full illumination.

"You hungry?" he asked over his shoulder.

"You got to promise me you won't tell my dad." Chase followed him.

The small room was still as ugly as ever.

The same scarred green Formica countertops above mustard-yellow cabinets that matched the walls, an old gas stove, a chipped white sink, and the folding card table that had always served as a kitchen table standing in the middle of the floor. Only the stainless-steel refrigerator with ice and water dispensers was new. It had been Scott's gift to the old man to replace the one that had died, which had stood in the kitchen since Scott had been a boy. He only hoped there was something edible in it.

"Your dad's my brother. I don't feel right about keeping this from him." Scott opened the refrigerator door as Chase, obviously appalled, went off on a rant that boiled down to the universal teenage lament of *That's not fair,* to which he half listened. As he would have expected, the shelves were stocked with beer, with a couple of wine coolers and a bottle each of vodka and gin thrown in. Food consisted of some leftover pizza — no telling how old it was — some tuna or chicken salad in a Saran Wrap–covered bowl that looked old, too, maybe half a package of sliced bacon, and some eggs.

Hey, he could make that work.

Grabbing the bacon and eggs, he turned toward the stove, shutting the refrigerator door with a nudge of his arm.

"You like bacon and eggs?" Setting the food down on the counter beside the stove, he fished a frying pan out of the cabinet where they were kept, set it on the stove, and started making breakfast.

"You can't tell my dad! Especially about the truck."

"Oh, that's the part that's going to make him mad, is it?" If that was true, Ryan needed to rethink some things. "Not the beer or the pot? How about taking your friends to your grandpa's empty house to party? And let's not forget breaking in."

"We didn't break in. There's a key on the truck's key ring."

"So, you beat one count. Good for you." The smell of the frying bacon made Scott's mouth water. Come to think of it, he'd missed lunch.

"What do you want from me?"

Turning the sizzling bacon with a fork, Scott glanced at Chase over his shoulder. Perched on the counter by the sink, the kid looked tense and pale.

"I want you to wise up." Scott was surprised to find that this was true. "I want you to take a good, hard look at the path you're heading down and see where it leads. I want you to stay out of trouble, get yourself through school, and make something of yourself. Be a healthy, happy, successful adult."

"Like you?" Chase sneered. "My dad says you're a sanctimonious prick."

Scott succumbed to a half-smile. "Yeah, well, I won't bother to tell you all the things I've called him over the years."

Grabbing two paper plates from the cabinet, he split the bacon between them, then cracked four eggs — there were only four left in the carton — into the hot grease. A little salt, a little pepper, four slices of bread into the toaster, and the meal was well on its way to being done.

"Could you *please* not tell him about this?" That was the humblest Chase had sounded since they'd first locked eyes in the living room.

"He beat you up?" Keeping his tone carefully casual and busying himself with scooping eggs onto the plates along with the toast that had just popped up, Scott probed for information. He didn't really want to know this about his brother if the answer was yes, but for the kid's sake he needed to.

"N-no." Chase sounded doubtful. "Last time I made him mad, he backhanded me across the face. Course, I called him a son of a bitch and a hillbilly loser and spit at him first."

"Definitely a mitigating factor." Relieved to know that his brother hadn't quite sunk to their father's depths, Scott plopped the plates and a couple of forks down on the table, then grabbed two glasses and filled them at the sink. "Sit down and eat."

"I told you, I'm not hungry." Chase slid off the counter and approached the table. Scott, already seated, forked egg into his mouth.

"Eat anyway."

"Look, I'll make you a deal." Chase sat across from him, looking at him earnestly from beneath his blond fringe of hair. "If you don't tell my dad about this, I'll make sure my friends all show up in your office tomorrow morning like you want, and we'll all do whatever it is you want us to do."

"You think they won't show up otherwise?" Scott kept eating. Absently, Chase picked up a piece of bacon and started munching.

"I don't know. Probably not Austin. Maybe not Matt. You should've threatened to call his coach if you wanted to make sure he came. And Noah gave you the wrong phone number."

Scott smiled. "Did he? Well, I don't imagine finding the right one will be that hard."

"I'll get them all there and promise not to

drink or smoke pot or whatever —"

"Steal your dad's truck." Scott was on his second egg. Having polished off the first piece of bacon, Chase was tackling an egg, too. "Or drive any vehicle before you get your license."

"Okay, that, too. All of it. But I got to get me and the truck back before my dad misses us, and you got to not tell him about this."

"Your word good?"

Chase flushed. "Yes."

"Then we got a deal. Eat up. I need to get some sleep. And we're getting up early." He wondered how Lisa would react to a six a.m. wake-up call. Seeing as it was him making it, probably not well. On the other hand, she was getting a reliable vehicle to drive to work in.

"He's got an alarm that goes off at eight. He might not wake up, but . . ."

"You — and the truck — will be home before then. I have to be at work at eight, so I'll be dropping you off well before that." Scott finished his meal, waited for Chase to finish, then carried the paper plates to the trash can in the corner. Knowing there wouldn't be anyone in the house for a while to see to the garbage, he pulled the black plastic bag lining it out and knotted it with the intention of taking it out as he left in the morning. In the meantime, Chase, as he saw when he turned around, was washing the frying pan and silverware. The kid was standing at the sink because there was no dishwasher, and he was wrist-deep in soapy water.

Scott smiled inwardly. How bad could a kid who did the dishes without being asked be?

"Hey, Scott. Come look at this." Chase was frowning at something he was seeing through the window.

Scott came up behind him. He saw it instantly, without Chase having to say a word. A faint reddish glow with a kind of pulse to it lit up a small piece of the dark sky to the south. *What the hell?* He frowned as it took him a second or two to make sense of what he was seeing.

"Shit!" His heart gave a great leap as all of a sudden he knew. Pivoting, he ran for the front door.

"What?" Sounding bewildered, Chase ran after him.

Wrenching open the front door, Scott raced toward the Jeep even as he snatched his phone from his pocket.

"Grayson Springs is on fire," he threw over his shoulder at his nephew while he punched in 911. Snatching open the door to the Jeep, he threw himself behind the wheel as the emergency number rang fruitlessly and Chase scrambled into the passenger seat behind him.

9

"Nine-one-one emergency," the operator answered, her voice the maddening epitome of untroubled calm. Having hurtled down the lane like a rocket off a launching pad, the Jeep was just going airborne over the last rise before hunkering down to race between the double row of giant oaks that led to the house.

"Send the fire department. There's a house on fire. People may be inside." Keeping his voice even was an effort. Scott wanted to shout down the phone. "It's Grayson Springs." The whereabouts of the famous horse farm was presumably known to everyone within a fifty-mile radius, but at the operator's request, even as his sweaty palms clamped around the phone and the wheel and his heart pounded and his pulse raced, he gave the address. And repeated it for her, too.

All without outwardly losing his cool.

Suddenly the house's white façade popped into view, ghostlike in the moonlit darkness. In that instant before the trees swallowed the Jeep again, he could see the dark windows shining like countless staring eyes, the tall columns as stately as always, the pale sweep of the driveway curving up to the porte cochere — and the licking flames and billowing smoke rising from the roof. Of the north wing. Where Lisa slept. Where she had always slept.

His gut clenched. His breathing suspended.

"Damn." Chase sounded awed.

There were people on the lawn, Scott was relieved to see, as the Jeep shot out from beneath the avenue of trees. No more than gray shapes against the inky grass at that distance, their identities were impossible to determine.

She's there. Of course she is.

But telling himself that, and knowing it for a fact, were two different things. Slamming on the brakes as the Jeep drew even with them, throwing the transmission into park, he turned off the ignition, leaped out of the car, and ran across the manicured lawn toward where they were gathered, a distance of perhaps some two hundred yards from the driveway. He counted heads

was in her
ldn't get to

rld seemed
adrenaline
like speed

Frye, still
and looked
d."
his shoulder
n. Of course
n. Scott was
nd him as he
he house and
onto, among
ase that Andy
had no time
ound of sirens
the low stone
atio and, dodg-
, crossed the
Where the hell
ow long did it

the closest fire
nd getting them
minutes. On a
vas a good night.

stretched out on
s closed, ghostly
He would have
except a woman
her, seemingly
t aid, and you
dead woman,
ext to her, on
ng and wheez-
his shoulder,
saying some-
ern.
realized who

e drew close
strong. The
h to drown
nd presum-
se no one
rie flicker-

His heart

urgently,
e all but
ker. He
Where's

vild as
oward

the house.

"We think she's still inside! She
bedroom. Andy tried, but he cou
her."

For a moment, the whole wo
to shift into a slower gear. Then
kicked in. He could feel it rusl
through his veins.

"Go up — the back." Mr.
coughing, raised his head
around at him. "Front's blocke

"Stay here," Scott barked ove
at Chase. The kid didn't liste
the damned kid didn't liste
aware of him pounding behi
raced toward the far side of t
the side entrance that opened
other things, the back stairc
had been referring to, but h
to do anything about it. No s
yet, he registered, as he leape
wall that edged a small side p
ing wrought-iron furniture
stone pavers in two bounds.
was the fire department? H
take?

The bitter truth was that
station was in Versailles. A
there could take up to fiftee
good night. He prayed this v

The red glare of the fire was growing brighter. Bright enough so that this slightly overgrown section of yard where lilies on swaying stalks surrounded the trees and flowering bushes abounded had taken on the look of a garden in hell. This close, he could feel the fire's heat, hear its sharp crackle. At the thought that Lisa was trapped in there, a hard shiver shot down his spine.

God, let her be all right.

"You come one step inside this house and I'll tell your dad everything that's gone down tonight, you hear?"

He was at the side door as he growled the threat at Chase, who stopped, panting, beside him. A quick twist of the smooth brass knob confirmed Scott's fear: It was locked. A faint hope that Lisa might have exited this way died. She would never have stopped to lock it behind her. His every instinct urged him to kick the damned door down. But calm reason prevailed. With no time to do more than underline his words with a glare at Chase, he whipped his wallet out of his pocket, pulled out a credit card, and dropped the rest. He knew that door; he knew that lock. The door was solid wood in the way that hundred-year-old doors were solid wood; kicking it down would take some time. But the lock was modern. The lock was a simple push-button. The lock he could open with a credit card.

Sweating bullets and clenching his teeth in an effort to keep panic at bay, he gently slid the credit card between the doorjamb and the lock and jiggled it.

"Maybe she got out some other way." Chase was still breathing irregularly.

Maybe. Intent on what he was doing, he thought it without giving voice to the reply. But was he willing to take the time to run all over the damn huge grounds, checking to see if she was out there somewhere?

If he did and Lisa was inside, she could die.

To his great relief, the lock yielded with a click.

"Stay fucking here," he ordered Chase fiercely over his shoulder as he shoved the door open. "I mean it. If I'm not back by the time the firefighters get here, tell them where I went."

For just a second after he entered he was disoriented and had to stop to look around him. He hadn't been in this part of the house for at least ten years. The back hall was shaped like a capital T, opening straight ahead into the wider hall that bisected the ground floor of the north wing. To his right, the hall ended in a bathroom, he recalled. To his left was the door that led to the narrow chute of stairs that was his goal. The memory came to him in a flash, and he turned left and ran.

With only the moonlight pouring through the open door behind him for illumination, he reached the end of the hall and jerked open the door to the staircase. A plume of smoke greeted him even before his foot hit the stairs. The crackle and pop of the fire was suddenly much louder. The smell of burning was strong.

"Lisa!" he bellowed. Ducking to avoid the smoke that was thick enough at the higher elevation to sting his eyes, he leaped up the stairs two at a time.

And thought — wasn't sure but thought — he heard a faint answering cry.

"Help!" Lisa cried again, weakly, then succumbed to a fit of coughing so deep it felt like claws tearing at her lungs. Her head drooped as she gasped for breath. It felt heavy as a boulder, far too heavy for her neck to support. Her temples pounded. She felt dizzy, sick. There was a terrible metallic taste on her tongue.

If I could only lie down for a moment and rest. . . .

Probably she shouldn't waste her energy calling out anymore. Her voice was now so hoarse that she doubted it could be heard beyond a few feet away. Certainly if no one had heard her first terrified screams, they wouldn't hear her now. Her mother, Robin, Andy — where were they? Had they escaped? Or were they trapped, too?

Terror grabbed her heart at the thought. But there was nothing she could do for them. She was beginning to doubt that she was even going to be able to save herself.

I have to keep going. I have to get out.

Biting her lip in an effort to stay focused, she forced herself to keep moving, crawling like a baby down the hallway toward the back staircase at the far end of the north wing, the hardwood floor hurting her bare knees, the increasing heat of it beneath her hands scaring her. Smoke was thick overhead, so thick it had choked her when, upon first leaving her room, she'd tried to run through it, tried to escape in the opposite direction. The smoke had clogged her nostrils, burned her throat, filled her lungs, until she'd remembered that she needed to stay low. Bending double, she'd almost made it to front stairs, the big central staircase that wound up to the glass atrium and down to the first floor, when part of the ceiling collapsed in front of her. Just collapsed with no warning at all other than a *whoosh* of flames and the crash of falling timbers. Screaming, she'd barely managed to jump back in time. Sparks had showered her. Fire had roared up toward the hole that had opened in the roof.

I can't get to the stairs.

Panic had exploded through her veins even as she reeled away from the fiery wall that leaped to life in front of her. The smoke was so thick now that she could feel its oily texture against her skin, feel the weight of it as she sucked it into her lungs. Coughing, gasping for air, so fuzzy-headed she could barely think, she'd once again remembered that to escape smoke you stayed low, and so she turned and dropped to her hands and knees and crawled frantically away. The air was better near the floor. Hot and thick and faintly sulfurous but breathable. She hugged the wall on her left because heat radiated through the wall on her right, and she feared that at any minute more flames might burst through the plaster. Behind her, the ominous crackling noise filled her with terror. Her stomach knotted. Her pulse raced. She could feel the blazing heat on the soles of her bare feet, on the backs of her thighs. The fire was chasing her. If it caught up she would die. The fifty or so feet that she still had to go before she reached the stairs felt like fifty miles.

What if more of the roof collapses? Or even the floor?

The thought brought another wave of panic with it. Forcing it back, she willed herself onward, despite an alarming lethargy that was beginning to steal her will along with the strength from her muscles.

What she wanted most of all, beyond anything, was to just lie down.

I'm so tired.

Having been awakened by a loud *boom,* she'd still been groggy with sleep and had lain in bed, blinking into the darkness, trying to think what the sound could have been for the moment or two that, she realized now, had constituted her best chance for escape. She'd even contemplated going back to sleep — until she realized that her room smelled of smoke. Then several other things clicked simultaneously: a strange rumbling sound, an acrid taste in her mouth, the sense that something was wrong.

Realization, when it came, was horrifying: *The house is on fire.*

If something happens to me, it will kill Mother, she told herself now as her blood hammered against her temples and she coughed up what felt like another section of lung and her limbs seemed to weaken still more. The knowledge gave her the impetus she needed to keep moving.

You know where the back stairs are. Just a little farther . . .

Eyes burning, gagging on low-riding fingers of smoke that she couldn't help but inhale, heart pounding like it wanted to beat its way out of her chest, she crawled desperately toward the darkness at the end of the hall. The door there opened onto what had once been a servants' staircase, a narrow, steep flight of unadorned wooden steps that led up from the first floor.

The closed door was still maybe thirty feet away.

I'm not going to make it. The knowledge settled, hard and cold as a rock, in the pit of her stomach.

Even as she looked toward it despairingly, the door burst open and a man, painted orange by the flames, barreled into the hall. The fire behind her roared as if in anger. She felt a blistering burst of heat as, she realized, the rush of fresh oxygen fed the conflagration.

"Lisa!" His voice was so thick it was scarcely recognizable. His eyes fastened on her.

"Scott!" It was a choked cry. She started coughing violently again even as his name left her lips.

He won't let me die.

Bent low against the smoke, his arm covering his nose and mouth, he ran toward her. Stopping, bracing a hand against the wall, she tried to get to her feet. If she could only run to him, he would help her get away.

But she was too weak. He reached her before she could do more than get into a kneeling position. Snatching her up into his arms, he pivoted with her and started racing back the way he had come. Over his shoulder, she was stunned to see that runners of flames had advanced to within just inches of where she had been. Following in the path of those runners, the fire moved forward steadily. Her eyes widened on the seething wall of flame as it came after them, devouring everything — ceiling, walls, floor — in its path with ravenous fury.

Another couple of minutes and it would have swallowed me.

"Lisa. Put your arms around my neck." Scott spoke urgently in her ear as they reached the top of the stairs and he slammed the door in the fire's teeth. Coughing, Lisa used what felt like every last bit of strength and will that remained in her to comply.

Held tight against his chest, her arms locked around his neck now, feeling boneless as a rag doll, she buried her face in his shoulder in an effort to escape the smoke that swirled around them as he ran down the stairs with her.

A moment later they burst out the side door and into the night. Lisa felt the rush of cool air against her skin. Lifting her head, blinking because her eyes still stung, she inhaled deeply, thankfully. Immediately she started to cough, but she didn't even care. The familiar side of the house, the lilac bush beside the door, the swaying lilies, the rounded silhouettes of the towering tulip poplars high above that were blacker even than the starry sky, all confirmed it: They were outside. They had made it. They had survived.

Thank you, God.

It was only then that she realized she was shaking.

"Run around front and tell them she got out safely, would you?" Scott said in a strange hoarse voice, and she realized he wasn't talking to her. She caught just a glimpse of a long-haired teenage boy she didn't recognize as, with a nod, he darted off toward the front of the house to do Scott's bidding.

Scott wasn't running anymore, he was just walking and carrying her while she stared back at the house in shock. From this position, all she could see were the sharp angles of the roof, the still solid-looking exterior brick wall, the windows that remained, impossibly, she thought, until she remembered he had closed the door at the top of the stairs, a blank, shiny black. And the fire, bright and menacing, flitting along the edge of the roof. It was too terrible to watch, so she quickly averted her eyes. She could feel Scott's chest heaving against her as he alternately sucked fresh air into his lungs and coughed. Weak and dizzy, she clung to him, tucking her face into the curve between his neck and shoulder, coughing violently herself. Her emotions were in turmoil, but the strongest was relief: She was so profoundly glad to be alive. Trembling in the aftermath of terror, she tried her best to get herself under control. Gritting her teeth, she concentrated on stilling the spasms that raced through her muscles. It didn't help that she had to cough with nearly every other breath. She was just vaguely aware of the low stone wall, the furled umbrella, the table and chairs, the glider, as he reached the little patio at the side of the house. From there she couldn't see the flames themselves, but the roar and the smell and the orange incandescence that silhouetted the tall chimney at the edge of the roof and lit up the sky left her in no doubt that it wasn't, as she'd been hoping, as she'd been praying, all a bad dream: Grayson Springs was really burning.

Her heart clutched. Tears started to her eyes. She closed them, holding in the moisture, blocking out the sight. And coughed. And coughed some more.

10

"Christ." Stopping abruptly, Scott sank down into a chair, one of the wrought-iron ones at the far end of the patio. Shadows closed in around them, wrapping them in solitude. Lisa rested against him in utter despairing exhaustion as, despite her best efforts, a few tears leaked from her eyes. He smelled of smoke. So, she supposed, did she. His skin was faintly damp with sweat, and he was still breathing as though he'd just run a marathon. No doubt his heart still pounded just as hers did, although the frantic beat was slowing now. He felt strong and solid and wonderfully familiar, and she was glad of the comfort of his arms. The shivers that racked her were easing, and she curled more closely against him in an effort to absorb some of his warmth. She felt the glide of his hand as he stroked her hair, which was long and loose because she slept with it that way, and pushed errant strands back away from her face, tucking them behind her ear.

"Lisa, talk to me. Are you hurt?" Scott's ragged breathing was slowing. His voice was still hoarse, but it was at least recognizable now.

With an effort Lisa shook her head.

"Mother?" The single word was all she could manage. Even that caused her to cough so hard her lungs ached.

"She's out on the front lawn. Everybody got out. You're the last. Are you having trouble breathing?"

Relief that her mother and everyone else was safe made her feel almost weightless. She had the strange sensation of floating away, and she opened her eyes in an attempt to combat it. She found herself looking at the strong column of his neck, the dark underside of his chin, his wide chest in the white shirt that was bisected by her arm curving up to his shoulder. He was looking down at her so most of his face was in shadow, but she could see his eyes, see the tightness of his mouth, see that he was frowning at her. This was Scott the responsible, she reminded herself, and she felt some of the terrible tension leave her body as she realized that she could count on him to take care of her and whatever else arose that needed taking care of until she felt like herself again. Even as a teen he'd always been coolly capable, and that hadn't changed. The hideous vision she'd been harboring of her mother, who was unable to even get out of bed without assistance, being trapped in the flames, receded. But the fire was all too terribly real. . . .

Despite her best efforts, another stray tear or two trickled down her cheeks. Resting heavily against Scott, glad he was there, she took a deep, shuddering breath that once again made her cough violently.

"Damn it, Lisa, answer me. Are you having trouble breathing?"

From the sharpness of his tone, she guessed that she was facing something on the order of CPR within the next few seconds if she didn't respond.

"I'm okay. It's just" — cough — "the smoke."

He coughed himself. "You sure? You're not burned anywhere?"

His hand smoothed down her back as he spoke. As she felt its gentle slide, she realized what she was wearing: the satiny camisole and matching boxers she'd gone to sleep in. The set was a gleaming silver-gray, with spaghetti straps and a filmy lace insert between her breasts and tiny loose pants that ended just past the tops of her thighs. She was, in short, revealing a great deal of skin. But this was Scott, so it didn't really matter. Scott was many things, but he wasn't a pig.

"I don't think so." She coughed some more, then sniffed and blinked in an effort to control the tears that still wanted to leak from her eyes.

"Sit up and let me see." He unhooked her arms from around his neck and set her upright in his lap. Head swimming, she coughed again as their eyes met. Squinting at her through the darkness, he asked abruptly, "Are you crying?"

"No."

"Yes, you are. Hell, why shouldn't you cry? You have every right to." Lips compressing as if to keep himself from saying more, his gaze swept slowly over her from her hairline to her toes, clearly checking for any sign of injury. "I can't see squat. Can you move everything?"

"Yes. See?" Lifting her legs one at a time, she wiggled her toes for his delectation as his eyes slid down toward them. "And for your information, I'm not crying. My eyes are watering from the smoke."

"Oh, is that what it is?"

"Yes." As another coughing fit hit her, she

subsided weakly against his chest. Her head dropped back onto his shoulder, settling onto that wide expanse as if it belonged there. His arms came back around her, and for a moment she closed her eyes and allowed herself to simply feel safe.

"You could have been killed." His voice was suddenly harsh. "That was damned close in there."

She shivered. "I think you saved my life."

"I think so, too."

Glad to find she could, she smiled a little. *Typical arrogant Scott,* she thought, and opened her eyes. "Way to be modest."

"Is that a 'Thank you'? And by the way, modesty is overrated."

"That's your opinion. And yes, it's a 'Thank you,' " she said, and started coughing again.

"You're welcome. Quit talking. You need to put all your energy into breathing right now."

Wrapped in his arms again, she sat silently for a moment, taking his advice. Then a muffled crash and a bright flare that could only have been caused by shooting flames from another section of the roof collapsing made her wince.

"Don't think about it," he advised. "Just breathe."

night attendant for
er what looked like
,

ve movement to get
stalled her by stand-
arms. She wrapped
eck automatically as
h her, stepping over
ding toward the front
veight with ease, and
urprised — no, she
n't — at how strong

rry me. I'm perfectly

mebody with so
e that."
ut br

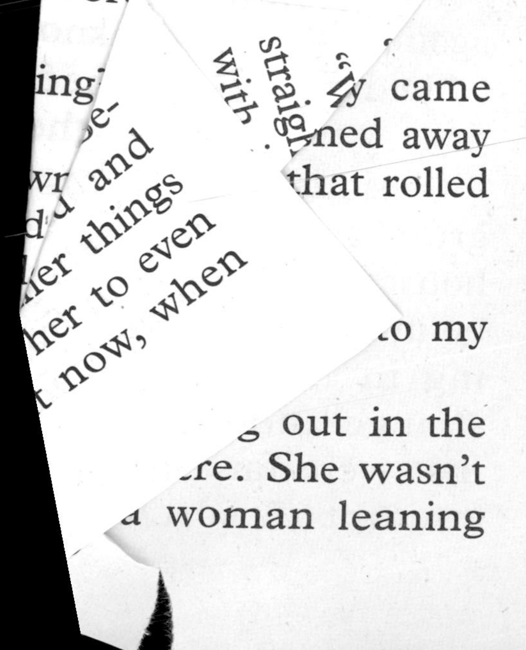

ing y came
ned away
that rolled

o my

out in the
re. She wasn't
a woman leaning

over her — you got
her now? — giving
some kind of first aid.

"Oh, no!"

She made an abort
off his lap, but he for
ing up with her in his
her arms around his r
he started walking wi
the low stone wall, stri
yard. He handled her
she was once again s
guessed she really was
he was.

"You don't have to ca
fine."

"I'd feel better if sc
medical training told m

She started to reply b
again.

"Did you say someth
dry.

"Seriously, put me do
gruff, as he approache
house. Once they rounc
be in view of anyone or
ing in his arms like
strange and a whole
that were far too con
attempt to sort thr

her head was swimming and her lungs ached and she felt absolutely sick with loss. But at the thought of what Robin and Andy would say if they saw them like this, she squirmed a little in protest.

"Scott . . ."

She felt him shrug. "Your call."

Stopping, keeping an arm around her waist for support, he let her slide to her feet. The thick, clipped grass felt cool and soft beneath her soles. The soft night air caressed her bare legs and arms. Her knees were wobbly, and for a moment she thought they weren't going to support her. If he hadn't been holding on to her, she would have staggered. He steadied her, and she leaned gratefully against him.

"You need to see a —"

The wail of approaching sirens made him break off and caused her to lift her head.

"Oh my God, they took so long." Inhaling, she coughed, but at least it wasn't as deep and wrenching as her cough had been before. The smell, the hideous burning smell, was growing stronger, and she didn't like to think what that meant.

"Too damned long." The grimness of his tone said what he forbore to add: If she'd had to wait for them to rescue her, she wouldn't have made it out.

The sirens were almost loud enough now to drown out the roar of the fire. They sounded close, and she wondered if the trucks had arrived. There was no way to know, because it was impossible to see the driveway from where they stood.

"This way. *Hurry.*"

The faint cry caused them both to look toward it. A teenage boy — Lisa was almost sure that it was the same one Scott had sent off with news of her rescue when they had first emerged from the house — burst into view around the corner of the house and dashed toward them, or rather, toward the side door, gesturing for someone behind him to follow. That someone turned out to be a man in a dark uniform who ran around the corner after him, carrying a satchel-type bag of some kind in one hand. Clearly a fire truck, or an ambulance, or something of that nature, had finally reached them. Lisa thought the man must be a paramedic.

"Chase, over here," Scott called, waving, and the kid changed course. "My nephew," he added in an aside for her ears alone. Lisa had known, vaguely, that his brother had married years ago and had a kid, but this was the first time she had ever seen him. Behind Chase, the man following changed course as well. Feeling two new sets of male eyes on her, Lisa was suddenly uncomfortably conscious of her state of undress.

"I need a robe," she said, more to herself than to Scott.

"This guy's an EMT," Chase announced as he arrived breathlessly in front of them. His eyes slid over her, widened, then quickly averted to Scott's face. "When you didn't show up out front, I thought she might need one."

"Good call," Scott said.

"Somebody hurt here?" Sounding faintly breathless, the EMT reached them and stopped, looking from one to the other. In the dark it was hard to be sure, but she thought he was about her age. She suddenly found her skimpy night attire extremely embarrassing, and was glad of the shadows that helped hide her.

"No," Lisa answered, pulling away from Scott and suppressing a cough as at the same time Scott said, "Check her out for smoke inhalation."

"Let me give you a listen." The EMT reached into his bag.

"I don't have time. I have to get to my mother." That was a firm negative, uttered as she started moving away. Her throat was raw, her lungs hurt, and she was a little dizzy, a little unsteady on her feet, but none of it mattered. She would have run to the front yard if she could have, but unfortunately, running seemed to be beyond her for the moment. But she could walk determinedly.

"They can check her out at the hospital," she heard the EMT say, presumably to Scott, and realized that they, plus his nephew, were right behind her. "But in my opinion, if she can walk and talk like that, there's no serious damage."

Rounding the corner of the house, Lisa immediately spotted the emergency vehicles: three fire trucks and two ambulances, sirens screaming, their stroboscopic lights sending bright red flashes of color through the night. A dozen or so firefighters in full gear swarmed toward the house. More emergency workers gathered around the figures on the lawn. They were small at this distance, but there was no mistaking who and what they were: her mother lying on her back in the grass with Robin and Andy and Lynn around her. A stretcher lay on the ground beside her, and even as Lisa watched, her heart suddenly in her throat, her mother was lifted onto it. The stretcher was then lifted, and Lisa realized that it was headed toward the ambulance.

"Wait!" she cried, then broke into a stumbling run. Scott was immediately beside her, grabbing her arm to provide support, running with her as he helped her stay on her feet. Robin, who was following the stretcher with the others, looked back at her cry. Lisa waved. Robin said something to the others, but no one slowed. Lisa managed to catch up just as the stretcher was being loaded into the vehicle. By the bright light inside the ambulance, she could see that her mother was deathly pale, her skin waxy-looking, her lips parted, her jaw slack. Strapped to the stretcher, she was covered to the armpits by a white sheet. The top few inches of her blue sleeveless nightgown were just visible above it. Her eyes were closed, and she appeared to be unconscious — or worse.

Fear clogged Lisa's throat. Her hands clenched. Her heart thudded painfully.

"Mother!"

Martha didn't respond in any way. Unable to get inside the ambulance because the paramedics who were still transferring her from the stretcher to the gurney were in the way, Lisa cast a frantic look around and encountered Andy's anguished eyes.

"What happened to her? Did she get trapped in the fire?"

"There was no fire where we were, just a

little smoke. We got her out fine. Then she just . . . passed out," Andy said. He was wearing a matched set of blue cotton pajamas. Beside him, Robin, looking equally distraught, wore a knee-length flowered nightgown. Only Lynn, in her white nurse's uniform, looked calm.

"Maybe the shock of it." Robin wrung her hands. "She saw where the fire was. She said your name and then . . ."

"She started shaking." Andy sounded shaky himself. "Then her eyes rolled back in her head, and . . . that was it."

"She may have had a small seizure," Lynn said.

Lisa felt a stab of dread. "Where are they taking her?"

"University of Kentucky Medical Center." It was in Lexington, Lisa knew. Lynn sounded fearful, and that scared Lisa anew. "They're best equipped to treat this."

"Oh my God." For a moment, as terror for her mother crashed over her in a near-crushing wave, Lisa felt faint. Then she forced herself to rally. She was all her mother had, and for that reason she had to stay strong.

"I'm going in the ambulance with her. I'm her daughter," she told the paramedics, who continued to bustle around their patient.

There still wasn't enough room for her to get in. One of them, a chubby, white-haired guy with glasses, slid his eyes over her, then looked at the rest of the group around her.

"Only one family member in the ambulance," he said, and went back to work.

"That's me." Putting one hand on the open door, Lisa prepared to scramble in.

"Here, take this." It was Scott's voice.

To Lisa's surprise, she felt cloth, lightweight and warm and smelling faintly of smoke, settle around her shoulders. A quick downward glance told her that Scott had taken off his shirt and given it to her. Letting go of the door, she thrust her arms into the sleeves gratefully.

"Thanks." Scrambling into the ambulance, clutching the edges of the shirt together, she looked back at Scott just as someone — Lisa presumed it was the ambulance's driver — started closing up the doors.

"We'll meet you at the hospital," Robin called, added, "Take these, too," and tossed a pair of slippers at her. Then the doors closed with a metallic clang. Gathering up the slippers, Lisa quickly found a seat on one of the molded benches built into the wall. She slid her feet into the slippers — they were blue terry-cloth scuffs that fortunately fit reasonably well — and started buttoning Scott's shirt and rolling up the too-long sleeves. It smelled of him, just faintly, and she wasn't even surprised to discover that the smell was comforting. The paramedics paid no attention to her: They were busy fitting an oxygen mask to her mother's face and hooking her up to an IV.

"How is she?" Lisa asked fearfully as the ambulance jolted into motion.

"Her vital signs are stable," the white-haired paramedic answered as he dropped onto the seat beside her. The other paramedic, a young, thin woman with short brown hair, said something from the opposite side of the stretcher, but the shrieking sirens made it impossible for Lisa to hear.

Her mother's arms were uncovered now — an IV line was inserted into one — and Lisa slid her hand around Martha's as the ambulance sped toward Lexington.

It felt cold and lifeless in her grasp.

"I'm here, Mother," she said, and only hoped that Martha could still hear her.

11

By the time all the diagnostic tests had been run and Martha had finally been admitted to the hospital and settled into a small private room, it was after nine a.m. the next morning. Martha's eyes were closed. Clear oxygen tubes ran into her nose. Her breathing was so shallow as to be almost undetectable beneath the blue blanket that was tucked in around her. The steady beep of the monitor she was hooked up to provided a modicum of reassurance to Lisa, who kept vigil beside the bed. For the moment, her mother slept. Lisa herself was so exhausted that her eyelids felt as though they had lead weights attached to them. She'd been treated for smoke inhalation and a couple of minor burns about the size of pencil erasers on the backs of her legs that had resulted from flying sparks. Other than that, her throat felt scratchy, her stomach was upset, and she had a thumping headache. But she was dressed, in jeans, a yellow tee with, ridiculously, a picture of SpongeBob SquarePants on it, and flip-flops, which had to count as a positive development, considering the outfit she had arrived at the hospital in. The clothes, along with the appropriate underwear, had been purchased by Robin during a hasty visit to the nearest open-all-night Walmart when Lisa could no longer tolerate being stared at as she walked around the hospital in Scott's shirt. The thought that she'd almost certainly lost nearly all her belongings in the fire was upsetting, so she tried not to think about it. Equally upsetting was the knowledge that her briefcase had been in her bedroom. So, too, had the Garcia file. And Katrina, in the dress that had so closely resembled Marisa Garcia's.

Did someone set fire to the house in order to get rid of the Garcia file? That was the question that wouldn't stop haunting her.

It wasn't impossible, but it was so unlikely as to verge on it. She was almost — *almost* — positive about that. That her interest in that long-ago disappearance could have triggered the burning of Grayson Springs was so paranoid that even considering the possibility boggled the mind, she decided, when the suspicion occurred, as it did for the first time in the middle of the night as she waited for one of several CT scans on her mother to be completed. The timing of the fire was coincidental, the probable loss of the evidence in the file unfortunate but not sinister. To believe otherwise was to do nothing less than question the very foundations of her life.

It was stupid, and she simply wasn't going to go there.

So, bottom line: As far as she was concerned, her biggest problem regarding the file was that she was going to have to tell Scott that she had taken it home.

He wasn't going to be happy.

Last night, he'd risked his life to save her. He'd carried her to safety, held her, comforted her, even given her the shirt off his back. Their often prickly relationship had shifted: The baiting and antagonism that had been the cornerstone of it for years had vanished. She'd felt — what? Safe in his arms? He'd felt something different than his usual half-annoyed aggravation for her, too. It had been there in his eyes when he looked at her.

Part of it was desire. She was a grown-up woman now, not a girl, and she was mature enough to recognize desire in a man's eyes when she saw it. And Scott definitely desired her. But then, she'd never really doubted that, on some fundamental level, he did, even if he never would make the slightest move in her direction.

For years there'd been an undeniable chemistry between them simmering just below the surface. But always she'd been the one who'd acted on it, chasing him, doing her best to entice him, trying to get him to want her, while he'd treated her like a stupid, importunate little girl who was more nuisance than anything else.

Last night something had changed. She'd felt that the guard he'd kept on himself all these years had dropped for long enough to let the way he really felt about her shine through.

The idea of it — of Scott openly wanting her — was actually kind of thrilling. Whenever she let herself think about it, her heart started to beat faster. Sleeping with Scott was something she had fantasized about during her teenage years. Now that she was all grown up, she was starting to get the feeling that it wouldn't take a whole lot of effort on her part to make that particular fantasy come true.

The thing was, though, there had been more than just sexual attraction for her there in his eyes. She couldn't quite put her

finger on what it was, but she knew what she'd felt in his arms — a sense of belonging.

That wrapped in Scott's arms was just exactly where she was supposed to be.

Not that any of it — desire, belonging, a sense of romantic possibility — was going to make any difference to her predicament, she told herself wryly: She knew Scott well enough to be sure that he was still going to be ticked off about the file.

Ticked off enough to fire her? She didn't *think* so. But she wasn't one hundred percent sure.

Something to worry about later, she told herself, and put Scott and the file and every other extraneous thing out of her mind as her mother opened her eyes for the first time in a couple of hours. With the head of the hospital bed raised to ease her breathing, Martha was almost in a sitting position.

"Hey," Lisa said softly, taking her hand.

Martha looked at her. For a moment she seemed to be having trouble focusing. Then her gaze sharpened and she smiled.

"Lisa."

"How are you feeling?"

"I've felt — better." A twinkle of rueful humor in her mother's eyes made Lisa feel a little more hopeful. That was the mother

she knew, and she experienced a brief uprising of relief. Then Martha glanced around and frowned. "Where — am I?"

Lisa's stomach tightened. She'd answered this same question at least three previous times. "At the University of Kentucky Medical Center."

"Oh." Martha accepted the information with an uncharacteristic lack of curiosity, then closed her eyes again.

Lisa waited silently.

Bright morning sunlight poured in through the cracks in the closed mini-blinds that covered the single window. A foam cup of coffee, the only pleasant smell among the cornucopia of antiseptic hospital scents, steamed on the stand beside her, perched next to the yellow plastic hospital pitcher of water, the phone, the remote, and a box of tissues. The coffee was courtesy of Andy, who had left maybe twenty minutes earlier to drive Robin back to Grayson Springs to check out the damage. They, along with Lisa, Scott, and Lynn, had been part of the group gathered around Martha in the hospital when they had received word at about two a.m. that the fire had been put out. Th cause, they were told, was under investig tion.

Lisa discovered that she was extrer

anxious to know the cause. Even though she was sure — sure — that it would be found to be an accident. Which would mean that it could have had nothing to do with the Garcia file. Which would, she discovered, be a huge relief.

If the fire was set to destroy the file . . . She didn't want to follow that thought to its obvious conclusion, but she couldn't help it: *It might have something to do with me.*

"You should — go home and — get some sleep." Martha's eyes opened again to focus on Lisa. Martha had regained consciousness not long after arriving at the hospital and had been awake several times since then, but thanks to the medication being pumped into her veins — at least, Lisa prayed her fogginess was due to medication — she seemed to only intermittently remember that the house had burned. Which was probably something to be thankful for. Her mother would grieve for the house she loved, just as Lisa was grieving. And at the moment Martha didn't need that kind of psychic pain.

"I'll go home later." She squeezed her mother's hand. It was cold — too cold — and dry. An insurance adjuster would be meeting her at Grayson Springs at about seven p.m., but other than that she meant to spend the rest of the day at the hospital, and to sleep there, too.

"You look — tired. I'll be — fine here. Really."

Martha's short white hair fanned out against the pillow like a bird's ruffled feathers. Her paper-thin skin seemed to have developed a myriad of new wrinkles overnight. Her eyes as they met Lisa's were red-rimmed and puffy, and had a disoriented look to them that Lisa found alarming.

"You know I'm not going to leave you."

"Annalisa." Martha managed a small smile. "I'm so — glad — you came home. When you were gone — I missed you — so much."

"I missed you, too," Lisa said softly, her heart aching. She'd been so young and self-involved when she went away to college that she had never even considered what it might have cost her mother to simply smile and let her go. Now that she'd grown up enough to realize this, she wished with all her heart she could go back through time and call more, visit more, come back sooner. But there was no changing the past; all she could do was be here for her mother now.

A quick knock on the open door made her look around in time to see a balding, fortyish man in a white lab coat step into the room. Nodding briskly at Lisa, he moved to her mother's bedside.

"Hello, Mrs. Grant, I'm Dr. Metz, Dr. Spencer's associate. Let's take a look at you."

Dr. Spencer was her mother's regular physician. "Where's Dr. Spencer?" Lisa asked.

"He's on vacation. He'll be back on Monday."

When the brief examination was over, her mother closed her eyes, took a deep breath, and seemed to fall almost instantly asleep. With a worried look at her, Lisa rose and followed the doctor out into the hall. They stopped in the busy corridor, and as hospital life went on around them Lisa regarded him anxiously.

"How is she?"

He shook his head. "We're still running tests. We won't know for sure until some of the results come back."

"She doesn't seem to be thinking clearly. Half the time she doesn't know where she is or remember that our house burned last night."

"Some confusion is probably normal under the circumstances. She suffered a trauma when your house caught fire, and then there's the ALS, which is complicating the diagnosis a little bit. My best guess is that last night she suffered a transient ischemic event" — Lisa looked at him questioningly — "basically a small stroke, which would account for her lapsing into unconsciousness at the scene and her confusion today. I'll be able to tell you more when the test results come back."

"And that will be?"

"Later today, possibly, for some of them. Others may take a little longer."

The cell phone in Lisa's pocket went off. It was her phone, which fortunately she had left in the workout room the night before, allowing it to survive the fire. Robin had brought it to her at the hospital, and Lisa had been so glad to see it that she had almost cried. So much else had been lost that it had suddenly seemed as precious as a recovered treasure. While she fished for it, Dr. Metz, giving her another nod, took the opportunity to escape. Of course he must be a busy man, with lots of patients to see, but she didn't feel that she knew much more than she had when he'd come into her mother's room. Certainly she didn't feel reassured.

"It's the Rink," the caller identified himself when Lisa, frowning after Dr. Metz with some frustration, said hello. "Uh, I gotta ask you something: Did you make off with that file we were looking at yesterday? The one where you're, like, the victim's twin?"

Lisa grimaced. *Busted so soon.* "Yeah, I did."

"Thought so." Rinko sounded relieved. "When I got to work this morning and it wasn't here, I freaked for a minute. Looked everywhere. Then it occurred that you might have taken it home to look at it some more. No biggie. Although you probably ought to be getting it back in here."

"Yeah, it is a biggie." Lisa leaned back against the wall and sighed. "Our house burned last night. I'm afraid the file burned, too."

"Oh, man." Rinko was silent for a moment, as if to let the news sink in. "I'm sorry about your house."

"Thanks."

Glancing up, she discovered Scott walking down the hall toward her, looking tall, broad-shouldered, handsome, and very much the big-shot DA in a navy suit, white shirt, and red power tie. He'd left the hospital at about three a.m. shortly after she'd been pronounced fine but not before telling her to take as many days off as she needed to deal with what had happened. Now, for whatever reason, he was back. As her eyes fastened on him, Lisa felt an instantaneous tingle of sexual awareness followed by a warm little glow that roughly translated to *Hey, I'm really glad to see you.* This was the first time she'd ever felt that particular combination of reactions to his presence, and they came as a not-unpleasant surprise.

Then she saw that he wasn't alone. In full lawyer mode — black skirt suit and pumps, blond hair pulled back, carrying a briefcase — Kane was with him, saying something to him, nodding earnestly at his reply. There was another suit-clad lawyer with them, too, a man — thirtyish, thin, glasses. Hendricks, that was his name. Like Kane, he was an ADA. As Lisa watched, Scott said something to his companions and made a "give me a minute" gesture. As the two of them obediently stopped with the obvious purpose of waiting for him out of earshot, he continued to stride toward her.

In that instant while she watched him walking toward her, an image flashed into her mind: Scott bare to the waist, as he had been last night after he had whipped off his shirt so that she could wear it to the hospital. At the time, she'd been too preoccupied to do more than subconsciously register the sight. Now she remembered vividly how muscular his shoulders were, and that his arms were as big and brawny as if he continued to do a lot of physical labor — or, alternatively, worked out. His chest was wide, with a wedge of dark brown hair and well-developed pecs that gave way to flat abs. It tapered down in a classic V to narrow hips, where his pants had interrupted the view.

She'd seen him bare-chested before — fairly frequently, actually — when they'd been kids. But there was a difference: Now he was a full-grown man.

Their gazes met. Lisa's pulse, which was primed to quicken, wasn't put to the trouble.

Ouch, she thought. *Reality bites.*

Whatever she might have thought she'd seen in his eyes for her last night was nowhere in evidence as she met them today. There was nothing personal in his expression at all. In fact, he looked like his usual maddening self again, hard and purposeful, all business, every inch the successful lawyer and her boss. If he was, as she'd so briefly enjoyed imagining, lusting for her body, he gave no indication of it now.

Clutching the phone tighter, she gave him a cool look in retaliation.

"Um, Buchanan's here," she said in a

lowered voice to Rinko. "I'm going to have to go."

"Oh, crap. Well, if it helps, you can tell him that we already uploaded everything that was in that file. All that was lost was . . ."

"The original documents," Lisa finished for him in a dry undertone as Scott reached her. Then, louder, she said, "Thanks. You're a prince."

"Who's a prince?" Scott asked as she disconnected. His gaze slid over her, and his impatient look was leavened by a flash of amusement. "Like the T-shirt."

She was suddenly conscious that without makeup and with her hair knotted into a haphazard bun at her nape, she was looking something less than her best. The reason she was conscious of it wasn't so much Scott, who'd seen her just about every which way there was to see her many times before this, but Kane, who from her spot some two doors away was eyeing her up and down. With dislike. That's when the other shoe dropped: The reason Kane was so consistently hateful to her was because of Scott.

Of course.

Obviously Kane had a thing for him. Interesting to realize that she felt Lisa might be a threat to that. Less interesting to acknowledge was her own instinctive spurt of antagonism toward Kane.

So, what does that tell you?

The short answer was: Nothing she cared to think about at the moment.

Strictly for Kane's sake, Lisa summoned a warm smile for Scott.

"Thanks. And the prince is Alan Rinko. He's a law student, and he's been working for you in Siberia since May."

Scott's brows rose. "Siberia?"

"Where you sent me yesterday. The basement, to sort through the cold-case files. Everybody in the office calls it Siberia, because you banish people to it when you're mad at them."

"First time I've ever heard it called that."

"I'm not surprised." Her voice turned tart. "They're all too afraid of you to say it to your face."

"What? That's not true."

"Want to bet? For your information, Mr. Boss Man, the whole office tiptoes around on eggshells when you're in a bad mood. Which the word is you have been quite a bit lately."

"Who says?" He sounded faintly defensive.

"Think I'm going to start naming names? No way."

"If you're not naming names, Princess, it's because it's not true."

"Believe what you want. And don't call me Princess." She gave him a blistering look, then shook her head and gave up. "So, what's happening with your dad? Did you get him out of jail yet?"

"I got him a lawyer, and I'm staying out of it. Listen, I don't have time for chitchat. I'm on my way to a meeting. We've got an informant who's apparently ready to spill his guts on McDonnell and Coley." As everyone in the office knew, McDonnell, a prominent local businessman, was under investigation for bribing Circuit Court Judge Arthur Coley to return a favorable ruling in a case involving McDonnell's divorce. It had the potential to be a very big, and very messy, case. "I just came by to give you some news."

"What news? No, wait, there's something I have to tell you first." Determined to put her transgression behind her, she wanted to get it out there and over with. "There was a cold-case file I came across yesterday that interested me. I took it home last night. Um, I'm afraid it probably burned in the fire."

His face tightened. If she hadn't known him so well, she thought, she probably would have started quaking in her boots about then, because he looked displeased, to say the very least.

"There's a rule about taking cold-case files out of the building."

"I know."

"You did it anyway." It wasn't a question.

"Yes."

"You get permission from anybody? Sign it out? Anything like that?"

"No."

"You know anybody caught taking cold-case files out of the building without permission is subject to being fired, right?"

"So, are you going to fire me?"

He hesitated, then looked disgusted. "What, and make it twice in two days? Are you going for some kind of record?"

"Scott . . ."

"You are a major pain in my ass, you know that? You want to tell me why you took that file?"

"The woman looked like me."

"What?"

"A local family disappeared about thirty years ago. Mother, father, two children. There was a picture of them in the file. The mother looked enough like me to be my twin. You should see it, the resemblance is amazing." She tried a small smile, which elicited no comparable response.

"I'm never going to see it, am I? Because it just burned up."

"There's a copy," she said with dignity. "The good news, as Rinko just informed me, is that the file had already been uploaded to the system when I took it. Everything in it was copied before it was destroyed. Including the picture."

She was almost sure.

"Wonderful. In fact, that'd make everything just peachy keen, except, number one, the file was not supposed to be removed from the building, and, number two, if by chance we ever get enough evidence together to identify a culprit and take the case to trial we'll need the original documents to get a conviction. Copies don't actually count."

"I know. I'm sorry. So, you're not going to fire me?"

He gave her a glinting look. "Consider this strike two."

This time Lisa's smile was genuine. "As in, one more and I'm out?"

"Fuckin-A, baby. And I mean it, so you'd best take care." His frown lightened fractionally. "So, how's your mother doing?"

"They think she may have had a stroke. Most of the time she doesn't seem to remember that the house burned last night."

"Which reminds me —"

He broke off as his cell phone began to ring. Fishing it out of his pocket, he identified himself and listened. As he did, he rolled his eyes toward the ceiling and looked harassed.

"Okay, I forgot all about them. Give me a minute here while I try to come up with something they can do. I'll call you back." Pressing a button to end the call with Adams, whose barely heard voice Lisa was certain she recognized, he frowned at Lisa, who was regarding him questioningly. "You wouldn't happen to have a suggestion for what I can do with a bunch of high school kids, including my dumbass nephew, who I caught partying in my old man's house last night, would you? Instead of busting them, I told them to meet me in my office this morning, thinking I'd come up with some kind of a junior-grade pretrial diversion program before they got there. But what with one thing and another" — as in, she thought, his rescue of her from a burning house, subsequent hours spent at the hospital, and whatever else he'd been doing in the meantime — "I forgot all about them, and now I've got somewhere I have to be and I'm drawing a blank here about what to do with them."

"Wait a minute. Let me get this straight. You caught some kids in your father's house last night? Before or after the fire?"

"Before. Right after I talked to you on the swing. That's why I was still around when the fire broke out."

"Oh." It hadn't even occurred to her to wonder about that, Lisa realized. Having Scott there at the exact moment when she had needed him had seemed so completely unremarkable that she hadn't thought to question it. "What do you mean 'partying'?"

"What do you think I mean? Smoking pot and drinking beer. Six of them, fifteen and sixteen years old, with Chase — my nephew — the ringleader."

"You didn't call the cops."

Remembering her own teenage partying days, she felt a residual tickle of gratitude. Knowing Scott's own attitude toward that kind of underage fun — he was agin it, to put it mildly — his restraint surprised her.

"Nope."

"You're a nice man, Scott Buchanan." She smiled at him again, with genuine warmth this time. Then, remembering various incidents over the years, she temporized. "Well, occasionally."

"Careful, you don't want to get carried

away with the compliments." He grimaced, glanced down at his phone, then looked impatient. "Look, do you or don't you have any suggestions for what I can do with those kids? I got things to do and places to be here."

The proverbial lightbulb came on in her head.

"Send them to Rinko. In Siberia. They can help him upload the cold-case files. There are thousands of them. Without more help than he's been getting — which is basically whoever you're mad at — somebody'll be down in that basement working on them until the end of time."

He looked struck. "That's not a bad idea. They could actually do something use —"

Kane appeared behind him just then and laid a hand on his arm, interrupting. Her eyes met Lisa's. They were the opposite of warm.

"Hi, Grant." Her perfunctory smile matched her eyes. "Sorry to hear about what happened last night." She switched her attention to Scott. "Um, I hate to interrupt, but Gamboli just called me to see if we're going to be much longer. He said his guy is getting antsy."

Scott's expression as he looked down at Kane was unreadable, but Scott had always been one to play things close to the vest. Still, as far as Lisa could tell, the attraction was all on Kane's side.

It was annoying to have to admit she was glad about that.

"Yeah, I'm coming." He looked back at Lisa, who, conscious of once more being the target of Kane's hard gaze, smiled at him again. Warmly.

He gave her a narrow-eyed look in response but didn't say anything.

"I can handle your wayward lambs for you. If you want, I'll call Rinko and set something up," Lisa suggested. "That kind of work I can do from the hospital."

"Yeah, you can. Okay, I appreciate it. Whatever you can arrange." He looked at Kane again. "You and Hendricks head on down. I'll meet you in the lobby. I won't be but another couple of minutes. I just want to say a quick hello to Mrs. Grant."

"Sure." Kane nodded her acquiescence, but she didn't look pleased as she turned and walked away.

"My mother's probably asleep," Lisa told him with an apologetic grimace.

"If she is, you can say hi to her for me. Like I said, I've got some news for you. This morning I put out a few calls to some people involved in the investigation of your fire. I got a call back from Greg Watson, who's now the chief detective on the case, just about half an hour ago. They're not positive yet, but they're working under the assumption that the cause was arson. I wanted to let you know before you got ambushed with it."

12

"I understand you've been under some financial strain." The statement — it wasn't a question — came from Woodford County Sheriff's Detective Greg Watson. "For one thing, you've got a pretty hefty mortgage on this place, don't you?"

Unable to believe what she was hearing, Lisa looked away from the burned-out shell in front of her to turn incredulous eyes on him. She'd already had a difficult day. Ambushed by reporters not long after Scott had left, she'd been surprised into saying that she'd been inside the house asleep when the fire had started before realizing her mistake in talking to them at all and clamming up. But it was too late: Her words had made the local news at noon, which had aired footage of the fire, complete with pictures of the damaged house, on all three channels. Since then, her cell phone and the phone in her mother's hospital room had been ringing off the hook. They'd been swamped with visitors, both welcome and unwelcome, to the point that she'd been forced to greet people who weren't part of her mother's inner circle at the door with the sometimes true and sometimes not claim that her mother was asleep, after which she would chat for a moment and then gently turn them away. She'd had to talk to her father by phone again and listen to his excuses about why he couldn't come to the hospital until she stopped them by telling him briskly that she was fine and her mother certainly didn't want to see him, so nobody needed him anyway. She'd had to deal with the insurance company, the police, the doctors treating her mother, and the hospital red tape. Confronted with the reality of her charred and damaged home, her chest ached with loss. Her throat was tight, and her stomach knotted from the knowledge that nothing was ever going to be able to put Grayson Springs back the way it had been. Now this deputy was giving her a hard time. She had to swallow before she could reply.

"There's a mortgage, yes."

Having showered and put on some makeup and loaner clothes that Nola had brought by the hospital for her earlier, she was glad to think that probably she was looking better than she felt. In deference to the swampy end-of-June heat, her hair was pulled back in a simple ponytail, and she wore lipstick and mascara only. Although Nola, who loved all things pink and ruffly, had been left to her own devices when choosing the clothes, she knew Lisa's taste well enough that she'd brought classics: a navy skirt and white polo, and a pair of slip-on sneakers.

"And you were having trouble making ends meet?"

Lisa took a deep breath, welcoming the anger that welled up inside her as an antidote to grief.

"You might as well quit beating around the bush and come right out and ask me if I set the fire, Detective." She was polite, but her voice had an edge to it. Detective Watson, a sandy-haired, lanky, fortysomething man of average attractiveness, average height, and, she was beginning to think, somewhat less than average intellect, blinked slowly at her, reminding her of nothing so much as a sleepy turtle. "The answer is no. I did not try to burn down the house I've lived in all my life, the house my family has lived in for generations and that my mother, who is terminally ill and wants to live out the rest of her days in, loves, the house that I will now have to try to restore to something approximating what it was before I can even begin to think about selling it after my mother passes away, for a little bit of insurance money."

"Quite a lot of insurance money, is what I've heard."

"I'm not sure of the amount, but believe me, whatever it is can't make up for *this.*" With a sweeping gesture she indicated the house, where a contingent of workers presumably called in by the insurance company was already trying to prevent further damage from the rain that was predicted to arrive overnight. Men in a crane worked with men on ladders to spread blue tarpaulins over the section of roof nearest to the part that had burned. Under Robin's critical supervision — Lynn was at the hospital with Martha — more were busy inside the house.

Watson turned his attention back to the scene in front of them. They were standing in the backyard, on the now trampled grass in front of the low brick wall that bordered the Baby's Garden. It was just before eight p.m., close enough to twilight so that the sunlight had softened and turned golden and the humidity had decreased to the point when it was just possible not to break into a sweat while standing still. The scorched smell that hung heavy in the air was strong enough so that the sweeter scent of the roses in the garden behind them was almost completely obliterated. Though her back was turned to the fountain, which operated on a timer that came on automatically at daylight and shut off at dark, Lisa could hear the soothing tinkle of falling water over the rumble and clank of the crane and the jumble of voices and other sounds. Like most of the grounds and the south wing of the house, the Baby's Garden was untouched. The center part of the house where the tarpaulins were being placed had sustained some minor burn and smoke damage but nothing that couldn't be repaired within a few days. There were scorch marks on the roof, and the white walls were black in places with plumy smears of smoke and soot, but structurally the center section was still sound and none of its rooms or their contents had been touched by the fire. It was the north wing, where her bedroom was located, that had burned. The outer walls still stood, as did the chimney on the far end, but the roofline looked as though a giant with jagged teeth had taken a huge bite out of it. What remained was black and charred. The inside was practically gutted, and what hadn't burned had suffered irreparable smoke and water damage. She'd lost everything that had been in her bedroom: her purse, with all her ID; her briefcase; her furniture; the majority of her clothes; her mementos, including the ceramic frog her mother had given her on the occasion of her first real breakup with her first real boyfriend — she'd been fourteen, tearful and tragic, and the frog had been presented in a little blue box tied with white ribbon along with a chocolate frosted cupcake (her favorite) and a note that read "You've got to kiss a lot of these to find a prince" — and the pink ballet shoes she'd worn when she'd taken classes as a little girl (ballet wasn't her best thing, but she'd loved those shoes), and . . . well, so many things that if she let herself think about them, she would burst into tears there and then.

Her dolls — including Katrina — were lost, too. The thought was worrisome.

So, with Detective Watson's eyes on her she did her best to block it out of her mind.

"You understand we have to ask these questions, ma'am, when we're investigating a possible arson," Detective Watson said in his slow southern drawl. "They're not meant to accuse you or anybody else."

Lisa could almost hear the unspoken *yet*

hanging in the air.

"What makes you think the fire was arson?" Lisa asked around the constriction in her throat.

Detective Watson shook his head, looking as tight-lipped and mysterious as a man who reminded her of a turtle could, but the insurance adjuster, whom she had driven out to Grayson Springs to meet and who had turned out to be a no-nonsense African-American woman in her fifties named Tracy McCoy, came up the path to join her and the detective in time to hear her question.

"They found traces of an accelerant." Ms. McCoy was carrying a red leather-bound notebook with a calculator attached. Lisa had watched earlier as, walking around the house, she had made ample use of both. "If you would start getting some estimates together, Ms. Grant, we'll see if we can't get the ball rolling for you."

"What kind of an accelerant?" Lisa could feel the blood starting to pound in her temples. She'd had almost no sleep, a quick lunch of hospital food, and more aggravation than any one human being should have to deal with in a single day. Add to that her worry for her mother and her grief over Grayson Springs, and it was no wonder that she was starting to feel as though her life was spinning out of control.

"Paint thinner. Isn't that right, Detective?" Ms. McCoy looked to Detective Watson for corroboration.

"Yes." Detective Watson sounded reluctant to part with even that much information.

"If you found traces of paint thinner, it probably wasn't arson." Relief bubbled in Lisa's voice. "There were painters in the house yesterday, in the north wing, the part that's burned. They would have had paint thinner, wouldn't they?"

"They would," Detective Watson said. "But . . ."

"There was *a lot* of accelerant. It was splashed on the walls and floor and —" Ms. McCoy stopped as Detective Watson frowned her down.

"Oh, all right," Ms. McCoy said to him. "But you know she isn't the one who did it. I've been doing this long enough where I can spot somebody attempting insurance fraud a mile off."

Detective Watson didn't look impressed. Without replying, he switched his attention to Lisa again.

"Can you think of anyone who might be angry with you or your family, or want to do you harm? Or any reason why someone might want to set fire to your house?"

To Lisa's surprise, an answer popped instantly, instinctively, into her head seemingly out of nowhere.

Well, see, there's this cold-case file I brought home from work, and I look just like the mother and . . .

For the briefest of moments, no more, Lisa considered mentioning the Garcia file. But if she did, she realized with a sick feeling in the pit of her stomach, what she might be doing was setting into motion a chain of events that she wouldn't like and couldn't control. What if, in some way she didn't even have the energy to speculate about at the moment, it turned out that she *was* somehow related to the missing family? Obviously, if the file had been the cause of someone setting fire to Grayson Springs, someone wanted to keep something about the family or their disappearance from coming to light. The question then became who, and what?

The who *is kind of obvious, isn't it? It has to be someone who knew I brought the file home.*

Which, in the quick mental tally she tried to do, made the list of suspects both short and well known to her. Terrifyingly so. Her heart clutched as a handful of names popped instantly into her head: She didn't want to go there.

Of course, what was far more likely was that she was being as overimaginative as Barty had often accused her of being, and the fire had nothing to do with the file at all. Detective Watson's suspicions notwithstanding, it might not even have been the result of arson. Paint thinner had been in use in the house, in the north wing, almost certainly. Didn't that mean the fire could have been an accident?

Yes, she decided. Relief made her a little light-headed as she mentally embraced the possibility.

"Ms. Grant?" Detective Watson was watching her closely.

"I can't think of anyone," Lisa said. Whatever the truth of the matter was, one thing was certain: She wanted to research the Garcia case a little more herself before bringing it to the attention of Detective Watson and his ilk as a possible reason someone might have set fire to Grayson Springs. If there did happen to be a skeleton she didn't know about in her own closet, she wanted to be the one to find it first.

If the fire was set because of the Garcia file, the reason behind it could tear my life apart.

The thought made her stomach knot. Curling her nails into her palms so hard they dug into her skin, she barely managed to stop herself from wetting her lips.

You're being ridiculous, she scolded herself.

"Rival horse farm owners?" Detective Watson continued inexorably, his eyes keen on her face. "A suitor you've recently broken up with? Anyone less than reputable you owe money to?"

Consciously but, she hoped, unobtrusively, she relaxed her clenched hands.

"Not that I know of. A definite 'no' to the suitor. And the money lender. And I don't see any reason why any of the farms around here would want to try to burn us out. We don't even own any racehorses anymore, and they're probably well aware that Grayson Springs will be put on the market eventually."

"Hmm." The sound Detective Watson made was noncommittal. Lisa wasn't sure whether he actually suspected her of something or not.

"Mrs. Baker said the old drunk lives up the road was on a bender yesterday." Ms. McCoy looked up from her notebook, where, pen in hand, she seemed to be adding up some scribbled figures. "She said he doesn't like you all."

"He couldn't have done it. He was in jail last night. Anyway, he'd be more likely to shoot our house up than burn it."

Lisa suddenly remembered the kids Scott had said he'd caught partying in his father's house last night. Could they maybe have done something like this out of pure teenage idiocy? But setting a house on fire went far beyond idiocy, and anyway, she didn't intend to make any accusations against anybody without some kind of compelling evidence. Let Detective Watson conduct his own investigation.

"I've got a check here to cover your immediate living expenses." Ms. McCoy pulled a rectangle of pale blue paper out of a pocket in the notebook, closed the pad, then handed the paper over. Lisa saw at a glance that it was a check for two thousand five hundred dollars. Fortunately, they were very old and valued clients of the insurance agency. "Temporary housing, food, any clothing or personal items that need to be replaced. Just keep your receipts. If you need more, you just call me. My number's right here on my card." She handed over her business card, which Lisa accepted with thanks. "If you want to call me tomorrow, I can give you a list of contractors we routinely work with. Or you can use anyone you prefer, of course."

"Where are you staying?" Detective Watson asked as, after a farewell handshake,

Ms. McCoy started walking away. "In case I need to reach you."

"I'm staying at the hospital with my mother for the time being." Robin was going to be sharing the manager's house with Andy when the two of them weren't taking shifts at the hospital, and Lisa guessed she'd better be thinking about coming up with her own temporary digs. So far, she hadn't had time. "Beyond that, I've made no plans. You can always reach me on my cell phone."

A uniformed deputy called to Detective Watson from the far side of the house, and with a murmured "Excuse me," he left her. Her business done, Lisa headed for the Jaguar, which the dealership had dropped off at the hospital earlier, while assuring her amid copious apologies that the vehicle was in tip-top shape now that the loose cap that had led to the transmission fluid inadvertently leaking out had been tightened and the fluid replaced. To say that she no longer had complete confidence in her wheels was an understatement, but the car had brought her to Grayson Springs and would, she hoped, convey her back to the hospital without mishap.

But first she meant to make a quick side trip.

A little before five she'd called Rinko. Her

stated purpose was to check on how the wayward lambs, as she now thought of them, were holding up in Siberia. He'd been upbeat and openly enthusiastic about the help, which she attributed largely to her happy notion of asking Jantzen to escort the kids down to the basement and provide Rinko with what help she could to get the new junior pretrial diversion program going. Then, as casually as possible, she'd asked Rinko to call up the Garcia file on the computer and give her the address of the house from which the family had disappeared.

"You planning to go check it out or something?" Rinko wasn't stupid.

Lisa had sighed. So much for keeping things on the down-low.

"Maybe. I have to meet an insurance adjuster at Grayson Springs tonight at seven, so I thought I might just drive by the house while I'm out. Unless I'm way confused about where it is, it's on the way, and . . . and . . . well, I just thought I'd go look it over. It's an interesting case."

She ended on a faintly defensive note.

"*Interesting*'s the word for it, all right." Lisa could hear Rinko tapping away at the computer keys as he spoke. "Hey, no worries, though: If I looked that much like some chick who'd disappeared thirty years ago, I'd want to eyeball the house she vanished from, too." Then he paused and seemed to consider it, although Lisa could still hear the tapping of keys. "Actually, if I looked that much like some chick, I'd have bigger problems than the fact that she'd disappeared. Like tits, to start with."

Chortling at what he clearly considered his own sparkling wit, he then gave her the information she'd asked for. Thanking him, she disconnected.

The house she sought was just inside the county line. Lisa had had a vague idea of where it was located from her quick perusal of the file before she'd gone down to supper, and it turned out she'd been right. Just as she'd thought, it was — sort of, kind of — on the way back into the city from Grayson Springs. But as she drove west along the narrow ribbon of rural blacktop that was home to a succession of trailers and small ranch-style houses set well back from the road on five- or ten-acre lots, the route started to seem eerily familiar.

What is this, déjà vu?

Glancing up at the canopy of ragged branches overhanging the road, looking sideways at the weed-choked ditches on either side, taking in the sagging wire fences and the scraggly yards and the unmistakable lack of prosperity of the area, she thought, *I've been here before,* with utter conviction.

Teetering on the verge of freaking out, she suddenly realized that the road seemed familiar because she — Lisa Grant, not the shade of Angela Garcia as she'd found herself half fearing — had indeed been this way before, and more than once. The road led to Carmody Landing, an old, under-the-radar tavern that wasn't too particular about carding its patrons. For that reason it was a favorite with the underage drinkers in the area, and she'd driven there with car-loads of her friends several times when she'd been in high school.

Making the connection was such a relief that she blew out a breath she hadn't realized she'd been holding.

Idiot, she scolded herself.

Still, when she reached the small brick house, all she meant to do was just drive past and take a quick, anonymous look. If there hadn't been a For Sale sign stuck out in the yard, she probably would have kept going just as she had intended. But seeing that the place looked empty, she couldn't resist: She turned the Jag around and went back, pulling slowly off the road and bumping up the long gravel drive that led to the house. Dingy-looking red brick, a low black roof with a couple of shingles missing, a tiny front porch huddled under a peaked overhang: Nothing seemed to have changed appreciably from the photograph.

There was an attached two-car garage, she saw, as she stopped opposite the walk that led to the concrete steps where the Garcias had sat for the picture in the file. The garage door, which was white and needed painting, was closed. The front door was also white and closed, with a flimsy plastic bag apparently left by some kind of door-to-door salesman hanging from the knob. A big picture window with drapes drawn marked the location of the living room, she was sure. There were two other windows, smaller, double-hung ones, which she guessed belonged to a bedroom or bedrooms.

There was no sign of life anywhere around the place. Turning off the ignition, Lisa got out of the car. The thick heat actually felt good after the air-conditioning. Long shadows from the strip of woods crowding close beside the driveway and running the length of the narrow, looked-to-be-five-acre property lay across the house and yard. Leafy foliage formed a dense wall at least fifty feet high, blocking all view of the setting sun, though orange and purple streamers streaked across the darkening sky. The height and size of the trees told her that they had almost certainly been there when the Garcias had lived in the house. Another similarly sized strip of woods on the far side of the house isolated the place from its neighbors, which made it reasonable that no one living nearby had heard or seen a thing the night the Garcias had disappeared.

Though a breeze had been blowing when she'd left Grayson Springs, now the air had gone perfectly still. Not so much as a blade of grass stirred as she headed down the walk toward the front door. Except for a high-pitched cicada chorus, there was no sound other than her own soft footfalls on the concrete pavers. Nothing passed by on the road. Not even a bird soared overhead. The sense of being cut off from the rest of the world was strong, and increasingly oppressive. As she neared the front steps, Lisa gave in to a sudden urge to cast a quick glance over her shoulder toward the woods behind her. A tingle along her spine, a prickling of the hairs on the back of her neck, made her feel as though someone was there among the trees, watching her every move.

Overimaginative. She could almost hear

Barty saying it.

Nothing but a stockade of brown trunks standing tall amid the undergrowth met her searching gaze. No one was there. *Of course* no one was there.

You're being an idiot.

But still the feeling of being watched was strong.

Why she didn't just turn around, get back in her car and leave, she couldn't have said. Certainly she did not expect to find anything that would tell her what had happened to the Garcias. Too many years had passed, and anyway, any number of families had probably lived in the house since, most of them in happy ignorance of the Garcias' existence. It was extremely unlikely that any trace of the missing family would remain. But still, she couldn't help herself. She felt almost irresistibly drawn to the house.

It bothered her that her heart was thumping and her pulse was racing as she reached the steps and stopped.

Get real. It's an empty house, that's all.

But that didn't keep her from studying the steps, from picturing the family perched on them as they had been in the photo: Angela here, her husband — what was his name again? — beside her, Tony here, little Marisa here. And the dog, Lucy.

Lisa froze as the dog's name popped into her mind.

How do I know that? Her mouth went dry even as she mentally grabbed for the most reasonable explanation with both hands. *Of course I read it in the file.*

And never mind that she didn't actually remember doing so.

The small, thirsty-looking bushes beside the steps were of recent vintage. She barely glanced at them as she went up the steps and, yes, tried the doorknob. It was locked.

Facing the fact that she wasn't going to be able to get inside the house without breaking and entering, which she wasn't prepared to do, flooded her with relief.

I can't get in. She tried to pacify the tiny voice in her head that seemed to be urging her to go inside.

Going back down the steps, she glanced almost longingly toward the Jag. It waited, solid and reassuring, its hunter-green paint gleaming faintly in the fading light. But instead of heading toward it, she went the other way, around the side of the house, toward the back. The kitchen would be in the back. There would be a back door.

I can try to get in there.

She could argue with herself all she wanted, she realized. Some part of her really, really wanted to go inside that house. Walking around the far corner so that she lost sight of the Jag, she found herself enveloped by the house's shadow, and shivered.

Call the Realtor, make an appointment, and come back another time with another human being.

That was the rational solution, and she absolutely intended to take her own advice. But first she just wanted to finish walking around the house, to get a sense of it without anyone else's presence interfering with her impressions. It was as if she could feel an invisible force drawing her on, like the pull of a magnet. Uneasy but persevering, she glanced at the double-hung windows. Two, one on each side, with a smaller window perfectly spaced in between: two bedrooms and a bathroom, probably. Judging from the size of the house and its age, she was guessing that it was the standard-for-the-era three bedrooms and one bath. The windows had pull-down shades that blocked her from seeing inside.

The backyard, she saw as she reached it, ended in a cornfield. No fence, just an acre or so of dusty crabgrass fading into row upon row of bright green cornstalks that were already stretching higher than her head. With the woods on either side, the result was that the backyard felt closed in. Oppressive, even. As if it harbored secrets.

The thought gave her the willies.

Okay, I'm leaving, she promised herself as her gaze ran along the back of the house: two double-hung windows, a pair of smaller side-by-side windows that were higher set — the kitchen? — and a jalousied door that opened onto a small wooden deck. The deck had almost certainly been added since the Garcias' time.

Something — a flash of movement? — caught her eye as she stepped up onto the deck. Quickly she turned her head to scan the section of the woods where she'd seen it. It was the same approximate spot where she'd thought she'd felt someone watching her before.

Is someone in the woods? Lisa caught her breath. She felt the prickle of cold sweat along her hairline.

But there was nothing. No face, pale among the shadows. No eyes shining through the foliage. There was no movement, not even the quiver of a leaf. Nothing at all. Just utter stillness and the same solid wall of trees that had been there all along.

See? No one's there.

But no matter how she sought to convince

herself of that, her body didn't seem to be getting the message. Her heart thumped. Her pulse raced. Her stomach tightened. If her hand hadn't already been reaching for the doorknob by that time, she would have abandoned her mission there and then. But her fingers closed around the smooth brass knob almost of their own volition and turned it — *turned it!* — even as the impulse to hightail it for the Jag grew ever more urgent.

The door was unlocked.

Oh my God.

Completely unable to draw back now that she was so tantalizingly close, she refocused all her attention on what she was doing and cautiously pushed the door open. Her breathing ragged, her heart jitterbugging in her chest, she looked wide-eyed into the gloom of the empty kitchen. That first glance took in a wall of old varnished wood cabinets, figured wallpaper, and a faux-brick linoleum floor. Remembering the blood that supposedly had been spilled there, her eyes fixed on the floor — *could it possibly be the same one?* — and then she jumped a mile high as the first imposing notes of Beethoven's Fifth split the air.

My phone.

The relief she felt as she identified the

sound was as palpable as the musty smell wafting toward her through the open kitchen door. Releasing the knob, digging her phone out of her pocket, she squinted at the display. The numbers were difficult to see with the house's shadow falling over her.

"Hello?" Unable to read the number that would tell her the caller's identity, she answered anyway. It could be the hospital or Joel or . . . well, since Scott had told her to take as much time as she needed off from work, there wasn't anyone she was trying to avoid, so it didn't matter.

There was no reply.

Frowning, she turned away from the door and started walking toward the edge of the deck in hopes of getting a stronger signal.

"Hello?" she tried again impatiently.

"I can barely hear you." The voice on the other end sounded as if the speaker was at the bottom of a well. So far out in the country, cell phone towers were few and far between. "Hey, it's Rinko. Where are you?"

She was just about to answer when a sudden rush of movement behind her snapped her head around. A gray blur exploded through the door. . . .

Screaming, heart leaping into her throat, she tried to get away, but it was too late. Even as the phone fell from her suddenly nerveless fingers to land with a clatter at her feet, something slammed hard into the side of her head.

Her knees collapsed, and she dropped like a rock into nothingness.

13

When Lisa opened her eyes again, she found herself looking up into Jantzen's worried face. It was close, and shadowed, and framed by a patch of sky that was slowly turning purple far above it as the twilight continued to deepen.

"She's conscious," Jantzen turned her head to report with relief to someone behind her.

"Think we should call nine-one-one?"

Lisa recognized the anxious voice even before the face just beyond Jantzen's shoulder came clear enough to be identifiable: Rinko.

"I don't know." Jantzen touched her arm. "Grant, can you hear me?"

Lisa summoned all her resources. "Yes."

"What happened?" Rinko asked.

Frowning made her head hurt, so Lisa abandoned the attempt and stared blankly up at the two of them without replying as she tried to work that out for herself. She'd headed out to meet the insurance adjuster at Grayson Springs, then . . .

"You probably shouldn't move." Rinko had his phone out. She could see it in his hand. The fingers of his other hand hovered over it. "So, do I call nine-one-one or not?"

"I don't know." Jantzen seemed to be peering deeply into her eyes, which briefly baffled Lisa. "Her pupils look normal," she reported back to Rinko, and Lisa realized Jantzen had been evaluating her pupil size to check for a possible concussion.

Lisa, meanwhile, had started to shake her head in reply to Rinko's question but had to stop. The movement was so discombobulating that she had to briefly close her eyes again.

"Oh, crap," Rinko said. "Did she faint?"

"No." Lisa opened her eyes before Jantzen could reply or Rinko could get carried away with his cell phone. There was a reason she didn't want him to make that call, but just at the moment, with her brain frozen like a balky computer and pain hammering her skull, she couldn't think what it was. She made a tremendous effort. "Don't call anybody. Just give me a minute, would you please?"

Her voice sounded weak. Lifting an unsteady hand in an attempt to pinpoint the source of the pain, she found a bump the size of a Ping-Pong ball rising just above her right ear, and winced.

"Did you hit your head?" Jantzen asked.

This time Lisa didn't make the mistake of moving. She took a deep breath and tried again to remember. She'd found the Garcias' house. . . .

"What are you two doing here?" The sheer unlikeliness of Rinko's and Jantzen's presence struck her in mid-rumination. She was, she saw, as her surroundings finally swam into full focus, lying on her back in what had once been the Garcias' backyard. The ground was hard, and sharp blades of grass pricked her bare arms and legs. Hair tucked behind her ears, a worried frown on her face, her tiered yellow skirt pooled around her like the petals of a daffodil, Jantzen knelt beside her. Phone in hand, glasses slightly askew, collar unbuttoned, and tie at half-mast, Rinko crouched just behind Jantzen. There were others present as well, roughly half a dozen people she didn't recognize, surrounding her in a loose semicircle. They were standing — tall as trees, from her vantage point — all looking down at her with varying degrees of concern. Her first impression of them was of a jumble of sneakers, flip-flops, denim, bare legs, T-shirts, and weird hair. Teenagers: almost certainly the wayward lambs. She felt a sense of relief as she made the connection.

At least her brain seemed to be beginning to function again.

"We started talking about the case when I called it up on the computer to give you the address. Everybody kind of thought it would be pretty tight if we could figure out what had happened to the family after all these years. The first step, obviously, was to come out and look at the house they disappeared from." Rinko still seemed on the brink of dialing 911. He gestured with the phone still clutched in his hand. "Your car was here when we got here, so we knew you had to be here, too. I called your cell phone, you answered, and then — *wow.* That was some kind of scream you let out. You weren't anywhere out front, so we ran around back. You were laid out on the ground here."

"You looked really bad," a plump blond girl with raccoon eyes said earnestly. "Real pale."

"Ashley thought you were dead. She screamed, too." The boy's voice — he was a tall, lanky kid with spiky black hair — was taunting. "Like a little girl."

"Shut up, Matt." The blonde — presumably Ashley — glared at him.

"What? You did," Matt protested.

"Can it, guys," Rinko ordered, shooting them a quelling look.

The house was to her left, Lisa saw, as she glanced in that direction. That was what Rinko had been gesturing at, obviously. She lay in its shadow. From her position, it seemed probable that she'd fallen down the two shallow steps that were attached to the deck. Was that why she had screamed? The kitchen door was ajar, providing a glimpse into the dark interior. Seeing that, Lisa suddenly felt cold all ovcr.

In a flash she remcmbered everything: She'd opened the back door of the house, and then her phone had rung. When she turned away to answer, something — *someone* — had attacked her.

"Somebody hit me. There was somebody in the house and I opened the door and I —"

She broke off as all of a sudden it occurred to her that whoever had attacked her was probably not far away. Jackknifing into a sitting position, she was assailed by a wave of dizziness so strong she swayed. If she hadn't felt such an acute sense of urgency, she would have slumped back down to the grass again and lain there unmoving for pretty much the rest of her life. Instead, fighting to clear her head, she braced a hand on the ground and glanced anxiously around.

"Did you see anybody? Somebody running away? Or maybe a car leaving? Anything like that?"

"No." They were all shaking their heads as the world finally stopped dipping and spinning around her and they came into focus again.

"There was no one here when we got here." Jantzen must have seen that she was having difficulties, because she put a steadying arm around her. Lisa accepted the support gratefully. "Just you."

"Okay, now I guess I really should call nine-one-one." Rinko started punching in the numbers once more.

"No!" The sharpness in Lisa's voice stopped his finger in mid-punch. He looked at her questioningly. "Don't call anyone. I don't need medical attention, I promise."

"At the very least we should call the police." Jantzen frowned at her. "If somebody hit you . . ."

"I may be wrong about that," Lisa lied desperately. As her thoughts became clearer, one thing she was fairly sure of was that she didn't want to call official attention to what had happened. Obviously she had surprised someone inside the house. It was possible that whoever it was had been in the midst of a random break-in, maybe a drifter or even a couple of kids or — well, somebody engaged on their own nefarious business that had nothing to do with her and just didn't want to be caught at it. It was also possible that her attacker had been inside the house for the same reason she had stopped by — because the Garcias had once lived there.

Is there a connection?

Yesterday she had taken the Garcia file home. Last night Grayson Springs had burned. Today someone inside the supposedly empty house the Garcia family formerly lived in had leaped out at her when she had surprised them and had knocked her unconscious.

Coincidence? God, she hoped so. Because if it was anything other than coincidence, she had stumbled onto something she was probably better off not pursuing.

If my interest in this case is stirring up such a reaction, it can only be because there is something there to find.

The thought lay before her like a nearly invisible thread. She mentally stared at it in the full knowledge that if she picked it up and followed it, it might lead her back to the answer to what had happened to the Garcias.

And why she looked so much like Angela.

Do I really want to know?

Every instinct she possessed screamed that the best thing she could do was just leave the matter lie.

Never ask a question unless you're sure you want to know the answer. It was one of the first things she'd learned in law school.

Do I want to know the answer to this? Ah, that was the question.

"Could we get out of here?" The other girl, who glanced around nervously as she spoke, had short black hair and a short denim skirt that revealed thin, knobby-kneed legs. "This place is starting to creep me out. Anyway, I told my grandmother I'd be home by dark."

"What difference does it make if you're home by dark or not if you're out getting pizza? It's not like you're going to be outside." A boy with a Veronica Lake–style sweep of medium brown hair gave the girl who had just spoken an impatient look out of his one visible eye.

"But we're not out getting pizza," the blonde pointed out. "We already did that. Now we're out here in the middle of nowhere, where there's maybe some kind of murderer on the loose, to check out a house where a family might have been killed. I'm with Sarah: I think we should leave."

"What, do you think there's been a murderer hiding inside the house for thirty years? What is this, *Friday the Thirteenth?*" a boy snorted. He was thin, with shaggy, fair hair, and Lisa recognized him with a quick widening of her eyes: Scott's nephew. What was his name? Oh, yeah. Chase.

"She didn't say that," the black-haired girl — Sarah — defended her friend. "Anyway, *something* happened to her." Sarah's eyes rested significantly on Lisa.

"I think I must have fallen down the steps and hit my head," Lisa said as all eyes turned to her. Until she had more time to think the possible ramifications through, she didn't want to get the police involved in anything to do with the Garcias, which was what was going to happen if she told the truth.

"So, you're saying nobody hit you? Nobody was in the house?" Rinko looked at her with a skeptical frown.

"My father's always saying I'm way too imaginative. I . . . thought at first that was what had happened, but now that my mind's a little clearer, I think I must have just fallen down the steps." Lisa tried offering a helping of apologetic smile to go along with that lie. The smile felt lopsided. God, she was developing the mother of all headaches, which was no surprise, considering the size of the bump. "I'm with Sarah — is that your name? — too. I think we should leave."

Sarah acknowledged her name with a nod.

"Oh, sorry, I thought you knew these guys." Rinko rattled off their names one after the other as he pointed to each kid in turn. "They're wicked smart, and they're going to be a big help with the files. We worked it out so that they're going to come in for a couple of hours a day a few days a week. And Jantzen's going to help, too. But this here is strictly extracurricular. You know, kind of for fun."

"Great." Mentally gritting her teeth against a fresh wave of dizziness, Lisa managed to stand up. Her head pounded, and the world swam around her, but she planted her feet and stood fast. Gingerly, she touched the bump and winced. She couldn't help it: She found herself once again looking at the house. "Um, maybe somebody could shut the door?"

"I'll do it." They all watched as Chase scampered up the steps to the deck. Reaching the door, he looked back at them. "You want me to lock it, right?"

Lisa had a lightning mental vision of herself returning to the house alone and, entering through the back door, which she had told Chase not to lock, exploring the interior of the house. Her verdict?

Not gonna happen.

"Lock it," she decreed.

Chase nodded, did something to the inner knob, which she presumed involved engaging the lock, and closed the back door. Only then did it occur to Lisa that maybe there had been some evidence of her attacker on the smooth brass surface, such as fingerprints. But the last thing she wanted to do was trigger an investigation, so she said nothing as Chase rejoined the group.

"If you don't want me to call nine-one-one, can I drive you to a hospital? You should at least get your head looked at." Rinko tucked his hand beneath her elbow for support as they all began to move toward the driveway, which would be visible just as soon as they rounded the corner of the house.

"I'll drive her. You've got to take these kids home. It's your van," Jantzen pointed out. "And I can't drive a stick shift. Remember, I told you that."

"Oh, right." Rinko glanced at Jantzen, then hesitated. Reading his face, Lisa was pretty sure she knew what he wanted to say next. Lack of confidence kept the offer from emerging.

"Maybe Rinko could teach you sometime," she said to Jantzen on his behalf. "Being able to drive a stick shift is a useful skill." One she didn't have herself and had never actually needed, but never mind. Probably Jantzen would find it useful. "Look, I can drive myself. And I'm headed to University Hospital, because that's where my mother is, and if I feel the need I'll have someone there look at my head. Anyway, you're going into Lexington, aren't you? You'll be right behind me if I should need help."

As they rounded the corner of the house and her Jag and Rinko's van came into view, Lisa realized she wasn't the only one casting covert, nervous glances around. Nearly everyone else was, too, even the outwardly macho boys.

Maybe they all felt what she did: that someone was watching them. Someone who was hidden in the trees. Her heart picked up the pace again as her gaze fastened on a particularly dense clump of undergrowth.

Did I just see something move there?

What felt like an icy finger slid down

Lisa's spine. Staring with all her might, she barely repressed a shiver. There was definitely no movement whatsoever now that she was looking. She couldn't see anything but fat, leafy bushes and closely packed tree trunks and a tangle of weeds and dangling vines.

"It's like you can feel their ghosts." Hanging on to Ashley's arm now, Sarah was wide-eyed as she looked back at the house. Her words expressed Lisa's sentiments exactly.

"Ghosts? If you're talking about the Garcias, they might not even be dead. For all you know, they're off living the good life in California or someplace," Austin said scornfully.

It was possible, Lisa knew. So why did she feel certain that it wasn't true?

"You are so insensitive." Ashley shook her head in disgust. "Of course they're dead. Or somebody would have heard from them by now."

"What, do you think everybody's like E.T.? 'Phone home, phone home'?"

"Shut up, Austin," Sarah said.

And on that note they reached the vehicles and quickly piled in.

Even as they pulled out of the driveway and peeled out in tandem toward Lexington, Lisa couldn't get the feeling that they were being watched out of her head.

14

"This place looks like shit." Scott stood in the middle of the small living room, watching his brother chew hungrily on a slice of the pepperoni pizza Scott had brought with him. It was around ten-thirty p.m., but he'd just gotten there because, hey, he had to work, and tonight work, as it usually did, had run way late. Ryan's flophouse of a one-bedroom apartment was on the top floor of an old brick house on Maxwell Street, and noise from the other tenants penetrated the thin walls. The overhead light was on in the kitchen and a lamp was on beside the couch, but still the place was gloomy-dark. Trash — fast-food wrappers, empty soda and beer cans, old newspapers, you name it — littered every flat surface, including the floor. Discarded clothes draped the furniture and the half-wall that separated the living room from the kitchen. A faint sour smell hung in the air. From where Scott stood, he could see used pans and dishes and utensils piled in the sink. A loaf of bread spilled slices onto the counter. A tub of butter and a jar of jelly — the jelly had a spoon sticking out of it — waited lidless nearby. A carton of milk — he presumed it was empty — lay on its side next to the jelly. A good portion of its contents was on the kitchen floor, he saw as he glanced beneath it, which, as the spill looked to be at least a day old, probably accounted for the smell.

"You come over here to tell me you've got a problem with my housekeeping?" Ryan gave him a less than loving look. He was sitting on the couch, where he'd been watching TV until Scott had picked up the remote and turned it off, saying, "I need to talk to you." Then Scott had gotten distracted by the mess.

Now Scott answered, "Among other things."

Ryan picked up another piece of pizza from the box on the coffee table in front of him. "You don't like the way the place looks, go away. I ain't blocking the door."

Scott's lips thinned, but he didn't reply. A couple of discarded plastic grocery bags lay crumpled on the small round dining table that sat just this side of the kitchen wall, making the room a living room–dining room combination, he supposed. Grabbing a bag, he opened it with an impatient snap and started scooping trash into it. Finishing off his second slice of pizza, his brother gulped part of a Coke from the six-pack Scott had also brought and watched his efforts to dig him out of the mess broodingly.

"Since when did you give a damn what my place looks like?" Putting down the soda, Ryan started in on another slice of pizza.

"Since I walked in the door and practically got knocked down by the smell." Scott realized he was going to run out of bags before he ran out of garbage. Well, maybe there were more in a kitchen cabinet or something. He headed that way to see. The sight of the butter and jelly sitting out was too much for him. Removing the spoon from the jelly, he tossed it in the sink — the clatter made Ryan jump — screwed the lid back on, and opened the refrigerator. As he put the butter and jelly back where they belonged, he took stock of the refrigerator's contents: beer, some old-looking bologna, two hot dogs remaining in a leaky package, a half-empty jar of pickles. Chase hadn't been kidding when he'd said there was nothing to eat in the house.

"When's the last time you went to the

grocery?" Scott asked over his shoulder.

"Get the hell out of my refrigerator," Ryan growled.

"I see you've been feeding your kid real good." Scott closed the refrigerator door. "Bologna and pickles, real healthy stuff."

"Look, the only reason I let you in is because you brought pizza with you. It sure wasn't so you could tell me how to run my life."

"You short of money?" The puddle of milk on the floor revolted Scott. Grabbing some paper towels, he wiped it up.

"Hell, yes, I'm short of money. I'm always short of money. Who isn't? And no, I don't want any of yours. I got enough for damn groceries. It's just easier to eat out."

"Or not." Scott's voice was dry as he looked his brother over. Ryan was bone-thin. At least a week's worth of scruff covered his cheeks and chin. His usually short brown hair was longer than Scott had seen it in years, and scraggly. Shades of the old man, he was wearing a wife-beater with baggy jeans kept up by a belt and looked so down-and-out that Scott wanted to shake him. "The kid needs to eat. Like, regular meals."

"What the hell do you know about anything, anyway?"

"I hear Gayle got remarried." Locating a half-full box of garbage bags under the sink, Scott dragged one out, tossed the wad of damp paper towels in, and started filling it as he got to the heart of the matter.

Ryan stopped chewing to glare at him. "Where'd you hear that?"

Scott dumped what was left of the milk down the sink and added the empty carton to the bag. "Chase told me."

Blue eyes that were the same color as his own darted around as much of the apartment as Ryan could see.

"Chase ain't here."

Clearly he hadn't been entirely sure without glancing around.

"You know where he is?" If anything had been needed to underline his brother's less than attentive parenting style, that glance had done it. Scott's tone made the question a challenge. With the garbage bag full now and no ties in sight, he knotted the top. Walking back into the living room carrying an empty one, he shook it open and continued the cleanup.

Ryan put the half-eaten slice back in the box, folded his arms over his chest, and glared at him. "What's it to you where my kid is?"

"He's not with Gayle. He's not here. So,

I'm asking: Where is he?" An armful of old newspapers, a couple of McDonald's bags, some candy wrappers and beer cans later, and Scott could actually see most of the floor.

"Hangin' with his buds. It's summer. That's what kids his age do. Listen, if you're so interested in kids, have one of your own and leave mine the hell out of it."

"You got a responsibility to him." Having filled it, Scott tied that bag off, too, and carried it into the kitchen.

"I told you —"

"Cut the crap, Ryan." Coming back into the living room, Scott pulled some clothes off a worn blue La-Z-Boy, tossed them on top of the dividing wall with a bunch of others, and sat down, looking intently at his brother. "I can tell looking at you and looking at this place that you've been on a days-long bender. We both know what having a drunk for a dad is like. You really want that for Chase?"

Ryan stiffened. "You want to tell me what business that is of yours?"

"You're my brother. He's my nephew."

Animosity flared in Ryan's eyes. "And you're Mr. Perfect, aren't you? Just like you've always been. Mr. Never Put a Foot Wrong in All His Life."

Scott's eyes narrowed. "You can shove that up your ass."

"Fuck you."

"You're a drunk."

Their eyes locked.

"Just 'cause I drink some don't make me a drunk."

"You trying to bullshit *me?*"

Ryan's face tightened. "Get the hell out of here, why don't you?"

"Nope. I'm here, and I'm staying until I've said my piece. Unless you think you can throw me out."

They exchanged measuring looks. Since he'd hit about fifteen, Scott had always been taller and more muscular than four-years-older Ryan, and the knock-down, drag-out fighting that brothers typically did growing up had ended. From Ryan's expression, the knowledge that he was no physical match for his little brother continued to tick him off.

"Prick," Ryan muttered.

"Hitting your kid is a big no-no nowadays. I don't care what kind of little shit he's being. You do it again and you can expect a visit from Child Protective Services. And me."

"Who said I hit my kid?"

Scott didn't reply, just sat there looking at

him. For a long moment neither of them spoke.

"I'm going through a hard time right now, all right?" Ryan burst out.

"Yeah," Scott said. "I know. Gayle getting remarried is a tough one."

Ryan swallowed. "I always thought I'd get her back one day."

"I know."

"You don't know." The look Ryan gave him was bitter. "You've never been married. Just like you've never had a kid. Hell, you damned well live alone. I've been through enough AA programs to know why, too: You got trust issues. You're never going to put your heart on the line enough to fall in love."

Knowing Ryan was trying to get under his skin, Scott let the psychobabble pass.

"Your marriage may be over, but you still have the kid. You've got to get yourself straight for him. You remember what it was like for us, living with Dad."

Ryan's expression turned bitter. "Mean old bastard. I hope he rots in jail. They going to keep him this time?"

Scott shook his head. "They're going to let him out tomorrow. On bail. They set it at fifty grand."

"Shit. You got that much?"

"I'm not posting it. It's a property bond, and believe it or not, his farm's good to cover it. The only reason he's not already out is I got the lawyer I hired looking to see if the judge won't set him going into some kind of live-in rehab program as a condition of bail. He doesn't go to rehab, he stays in jail until trial."

Ryan grimaced. "That's a waste of time and you know it. No damned rehab program exists that can change him."

"Probably not."

"I don't —"

Ryan was interrupted by the opening of the apartment door. With the dimly lit hall visible behind him, Chase stood there, one hand on the knob, his eyes widening as he took in both his father and uncle sitting a few feet apart, looking at him. Scott felt a flicker of amusement as alarm flashed in Chase's eyes. It didn't take a genius to realize the kid was panicking in case he was being told on. Having managed to get both Chase and the truck back to the apartment without Ryan's knowing that either of them had gone anywhere, Scott hadn't seen his nephew since.

He gave the kid a sardonic smile.

"Hey." Recovering, Chase pulled his key from the lock, then closed the door and walked on into the room, tucking the key back into his pocket as his eyes slid away from Scott's face to fasten on the box on the coffee table. "Is that pizza?"

The panic Scott had seen was gone. Chase, he realized, was good at putting on an insouciant front. Just like, he reluctantly recognized, he himself once had been.

Never let 'em see you're scared. God, he remembered that.

"Yep," Scott said as Chase, with another lightning, faintly wary glance at him, helped himself to pizza.

"Where you been?" Ryan demanded.

"Out." Attacking the pizza with enthusiasm, Chase met his father's eyes. Something in Ryan's expression must have told him that more was required, because he added, mumbling around a mouthful, "I was with some friends from school."

Ryan shot Scott a triumphant look. "See?"

Brows raised, Chase was looking around. "Who cleaned up?"

"I did," Scott said. "You know, I came by to tell your dad about a program I'd like you to join. A bunch of kids your age working a few hours a week this summer at the prosecutor's office."

His nephew's eyes collided with his.

"You gonna pay me?" Chase asked cheekily. The kid had balls, Scott had to give him that.

Scott shook his head. "This is more like an internship. Give you something to do. Keep you out of trouble."

There was the smallest edge of meaning to that last.

Chase grimaced as Ryan looked at Scott. "You didn't say anything about that."

"I got sidetracked." Scott turned his attention back to Chase. "Sound like something you might find interesting?"

Chase's eyes flickered. Scott was pretty sure he knew what the kid was thinking: *Like I've got a choice.* But for his father's consumption, Chase nodded.

"I guess."

"It okay with you if he comes into the office for a couple of hours a couple of times a week?" Scott asked his brother.

Ryan looked at him kind of hard. Then he looked at Chase, who was just finishing up his second slice of pizza, the same way.

"Why the sudden interest in my kid?"

Out of the corner of his eye Scott saw that Chase was once again looking apprehensive. It was a fleeting expression, as quickly gone, and Chase was once again wolfing down pizza as if it was the most important thing in his life.

"Like I said, he's my nephew."

Ryan shrugged. "If he wants to, it's okay by me."

"Great." Scott stood up. "Well, that's what I came by for. Chase, why don't you help me carry this trash down, and we can go over some times and dates on the way?" Chase looked less than enthused, but he picked up the trash bag Scott hauled out of the kitchen and then, carrying it, followed Scott toward the door. With a hand on the knob, Scott looked back at his brother. "I'll be in touch about Dad. And the other things we talked about."

"Looking forward to it," was Ryan's caustic response.

"So, what else did you and Dad talk about?" Chase asked as he followed Scott down the three flights of stairs to the street. Scott shrugged by way of a reply. Music from the apartments on either side boomed in the stairwell. A couple of college-age kids carrying bicycles came through the building's front door as he and Chase exited. They said hi to Chase, who they obviously knew, and he nodded back. Then Scott and Chase stepped out into the relative quiet of the night.

"Where does the trash go?" Scott looked around at his nephew.

"Around back." Chase led the way around the side of the building. Maybe twenty feet separated the huge old Victorian from its similar neighbor, and the resulting passageway was dark as a tunnel so late at night. At the end of it was an alley that, thanks to the pale moon floating high overhead, was at least light enough so that they could see where they were going. Dumpsters and trash cans crowded close to run-down garagcs. Reaching the nearest dumpster, Chase heaved his bag inside.

"Did you tell him about me?" Chase asked as Scott followed suit.

"About you stealing his truck, or about the beer-and-pot party you were having with your friends at Grandpa's place?" Scott headed back around toward the front of the house as he spoke.

Chase kept up. "You know."

"Nope. Although I did mention that you told me about your mother getting remarried, so I guess you're going to have to say that you ran into me somewhere if your dad asks about that."

"That's no big deal." Scott could hear the relief in Chasc's voice. "I can say I saw you on the street or something, and you stopped to grill me about him. He says you're always sticking your nose in where it isn't wanted, anyway."

"Good to know." It occurred to Scott that by Kid Raising 101 standards he should probably be telling his nephew not to lie to his dad, but given that both of them were already sliding together down that slippery slope, he didn't see much point in worrying about it.

A small front yard bisected by a brick walk led to the street, which was narrow, lined with more once grand Victorian houses, most of which had been turned into low-rent apartments, and had cars parallel-parked on both sides. A single yellowish streetlight glowed on a corner. With that, the moon, and numerous lighted windows, the street was fairly well illuminated.

"So, did all your friends show up at my office today?" Scott asked as they reached his Jeep and he beeped the lock.

"Yeah, they did. Is that why you came by tonight? To check up on us?" Chase's voice took on a belligerent edge.

"To check up on *you.* Did you think I wouldn't? And just so you know, I'm going to keep checking up on you from now on. You do something you're not supposed to, and I'm going to be on you like a duck on a june bug." Scott gave the kid a stern look as he walked around the front of his car to open the door. "Get in."

Chase went wide-eyed. "Get in?"

"You heard me. There's a Thorntons not far from here. I'm going to run you up there real quick."

"I don't have any money."

"Would you quit arguing and get in the damned car?"

Chase got in. Scott did, too, and drove off down the street while his nephew eyed him uneasily.

"You need milk, bread, cheese. Maybe some bologna. Cereal. Doughnuts." The Thorntons anchored an intersection about half a mile away. Reaching it, Scott parked, and he and Chase went into the store. At the entrance, Scott grabbed a couple of plastic shopping baskets and handed one to Chase. "You go that way, I'll go this way. We'll meet in the middle. Get anything you see that I told you, and whatever else you want. Let's make this quick."

Chase obeyed, and their shopping trip took maybe five minutes, max. When they were back in the car heading for Ryan's apartment, Chase shot him a sidelong look.

"My dad's probably going to be pissed that I let you buy us this stuff."

"Tell your dad he can —" Scott broke off before he could add "stick it up his ass," which was what hovered on the tip of his tongue. Instead he segued into, "Call me if he has a problem with it. Tell him it wasn't your fault. I made you come with me."

"That's just going to make him pissed at you."

Scott laughed. "I guess I'll just have to live with that." They were on Maxwell Street now, and as he pulled up in front of the apartment building and stopped, he looked over at Chase. "You need anything else, or anything comes up with your dad, you call me, understand?"

"Sure." From the tone of that, Scott doubted he was going to be getting many calls. Having gathered the grocery bags, Chase was just about to get out of the car when he paused with his hand on the handle to add, "Oh, by the way, I saw your girlfriend tonight. You want to go around checking up on people, you probably ought to be checking up on her about now."

Not sure who he was talking about, Scott squinted at him through the darkness. "My girlfriend?"

"You know, the babe. With the legs. Lisa. We went to this house that some family disappeared from like forever ago — the girls and Rinko made up this club, they want to take on figuring out what happened to that family as kind of a project — and she was there when we got there, just lying in the grass out there in the backyard like she was dead or something. First she said somebody in the house clobbered her over the head, then she changed her mind and said she fell." Chase shrugged. "Whatever, she was knocked cold. She kept rubbing this place over her ear like it hurt." He demonstrated, pushing his fingers through his hair above his right ear.

"What?" Scott stared at Chase, who shrugged again, as if disclaiming all responsibility. "Is she okay? Where is she now?"

"She was up walking and talking a few minutes after we got there, and she was able to drive herself back to Lexington, so I guess she's okay," Chase said. "But I don't have a clue where she is."

Luckily, Scott did. His thoughts in turmoil, he stared at Chase without really seeing him.

The idea of Lisa being knocked cold, however it had happened, wasn't sitting well with him at all, he discovered.

"Thanks for telling me. Go on back in now. And stay there."

"Of course I'm going to stay there. Dad's awake. I only take his wheels when he's passed out."

Lips thinning, shooting his nephew a warning look but not wanting to take the time to deliver the lecture that bit of provocation clearly called for, Scott waited impatiently until Chase was out of the car and safely back inside the building. Then he headed for University Hospital, driving through the narrow streets with a barely controlled ferocity that was a symptom of his inner unease.

What the hell had she been doing to get herself knocked out?

Whatever had gone down, if he knew Lisa, right now she'd be there at the hospital with her mother.

She was, just as he'd expected. As soon as the elevator reached the fourth floor and he stepped out he saw her. At this time of night, the long, blue-painted hall was nearly deserted except for a nurse pushing a squeaky-wheeled cart into a room just ahead of him. The lighting was bright, the air-conditioning was cold, the place smelled like antiseptic. Lisa was farther down the hall, standing with her back to him just outside her mother's room. Her long black hair spilling down her back, dressed in a pair of loose gray sweatpants and a nondescript white T-shirt that she somehow managed to make look sexy as hell, she seemed to be feeling right at home. Loverboy had his arms around her. She was pressed up against him tighter than a stamp to a letter, kissing him for all she was worth.

Big surprise: He didn't like what he was seeing at all.

15

"Peyton."

It was a curt greeting, uttered in Scott's voice behind her. The sheer unexpectedness of it made Lisa jump. Her lips had just pulled away from Joel's as she finished answering his good-night kiss. Stiffening at the idea that they were under observation from Scott, no less, her arms dropped away from Joel's neck more quickly than they otherwise would have. She hated to acknowledge that she felt absurdly self-conscious as she turned to face Scott.

Their eyes met. The glint in his was disagreeable.

"Buchanan." If anything, Joel's voice held less enthusiasm than Scott's. The two had never liked each other, going all the way back to the time when teenage Joel had frequently roared up to Grayson Springs in the new BMW convertible that had been his sixteenth birthday gift from his parents, honking for her to come out, usually with the car packed with the kids who were part of their crowd, only to encounter the older, bigger, openly contemptuous Scott working on the property. Until Scott had taken to calling him Loverboy — a development that dated to the kiss Scott had observed from his office window — his preferred name for the patrician-looking Joel had been Richie Rich. Joel, for his part, had referred to Scott as "the yard guy."

That was then. This was now.

Neither offered to shake hands.

Pushing her hair away from her face with one hand, Lisa gave Scott a questioning look.

"I came to see Miss Martha." Scott remained unsmiling as he answered her unspoken question. Probably his having seen her kissing Joel was part of the reason he looked so grim. She was perfectly aware of his dog-in-the-manger tendency: He might not have any plans to kiss her himself, but he sure didn't like to see her kissing other guys. This was nothing new; that's the way he had always been. The thought made her frown at him.

"It's kind of late, isn't it?" The abruptness of her tone was payback for the hard look he was giving her. Her gaze slid over him.

Five-o'clock shadow darkened his chin, she saw, and his hair was starting to wave, as it tended to do after a long day in this kind of heat. He still wore the same suit he'd had on earlier but had taken off the tie, and he looked big and broad-shouldered and surprisingly formidable for a man in a suit. He also looked tired. Of course, she knew how he'd spent a great deal of the previous night, and clearly he'd worked all day. Who wouldn't be tired? She was exhausted herself, among a whole jumble of other things that she was being very careful to keep from thinking about for the moment. Glancing from him to Joel, she couldn't help comparing the two. Her boyfriend's features were more refined, his jaw less pugnaciously square, his blue eyes deeper and less hooded. His blond hair gleamed gold in the unforgiving overhead light. He and Scott were about the same height, but Joel had a slimmer, more elegant build that his trimmer-fitting, European-cut navy suit made the most of. There was no doubt about it, Lisa decided: Taken feature by feature, Joel was definitely the handsomer man.

But Scott was sexier. Sexy enough for her heart to start beating a little faster just because he was there.

"I've been busy. If it's not convenient, I can always go away and come back some other time." Scott's tone was as hard as his expression. If she hadn't been a mature adult, she might well have succumbed to the urge to stick out her tongue at him.

Just then the nurse whose arrival at her mother's bedside to check on the patient had driven Joel from the room emerged through the open door and, finding the three of them gathered there in the hall, smiled impartially at them.

"Looks like she's up for a while," she said cheerily to Lisa as she passed. "Hope you like *House,* because she's settling in to watch a marathon."

"Thanks," Lisa called after her, while Scott's expression turned mocking.

"So, do I go in or not?"

"Knowing your mother, she'll probably be glad of the company," Joel said, and was rewarded for his interference when neither of the principals to the conversation so much as glanced at him.

Instead, Scott lifted his brows at Lisa.

"Since it seems she's planning to stay awake, I'm sure she'll be glad to see you. Go on in." Gesturing toward the open door of her mother's room, Lisa ostentatiously waited until he had disappeared inside before turning back to Joel. The fact that it cost her an effort to switch gears underlined how truly tired and overwhelmed she was, but she summoned her inner resources and deliberately warmed her expression and voice for Joel. That some of that warmth might have been for Scott's benefit, just in case he was listening — which, knowing him, he probably was — she preferred not to acknowledge. "Listen, thanks for coming. You could have waited until tomorrow, though. You didn't have to come straight to the hospital from the airport."

"Sure I did. You're my girl. When you're in trouble, I'm there." Taking both her hands, Joel smiled at her, his sunny blue eyes possessive. Lisa smiled back without disputing the "You're my girl" statement, which she normally would have done in the interests of not letting Joel take too much for granted, again because she was pretty sure that Scott could, if he wished, overhear. Joel brought each of her hands to his mouth in turn and kissed the knuckles. Aware of the interested gazes of a couple of nurses at the nurses' station opposite, feeling suddenly totally grumpy and not in the mood to sort out the reasons why, she could have done without the gesture, which she knew she should have been thinking was romantic.

But she kept her smile, then discreetly pulled her hands away as soon as she could.

"You better go. It's getting late."

The good-night kiss Scott had interrupted had been because Joel was on the verge of leaving. But now Joel hesitated, glancing significantly toward the open door of her mother's room. A murmur of voices — Scott's and her mother's — could clearly be heard through it.

"I can stay for a while, if you want." It was clear Joel didn't much like the idea of leaving while Scott remained. He'd always been faintly jealous of Scott's presence in her life, platonic and at times downright friction-filled as it was.

"I don't. I'm sure Scott will just stay a few minutes, and then I'm going to shut the door to visitors. My mother can watch *House* if she wants. I'm going to sleep." She would be sleeping on the cot the nurses had brought in for her, just as she had the night before. It was already set up in a corner of the room. Tomorrow she guessed she was going to have to rent a hotel room nearby to use as a base and then shop for clothes and other necessities, but for tonight she was still showering in her mother's bathroom and living out of the suitcase Nola had brought her earlier.

"If you're sure you don't need me . . ."

"I am."

"Okay, then. But only because I have to drive to Cincinnati first thing in the morning." Joel smiled and drew her close for another quick kiss. Then, releasing her, he started walking toward the elevators. Not really wanting to join her mother and Scott just yet, Lisa stayed where she was, rubbing her temples in an attempt to relieve the throbbing headache that nagged at her still. He was about halfway to the elevator bank when he turned around to call to her, "We're still on for Saturday, right?"

"I don't know." Lisa's hands dropped away from her head. She'd said nothing to anyone outside of the little group of people who had found her about the blow she'd suffered. "I'll have to see how it goes. I'll call you if there's a problem, okay?"

He acknowledged that with a wave. Then a faint *ping* announced the arrival of an elevator, and he hurried to catch it.

When he was gone, with no further excuse not to, Lisa turned and went into her mother's room. Her first impression was that it was surprisingly peaceful, more peaceful than it had been all evening. Of course, now there was only one slightly unwelcome but all-too-well-known-to-her

Scott's mouth twisted.

"But I want you — to go back to work." Her mother's fingers tightened on hers. "And I want you — to go to the dance. All those — things. I like — hearing about your — doings. Any number of — people — can sit with me. But you — my heart goes with you — wherever you are. Knowing you're out — doing things — brightens my day."

A lump formed unexpectedly in Lisa's throat. "Mother . . ."

"Don't you — feel sorry — for me — Annalisa. I've had — the most wonderful life. Now I want you — to live yours."

Against her eyelids, Lisa felt the sudden sting of tears.

"Mother . . ." she said again, helplessly.

"You can take tomorrow off, and then I'll expect you back at work on Friday." Scott's tone was maddeningly authoritative. Because she was annoyed with him, because she shot him a look that was meant to be read as *You know what you can do with that,* because he gave her an infuriating little smile in return, the urge to cry receded.

Which was a good thing.

"And then — you're to go to the — country club — on Saturday." In its own way, her mother's voice was as commanding as Scott's.

visitor, where earlier the room had been full of her mother's friends, most of whom she didn't know particularly well and all of whom seemed to be dying to talk to her. The TV was on, but its volume had been muted. Chilled to the bone after her shower, Lisa had personally turned the air conditioner down earlier, so now its hum was barely audible. And the corridor outside was empty.

After the day she'd had, the relative quiet was a welcome relief.

But she still had to deal with Scott.

Flanked by banks of softly glowing hospital monitors, he stood on the near side of the bed with his back to the door, holding her mother's hand, nodding at something she was saying to him. Lisa clearly heard him reply, "You know I will," and then he broke off to glance over his shoulder as he became aware of her entrance. But it was her mother who spoke to her.

"Annalisa. I want you to — keep your date — Saturday." Martha's tone was unusually stern.

"It's just the Fourth of July thing at the country club." It vexed Lisa to realize that Scott was now privy to information about her date. Clearly her last exchange with Joel had been overheard. Scott regarded her without expression, but she knew how his mind worked. He would be mentally sneering at her relationship with Joel. She kept her gaze focused on her mother. "If I'm going to leave you for any length of time, Mother, it'll be to go back to work, not to a dance."

"You should go — back to work. And you should — go to the dance, too. There is — nothing wrong with me — that wasn't wrong with me — before." Martha took a deep breath. It pained Lisa to realize how much effort it cost her. "I have Andy — and Robin — and Lynn — and any number of friends — to sit with me. I want you — to go about your — normal life."

Lisa walked around the foot of the bed to her mother's other side, which put her directly across from Scott. Glancing at him only briefly, she took her mother's cold hand. It was almost clawlike now, and she hated it that she could feel the bones through the skin. Dressed in a blue hospital gown that left her neck and arms and most of her collarbone bare, Martha looked as fragile as a dry leaf. Her white hair made her face seem almost gray in contrast, and she was so thin that she barely made a hump beneath the blue blanket that was tucked beneath her armpits. Lisa realized

with a pang that her arms were practically skeletal. Looking at the various tubes and needles taped to them, her heart ached.

"Until we get the test results back —" Lisa began, unconsciously chafing her mother's hand in an effort to warm it up.

Martha interrupted. "What difference — can any test results — possibly make? We already know — I'm dying. What are they — going to tell me — that's different?" A flash of her old feisty spirit showed in her eyes.

That was so very true that for a moment Lisa was rendered speechless.

"Miss Martha's right, you know. You can't just sit here night and day." Scott's tone was brusque. "It's not good for either of you. You should come back to work. The job won't wait forever."

Lisa gave him an indignant look that silently, because she didn't care to say it out loud in front of her mother, told him that she didn't appreciate his lack of sensitivity. Given that she'd revealed the direness of their circumstances to him when she'd had to practically beg him for the job, the implied threat struck a wrong note with her, too.

"I'm sure I can count on you not to fire me," she said lightly.

"Fine." Lisa didn't frown at her mother, but the covert look she shot Scott was deadly. "Work on Friday, country club on Saturday. Got it." In defcrence to her mother, she swallowed the rest of what she felt like saying. Most of which would have been directed at Scott, anyway.

"I've got to go. I just came by to see how you're doing." Scott's voice was gentle as he addressed Martha. Squeezing her hand, he let it go as his attention turned to Lisa. "Walk me out, would you?"

Typical Scott; it was more of a command than a question. From his expression, she inferred that he had something he wanted to say to her. Which worked for her, because she had something she wanted to say to him, too. With a quick smile for her mother, she followed him out the door, which she closed behind her just to make sure her mother couldn't overhear. There was only one nurse at the nurses' station now, and her profile was turned to them as she talked on the phone. Down the hall, a janitor wielded a mop. Other than that, the area was deserted. They were, to all intents and purposes, alone.

16

"What do you mean you expect me back at work on Friday?" Lisa attacked first, in a hushed voice that nonetheless was sharp with indignation. The look she gave him sizzled. "In a situation like this, I'm entitled to take personal days off. I checked with human resources just to be sure. And if you recall, just last night you told me to take as long as I needed."

"Yeah, well, I changed my mind. The work's piling up. I got an office to run, and the reason I hired you as a research assistant is because we need a research assistant. If you can't come back to work by Friday, I'm going to have to get someone else."

"I can't believe you're threatening me. My mother needs me!"

"No, she doesn't. Having you sitting there beside her hour after hour worries her to death. She feels like you're sacrificing your life to take care of her."

"And how would you know that?" Even as she snapped the words at him, realization dawned. "Did she tell you that? Is that what you two were talking about in there?"

"Maybe I'm just an astute observer of the human condition."

"Bullshit." She glared at him. Then as she read the truth in his eyes her shoulders slumped a little. "I know she worries about me. I still feel like I need to stay with her."

"The sooner your life gets back to normal, the happier she'll be. And from what I've gathered, she's in no immediate danger."

"We're still waiting for test results." She sighed, reluctantly accepting the truth of what he was telling her. "Okay, fine. I'll be at work on Friday."

"Wonderful. Which brings us to what I wanted to talk to you about: How's your head?"

She frowned. "What?"

"Your head. You know." Reaching out, Scott touched very close to the area over her ear where the bump was still tender. "The place where you got hit."

Lisa jerked away from his hand. "Who told you that?"

"A little bird."

"Rinko, I'm guessing. Or your nephew."

"So, you want to tell me about it?"

"No." Her answer was stark. She'd already considered, and discarded, the idea of confiding in Scott. If she did, he would put two and two together, and probably sooner rather than later arrive at the same place she had herself. Although it seemed almost too incredible even to allow herself to believe, she was beginning to feel convinced that the fire, and the attack that had left her unconscious, had happened because she was suddenly interested in what had happened to the Garcia family.

Which was because she had a terrible gut feeling that what had happened to the Garcia family had something to do with her.

Which, if it were true, brought up all kinds of appalling possibilities that would leave her where, exactly?

She didn't know. She did know she was pretty sure she didn't want to find out. But she also knew that this was something she just wasn't going to be able to leave alone.

"This wouldn't have anything to do with the cold-case file you took home, would it? The one where the woman who disappeared looked like you? The file that burned up in the fire?"

Lisa looked at him mutely. It was clear from his expression that he knew her well enough to read the truth in her silence.

"You got hit over the head." His eyes were keen on her face. "Hard enough to knock you cold. You were found unconscious in the backyard of the house the cold-case family disappeared from. Which you were checking out because you look like the missing woman." He broke off to lift his brows at her. "How'm I doing so far?"

The sour look she gave him was his answer.

"Batting a thousand, I see." Folding his arms over his chest, he rested a shoulder against the wall. "So, you want to fill me in on the details?"

She glared at him.

"I can keep on guessing, but it's late and I'm tired. Come on, Princess. If you can't tell me, who can you tell?"

For another long moment she hesitated. Indignation at being called a name he knew annoyed her and an innate caution that took fright at the idea of letting anyone else in on what she half suspected warred with her realization that he had hit on the truth: Out of her circle of family, friends, and acquaintances, he was the one person — the only person — both who could help her and whom she could trust.

If she didn't tell him, she would be going it alone. And maybe, under the circumstances, that wasn't too smart.

"I walked around the house." She capitulated ungraciously. "When I checked the back door — okay, I was going to go inside, I know it was wrong and stupid and everything else you can think of to call it, so don't get started — it was unlocked, and I opened it. Then my cell phone rang. It was Rinko, who had apparently just pulled into the driveway with that group of kids you're trying to scare straight. I turned away from the door to answer my phone. There must have been someone already in the house, someone up to no good, because I felt kind of a rush of movement behind me before something slammed hard into the side of my head and knocked me out." She took a breath. "There you go. That's the whole story. Now you know."

He looked at her thoughtfully. "You didn't call the police."

"No."

"Any particular reason why not?"

"Because I didn't want to have to explain what I was doing there, okay?"

"And you didn't want to explain what you were doing there because you're afraid that the fact that the missing woman looks like you means something, right?"

Scott, damn him, had always been too

perceptive where she was concerned.

"What could it mean?" she burst out. Now that he'd hit the nail on the head, she found the prospect of him probing at the possibilities terrifying. "That maybe Angela Garcia and I are distant cousins or something? That everybody has a doppelgänger, like they say? It's an interesting coincidence, but that's all it is."

He studied her. "Then what exactly are you afraid of?"

"Nothing." Her tone was fierce.

"You took the file home with you, and your house burned, destroying the file and nearly killing you in the process," he said slowly, his eyes intent on her face. "You went by the house where the family disappeared just to check it out and got knocked unconscious by an unknown assailant. That could be just a run of bad luck, true, but let's say for a moment it isn't. Let's say it's all connected to your discovery of the file and subsequent display of interest in it. Hypothetically."

Lisa took a deep breath. She felt as though she were teetering at the top of the proverbial slippery slope.

"Hypothetically," she agreed.

"Who knew you took the file home?"

That was a logical first question, one Lisa

had already been halfheartedly trying to work out for herself. Trust Scott to cut right to the heart of the matter.

"Not very many people. I've been trying to think." She did a quick visual sweep of the hall. Most of the doors were closed. There were now two nurses at the nurses' station, and they were conferring over a pile of charts spread out on the counter. Another nurse was pushing a cart toward them, stopping at every room as she came. The janitor, still wielding his mop, had nearly reached the end of the hall. No one was paying them any particular attention. Her eyes returned to Scott. "Rinko was the only one left in Siberia when I took the file out of there, but I'm pretty sure he had no idea I was taking it. While I was driving home, Joel called. I think I told him I had the file with me. It's possible he told his father, who was with him when he made the call, although I don't know why it would have come up. Then, you may have seen it."

"I may have seen it?"

"When my car broke down and you stopped. My briefcase fell open. The file was one of the things that spilled out. You had your hand right on it. At the time, I was surprised you didn't see it."

"I didn't," he assured her.

"You would say that, though, wouldn't you?" She gave him a small, faintly mocking smile, to which he responded with an acknowledging grimace. "After I got home, I took my briefcase up to my bedroom. It had the file in it. I got the file out. This is going to sound stupid, but I have — had — a doll that looked a lot like the little girl in the picture, and I wanted to compare the two. My father called while I was doing that, and I believe I may have mentioned the file to him and said I had it with me, but I'm not sure I told him that. I know I said something about the file and the Garcia family, though." She shot him a quick, defensive look. "Actually, I asked him if I was adopted."

"If you were adopted?" Scott looked mildly astounded. Then he frowned at her. "Is that what you think this is about?"

Lisa shook her head. "N-no. I mean, it was just a sudden thought I had but — no. In any case, Barty assured me that I wasn't, and then my mother showed me my baby book. It was all there, all the pictures, her being pregnant, me being born, the hospital, everything. The whole nine yards."

"Okay, so it's possible your father may have known you had the file at home. Who else?"

Lisa sighed. "This is where it gets tricky. When I went down to supper, I'm almost positive I left the file open on my bedroom floor. After that, I suppose anyone who was in the house could have come into my room and seen it. Andy and Robin were there, and so was Lynn Carter, my mother's nurse, whom you met. Plus we had some painters working not far from my bedroom. Remember that big oak that fell on the house in May? They were finishing up the last phase of the repair work. There were five or six of them, I think. Any one of them might have seen it, if they'd walked into my bedroom for whatever reason. By my count, that's fourteen people who possibly knew I had the file and where it was. Along with anyone they may have told."

Scott's brow had slowly furrowed while she'd been speaking.

"You said the contents of the file had already been entered into the computer when you took it home?" he asked.

Lisa nodded. "Everything should be on there, thank goodness. Wait till you see the picture. You won't believe how much I look like her."

Even as she said it, she knew she was assuming Scott would want to see the picture. That he was in this with her now. It was, she realized, a good feeling. Comforting. Reassuring.

He still frowned.

"Once the file was logged in to the system, it was supposed to be tagged with a security device before being re-stored. One of those little plastic stick-on things like they use in library books. Did you see anything like that on it?"

Lisa shook her head. "If it was there, I didn't notice it."

"Well, it should have been there, and if it was, it would have registered the file number and name when you carried it out the door. If the system worked like it's supposed to — and I know that's a big if — potentially anyone on the building's security staff could have known that it had been taken out of the building, and probably could have figured out that you had taken it."

"Great. How many people are we talking about?"

Scott shook his head. "I don't know. I'll check it out."

The cart rattled past, making Lisa, who was already on edge, jump. The nurse pushing it gave them a curious glance and then a quick smile as she stopped outside Martha's door to knock on it briefly.

"Go on in," Lisa told her.

"Staying the night again?" the nurse asked, opening the door, and Lisa smiled and nodded.

The nurse pushed the cart into the room, leaving the door open behind her. It was a routine check, Lisa knew, but still she felt she needed to be in there. With her mother's hesitant speech and impaired mobility, some of the hospital staff had a tendency to treat her as if her mind was impaired, too.

"I need to get back to my mother," she said to Scott.

Scott nodded, but he seemed to be deep in thought. Then, as she started to turn away, he caught her arm. The warm curl of his hand around her bare skin caused her breath to catch and her pulse to quicken. Such a sudden, intense reaction to his touch was new. Disconcerted by it, her eyes flew to his face.

"You're spending the night in Miss Martha's room?" If he was feeling anything like she was, he didn't show it. She pulled free of his grip and folded her arms over her chest in a kind of instinctive self-defense.

"Yes."

"Don't go outside again tonight. Not to get something out of your car or for any other reason, hear?"

"I wasn't planning to, but why?"

"Either you're really unlucky lately, or our hypothetical scenario isn't so hypothetical after all. Whichever one it is, you don't want to be running around by yourself in the dark."

Lisa's eyes widened as she forgot all about the way his hand wrapped around her arm had made her feel. "Are you saying you think I'm in danger?"

That was the thought she'd been shying away from, the one she didn't want to face. Now she had no choice.

"Let's say I'm starting to think it might be a possibility."

A thrill of dread ran through her. "Scott . . ."

"Miss Grant?" The nurse put her head out the door. "Your mother is refusing to take her sleeping medication. If you could help me with her . . ."

Distracted, Lisa glanced around. "She doesn't want to go to sleep right now. She apparently wants to watch *House*. Give me a second, and I'll be right there."

Looking disapproving, the nurse withdrew. Lisa turned her attention back to Scott, who was frowning at her.

"I want you to leave this case alone. Don't talk about it to anyone else, and don't go poking around in it anymore. I'll get it checked out for you," he said before she could say anything else.

"But I don't want anybody else checking it out," she protested. "Just in case . . ."

Her voice trailed off. The truth was, she didn't want to examine her burgeoning suspicions closely enough to put what she feared into words. Not that she knew, exactly, what it was she did fear. It could, however, be summed up in two words: nothing good.

"Trust me, would you please? I'll make sure that whatever's done is done discreetly, and I'll keep your name out of it. Stay in your mother's room for the night, and leave that damned case alone. And if anything comes up that makes you nervous, call me. I can be here in ten minutes. My apartment is right down the road."

"Okay, fine," she said, although not without misgiving. She wasn't sure about turning anybody else loose on the case, even if it was done discreetly. But she knew from experience that arguing with Scott was an exhausting experience that she didn't feel like entering into at the moment. At the various and assorted memories that conjured up, she smiled at him, a quick, wry smile that to her surprise caused his eyes to narrow and his mouth to tighten as if something had suddenly displeased him. Before she could even begin to figure out what, they were once again interrupted by the nurse.

"Miss Grant . . ."

"I'm coming." With an apologetic grimace for Scott, Lisa turned away. "I really have to go."

Then, with one hand on the open doorjamb, she glanced back at him.

"Thanks," she added softly.

"Anytime."

Even as she went to her mother's assistance, she was aware of him heading toward the elevators, walking with that easy, athletic grace she had always associated with him. When she was inside the room, dealing with the sleep issue, when she knew he had gone, she was surprised to find that despite the presence of her mother and the nurse, she felt very alone. And far too vulnerable. And just a little bit afraid.

17

Okay, you can forget reincarnation.

That was Lisa's first relieved thought when she saw that the Garcias had disappeared on May 1, 1981, almost a month after her own birth. Not that she had ever believed such a thing was even remotely possible, of course.

The great thing about the combination of wireless Internet and laptops was that she could do all kinds of research from just about anywhere, Lisa reflected as she read the date one more time late the following morning. For example, while she was sitting in one of the uncomfortable plastic chairs that lined the waiting area outside the MRI room with a smattering of other patients' relatives, killing time while her mother was inside, having yet another scan done. That was where she was when she discovered that the snapshot of the Garcia family that had been taped to the inside of the folder had been taken on the day they had moved into the house from which they had disappeared eight months later. Before that, they had lived in Arlington, Virginia, for a number of years.

She'd had Rinko e-mail the case file to her (and never mind that Scott had told her to leave the case alone; she was far too emotionally invested in it to obey, and besides, when had she ever just meekly done what Scott told her?). Reading the various documents, she was riveted when she stumbled across the information that Angela, before moving to Lexington, had been a radiology technician at Saints Mary and Elizabeth Hospital in Silver Spring, Maryland, which was, like Arlington, practically a suburb of Washington, D.C. The coincidence of the woman she so closely resembled having worked at the hospital where she had been born made her pulse quicken, but since she'd been born in Silver Spring in April 1981 and Angela and her family had been living in Lexington for months at the time, there didn't seem any way to forge a connection between the two happenstances, as tantalizingly significant as the fact seemed to be.

There's no mention anywhere of the dog's name. No mention of a Lucy at all . . .

"Miss Grant." A female voice dragged her attention away from her laptop.

"Yes?" Lisa looked up to find a plump gray-haired woman in a white lab coat standing in front of her. She recognized her as one of the phalanx of doctors who'd been treating her mother but couldn't quite place her otherwise. She was saved by a plastic name tag identifying her as Dr. JoAnn Dean, head of radiology. Oh, yes, now she remembered.

"I just wanted to let you know that as far as we can tell, your mother has not had a stroke. What we think occurred is that stress combined with her weakened condition caused several small blood vessels to pop in her brain, resulting in the loss of consciousness she experienced. There should be no lasting damage from that, and if the other tests come back negative and we can get her back physically to where she was before, she should be able to be released from the hospital in a few days. Maybe as soon as Monday."

Lisa felt a wave of thankfulness ease something inside her that she hadn't even realized was gripping her heart like a tight fist. What that rush of emotion told her was that, as braced as she had thought she was for her mother's passing, she still wasn't ready. Not even close.

"I'm so glad. Thank you for telling me."

Dr. Dean nodded and talked for a few minutes about the physical therapy her mother would be getting to strengthen her enough so that she could once again get around in her wheelchair. Then she left, and Lisa returned her attention to her laptop and the Garcia family.

The husband, Michael, had been working at a service station on Winchester Pike at the time of his disappearance, according to the initial police report. He had a rap sheet with convictions for a number of mostly petty crimes ranging back to his teenage years. The most serious, receiving stolen property, had resulted in him spending time in jail just before they had moved to Lexington. Not a lot of time, just ninety days, but still Lisa wondered if it had something to do with the move.

A handwritten police note clipped to the rap sheet suggested that Michael's background be investigated further for possible connections to the disappearance. Paging through the rest of the file, Lisa could find no evidence that this had been done. After nearly thirty years, though, it was only to be expected that the file would be less than complete. It would have gone through a lot of hands before being finally filed away as the leads petered out and the trail went cold, which meant there would have been ample opportunity for things to get lost.

The lead detective on the case was a Lexington police officer named Dean Graves. Although the note suggesting further investigation of Michael Garcia's background had not been signed, Lisa thought, from matching it to other handwriting throughout the file, that he had written it. Talking to him was a logical next step, but a quick scan of police records revealed that he had retired in 1995 and had since died.

That was the trouble with cold cases. People died, or moved, or forgot. Documents got misplaced. Evidence was lost. And after a while the case got buried under the sheer avalanche of new crime.

Where it was eventually forgotten, as this case would have been forgotten if Gemmel had not noticed and been intrigued by how much she looked like Angela Garcia.

Lisa found herself almost wishing Gemmel hadn't noticed.

Certainly she would be sleeping better at night.

There was a Christmas picture of the children in the file, the kind of inexpensive professional photograph that would have been taken at one of those talk-to-Santa setups in a mall. Probably in Lexington, because the children looked to be approximately the same age that they had been when they had disappeared. Perched on Santa's lap, Marisa, wearing a Christmasy plaid dress and red tights, was looking down at a small stuffed reindeer in her lap. Her brother, Tony, in a red sweater and black pants, stood by Santa's knee, staring solemnly in the direction of the camera. Like Marisa, he was a sturdy, rosy-cheeked, black-haired child. Handsome and a little mischievous-looking. A shiver went up Lisa's spine as, taking a closer look, squinting past the glow of her laptop screen and enlarging the picture as best she could, she was able to determine that his eyes were brown.

A warm caramel brown.

Like mine.

At the thought, her stomach tightened. But then, of course, she reminded herself, golden brown was in no way extraordinary. After all, in a world in which approximately half the population was brown-eyed, how many shades of brown could there be?

Because Marisa was looking down, her eye color was impossible to determine. Suddenly desperate to know, Lisa searched through the file, scanning every page for a mention of Marisa's eye color. She knew that it had to be part of the record, because a detailed description of the child would have been taken and sent to the media as well as law enforcement across the country, but if it was in the file she couldn't find it.

In her mind, she'd pictured Marisa's eyes as blue, but she realized that was strictly because the doll Katrina's eyes were blue, and she'd extrapolated the color to the child. But if Marisa's eyes were caramel, too . . .

What? Then she was Marisa? Was that what she secretly suspected? Lisa shook her head at herself. It was impossible, and not only because she had seen the photographic proof of her own birth, or because her existence had been carefully documented from the time her mother had first begun to swell with pregnancy to some snapshots Robin had taken of Lisa with Martha last week. The age difference alone ruled that out.

Still, she couldn't stop looking at the photo.

There was a picture in her baby book of herself with Santa at about four years old that Lisa had never really been aware of until she and her mother had gone through the album together on the day of the fire. It had been well on its way to fading into the dim recesses of her memory until now.

That picture of herself looked enough like this picture of Marisa that they could have been taken of the same child.

Lisa's heart started to beat faster. She was still staring down at the picture when her mother, on a gurney, was rolled out of the MRI room.

Glancing up at the sound of the gurney's wheels, Lisa quickly closed the laptop, slid it into her tote, and stood up.

"Good news," Lisa greeted her, falling into place beside the gurney after a quick smile for the orderly who was pushing it. "Dr. Dean said you haven't had a stroke. They're going to schedule you for some physical therapy, and then, when you're a little stronger, they're going to let you go. Maybe as early as Monday."

"That's — wonderful. I can't wait — to get home." Her mother's eyes grew misty, and Lisa realized that Martha was fighting back a sudden welling of tears. "I was afraid I was — going — to die in here."

"No way." Lisa wrapped her fingers around her mother's as a lump rose in her own throat. The truth was, she had been afraid of that, too.

A little later, very casually, she asked her mother if she remembered anything about a family by the name of Garcia who'd gone missing from the area about thirty years ago.

For a moment Martha frowned, and Lisa had thought she was going to say no. Then her brow cleared. "Yes — I do."

The answer was surprising enough to send a tiny chill through Lisa. Unsure how to proceed — the last thing she wanted to do was cause her mother any distress — Lisa met her mother's eyes. There was no trace of self-consciousness in them that she could detect. No trace of the nervousness she should have been feeling if she'd been keeping a lifelong guilty secret from her daughter and suspected she was about to be called on it.

"Did you know them?"

"No. But — there were children involved — and I was a — new mother. It was — all over TV. And — the papers. At the time. I remember thinking it — was very sad. Why? Have they — turned up?"

Still watching her mother closely, Lisa shook her head. "I came across a file on the case at work, is all."

She hesitated, tempted to pull her laptop out of her tote and show her mother the pictures. But illness had made Martha fragile, and seeing how much the daughter she adored looked like the missing family might well worry her.

It might even stir up things best left unstirred.

Even to have such thoughts was unsettling. Lisa felt as though she were tiptoeing her way through a minefield. One wrong step had the potential to set off an explosion that could be catastrophic.

"That must be — so interesting. Sometimes I wish — I — had had a career." Martha's tone was wistful. Knowing her mother well enough to be convinced by her words and manner that she wasn't hiding anything, Lisa allowed herself to be led down the trail of gentle reminiscences that Martha embarked on.

When her mother was wheeled away for her first physical therapy session shortly after three p.m., Lisa left the hospital to run some much-needed errands. The first thing she did was, finally, get a room at the Marriott down the street and move her suitcase into it. If she was going back to work tomorrow, she needed a base other than the hospital. Then she did a little shopping, acquiring such necessities as underwear and toiletries, and a very basic wardrobe.

Finally she drove out to Grayson Springs.

Detective Watson had called and asked to meet with her there, and she had agreed, although not without some misgivings: From his tone, she was sure that he had more questions, and maybe even more suspicion, for her. But she wanted to pick up some things, including her baby book and other photo albums, and because she felt uneasy about going out to the house or anywhere else that was kind of isolated on her own, she considered that the safety Detective Watson's presence promised outweighed any unpleasantness he might have in store for her. With an eye toward getting the most out of her visit, she also made an appointment to talk with the contractor she had selected to restore the house. Among other things, she wanted his opinion on whether it would be possible for them to move back into the house after Martha was released from the hospital. Once Lisa had begun thinking the matter over, she had started to be horribly afraid it would not. There had been so much damage, and there was so much work to be done, that it was possible that she would have to find some other place for herself and her mother to live until at least some of the repairs were completed. She immediately thought of the manager's house, where

Robin and Andy were staying, but just as quickly ruled that out. An old farmhouse much like the one Bud Buchanan lived in, although in far better shape, it was totally unsuitable for a woman in a wheelchair.

The problem was that although Dr. Dean's verdict today had felt very much like a reprieve, the hard truth remained that Martha didn't have a lot of time. Lisa wanted her to be able to spend as much of that time as possible in the home she loved.

When she crested the rise in the long driveway to be greeted by the scorched and damaged outline of the roof against the sky, Lisa's heart sank. The house's once pristine façade was seared and black in places, and beside the columned porch the bucket of a bright yellow cherry picker hoisted a man toward the gutted second floor. More trucks were parked in the driveway, and workers swarmed around the place like bees. The grass was rutted, the windows grimy with smoke, the front door standing open. Seeing Grayson Springs so terribly brutalized made her ache with loss. Her eyes stung and her throat grew tight remembering the house the way it had been.

But there was no undoing what had been done. Blinking away incipient tears, she steeled herself to accept the situation as it was and deal with it.

The contractor who was waiting for her confirmed what she instinctively knew: It would take months to bring Grayson Springs fully back to life. Even to get the part of the house that the fire had left undamaged livable again would require weeks of work, because of havoc wrought by water and smoke and the destruction of such essentials as the electrical, heating, and air-conditioning systems.

The hard truth was that her mother would not be able to go home right away.

Detective Watson, as it happened, wanted to ask about the smoke detectors. It seemed that the semi-melted remains of two of them had been recovered. From their location in the debris, he believed that they were the ones from either end of the second-floor hallway ceiling in Lisa's bedroom wing.

"Who was responsible for seeing to their maintenance?" he asked.

Lisa frowned. They were standing near the porte cochere with a bustle of activity going on around them. It was hot and humid, and the terrible burned smell that she was actually starting to grow almost accustomed to hung in the air. There was also a great deal of noise. The contractor and his crew were on the far side of the house, yelling back and forth. A chain saw roared from the front yard. An arson team was at work inside, and she watched as plastic bin after plastic bin of blackened items was carried past to be stored in an outbuilding until investigators could go through them.

"Robin — Mrs. Baker, I suppose. Or Mr. Frye. Really, anyone who thought of it. Why?"

"Far as we can tell, the batteries were missing. From both."

Lisa felt an icy tingle run down her spine. It was possible that the missing batteries were an accident, of course. Somebody took them out, meant to replace them, and never got around to it. But how likely was that?

Her stomach tightened. Her heart started to thud. She could feel her body reacting, and she did her best to keep it from showing. "You really think it was arson?"

"We wouldn't be doing this if we didn't." Detective Watson did his sleepy-turtle blink at her. "You said you were in bed asleep when the fire started. If they didn't have batteries, the smoke detectors definitely weren't working. So, you want to tell me how it was again that you woke up and became aware of the fire?"

"Oh, for goodness' sake." His suspicion of her was as tangible as a blast of cold air. "If it was arson, I didn't do it, I promise you."

"If you could just answer the question, Miss Grant."

Lisa gave up and gave in. She had nearly finished with one more recounting of how she had awakened to smell smoke when something atop one of the bins being carted past caught her eye.

"Stop," she broke off to say sharply to the uniformed deputy who was carrying the bin. As he obediently stopped, frowning at her, she walked toward him. "I — that's mine."

"That" was Katrina. The doll's face was smudged with soot, and her hair was singed so that the ends frizzed around her neck. Her clothes were dirty and scorched in places, and her tights and shoes were missing. It was obvious from the discoloration and flatness of the dress's nap that she'd been soaked with water that had then slowly dried. But she was still perfectly recognizable.

Almost convulsively, Lisa picked her up out of the bin, her hands closing around hard plastic arms clad in now stiff blue velvet. As she was tilted upright, the doll's eyes flew open. Lisa's heart gave an unexpected leap. For a moment she had the eerie impression that Katrina was staring at her.

Get a grip.

With Detective Watson's permission, she took Katrina with her when she left. But during the drive back to Lexington she became spooked enough by the doll's vacant blue gaze to lock her securely in the trunk before she went back into the hospital.

It felt, Lisa decided with a shiver, like having a ghost riding with her.

18

"You bought that at Walmart?" Nola looked incredulously at Lisa's airy white linen jacket, which she wore over a simple white tee with a pair of black slacks. "I don't believe it. It's actually cute!"

"They have some nice things. You just have to look. You ought to try shopping there. You might be surprised." Hiding a smile, Lisa took another small bite out of what remained of her scoop of tuna salad. The tuna, presented on a bed of lettuce surrounded by juicy red tomato slices, was delectable, and she was determined to savor every last morsel. It was also pricey enough to be a splurge she allowed herself only rarely now. She and Nola were seated in a booth at one of their favorite restaurants, Fortuni's, which was located in the middle of Lexington's chicly revitalized downtown. It was Friday lunch hour, and the place, which was popular with the legal community because it was near the courthouse, was crowded and noisy. As she had to be in courtroom nine at the prosecution's table complete with paperwork at one, and it was now twelve-thirty, they were just finishing.

Nola, the Saks, Neiman's, and expensive boutique shopaholic, dismissed Walmart with a shudder. "Sweetie, forget Walmart. I brought you two big boxes full of the good stuff. Lucky we wear the same size."

Lisa grinned at her friend. They did wear the same size, although Nola was two inches shorter and considerably curvier where it counted. But they had wildly different tastes and coloring. Blue-eyed, with a crop of platinum-blond curls that spiraled to her shoulders and the kind of round-cheeked, pert-nosed beauty that made her look like a teenager at twenty-eight, Nola favored bright colors, silky textures, low-cut tops, short skirts, and clingy dresses. If there was a pantsuit in her wardrobe, Lisa had yet to see it. The only thing they agreed on was shoes: They both favored sinfully expensive high heels. Trust-fund-baby Nola could still afford them. Lisa unfortunately couldn't.

"Remember, I'm a lawyer. I work in a very conservative office."

"Hey, the stuff I brought you is classic. Timeless. It can go anywhere." Nola's eyes twinkled at her. "Which is why I'm giving it to you. They're basically my mistakes. Who wants to be boring?"

"Oh, thanks a lot."

"You know I mean it lovingly. Oh, wow, look who's here!"

She was staring over Lisa's shoulder. Lisa, who had her back to the door, turned to look. At first, scanning the crowd gathered behind the hostess's stand, she didn't think she saw anyone she knew.

"I don't . . ." she began.

"They're on their way to a table." Nola was already waving. "Oh my God, he is so hot. Tell me you don't think so."

"Who are we . . . ?" Lisa's voice trailed off as she spotted Scott. In that single glance she saw that he was wearing a medium-blue suit, that he was with some people from the office, and that the whole group was following one of the black-clad hostesses toward the private back room that was mostly kept for VIPs, which, as the local DA, Scott now was.

And he was, indeed, looking hot.

Having seen them, Scott acknowledged Nola's newest wave with an uplifted hand, said something to the group around him, and headed toward them. Lisa recognized some of the people he was with — Pratchett, Ellis, and Kane, who shot her a dirty look — and lifted a halfhearted hand toward them in greeting. Everybody except Kane waved back.

Well, screw Kane.

"Don't forget he's my boss now," Lisa turned back to hiss.

"How hot is that?" Nola's grin was wicked. "Have you jumped him in the office yet?"

"No!"

"Don't tell me you haven't thought about it."

"No, I actually haven't."

"I bet the sex would be phenomenal. He is such a stud. All those muscles —"

"Nola." Lisa was acutely aware of Scott approaching. The last thing she wanted was for him to overhear. "Hush."

She of the tawny complexion who never blushed could feel her face heating as Scott neared the table. It was all because of Nola's nonsense, of course, and she shot her friend a killer look that she hoped would be sufficient to keep the coming conversation at least approximately G-rated. She hadn't seen Scott since Wednesday night. He'd called her yesterday to tell her that he had a copy of the Garcia file in front of him, that she did indeed bear a marked resemblance to the woman in the picture, and that he was, as he had said he would, having someone look into the case further. When she'd made a sound of alarm, he'd promised that he'd kept her out of it, and would continue to keep her out of it, until they had some idea of where any leads that might turn up were going to take them. Then he'd once again told her to leave the case alone. When she had demurred — actually, what she'd said was "Yeah, right" — he'd told her it wasn't a request, it was an order. This she had considered a piece of typical Scott arrogance, and told him so. His reply was something along the lines that this was work-related, not personal, and she had damned well better do as he said. The upshot had been that she'd hung up on him. Last night he'd stopped by the hospital briefly, but she'd been downstairs in the cafeteria grabbing a late dinner with Andy and had missed him. This morning she'd gone back to work, where she'd been so snowed under that she hadn't resurfaced until lunch, which she would have worked through if she hadn't had plans with Nola. But even if she had hoped to see Scott at the office — which she hadn't — it wouldn't have mattered, because he'd spent the morning somewhere else.

Now, despite their recent quarrel, despite everything, she discovered that she was too glad to see him for her own peace of mind.

"Scott!" Nola shot up to give him a big hug as he reached their table. She was her usual sexy self in a hot-pink sleeveless blouse with a black mid-thigh-length skirt that bloomed with pink hibiscus, along with tons of jewelry and sky-high heels. With her curves pressed against Scott's powerful frame, she looked as impossibly feminine as a Barbie.

"Nola." Scott suffered the hug more than returned it. He'd always been a little stand-offish where Nola, who was nothing if not predatory toward the men she was attracted to, was concerned. His eyes met Lisa's over Nola's shoulder. "Hello, Lisa."

"Hello, Scott." She narrowed her eyes at him. He smiled at her, a slow, intimate smile that made her heart start to beat a little faster.

Good God, I'm as bad as Nola.

At the thought, her brows snapped together. Maddeningly, his smile widened.

"I hear you're quite the hero." Nola released him to slide, with obvious reluctance, back into her seat.

"How so?"

"I told her how you rescued me from my

burning house." Lisa flicked a glance up at him. "Scooped me up in your arms and all that. She practically drooled."

"Yeah, well, every now and then I have to get my knight-in-shining-armor fix in. You know how it is."

Nola giggled.

Lisa didn't. "What does that make me, the damsel in distress?" she asked tartly.

"More like the princess in the tower." Their eyes met.

Before she could reply, Nola turned her best high-wattage smile on him. "I haven't seen you in forever. Why don't you join us?"

"He's with some people." Lisa barely resisted the urge to kick Nola under the table. "Besides, we're almost finished."

"I was just thinking about ordering dessert."

That was news to Lisa, as Nola, who was perpetually on a diet, never ate dessert, and she knew perfectly well that Lisa, who sometimes did, didn't have time. Pretending not to see Lisa's look of surprise and smiling for all she was worth at Scott, Nola did a subtle wriggle and back arch that made the most of her curves. It was one of her trademark come-hither moves. Lisa reckoned she must have seen it a thousand times over the years. Scott's eyes dipped just as they were supposed to, and Lisa realized he was doing exactly what countless other males before him had done: taking in the view. Nola's neckline plunged to a deep vee that Lisa had little doubt provided Scott, from his vantage point above them, with a bird's-eye view of a copious amount of grade-A cleavage. Which was just what Nola wanted, of course. She was a shameless flirt, always had been, always would be, and used her ample assets to maximum advantage. She'd been after Scott since she'd first hit puberty, so far without success. Until this moment, Lisa had always rather admired Nola's aggressiveness toward the men she set her sights on. In private moments, Nola would wickedly sing "What Nola wants, Nola gets" about the men she was after, and Lisa would always laugh along, because it was pretty much true.

But this time she wasn't quite so amused. Not when Nola's sights were turned on Scott.

Though why it should bother her so she refused to let herself even begin to think about.

He must have felt the weight of Lisa's gaze, because his eyes lifted suddenly to meet hers. She couldn't help it: The look she gave him was downright frosty.

"Anyway, I guarantee we're much more fun than the people he's with," Nola added. "They don't look exciting at all."

"Not polite," Lisa warned her through a smile that she devoutly hoped didn't look as stiff as it felt.

Nola ignored her.

"I wish I could." Scott was once again looking at Nola — in the face this time — while the slightest of smiles touched his mouth. Lisa found she didn't much like that smile. It was, she suspected, a reaction to her own cold glare. "But unfortunately it's a business lunch. Much as I might like to, I can't skip out on it. Not even to join two such beautiful ladies."

At that piece of blatant, un-Scott-like flattery, Lisa's smile turned into more of a sneer. Not that anyone noticed.

"That's too bad." Nola made a charming little moue. Then her eyes brightened. "You know, come to think of it, I am *so* glad we ran into you. Mark Thomas — you remember Mark Thomas? — and I were supposed to go with Lisa and Joel and some other friends to the Fourth of July party at the country club tomorrow night, but, um, I just broke up with him, so that's out. But I still want to go. Which means I need a date." Her smile beamed brighter than ever. "You could take me. If you wanted to."

Lisa heard that with something very close to horror. Like Nola's, her eyes fastened on Scott's face. She had a feeling that the expression in hers was quite different, however. *Appalled* probably would come closest to describing it.

Scott's smile widened. "Definitely I want to."

For an instant Lisa couldn't believe what she was hearing. She was sure her jaw dropped. Fortunately, Scott was smiling at Nola, and neither of them was looking at her at all.

"Really?" Nola's tone was suddenly that of a thrilled little girl. But she made a quick recovery. "That's wonderful. We'll have such a good time, I know. The country club puts on the most amazing bashes."

Lisa remembered that Scott had never, to her knowledge, been to one. The country club was very exclusive, and unless you were a member or the guest of a member, you didn't get in, period. As a girl, she'd swum there, played tennis there, gone to dances and parties and Fourth of July celebrations there, year in and year out, without even thinking about it. It was part of the fabric of her life. But not Scott's. Never Scott's.

"How about I call you later and we work

out the details?" He was still smiling at Nola. To her own annoyance, Lisa found herself suddenly feeling very much like a third wheel, and she didn't like the sensation. And what she really didn't like was the fact that she didn't like it.

Nola beamed back at him. "Do you have my number?"

"If I don't, I'll find it." He threw Lisa a smiling glance that made her think that he might have some small inkling of the depth of her displeasure. Immediately, she schooled her expression. The last thing she wanted to do was glare at him. "You don't mind me horning in on your date, do you, Princess?"

Lisa was spared having to answer as the waitress came up to their table.

"Anything else, ladies?" she asked.

Lisa shook her head. "Just the check, please." Her voice was probably crisper than it needed to be, and she vowed to work on that, too, before she said anything else.

"What about dessert?" Scott asked.

"I guess not today." Nola should have been an actress: She sounded genuinely regretful. It was all Lisa could do not to roll her eyes.

"I hate to eat and run, but I have to go." As the waitress left the check, Lisa pulled out a twenty — she knew exactly how much her share was, because she almost always got the tuna plate — and put it down on the table. "I have to be in court at one, and I don't dare be late."

"Yeah, I hear your boss is a real hard-ass," Scott drawled, making Nola giggle again. The sound grated on Lisa like fingernails on a blackboard. Sliding from the booth, she shot Scott a withering look. He was the one she was finding excruciatingly annoying. Nola, bless her man-eating little soul, was just being Nola.

"Lisa, wait! Don't leave without letting me give you those boxes," Nola called after her as Lisa, with a nonchalant "Bye" and a wave for the pair of them, started to weave her way between the tables and toward the door. A glance back told her that Nola, following, was just a couple of yards behind her. Scott still stood beside the booth they had just vacated, saying something to the waitress. Realizing where her eyes were resting, she jerked her gaze forward again. Then, with Nola catching up, she did her best to eradicate the grim look from her face. As she pushed through the door and into the wall of bright, blazing humidity that was the parking lot, Nola was right behind her.

"Sweetie, I'm not stepping on your toes or anything, am I?" Nola sounded faintly breathless. Lisa realized she was walking too fast for a woman calmly exiting a friendly lunch, and slowed down. "If I'd thought you wanted him, I never would have asked him out. You know that."

Clearly, Lisa realized with chagrin, her displeasure had been visible, and knowing Scott, she doubted he had missed it, either. *Damn.* Pinning a smile on her face, working hard to recover her equilibrium, she glanced sideways at Nola, who had fallen in beside her as they walked across the crowded parking lot toward where their cars were parked side by side.

"I'm not interested in him."

"Are you sure? 'Cause I have to tell you, you're putting out some pretty strong vibes that say otherwise."

A sharp blast from a car horn somewhere nearby made Lisa jump, an overreaction that wouldn't have happened if her nerves hadn't been so on edge. Almost immediately identifying the sound, she was annoyed at herself. Fortuni's was located on a corner, and the intersection in front of them teemed with midday traffic. The swoosh of tires and the stop-and-go sounds of vehicles braking for the light served as background noise for the click of their heels on the asphalt. The smell of gasoline-tinged exhaust hung heavy in the air. The new, twenty-story bank building across the street was fronted with mirrored glass that gave off a glare so blinding that Lisa had to shade her eyes with her hand. Was it any wonder that she was getting back the headache she thought she had controlled with regular doses of Tylenol?

"Lisa?"

Okay, be cool.

Lisa made a face. "It's just that he irritates the bejesus out of me sometimes. Did you hear those 'Princess' cracks? He's been calling me that for at least a dozen years, it ticks me off every time, and he knows it. Which is why he does it, of course."

"Oh." Nola didn't sound totally convinced. "I'd forgotten how you two always used to snipe at each other. Um, but if it is a problem, just tell me. I'll call Mr. Hunky District Attorney and tell him it's a no-go so fast it'll leave a vapor trail. Bro's before ho's, or whatever the female equivalent is, that's my motto."

Lisa had to laugh. Nola would, she knew. All she had to do was say the word.

Not in this lifetime.

"No, it's fine. Though I have to say, when you were asking *my boss* out, did it never occur to you that it might be a little awkward for me to go on a double date with him?"

Nola gave her a mischievous look. "You know, when I asked him out, I was thinking more about the *hunky* and less about the *district attorney.* And I definitely was not thinking anything about *my best friend's boss.*"

"I take that as a no."

"Yeah, it's a no. But I don't see why Scott being your boss matters particularly. What, were you planning to get hot and heavy with Joel in the middle of the dance floor? Wait till I tell him, he'll be thrilled." Nola stopped as she reached her white Lexus and pressed a button on her key ring to pop open the trunk.

"No, I wasn't. And don't you dare." Lisa knew that Nola and Joel frequently ran into each other in the course of their workdays. Knowing Nola, that was just the kind of thing she would say to him. "It's just awkward, is all."

Walking on to where the Jaguar practically sparkled in the sunlight, Lisa popped her trunk, too, to facilitate the handing over of the big brown cardboard boxes full of clothes, one of which Nola was already lifting from her trunk. It wasn't particularly heavy, Lisa discovered, as she took it from her and carefully put it in her own trunk on the opposite side from where Katrina lay, flat on her back, eyes closed, next to the pile of photo albums she had rescued. Glancing quickly away from the doll, which was taking on the uncanny ability to instantaneously creep her out, she was glad to be distracted by Nola's thrusting the second box into her arms. She was just putting it down beside the first when a voice behind her said, "Lisa?"

She knew that voice. Stiffening, she let go of the box as if it was suddenly filled with lead, and turned to find Barty, tall and craggily handsome, blue eyes sparkling, silver hair styled to shining perfection, smiling that big crocodile smile of his, as though he were actually glad to see her, when she knew perfectly well that he was secretly cursing the fate that had brought them to this same small parking lot at the same time, striding toward her. The sad thing was, he looked like a judge, distinguished, responsible, honorable, which just went to show how deceptive appearances could be. Her last contact with him had been a phone message he'd left for her, telling her to call him if she or her mother needed anything. It was so obviously a duty call that she hadn't even bothered to return it. Now everything about him, from his expensive suit to his carefully maintained tan to his aura of abundant good humor, set up her back. He looked a good decade younger than his sixty-eight years, too. Lisa thought of her mother and felt her hackles rise.

"Barty." Her voice was flat. As he reached her, he looked for a moment as if he was thinking about hugging her, but something in her expression must have dissuaded him, because he stopped short. "I thought you couldn't do lunch today because Todd had a track meet. Or — oh, wait — was it because your trial was running long? I never can keep your stories straight."

Beside her, she could feel Nola, who knew how she felt about her father, moving closer in support.

Barty's smile never faltered. He didn't even have the grace to blink. "The track meet finished up early. You know it was at Paul Dunbar" — one of Lexington's big public high schools — "so I was in town. Afterward, Jill and Todd headed on over to Danville to look at Centre College, so it just so happened I was free. Then Sanford called, and the long and short of it is we decided to stop in here for a quick bite before I headed home."

"I was sorry to hear about your fire, Lisa." Sanford Peyton nodded a greeting at her before transferring his attention to Nola. "Hello, Nola."

Until that moment, Lisa hadn't noticed him, but there he was, standing at Barty's shoulder like the perpetual wingman he was. Joel's father had none of his son's good looks, although he could be very charming when he chose. Balding, barrel-chested, and still powerful-looking at about Barty's age, with a fringe of short gray hair and some serious jowls, he had the look of a mafia enforcer gone to seed. As a longtime close friend and business associate of Barty's, he was someone Lisa had known all her life. As Joel's father, he was someone she saw with some frequency, certainly far more often than she saw her own father. Aside from his tendency to bully Joel, she actually knew nothing bad about him. But that and his friendship with Barty were more than enough to keep him off her favorite-persons list.

"Thanks," she said. Nola, whom Lisa was convinced could not help herself where single men — Sanford was a widower — were concerned, beamed at him as she said hi.

"Nola, that's right." Barty sounded delighted. It hadn't escaped Lisa that he'd been giving her bodacious friend a covert once-over, and her lip curled. "Nola Hampton. I remember now. Lord, I haven't seen you since you were in high school. I —"

"I hate to interrupt, but I have to get going. I have to be in court at one." Turning to close the trunk, Lisa cut Barty off without compunction. She glanced at Nola, whose legs were right up against the bumper. "Better move."

"Oh. Right." Nola took a couple of steps back out of the way, and Barty, who was just getting going again on how amazing he found it that the two of them were now all grown up, broke off in full spiel.

"My God, what's that?" he croaked. His tone was odd enough so that Lisa, who had a hand on the trunk just about to slam it closed, turned to frown at him instead. His eyes were fastened on Katrina. He wasn't moving, barely seemed to be breathing. In fact, the best word she could think of to describe his expression was *stunned.*

19

Lisa watched him, riveted. She was ready to swear that beneath his tan, Barty's face had paled.

"My old doll," she said slowly, never taking her eyes off his face. "One of the few things of mine that survived the fire."

"Oh. Oh." Barty wrenched his eyes away from Katrina, took a deep breath, and met Lisa's gaze. "Of course. Your doll. I don't know what I was thinking. It just — it's burned and . . ."

Sanford took his arm. If he'd noticed anything unusual in Barty's manner, his easy smile at Lisa didn't show it. "If Lisa has to be in court by one, we'd best be letting her get on her way."

Barty glanced at him. Then he looked back at Lisa.

"Of course we should." He seemed recovered now. At least — had there been beads of sweat on his upper lip before he saw

Katrina? Lisa couldn't remember. But there definitely were now. "As I can tell you from personal experience, judges hate it when anyone's late to court." He glanced down at his watch. "It's already twelve-fifty, so —"

"I've got to go." She had no time to waste. Why Barty was behaving oddly was something to ponder later. For now, her job had to be her priority. She slammed the trunk closed and called hurried farewells as she jumped into her car. As she pulled out of the parking lot, she glanced into her rearview mirror. Nola was gone, but Barty and Sanford still stood in the parking lot exactly where she had left them, looking after her, deep in conversation.

What were they talking about? She couldn't be sure, but something about seeing Katrina had shaken Barty to the core.

The thought made Lisa feel cold all over.

Had Sanford seen Barty's reaction, too, and were they even now talking about it as they watched her drive away?

She thought the probability was strong, but there was no way to be sure, and in any case, she couldn't worry about it now. There was simply no time. She was on the verge of being late to court, and that just could not be allowed to happen, not twice in one week. Pulling into the courthouse parking lot, jamming the Jaguar into the sliver of space that remained between the yellow lines surrounding a dumpster and a poorly parked pickup, she snatched her newly purchased briefcase from the backseat and ran for the building and courtroom nine. The clock was just striking one as she slid into her seat at the prosecution table. Leroy Jones, the mercifully affable ADA who was the lead on the case, grinned at her.

"I knew you'd make it," he mouthed. Then the judge entered and the bailiff called, "All rise!" and they did.

It was an embezzlement trial in which a church secretary was accused of siphoning off more than a hundred thousand dollars from the parish's building fund. A plea bargain having been offered and refused, the Commonwealth was going for broke. It was a standard prosecution tactic, designed to scare the next defendant offered a plea bargain into accepting and thus saving everyone the time and expense of a trial. Lisa spent the next couple of hours whispering into Jones's ear explanations of relevant material in subpoenaed bank records, credit-card statements, e-mails, and telephone bills. The defendant had a gambling problem, and Lisa had checked every casino within a day's drive to find dates and amounts that corresponded roughly with the missing money. The upshot was that they had the woman cold. The plea bargain had included four months behind bars. A conviction would probably net the defendant three to five years. And they were going to get the conviction, Lisa was sure.

If so, it would be a harsh lesson aimed more at the public defender than the defendant.

By the time the case had gone to the jury and Lisa was back in her cubicle, it was getting on toward five. Five o'clock on a Friday, and every single desk around her was still occupied. Casting a single wistful glance at the clock while the memory of her previous job with its five-o'clock quitting time danced in her head, she tuned out all the hustle and bustle of the grunt room where the research assistants and administrative assistants and paralegals labored in busy anonymity and got down to dotting her *i*'s and crossing her *t*'s for the next case on her agenda. She'd been working on it off and on for the past month, and basically what she was doing at the moment was double-checking what she'd already done. It involved putting everything else out of her mind and being very, very careful to make sure that every single fact was in order. The material was in the system, having been sent to the defense in a timely fashion as part of the discovery process, but the case went to trial on Monday and the ADA was Kane. In other words, no screwups would be tolerated.

"So, how'd the trial go?"

Scott's voice behind her made her start. Lisa looked around at him in surprise. He had never spoken to her or even so much as acknowledged her presence in this big common room before, yet now here he was, standing in the opening of her cubicle as casually as if he did this every day. With his suit jacket on, he was broad-shouldered enough to block her view of most of the rest of the room. Conscious that the eyes and ears of her fellow cubicle dwellers must be zeroing in like heat-seeking missiles on such a gossip-worthy occurrence as the boss stopping to chat with one he had heretofore treated as invisible, she squelched the urge to scowl at him and instead rolled her chair — it was on wheels — back a little so that she could look at him without breaking her neck.

"It went well. I'm very confident the jury will come back with a guilty verdict."

There you go: tone and expression both

professional as hell. She was proud of herself.

"That's what Jones said."

Then why ask me? is what she almost replied — and sharply, too — but remembered just in time that he was her boss and they were at work, with, quite possibly, many ears listening in.

"Did you want something?" she asked instead, still coolly professional. He smiled at her. With the bright overhead light casting his blunt features into harsh relief and emphasizing every tiny crinkle around his eyes, he shouldn't have looked handsome enough to make her stomach flutter. But he did.

"I can't find Nola's phone number."

It was all she could do to keep from stiffening in indignation.

"Are you *really* asking *me* for it?"

Okay, there was more than a hint of a snap in her voice. It was not something she wanted him to pick up on. *Dial it back.*

"If you wouldn't mind."

Lisa sizzled inwardly and said, "814-9034."

This time her tone was as sweet as pie.

He pulled his phone out of his pocket, repeating, "814-9034?" Tapping away, he entered the number into his phone's memory.

"That's right." Her smile felt as though it was hurting her face.

"Thank you." He put his phone away. "I saw your father today, by the way. At Fortuni's. He came in not long after you and Nola left."

Barty as a topic of conversation was only slightly more tolerable than Scott's upcoming date with Nola, she discovered.

"I saw him, too. In the parking lot." Her tone was not encouraging. She thought about telling him about Katrina, and Barty's reaction to the sight of the doll, but she didn't. The story was too complicated and there were too many ears to hear, and anyway, she didn't particularly feel like confiding in Scott at the moment. Although it was galling to face the reason why.

He studied her. "You know, I'm getting the feeling you're mad at me."

Ya think? That's what trembled on the tip of her tongue, but she swallowed it. Instead she gave an elaborately indifferent little shrug and said, "Why would I be?"

"You tell me."

"I'm not, so I can't. Look, I have to get this finished. Do you mind?"

She ostentatiously turned back to her work, rolling her chair around so that she was once again foursquare and solid at her desk, looking at the computer in front of her without registering a thing that was on the screen. Boss or no boss, it was a gesture of obvious dismissal.

"I hear you went out to Grayson Springs yesterday."

So much for her attempt to get rid of him. He was inside her cubicle now, all the way inside — standing right behind her, in fact. Even though she wasn't looking at him, she could feel his presence with every nerve ending she possessed. Her fellow workers must be agog. She only hoped they didn't strain their ears too badly, trying to overhear. Once a visitor was actually inside a cubicle, the semiefficient soundproofing semi–kicked in.

Provoked, she rolled her chair around again so that she could see him. He had to step back out of the way, which still left him so close that she had to tilt her head back to meet his gaze. "So?"

"Watson says he's ninety percent sure it was arson."

That made her stomach clench. "When did you talk to him?"

"He called me about an hour ago."

"What, he's giving you personal updates now?"

"Hey, he and I go way back. And he knows I've got an interest in this."

"Did he happen to mention that I seem to be his chief suspect?"

Scott smiled. It was a small, wry, barely there kind of smile that curled his lips and narrowed his eyes and was sexy as hell. Her response to it was immediate and visceral.

He is *hot,* she thought. Then, *Damn Nola, anyway.*

"He did mention something about that, yeah. Then I reminded him that you were the one person in that house who almost didn't make it out alive, and he seemed to see the point I was making: If you were going to burn your house down for money, you would have made damn sure you weren't in it at the time."

"Very true. Thank you."

"You're welcome."

Remembering how much she really didn't like him at the moment, she gave him a disagreeable look. "Is there something else you wanted? Because if not, I really do need to get back to work. I'd like to get out of here by at least, say, midnight."

"Actually, there is." If he caught the sarcasm — and she knew he did — he gave no sign of it. "You have plans tonight?"

At that, her hands tightened around the

arms of her chair. Her eyes locked on his. For a minute there, she almost thought he meant it. Then she knew he did not.

"I hope that's not a prelude to you trying to ask me out to dinner or something, because if it is, the answer's no." Her tone was deliberately flippant. To mask her disappointment? God, she hoped not.

"You must have forgotten my rule: I don't date people who work for me, remember?" As her eyes flared at him, he smiled. "I just wanted to remind you to be careful. Get inside before dark. Don't go into deserted areas by yourself, that kind of thing."

"Don't worry, I'll keep Joel with me at all times."

He didn't take the bait. "You do that." A tiny sound from the direction of his pocket had him digging his phone out and glancing down at what she was pretty sure was a text message before he looked at her again. "I've got to go. I'm driving my dad down to a rehab center in Nashville. I'll be back tomorrow."

"Oh." Some of her annoyance at him was replaced by concern. That would be a difficult trip, she knew. "I hope everything goes all right."

"Yeah." He gave her a look. "You keep that fire in mind, you hear? Don't do anything too stupid."

Then he turned and began to walk away.

As she started to get mad all over again at the implication in his words, Lisa realized that the real reason he'd sought her out was not to get Nola's phone number at all. That had been merely a tease, entered into because he knew her well enough to be sure it would get a rise out of her. He'd come to her here in the common room, where he'd never approached her before, because he wanted to let her know he was going to be gone and he was concerned for her safety. As she absorbed the truth of that, she felt the hard little knot of what she had steadfastly refused to admit was jealousy that had been there in her chest since lunch ease a little.

"Jackass," she said to his retreating back. It was a name she'd called him dozens of times over the years. At least this time her tone was mild.

He stopped, pivoted, and looked at her without saying anything for a moment. Then he gave her another wry little smile, lifted a hand in farewell, turned, and left.

"Lisa?" No sooner was Scott out of sight than Gemmel appeared in her doorway, refocusing Lisa's attention in a hurry.

"Yes?"

"Are you okay?" Jantzen breathed, materializing behind Gemmel and looking wide-eyed at Lisa over Gemmel's shoulder.

Lisa frowned. "Yes, of course."

Glancing almost furtively in the direction in which Scott had disappeared as if to make sure he was really gone, Gemmel stepped into her cubicle. Jantzen was right behind her.

"Did you just call Buchanan a *jackass?*" Gemmel regarded her with something that looked very much like awe.

Oh, God, Lisa thought. When she'd said it she'd forgotten that she might be overheard. She didn't reply, just looked at Gemmel in consternation. Admitting to having called the boss a jackass was probably not something she wanted to do. The story would fly around the office, and it would focus attention on the relationship between Scott and herself, which would benefit neither of them. Behind Gemmel, other curious coworkers appeared, one after the other, until it seemed as though half the office was crowded into her cubicle, staring at her.

"Balls of *steel,*" Gemmel crowed in approval, apparently taking her silence for assent.

"She called Buchanan a jackass."

"Did he fire her?"

"What did he say?"

"What did he do to make her call him that, is what I want to know."

"New girl *rocks.*"

"Not for long, I imagine."

Her coworkers were, for the most part, talking to one another rather than her while eyeing her with the kind of horrified fascination they might have shown for a two-headed calf.

"Tell us *everything.*" Jantzen was wide-eyed.

"There's nothing to tell." Lisa looked at her associates waiting eagerly for the dirt on the conversation, sighed, and did the only thing she could do under the circumstances: She lied. "It was a joke, okay? I called him that as a *joke.* He knew that and was fine with it."

Not that she thought any of them really believed her denial, but at least she had done the best she could, she reflected, as she drove out of the parking lot shortly after eight o'clock. She was dead tired, hungry, and less than happy about the prospect of her upcoming Fourth of July double date. Friday-night traffic was heavy — there was a Heart concert at the downtown stadium — and she was dealing with the stop and go of Nicholasville Road on her way to the hospital when the memory of Barty's odd reaction to Katrina changed her mind. Something about the doll had shaken him badly, she was sure. Katrina was in her trunk, and Barty knew it. How hard would it be to break into her trunk and steal the doll while her car was parked overnight in the dark and shadowy hospital parking lot?

Not hard, was the answer.

Therefore, just to be on the safe side, she stopped by the hotel, emptied one of the boxes, put Katrina rather gingerly into it, and carried her up to her room for safekeeping. Barty — or more likely, someone working for Barty — might dare to break into a car trunk. Breaking into a hotel room in the teeth of security and the ubiquitous surveillance cameras was a whole different proposition. Anyway, he would have no idea where the doll was, so having tucked her, still in the box, into the darkest corner of the closet, Lisa was satisfied that Katrina would be safe. While she was in the room, she took a quick shower and changed into clothes suitable for sleeping over at the hospital, then carried in the things Nola had given her. Since the one box she'd piled everything into was brimming over, she quickly hung them all up. The clothes were beautiful, brighter and slinkier than she was used to but still relatively subdued, considering that they were Nola's. Three pairs of sky-high heels, one black, one nude, and one a deep scarlet that exactly matched a particularly gorgeous scarlet silk dress, and some funky costume jewelry — Nola loved piling on jewelry — completed the offering. She hurried, conscious of the clock ticking away the minutes until nightfall, but still everything took longer than she'd thought it would, and by the time she left the hotel, it was starting to get dark. A luminous orange line on the western horizon was all that remained of the sun. The sky was purpling. One or two stars had already popped into view.

Get inside before dark. She could almost hear Scott's voice echoing in her head. The unsettling thing was, just the thought of being outside at night made her pulse speed up.

If the fire really was arson, and she and her mother, the only ones who stood to benefit from the insurance money, weren't guilty, then what could the motive have been other than the file?

There *were* other possible motives. Such as a neighbor who coveted their property trying to burn them out, as Watson had suggested. Or maybe a developer — several developers had contacted her mother about selling over the years — hoping to make his next offer easier to say yes to. Or maybe one of the painters had stolen something and had set the fire to cover up the theft. Or in a pinch, there was always your typical unfriendly-neighborhood-arsonist theory.

Now that she'd gotten started, she could go on in this vein for days, which, she discovered, was actually kind of reassuring.

If the file was the motive, then the whole scenario, from the list of possible suspects to what the guilty party was trying to cover up, became too awful to think about.

One thing stood out in her mind, though: the way Barty had reacted to Katrina.

She couldn't force her brain around what that might mean. She was too tired, too anxious, and too hungry.

That last, at least, was easy to remedy.

Because she was sick of hospital food, she pulled into a McDonald's drive-thru a couple of blocks from the hospital. She was already drinking her Diet Coke and eating her Filet-O-Fish as she waited at the exit to rejoin the flow of traffic. It was twilight now, and headlights slashed past in both directions, making it seem even darker than it was.

Probably that was why she noticed the white Ford Explorer: It didn't have its lights on yet. As she pulled out, she spotted it in her rearview mirror and frowned. Then her eyes widened. She couldn't be positive, but she was almost sure that the same vehicle had been parked in the hotel parking lot not far from where she had been busy emptying the Jaguar's trunk.

She wouldn't have noticed it then, except that she'd kept getting the creepy feeling that she was being watched. After glancing around and seeing no one except a few perfectly innocent-looking people coming into and out of the hotel, she'd let her eyes wander over the surrounding vehicles, of which the Explorer had been one.

The only one with tinted windows, which meant she hadn't been able to see inside.

Edgy as she was, that had been enough to make her take notice of the license plate: DFY 347.

Stopping for the last red light just before she was to turn into the hospital parking lot, Lisa craned her neck in an attempt to get a look at this Explorer's license plate. It was several cars behind her. She couldn't see. . . .

The light turned green, and she had to go into the hospital parking lot. Slowing immediately, she watched through her rear-view mirror to see what the Explorer would do.

Staying with the flow of traffic, it drove on past. But she did get a glimpse of the license plate. Not enough to see it all. From her angle, only the last two numbers were visible.

Forty-seven. What were the chances that there were two white Ford Explorers in the vicinity with license plates bearing the same last two numbers? Slim and none, she thought. It had to be the same vehicle.

At the realization, her pulse kicked into overdrive and an icy shiver raced over her skin.

Then she saw the Explorer turn into the next hospital entrance just a little way up the street, and her heart practically leaped out of her chest.

20

Fighting a burst of panic, Lisa swiftly parked in one of the spots reserved for emergency-room visitors — it was within fifty feet of an entrance and bathed in light — and ran inside. Once the sliding glass doors closed behind her and the noise and activity of the crowded waiting room swallowed her up, she felt safer and slowed to a walk. Glancing compulsively behind her as she headed for the elevator bank at the end of the hall, where, thank goodness, at least a dozen people were waiting, she saw no one suspicious. Gradually her heart ceased its frightened thudding. Her breathing normalized.

But for the first time, the idea that she might be in danger felt real.

I should call the police. That was the thought at the forefront of her mind as she rode up to her mother's room on the fourth floor, but she already knew she wasn't ready to do that. Why? For the same reason she didn't tell Watson about the file.

If her resemblance to the Garcias meant something, she wanted to be the one to figure it out before deciding what to do.

Andy was in her mother's room. The two of them were watching a tennis match with the ease of the old friends they were. Martha, who was clutching the remote, turned the volume down at Lisa's entrance, while Andy got to his feet.

"Hello, Mother. Andy." With a quick smile for the pair of them, she immediately looked toward the window. The blinds were open. Given that the room was brightly lit, anyone looking up from the parking lot below should be able to see in. The thought made her shiver.

"Lisa," Andy greeted her with a nod. Under the guise of hugging him, which she did, a quick hug that was warmly returned, she moved around the bed to where he stood beside the window and looked out. The yellowish glow of the security lights lit up the parking lot in sections. It was nearly full, with a number of vehicles circling in search of a space. All she could really see of any of them were their headlights; the vehicles themselves were impossible to identify. It didn't matter. When Andy released her, she moved the step or two past him needed to reach the window and unobtrusively closed the blinds.

Neither he nor her mother seemed to find anything to question in that.

You're safe now, she told herself in an attempt to quiet her jittery heart, and vowed not to leave the hospital again that night. She immediately squelched an urge to call Scott and tell him what had happened. *Nothing* had happened, she reminded herself, except that a white SUV had been in two of the same places she had been. Following her? Possibly. Just as possibly not.

Calm down. The last thing she wanted to do was upset her mother. *I'll look up the license plate number later.*

"I used to — love tennis," Martha said wistfully as Lisa, doing her best to put the incident out of her mind for the time being, dropped a quick kiss on her thin cheek.

Andy grinned. "You used to look mighty good in those little tennis skirts, too."

"I did — didn't I?" Martha smiled back and then turned her attention to Lisa. "So, how was — your day?"

By the time she and her mother had caught each other up on the (edited, in Lisa's case) events of their respective days, Andy was long gone. Claiming that she'd been able to find no other place to park, Lisa had asked him to move her car from the time-restricted spot outside the emergency room, which he had done, returning her keys to her before leaving for the night. Mrs. Wettig, a friend of her mother's, stopped by for half an hour, and an orderly came in to set up Lisa's bed. Only then, when she and her mother were finally left alone, did Lisa turn to the subject that had been bothering her since lunch: Barty's reaction to Katrina.

She did her best to approach it delicately.

"Do you remember one of my dolls, a big one with black hair and blue eyes and a blue velvet dress? I named her Katrina."

Lisa was sitting beside the bed, in the chair Andy had vacated earlier. Her mother was once again holding the remote, and the two of them were watching the news and talking over it. The thought of bringing Katrina in so that the sight of the doll might jog her mother's memory was tempting, but she was afraid Martha might find in Katrina's singed and battered state a distressing reminder of the fire, even if the doll meant nothing else to her.

Martha frowned. "You had — so many — dolls. It's hard to — remember one in — particular. Why?"

"I just wondered when I got her, is all. I can't remember."

"You got dolls for — your birthday — and Christmas — always. Every time — someone asked — what you would like — I always said — a doll. You — loved them."

Lisa smiled. Birthdays and Christmases when she'd been a child had been magical. Her mother had worked hard to make each special occasion truly special. At the time, she had taken it for granted.

"I was spoiled rotten, wasn't I?"

Martha smiled, too. "Not rotten. Maybe a little — spoiled. But I loved spoiling you."

Lisa hesitated. Bringing Barty into the conversation wasn't something she wanted to do. She and her mother rarely spoke of him, because Lisa didn't like to think about him in general and her mother's reminisces of the brief time they had been a family invariably made Martha sad. But tonight, because of Katrina, Lisa needed answers.

"Did — my father" — Martha hated it when she called him Barty — "ever give me any dolls?"

Martha smiled. "He was always — giving you dolls. He was — crazy about you."

Her words smote Lisa to the heart. She felt them as an actual physical blow.

"So, what happened? Why did he leave us?" The questions were out before Lisa could stop them. She had never before asked her mother why Barty had so thoroughly dropped out of both of their lives. She was too proud, and to even acknowledge her father's abandonment enough to ask about it brought too much pain.

"Oh, Annalisa." Her mother regarded her with so much compassion that Lisa ached inside. Gritting her teeth, she did her best to will away the hurt. "It wasn't you — he left. It was — me."

"He left me, too. He left both of us." Lisa had to fight to keep her voice steady, but she managed it. "He left our family."

Her mother sighed. "He left — me," she repeated firmly. "We'd been married for — six years — when you were born. We both wanted — children. I kept — trying and trying — to have a baby — but it didn't happen. By the time — I — finally got pregnant — with you — it was like — a miracle. He was a — congressman by then — you know. He was — running for the — Senate. It was such an — exciting time. Sanford was his — campaign manager — and Jean — Sanford's first wife, she's been dead now for — fifteen years, poor thing — was pregnant too — with Joel. She and I — stayed together — in the house in — Silver Spring — while they flew back and forth — campaigning. Then — you were born. You were premature, a seven-months baby. I was so — worried about you — that I — took you home — to Grayson Springs. Mama and Daddy were — still alive then — and they took care of — both of us. But Bart — didn't like it — that I — ran home to — my parents. That caused — trouble between us. Daddy — didn't like him. He said Bart only — married me for my money. At the time I — thought he was wrong — but later I — wasn't so sure. Then Bart — lost the election. He was still a congressman — still traveling back and forth — between Washington and Grayson Springs. But I could tell he — felt like — a failure. And — he changed. He and Daddy — couldn't get along at all. Bart wanted me — us — to move back to — the house in Silver Spring. But Mama — was ill. I couldn't leavc her. And so — you and I stayed. Bart and I — saw each other — less and less. By the time — Mama and Daddy died and — Bart lost his congressional seat — and moved back to Grayson Springs — our marriage was — over. We divorced — the next year."

"But he never came to see us after the divorce." Now that the wound had been reopened, Lisa could not keep at bay the hurt she had denied for years. It welled up inside her, corrosive as acid. And instead of "us," she was ashamed to admit, what she really meant was "me." *He never came to see me.*

"I know." Martha wet her lips. Her eyes were infinitely sad, and Lisa knew that the sorrow in them was for her. "He's behaved — badly — to you. But I think — it's because — to see you he had — to deal with me. By the time we — divorced — he'd gotten to where — he couldn't stand — me."

It was no excuse for never visiting a daughter, and the ache in Lisa's heart intensified. But then the familiar anger Lisa always felt when she thought of Barty welled to the surface. She welcomed it as an antidote to the sudden stinging rawness inside her.

"He's a very stupid man, then." Lisa's voice was firm; her head was high.

Her mother smiled. "I've thought that — for years. Lucky you — take after me."

Lisa had to laugh, and as she did, the hard little knot inside her chest eased.

"Lucky," she agreed.

Then she allowed the conversation to move on to other, less fraught, topics, until they were interrupted by the nurse, who appeared like clockwork with Martha's sleep medication. By the time Martha finally fell asleep, Lisa was too tired to do anything but curl up on the cot and go to sleep herself.

At least in the hospital, in the midst of so many people and so much activity, she felt safe. If she had been sleeping in her hotel room, as her mother had urged her to start doing, she knew she would never have been able to close her eyes. Being alone right now was the last thing she needed.

Fear had crept into her life, tainting everything.

The next morning, while Martha was in rehab, Lisa used a computer program from work that was installed on her laptop to run the white SUV's plate. It was registered to a company called Diurnal Plastics, with a post office box address. When she ran the company name through all the usual databases, though, she hit a brick wall: There was no information on it. Which meant one of two things: Either Diurnal Plastics was too small and too new to have left digital fingerprints or it was a sham company meant to hide the true ownership of the SUV.

It was impossible to be sure, but if she was voting, she would go with the latter.

The knowledge set her nerves on edge.

Because it was the Fourth of July and a national holiday, there was only a skeleton staff at the hospital. After that single rehab session, Martha had no further tests and nothing to do except chat or listen to music or read or watch TV. Because she expected to be out until the wee hours of the morning, Lisa had made arrangements for Robin to spend the night at the hospital with her mother while she slept in her hotel room. Now that the idea that someone might be following her had planted itself in her brain, staying at the hotel all by her lonesome seemed less and less attractive.

You're being ridiculous, she told herself. *Have Joel walk you up to your room and stay while you check it out, then say good night and lock the door behind him. You'll be safe as houses.*

She knew she was right. Still, when Robin arrived at seven and Lisa drove back to the hotel to get dressed, she was jittery the whole time, despite the fact that it was still full daylight and there were all kinds of people out everywhere celebrating the holiday with parades and picnics and preparations for the fireworks displays that would explode all over the city as soon as it was dark. But although she looked in her rearview mirror every five seconds and kept a wary eye out all around, there was no sign of the white SUV. Or of any other vehicle that could possibly be suspected of tailing her, either.

Still, by the time Lisa let herself into her hotel room, her palms were sweating.

There was just one more thing she had to do before she could take a shower and dress for the party: check to make sure Katrina was safe.

Sliding back the closet door, opening the lid on the box, she discovered that she was holding her breath and deliberately let it out. Of course Katrina was there, just where she had left her, lying in the box with her eyes closed, looking for all the world like a corpse in a coffin. The image bothered Lisa so much that she couldn't leave the doll in that position. Instead she picked her up — Katrina's eyes flew open unnervingly — then hesitated, unsure what to do with her. Putting her out in the bedroom was a nonstarter, but keeping her shut away in the closet wasn't much better. Either way, Lisa realized to her chagrin, the doll had her thoroughly spooked.

A glance at the clock by the bed told her that she had an hour until Joel was supposed to pick her up. No time to do anything, really, except shower and dress.

Lisa was reluctantly putting Katrina back in the box when a mark stamped into the sole of the doll's foot caught her eye.

Eyes widening, she ran the ball of her thumb over the mark's raised lines, then lifted the doll so that she could look at it more closely.

A heart with the letters MBF inside it. After all these years, it was worn and faint but still just legible enough for her to make it out.

The mark did not ring a bell.

Another glance at the clock confirmed it: She did not have time to turn on her computer and research the mark. Unless she wanted Joel to catch her in the shower — and she didn't — she needed to hurry.

Locking the bathroom door behind her as, she realized, a protection against the malevolent and mobile Katrina she could not help imagining more than from any possible human intruders, she showered and did her hair and makeup. When she emerged, cautiously, she slid into her underwear and hurried to the closet with one eye on the clock. The box was still closed — what, had she expected something different? — which, she hoped, meant Katrina was still inside. Shaking her head at her own idiocy, she fought the urge to check. She didn't have time to worry about the doll at the moment. Her eyes fell on the scarlet dress Nola had given her. Taking it out, she slipped it on, then looked at herself in the long mirror on the closet door.

She looked good.

The deep red wasn't a color she usually wore, but it suited her, as did the style, sleeveless and slim, with a short skirt. The matching heels, which she wore without hose, made her legs look long and shapely and very tan. It was a lovely dress, a siren's dress, and as she looked at herself in it, Lisa felt a flutter of excitement. Butterflies took wing in her stomach. Her heartbeat quickened.

All because she was anticipating the effect the way she looked would have on a certain man, she realized with some chagrin, even as a knock on the door announced Joel's arrival.

Making a face at herself, Lisa abandoned her mirror image to pull the door open.

"Yowzers," was Joel's most gratifying reaction as his eyes slid over her, and then as she smiled at him he bent to drop a quick kiss on her lips.

Even with his lips on hers, her pulse didn't budge. Her heart didn't speed up. Her stomach didn't flutter.

Disagreeable as it was to acknowledge, Lisa had to face it: The man whose possible reaction to her appearance had made her go all jittery inside wasn't Joel.

It was Scott. Who would be coming to the country club as Nola's date.

21

She was wearing red, and she was so beautiful that just looking at her made his body tighten.

Nola was at her sexy best, leaning against him, giving him an eye-opening view of her ample assets all but bared by the halter top of the slinky little dress she wore, her blond curls brushing his shoulder, her bare thigh pressing meaningfully against his under the table with only the thin cloth of his charcoal suit pants separating her skin from his, her flowery perfume drifting around his head.

His for the taking, as she'd made abundantly clear.

And yet he had eyes only for Lisa.

Who was threading her way through the crowd toward where he and Nola and two other couples sat at one of the glass-topped garden tables ringing the pool, responding to greetings from acquaintances right and left, her slender body as graceful as the smoke curling skyward from the flickering tiki torches that lit the darkness, her legs looking two yards long as they flashed beneath her short skirt, her long, loose hair blacker even than the night sky and rippling like the surface of the water just a few feet away as, smiling, she turned her head to say something to the man behind her.

Peyton, of course. The jerk even had his hand on her waist.

Scott's hand tightened around his glass. If it had held anything stronger than ginger ale with a twist, he would have knocked it back about then. Unfortunately, it didn't.

"There they are." Nola spotted the newcomers and waved at them. The others at the table — Macy and Thornton, Alexis and Ben, all possessing last names he couldn't remember — joined in, waving and calling hello as Lisa and Peyton approached. They were all old friends, everyone at the table. They were all scions of elite Bluegrass families, all long-standing members of the country club, all regulars at this Fourth of July extravaganza. All except him.

One of these things is not like the others. . . .

"Sorry we're late." Lisa made the smiling apology to the table in general as she and Peyton reached it. Her eyes just touched Scott's as she dropped down into the white wrought-iron chair opposite his that Peyton pulled out for her.

"Get lost?" Scott couldn't help it. The gibe, muttered half under his breath and directed squarely at Lisa, came out before he could stop it.

Her eyes held his as Peyton settled into the chair beside her.

There were eight of the deeply cushioned chairs around each of the sixty or so tables ringing the pool. Another layer of tables for eight were positioned around the outer layer of the pool deck. A third section of larger, family-style tables circled the nearby kiddie pool. All were full, with tuxedoed waiters and black-dress-and-white-apron-clad waitresses weaving deftly between them. A tented buffet and bar had been set up between the two pools, and a line of women in cocktail dresses and men in suits snaked away from both. The smell of grilling meat mixed with the faint scents of citronella and chlorine. Laughter and the sounds of many voices all talking at once filled the air. Another vast white tent covered the brick patio directly behind the antebellum mansion that served as the clubhouse. The patio had been converted for the night into a dance floor. It was lit by thousands of twinkly white lights that covered the interior ceiling of the tent, swirled around the tall support poles, and wrapped the nearby trees and shrubbery. More white lights festooned all the outdoor seating areas, including just above where they sat. A live band played "Margaritaville" with verve, and a few couples already danced energetically to it. Beyond the tent, the golf course stretched, black as velvet in the darkness. According to the card on the table, at eleven-thirty p.m., which was still an hour and a half away, it would be the site of a fireworks display. As befitted the ultra-exclusive nature of the establishment, it was billed as the largest in the region.

"I stopped by the hospital to show my mother my dress. I always wear pants, and I knew she'd like to see me in it."

In contrast to his, Lisa's voice wasn't lowered. Or edgy. Her eyes met his blandly. That very blandness — so un-Lisa — told him that she hadn't missed that he was in a piss-poor mood. He was also aware that she undoubtedly had a good idea of the cause.

They knew each other too damned well, was the problem.

"I knew that color would look great on you." Nola beamed at Lisa. Her gaze slid to Scott. "Doesn't she look great?"

"Beautiful." He spoke the truth without

inflection. His eyes switched to Nola, who was, after all, his date, and he dredged up a smile. "So do you, in case I forgot to mention it."

"You did, but I forgive you." Nola crinkled her nose coquettishly, and he smiled at her again. He liked Nola, found her attractive, was amused by her forwardness, but he already knew that nothing was going to come of this night except this one date. So, he suspected, did she.

Hell, the sad truth was that he'd accepted only to needle Lisa, because of the horrified look on Lisa's face when Nola had invited him. If he had not been fairly certain that Nola had pretty much known the score going in, he would have been feeling ashamed of himself about now.

"Anyone else want a drink?" Peyton looked around the table as he signaled a waitress. "Lise, the usual?"

Scott discovered that he didn't enjoy learning that Peyton called her "Lise." Or that he knew her "usual," whatever the hell it was. When she was with him, she pretty much stuck to iced tea. Or a soda or coffee. Something nonalcoholic.

Because she knew him.

"Sounds good. Thanks," Lisa replied. As the waitress arrived and took their drink order, Lisa looked at Scott again and frowned.

"What happened to your face?" she mouthed.

She was referring to the fresh, two-inch-long scrape just below his left eye, he knew.

"Ran into a door." Without bothering to lower his voice particularly, he told her the same lie he'd told Nola and everyone else who'd asked, because the truth wasn't something he wanted getting all over this small, gossipy, next-door-to-inbred town. The truth was ugly, and there was no room for ugly in the glittery never-never land he was at that moment pretending to be a part of.

"A door?" Lisa looked skeptical, but then her attention was claimed by Macy at the far end of the table, asking about her mother. Lisa answered and then amplified her answer in response to another question, and the conversation turned general as the drinks arrived. Lisa's "usual" was a cosmopolitan, Scott noted with a glance. As she picked up her glass, her eyes slid to his face.

I've got no problem with anyone who's of age *drinking. It just doesn't do it for me.*

He'd said that to her a long time ago, when he'd come across her and Nola and a number of their girlfriends — he didn't think Macy or Alexis had been part of the group, but he wasn't a hundred percent sure, as all the hot chicks who hung with Lisa had started to look alike to him by then — guzzling beer in one of the barns at about age seventeen. He'd been obviously disapproving, Lisa had laughed at him and offered him a beer, he'd turned her down flat, and she had called him uptight, among other things. Then he'd taken the booze away from them and dumped it out.

From the way she watched him as she took that first sip of her cosmopolitan, he had a feeling she was remembering that long-ago night, too.

"Lisa tells me you've been keeping her pretty busy lately." Peyton was talking to him, making a stab at casual conversation, although the two of them had always had about as much use for each other as a cat and a dog.

Quashing his instinct to give the guy a hard time, Scott searched for what he considered to be a relatively pleasant tone and found it.

"Office is jumping."

"You're lucky to have the work." Peyton shook his head. "Our business is way down."

"Is it?" Scott deliberately relaxed back in his chair and settled in for what he could tell already was going to be a long night. Through the table's glass top, he watched with slightly sour appreciation as Lisa crossed long, slim legs. Then Peyton's hand settled on her knee, and Scott found himself gritting his teeth.

"Off about fifty percent, if we're lucky."

"Damned recession." Nola said it cheerfully. Beneath the table, Lisa's legs shifted, Peyton's hand dropped, and Scott was once again able to look at the guy without wanting to deck him.

"Crime's the one thing that's pretty much recession-proof," he drawled, and Nola laughed.

"Hey, Joel, you all ever get that shopping center you were building out in Versailles finished?" one of the men — Ben, he thought — spoke from the other end of the table.

Joel nodded. "Now we're working on getting it all rented out."

"My company's a tenant. We just opened an interior design store in there named Ruffles." Nola grinned at Joel. "Now, if we could just get the developer to give us a break on the rent . . ."

Joel replied, Nola said something else, and suddenly everybody was talking. Under the cover of the general conversation, Lisa leaned toward Scott. His eyes flicked over her. Her hair was sliding over one shoulder, resting against her tawny skin and the vibrant red of her dress like a swathe of shiny black satin. Because she was leaning toward him, he could just see the first gentle slopes of her breasts and the suggestion of cleavage between them. Instead of being red to match the dress, as he would have expected, her lipstick was some barely there color that shimmered in the torchlight and made her parted lips look sexy as hell. The dark fringes of her lashes cast shadows on her cheeks. Her eyes gleamed gold at him.

Beautiful didn't begin to cover it.

"So, did you get your dad settled?" she asked in a voice meant for his ears alone. There was so much talk and laughter around them that she was confident of not being overheard.

Still moodily studying her, he wasn't feeling much like chatting, but he answered: "Yeah."

"Is he what happened to your face?"

Again, they knew each other too well. She'd been witness to a lot of his physical scars over the years, most all of them from the same source. Once upon a time, he'd found it embarrassing.

His shrug was an admission. "He changed

his mind about going about halfway there, and when I wouldn't turn the car around, he punched me. With a set of car keys."

Lisa eyes widened. She drew in a breath. "He barely missed your eye."

"He's getting old. His aim's going."

"That's not funny! The mean old bastard ought to be put away for the rest of his life."

She looked so indignant on his behalf that Scott smiled at her.

"What mean old bastard?" Peyton turned back to ask.

Scott didn't say anything. Lisa looked momentarily flustered. Even though she'd raised her voice at the end, he knew she'd meant their conversation to be private, that she hadn't intended to be overheard. He waited to see if his unfortunate family situation was now going to become the subject of general dinner-table conversation.

"A guy in the system." Lisa's vague answer was dismissive. Her gaze slid to Nola, who was now listening in again, too. She gave her friend a quick, rallying smile. "Did you persuade this cheapskate to lower the rent?"

The sudden gaiety in her voice was meant to start a whole new round of conversation, Scott realized. He was glad to have confirmed that she considered the private things they knew about each other private.

Not that he had really doubted it, or her, in that regard.

"No." Nola gave Peyton a mock-indignant glance, to which he threw up his hands.

"It's not up to me," he protested. "It's my dad's company. He's here somewhere. Talk to him."

Nola replied, but Scott missed it because Peyton's hand was riding Lisa's knee again.

"How about we all head for the buffet?" Macy — or maybe it was Alexis — suggested. He was having trouble keeping them straight, although one was a blonde and the other was a redhead. He kind of vaguely remembered them as part of Lisa's wild teenage crowd, but beyond that less than solid fragment of recollection, they were attractive strangers whom he was perfectly willing to let remain that way.

"I'm starving. Aren't you?" Rising with a supple undulation that was meant to make him take notice of her curves, as Scott was perfectly aware, Nola latched on to his arm with a smile when he stood up with the rest. As she leaned into him, all warm, willing flesh draped in bright turquoise silk, he managed to smile back — it wasn't that hard, he discovered, as long as he kept his attention fixed strictly on Nola — while coming up with a suitably agreeable reply.

Summoning his inner gentleman, reminding himself that by accepting her invitation he'd made Nola his responsibility for the evening, he set himself to showing her as good a time as possible while ignoring everything that might have bugged him if he'd let it. Which wasn't easy: Peyton held Lisa's hand, slid his arm around her waist, dropped a kiss on her shoulder.

And that was just while they were walking to the buffet line. Once inside the tent, Scott found that he knew a surprising number of people — Lexington's wheelers and dealers tended to be members of the country club — and was distracted enough by the conviviality he had no choice but to engage in to lose track of Lisa. When he and Nola returned to the table, though, she was already there, with Peyton, of course, beside her. Sitting down, he discovered that Peyton's hand was on her knee again.

Hostile didn't even approach how he felt as he worked to keep his eyes off Lisa's legs, hold up his end of the conversation, and eat his way through whatever tasteless food he had piled on his plate.

Without reaching under the table, grabbing Peyton's hand, and breaking his damned wrist.

Unlike himself, Lisa was downright animated. Merry, even. Talking and laughing all through dinner. Leaning into Peyton, letting her head brush his shoulder, offering him tidbits from her plate. By the time they were finishing after-dinner drinks, Scott felt as though every word he said was being forced out through clenched teeth.

Being dragged away by Nola to the dance floor was almost a relief.

He could handle having Nola plaster herself against him, handle having his earlobe nibbled and the back of his neck stroked, handle the smoldering looks she gave him and the way her cheek nuzzled his jaw. All that was par for the course, and he didn't have any real trouble keeping the fun from going any further than he wanted it to go. At any other time, he might even have found himself getting into the spirit of things: Nola was luscious enough to make any man in his right mind salivate.

Unfortunately, at the moment he didn't seem to be in his right mind. He danced with Nola, and he danced with Macy and Alexis, and with a number of other women, too, some of whom he even knew, slow dances, fast dances, dirty dances, plus everything in between, and barely registered a lick of it. He was a good enough dancer, having made a deliberate decision to master the basics, just like he'd mastered golf and tennis, too, because they were upper-crust skills that might prove useful to him in what he had made up his mind a long time ago was going to be his climb to the top. But except for the occasional mild turn-on it afforded if the woman in his arms was hot enough, he didn't particularly enjoy dancing at the best of times, and tonight he didn't enjoy it at all.

Because of Lisa.

She and Peyton were practically necking on the dance floor. She danced with other men, too. There was a lot of partner swapping going on, and she seemed to get pretty friendly with everyone she was with. But it was Peyton who really got his goat.

It was Peyton whose neck she wrapped her arms around. Peyton she was going pelvis to pelvis with. Peyton who let his hands slide down to her ass.

Seeing that, Scott felt a spurt of pure rage. It was primitive and illogical and stupid as hell, and there was absolutely nothing he could do about it. He had come tonight primarily to irk Lisa, had ended up being tortured himself instead, and was now fed up to his back teeth with the whole situation.

"Excuse me a minute, will you?" he asked

his partner. Who happened to be Nola, although she could have been a Keebler elf for all the awareness he'd had of her. When he escaped, he headed for the men's room, which was in the lower level of the club-house, and when he left there he lingered in the darkness outside the tent for a minute, just to get a few perspective-enhancing breaths of fresh air.

What's wrong with you? You know what a flirt she is.

He might know, but he didn't have to like it.

He probably would have stayed out there longer if he hadn't spotted a couple of lawyers he knew, walking with their partners up from the golf course, on a rough collision course with the area near the practice range, where he lurked. One thing he knew: He was in no mood to indulge in casual conversation at the moment.

Ducking back inside the tent, pondering the possibility of pleading work or a headache or anything to end the evening before he totally lost his cool, he ran smack into Lisa. From her direction, she must have been coming from the ladies' room. He saw her only at the last minute, just when they were about to bump into each other in the shadowy darkness at the far corner of the tent. To forestall a collision, he caught her upper arms just above the elbows.

"Oh!" It was a little sound of surprise. She looked up at him, her eyes widening as she recognized him. "Scott."

From the corner of his eye, he saw Peyton bearing down on them. That he'd spotted them, and that Lisa was his target, Scott had no doubt.

His hard-won perspective dissipated, just like that.

"Dance with me," he said.

It wasn't a question, and he didn't wait for an answer. Instead he pulled her out onto the floor and into his arms.

22

The truly maddening thing about it was that in Scott's arms was just exactly where she wanted to be.

They closed hard and strong around her, pulling her against him without giving her a chance to protest. Because he was Scott, she didn't want to. She relaxed in his embrace, her hands flattening on his chest so that she could feel the firm resilience of the muscles there beneath the smooth cotton of his shirt. Having the freedom to touch him like that was a luxury, and she reveled in it. Moving with him, and the music, she enjoyed the solid contours beneath her palms as she breathed in the scent of him: crisp and clean, as though he'd just come in from the outdoors. He was wearing his charcoal suit with a white shirt and pale blue tie, the one that matched his eyes. She'd been thinking all evening how handsome he looked in it, and how consequential. The hunky former farmhand was still hunky but now unmistakably a VIP. Through his clothes she could feel the heat of his body, and it lured her closer. Sliding her hands slowly and with deliberate sensuality up to his shoulders, she curled her arms around his neck and nestled against him, acutely conscious of how unyielding his chest felt against her breasts, experiencing the instant reaction of her nipples to the contact with a stir of pleasure. His hips were so close that she could feel the brush of his lower body against hers; his belt buckle was a small, hard rectangle just above her belly button. His legs felt long and powerful as they moved with hers. The fine wool of his trousers grazed her bare knees and calves.

Her heart was suddenly beating way too fast. Her pulse was tremulous. Her stomach seemed to quiver. Everything about him, from the square angle of his clean-shaven jaw just above her eye level to the breadth of his shoulders to the sturdy warmth of his neck beneath her fingers, appealed to her. She liked the confident way he held her. She liked how big and muscular he felt. She liked that there was no trace of alcohol on the warm breath that just feathered her cheek.

Swaying with him to the slow, throbbing

beat of the music, her body started to throb most pleasurably in turn. Smiling slightly, she tilted her head back and opened her eyes to look at him. His face was in shadow because of the ceiling of tiny white lights that twinkled like a thousand stars overhead, but as he met her gaze she could tell one thing for sure: He wasn't smiling back at her.

"Do you deliberately *try* to turn men on?" His low voice had a definite edge to it. "Or is it something you just can't help?"

His tone might be disagreeable, but his body language — the way his head bent close to hers, the possessive splaying of his hands across her back, the intimacy of his movements — told her that he was as much a prey to the heat flaring up between them as she was. The difference was, he was fighting it. As usual.

She gave a little gurgle of laughter. "Wait a minute. Are you *admitting* I'm turning you on?"

"Of course you are. You know it, too. And you're loving every minute of it, aren't you?"

"Maybe. All right, yes, I am loving it. And so are you, underneath all your bullshit. You think I can't tell what you're thinking? I can."

"Baby, if you knew what I was thinking,

you'd run for the hills."

Slowly she shook her head. "I wouldn't run."

There was the briefest of pauses. "Now that's a hell of a thing to say to me."

"At least I'm honest about what I want."

Smiling at him, she pressed deliberately closer yet. He hadn't been kidding: The proof of his arousal was right there between them now, impossible to mistake. He knew she felt it: His lips thinned and his jaw tightened even as he slanted a glinting look down at her.

"Just so you know, this isn't going to happen."

"I have no idea what you're talking about."

"Oh, yes, you do. You and me. No way."

She lifted her brows at him teasingly. "You could try relaxing and enjoying it."

"I might — if I wanted to wind up as one more notch on your bedpost."

"Now, that's insulting." Her tone was untroubled rather than angry or reproachful. Her arms tightened around his neck as he swung her around in a movement of the dance. His body was absolutely, unmistakably masculine, and she loved that it was. He was holding her so close to him now that she could feel his body heat radiating through his clothes, feel the slide of his shirt over his skin, feel the rigid length of him pressing solidly against her. Far too close for her to have any doubt that he wanted her badly, although she could also sense resistance in every tense muscle. "I'd be willing to bet anything you like that your bedpost has a lot more notches on it than mine."

Another brief pause. "Touché."

"I thought so."

His arms were taut around her. His hips and thighs molded her own. She could feel the tangible proof of his desire with every move they made. That pleasurable throb inside her turned into something that was hotter and more liquid, and her mouth went suddenly dry. Moistening her lips with her tongue, she met his gaze.

"This is nice, you have to admit."

" 'Nice' isn't quite the word I'd use." But the sudden huskiness of his voice gave him away. He was as turned on as she was.

"What word would you use, then?"

"Dumb."

"You don't always have to be smart, you know. Or in control."

She deliberately stroked the warm, smooth skin at the nape of his neck, her touch light and teasing. His lips firmed. His eyes darkened. His hold on her tightened. He swung her around again, and she clung to him. Her breasts snuggled against his chest. Her hips moved seductively against his. Her thighs pressed his thighs.

Her heart was drumming. Her bones were melting. Deep inside, her body quaked and burned.

"Are you sleeping with Peyton?" The question, growled into her ear, was abrupt, almost angry.

She tilted her head back to look at him. "What do you think?"

His fingers sank deeper into the firm flesh of her back. "I don't know. That's why I'm asking."

His eyes glinted at her, pale and hard as aquamarines. Nearby, other couples danced, some so close that a random wrong step would cause a collision. She got a whiff of some other woman's too-sweet perfume, heard laughter and the murmur of conversation rising and falling beneath the pulsing music, and was glad that they had somehow wound up near the center of the floor because of the relative privacy it afforded them. Even though it was supposed to be air-conditioned, it was too hot in the tent, or at least she was too hot. But probably, she thought, that had more to do with the way Scott was looking at her than the actual temperature.

He was looking at her as though he wanted to take her to bed.

"Nonc of your busincss," she said sweetly.

His face hardened. "He had his hands all over you tonight."

"*Really* none of your business."

"Damn it, Lisa . . ."

A muffled boom interrupted. The band stopped playing with a flourish. Somebody yelled, "Fireworks!" and everybody stopped dancing and began to move off the dance floor en masse. She and Scott stopped dancing, too, and looked around in some surprise, having been too caught up in each other to pay much attention to anything else. But she made no move to free herself, and he wasn't releasing her.

"Lise, there you are!"

Joel was coming toward them to the accompaniment of another loud boom, threading his way through the crowd that was exiting the tent. As his genial expression turned into a frown, Lisa realized that she was still wrapped in Scott's arms, still pressed up against him as snugly, as if they were glued together, still all gooey and shivery inside from the electricity they had generated together.

Still weak at the knees with wanting him.

She knew instantly when Scott saw Joel. The arms around her hardened to iron. The expression on his face turned ugly.

"Scott, let me go." It was a quiet order, issued as her arms slipped from around his neck. He didn't budge. "Scott."

At that he glanced down at her, then let her go. As his arms dropped, she moved away from him to join Joel. Behind Joel, she saw, came Nola, with Alexis and Ben and Macy and Thornton trailing after.

If there was any kind of scene here — and from the way Scott was looking at Joel, she feared there might be — news of it would fly all over the county within the hour. Not good for any of them, and especially not good for Scott, with the public office he held.

"Come on, we're missing the fireworks." Catching Joel by the arm, she all but dragged him away from Scott toward the outdoors. With a single wide-eyed glance at her, Nola went past them, toward Scott, Lisa thought, but she didn't look around to make sure. Fireworks were exploding over the golf course one after the other now, *boom, boom, boom, BOOM,* flashing lightning bolts of color across the interior of the tent.

"Do you have something going on with

that guy?" Disbelief tinged with outrage in his voice, Joel looked at her askance as they emerged into the darkness. A slight breeze had arisen, carrying the scent of gunpowder from the fireworks on it. Despite its acrid smell, she welcomed its cooling breath against her overheated skin.

"No more than I ever did," Lisa said shortly. This was a subject she didn't feel like discussing, not right now, not with Joel. Her fingers dug into his arm through the sleeve of his natty summer suit to hurry him toward where the assembly sat on specially provided blankets or chairs or stood to watch the fireworks. "We've known each other forever. He gave me a job. Right now he's my boss. That pretty much tells the story."

The sound Joel made was practically a snort, and it conveyed a considerable degree of skepticism, but he didn't say anything more, for which Lisa was thankful. She was thankful, too, that Scott, now in Nola's hands, kept his distance. Nola wasn't so reticent, however. When they were all out on the golf course staring up at the bright bursts of pinwheels and rockets and umbrella-like cascades exploding against the black velvet sky, Nola left Scott's side — he stood on the edge of the group, watching the display silently, his hands in his pockets, his profile looking as if it had been carved from stone — and came over to her.

"Sweetie, I'm releasing our friend back into the wild, so if you want to go after him, feel free." Nola was practically whispering in her ear.

"What? Nola . . ."

"You should totally go for it. He couldn't take his eyes off you all night. And that thing you two did on the dance floor — that was hot."

"We *danced.*"

"Uh-huh."

Lisa gave up on trying to act as if she didn't know what Nola was talking about. "Anyway, nothing's going to come of it. I practically invited him to sleep with me, and you know what he said? 'You and me. No way.' "

"Sounds like a bad case of wishful thinking on his part." Nola gave her arm a sympathetic squeeze. "I know what I saw, believe me. That man's got it going on for you big-time."

Suddenly conscious of how many interested parties were standing nearby, Lisa rolled her eyes at her friend but didn't say anything more on the subject, preferring to steer the conversation in a more general direction just in case the multiple explosions overhead weren't ear-splitting enough to cover their voices.

After the fireworks ended in a final Technicolor display that lit up the sky, the party broke up, with each couple going their separate ways and without her saying another word, or so much as exchanging a glance, to Scott. As Joel drove her back to the hotel, Lisa thought of how unlikely it was that she would get any appreciable sleep alone in her hotel room with Katrina in the closet and thoughts of unknown assailants, white SUVs, etc., in her head. Then she thought of a possible remedy for her problem — i.e., not sleeping alone in her hotel room — which would involve having Joel spend the night, which, knowing him, he was already thinking about trying to make happen. Finally she acknowledged something else that she'd known in at least part of her mind for some time: The thought of sleeping with Joel left her cold.

It was never going to happen.

That being the case, it was time and past to face up to it and move on.

Half an hour later, Joel dropped her off at the hospital's well-lit main entrance, roaring away in his Porsche without even waiting to see if she'd made it safely inside.

Grimacing as she looked after the car, Lisa decided she couldn't blame him, especially since he had no idea in the world that she might actually be in any kind of danger. Hurrying inside, glad of the security guard on duty in the lobby and the number of people moving around the halls even though it was nearly one a.m., she slowed her step as she headed for the elevator, then took a deep breath as she joined the few people waiting for one to show up. When an elevator finally came, she rode up to the fourth floor with a janitor pushing a cleaning cart and an elderly couple who giddily announced to both Lisa and the janitor that their granddaughter had just had a baby. Smiling her congratulations at them, Lisa got off the elevator with the intention of telling Robin, who was spending the night in Martha's room, that she would sleep there instead and Robin could go ahead and leave. In the morning, she would take a taxi back to the hotel. She just couldn't face being in that room alone tonight.

But what she found when she opened the door to her mother's room changed her mind. Defying all her expectations, the room was dark, the TV was off, and both her mother and Robin were sound asleep.

Robin even snored.

For a moment Lisa, nonplussed, stood at the foot of her mother's bed with a shaft of light from the hall providing the only illumination. Then she finally, reluctantly faced the truth: She couldn't stay. Waking up Robin from a sound sleep and asking her to leave wasn't something she was going to do. Not at such a late hour. She herself was going to have to leave instead. As in, go back to her hotel room and sleep in it all alone like a big girl. She would call a taxi to meet her at the front of the hospital, which subsequently would let her off at the Marriott's well-lit front entrance. Not risky at all.

With that plan in mind, Lisa quietly left the room, closed the door behind her, and started, slowly and reluctantly, to walk back toward the elevator bank, fishing in her purse for her phone as she went. The hall wasn't empty. A nurse and an intern conferred over a chart outside one of the rooms, and another nurse was on duty at the nurses' station. An elderly man in a cardigan sweater, worn presumably to combat the hospital's air-conditioning, because it was hot and sticky outside, walked toward her from the direction of the elevator bank carrying a plastic bag of food from Taco Bell. Lisa was just registering the spicy scent when she saw that another man had gotten off the elevator, too, and was coming toward her with the slightest of wry smiles on his face.

Scott.

Her eyes snapped open with surprise, and she forgot all about her phone. She'd been feeling sleepy, and slightly headachy, and even a little lonely and scared, but all that vanished in an instant. Her steps slowed as she waited for him to reach her.

"My mother's asleep," is how she greeted him.

"I didn't come to see your mother." He stopped in front of her, and for a moment they looked measuringly at each other. His hair was waving a little — proof of the humidity — and the scrape on his cheek stood out starkly in the unforgiving light. His eyes were slightly bloodshot, there were lines in his face she hadn't noticed before, and stubble darkened his jaw. He still wore his suit, but he had unbuttoned the top button of his shirt and loosened his tie.

Lisa's heart started to beat faster from just looking at him.

"You can give me a ride to my hotel," she said abruptly, and stepped around him, heading for the elevator bank. "I was going to send Robin home, but she's fallen asleep in my mother's room, and I don't want to wake her up."

"No problem." He fell into step beside her.

"So, what are you doing here?" They reached the elevators, and Lisa pushed the down button.

"Well, see, I had a theory."

She gave him a sharp look. "What kind of theory?"

"Once I really thought about it, I figured I know you well enough to be fairly certain that if you were sleeping with Peyton, you wouldn't be coming on to me. And if you weren't sleeping with Peyton, you'd show up here. So, I decided to test it out."

Indignation infused her voice. "You were checking up on me."

"I was trying to prove a theory."

Her eyes sparked at him. "That's a load of crap and you know it."

"Admit it. My theory was right. You're not sleeping with Loverboy."

The elevator arrived with a *ping,* and the doors slid open. Stepping inside it, she cast him a fulminating look as he followed her in.

"You know what your problem is, don't you?" She gave the lobby button a savage jab, then turned to glare at him as the elevator lurched into motion. They were facing each other now. Her back rested against the polished brass wall. She folded her arms over her chest. “You’re jealous.”

“Insanely,” he agreed with a rueful little smile, astonishing her. Then he leaned forward and kissed her.

23

The touch of his mouth on hers made her heart lurch. It was so unexpected that for a moment Lisa couldn't move, couldn't breathe, couldn't respond at all. Her pulse drummed in her ears. Her stomach dropped clear to her toes. Every sense suspended. Then the reality of it hit — Scott was kissing her! — and her lips quivered and parted beneath his, and she closed her eyes and clutched at his shoulders.

And kissed him back.

His lips slanted across hers, warm and firm and fiercely hungry. His tongue came into her mouth, and she responded with a fierceness of her own. Planting his hands on either side of her head, he leaned into her, pressing her back against the wall with the whole long length of him so that she could feel every muscular inch. As the weight of his body pinned her in place, a hot spiral of arousal began to burn deep inside her. Arching against him, she gave herself up to the kiss she'd been waiting for for years.

The elevator door opened with another *ping.*

Opening her eyes, Lisa saw through a bedazzled fog that they had reached the lobby and there were people standing in front of the open elevator door waiting to board: two female medical types, either doctors or nurses, she couldn't be sure which; a man in a track suit; and a middle-aged woman holding a balloon. All stared in wide-eyed surprise at the entwined couple in the elevator, and in turn Lisa stared blankly back at them.

Just as she was recovering enough presence of mind to realize that (a) she needed to stop kissing Scott and (b) they needed to get off the elevator, he lifted his mouth from hers, levered himself upright, cast a quick, comprehensive look at their audience, and caught her hand, pulling her after him from the elevator. She gave the gaping onlookers a small embarrassed smile as she was hauled past them, then hurried after Scott, who kept her hand in a firm grip as he strode for the lobby and the exit.

Her heart was still hammering, her breathing was still erratic, and it was still hard to focus on anything besides the fact that he'd kissed her. But she took a deep breath and tried.

"Scott. Wait. Where are we going?"

"Somewhere private."

"I'm wearing heels," she protested. "The floor's slick. I can't walk this fast."

Not quite the conversation she had always dreamed of having with him after their first kiss, but needs must, as the saying went.

"Sorry." He slowed down, and she caught up. Then, as their eyes met, he smiled at her, a slow, intimate smile that had her melting inside just as quick as that. Her heart thundered anew. He was still holding her hand, and she loved how big and warm and strong his hand felt. "I forgot about the shoes. How you women can walk in those things is an eternal mystery to me."

She disregarded that and went straight to the point. "You kissed me."

"I know."

She waited in vain for more, then chose to abandon the topic for the moment as they reached the middle of the lobby and the big glass doors with the black night stretching endlessly beyond looming up in front of them.

"Stop a minute. I have to tell you — last night there was a white Ford Explorer. I think it was following me. It turned into the hospital. For all I know, it may be out there now. We need to be care —"

She broke off because they had reached the door by this time and he was pushing through it. Her fingers tightened urgently on his hand. She would have planted her feet, but given the slick terrazzo surface beneath her soles, it wasn't happening.

A wall of humid air hit her as she was propelled over the threshold. Outside, the entrance was lit by round white lights recessed in the concrete overhang, and she was instantly conscious of what a target they must make for anyone who might be waiting farther out in the dark parking lot for just such an opportunity.

"Scott —"

"It wasn't anything you need to worry about. In fact, you weren't supposed to know squat about it," he said. They were stepping off the sidewalk into the parking lot proper about then, and she was busy casting scared glances all around. As his words registered, she looked at him instead and frowned. "I asked a friend of mine to keep an eye on you while I was out of town. Make sure you got to the hospital safely, that kind of thing. He's a cop, he was off duty, he owed me a favor. I called it in."

Lisa stopped dead. He had perforce to

stop too, which he did, turning to look at her inquiringly.

"What?" he asked.

"You had somebody following me?"

"Yeah, I did. Don't tell me you've got a problem with that."

"Oh my God. That is so typical of the high-handed way you do things. You could have at least told me."

"I didn't have time. I was on my way out of town, remember? And I didn't want to have to spend the whole night worrying about whether or not you were okay. I had enough on my plate, believe me. Besides, I figured you'd probably just pick a fight with me about it."

At his urging, they were walking again by that time, heading into the dark recesses of the parking lot, where she could just see his Jeep among the scattering of waiting vehicles. The lights out there were far apart, set high on tall metal poles, and cast only the most meager of yellow glows. The moon was big and round and high overhead now, and the stars were almost as thick as the twinkling lights in the tent earlier. In the distance, occasional explosions gave evidence that all the Independence Day celebrations weren't finished. His hand gripped hers firmly, and Lisa tingled all over at the contact. At her age, to react so strongly to a man holding her hand was probably ridiculous, she knew. But this wasn't any man, this was Scott, and react she did.

"I do not pick fights with you."

"Baby, you've been picking fights with me since you were twelve years old."

Not wanting to prove his point, Lisa switched gears. "I ran his plates. They came up as being registered to a company called Diurnal Plastics."

"He does PI work on the side. I guess he likes keeping things on the down-low."

"I was scared to death!"

"I'm sorry about that. You weren't supposed to even notice he was there."

"Believe me, I noticed."

They reached the Jeep, and he opened the passenger door for her. Fixing him with a mildly reproving look, Lisa slid inside. No sooner had she settled into her seat than he leaned in and kissed her. It was a quick kiss, hard and possessive, scarcely more than a hot branding of her mouth by his lips and tongue, certainly nothing to make her senses go into instant meltdown. But they did.

Looking up at him as he straightened away from her, she was so entranced she forgot all about the off-duty cop in the Explorer.

Forgot about everything, in fact, except him and the way he made her feel.

"Put your seat belt on," he told her, and closed the door on her. As he walked around the hood of the car and she struggled to get her breathing under control, she did as he said.

"The Marriott?" he asked as he got behind the wheel, and she nodded.

"Thank you," she said after a moment. He had already started the car and was driving out of the lot.

"For?"

"Caring enough to ask somebody to follow me."

The smile he gave her was enough to make her stomach tighten. "You're welcome."

Except for the occasional slash of headlights through the interior, it was dark in the car, and quiet enough so that she could hear the swoosh of tires on the pavement. For so late at night, there was a surprising amount of traffic on the road, and she remembered again that it was the Fourth of July — well, the fifth of July now. Letting her head drop back against the smooth leather seat, she looked at him meditatively. Just the sight of that hard, handsome profile silhouetted against the window made her feel warm all over. She knew him so well and had wanted him for so long. A lifetime, it felt like.

And now, this.

"Okay, what happened to the whole 'You and me, no way' thing?" If there was a wary note in her voice, she considered that he'd earned it. "What's with you kissing me all of a sudden?"

"I knew you were going to want to talk about this."

"You were right. So talk."

"I've been in a filthy mood for almost a month now."

"So everyone at the office has been telling me. Now I, I just thought you were being your regular self." He made a face at her. "But I don't see what that has to do with why you kissed me."

"I've been in a filthy mood because of you. Since you guilted me into hiring you."

"I *guilted* you?" She was indignant.

"Don't interrupt." He threw her a semi-humorous look. "I figure it's like a dieter locked in a room with a Hershey bar. The dieter's going to fight temptation as long as he can. He's going to turn his back, he's going to grit his teeth, he's going to get cranky. But in the end, temptation is going to win every time."

"Are you comparing me to a Hershey bar?"

"Premium dark chocolate, baby."

"Let me get this straight: You're saying you kissed me because tonight you're fresh out of willpower?"

"More like I decided willpower is overrated." They reached the hotel parking lot, and he pulled in, circling the rows of parked cars as he searched for a space. "I kissed you because I've wanted to kiss you for most of my life. Tonight I just decided to quit fighting it. This thing between us — this attraction, whatever you want to call it — has been there ever since we were kids. Tonight it finally occurred to me that the really dumb thing to do would be to keep turning my back on it."

He said it in such a quiet, serious tone that butterflies overtook Lisa's stomach.

"So, now what?" Her heart speeded up like a marathon runner's as he found a space, parked the Jeep, and switched off the ignition.

"I guess that's pretty much up to you." He released his seat belt. "Come on, I'll walk you in."

I'm as nervous as a teenager. The thought came with its own little thrill.

He got out of the car. Before he could

make it around to her door she was out, standing up on legs that felt rubbery, taking a deep breath of too warm, too thick, exhaust-scented air. *Not exactly the head-clearing combination I was hoping for.* He smiled at her, and her pulse raced.

It's the middle of the night, Scott's walking me up to my hotel room, and he kissed me.

Heart thumping, she tucked her hand into the crook of his elbow. Neither one of them said anything as they walked into the lobby; past the male clerk at the front desk, who eyed them without any real interest; and caught an elevator. Then, when the elevator door shut and their only audience was the surveillance camera mounted high up in a corner, she turned into his arms as naturally as if she'd been doing it for years and lifted her mouth to his.

His mouth closed over hers, fire shot through her body — and the elevator stopped on her floor.

He let her go, and she led the way out of the elevator. But not before she noticed that he was breathing as unevenly as she was. Inside, she was shivery with anticipation. Her knees felt weak. Her stomach was in a knot.

I should play hard to get.

But the sad truth was that where he was

concerned, she was easy. And he knew it. Had known it for years.

"So, how did you leave it with Nola?" she asked with an assumption of ease as they started down the hall. They weren't touching any longer. Instead they walked side by side.

"I don't think she's expecting me to call anytime soon." His voice was dry.

Lisa glanced at him. His breathing was under control now. Typical Scott, he looked large and tough, very composed, very much the man in charge. Unless you knew him really well, you wouldn't notice that his eyes were darker than normal, his jaw harder, his cheekbones a little flushed. But she knew him very well indeed.

I bet the sex would be phenomenal. She could almost hear Nola's words in her head.

At the images this conjured up, her body tightened deep inside.

It required a rcal effort to keep her voice light. "She told me she was releasing you into the wild, so if I wanted you, feel free."

"Did she?"

"She'll be glad to know I took her up on it."

"Going to tell her all about this, are you?"

"I don't kiss and tell."

"That sounds like it should be my line."

"Hey, I can be a gentleman, too."

That made him smile, a quick smile that curved his mouth and brought an amused gleam to his eyes. She was suddenly acutely conscious of how very sexy he was, and felt a new rush of heat.

The long hall with its double row of doors was deserted. Their shoes were soundless on the thick green carpet. The wallpaper was a tasteful, figured pale green, and the lighting was just bright enough to keep guests from stumbling over discarded room-service trays or bumping into console tables holding huge vases full of artificial flowers, both of which they passed. There was a slight, faint scent of potpourri. The air-conditioning hummed, but beyond that and their voices, there was no other sound. If anyone else was awake anywhere on the entire floor, it was impossible to tell. It felt as if they were totally alone.

"So, how'd you leave it with Loverboy?" There was absolutely no intonation to his voice, which, with Scott, meant a great deal.

"I left it."

"Meaning?"

"I don't think he likes me very much right now."

They reached her room. Lisa looked at the white-painted door with the discreet number on it and felt her mouth go dry.

Nola, I think I'm about to find out about the sex.

The thought came with a thrill that shot clear down to her toes.

"What, did you two have a fight?"

"Not really." Extracting her key card from her purse, aware of him looming behind her with every nerve ending she possessed, she put the card in the slot, watched the tiny green light come on, turned the knob, and opened the door. Then, heart hammering, she looked at him over her shoulder. "Want to come in?"

His eyes were dark and unreadable.

"Sure," he said.

24

"So, if you two didn't have a fight, what happened?"

He was inside her room, in the narrow part just beyond the door, with the closet on one side and the bathroom on the other. He stood waiting for her as she flicked the switch that turned on the bedside lamp in the main part of the room and closed the door behind them.

"What do you think happened? You." Her tone was acerbic. Having shot the dead bolt, she turned to face him. The area where they stood was shadowy but not really dark. He stood foursquare in front of her, tall and broad-shouldered enough to block her view. Beyond him, she could just see the feet of the two double beds with their brown-and-gold coverlets that reached all the way down to the beige carpet. Because she hadn't yet slept in the room, the beds had not been touched. At the thought that at least one of them soon would be, her heartbeat quickened.

A smile just curved his mouth. "Good."

She walked into his arms at exactly the same time as he reached for her. Electricity shot through her, hot and wild as a bolt of lightning as their bodies came together like two parts of the same whole. The solid strength of him against her made her go all light-headed. Her arms went around his neck. She lifted her head, and Scott bent his. Their lips met. That first kiss was almost gentle, almost tentative, a soft brushing of mouths, a brief meeting of tongues. But even that fleeting contact made her feel that she had just contracted a system-wide fever. Her breasts swelled against his chest, and her body caught fire.

Oh my God, I'm kissing Scott, she thought, and her eyes popped open just to verify that it was true. His eyes were open, too. He quit kissing her to look at her, his mouth hovering scant millimeters away. She could feel the uneven warmth of his breath against her lips. For the space of a couple of heartbeats they simply stared into each other's eyes. She saw the hot flare of passion in the depths of his, the dilation of his pupils, the sudden heaviness of his lids. Then he kissed her again, a sexy kiss burning with more than a decade's worth of pent-up longing, and she closed her eyes and pressed herself against him and kissed him back for all she was worth.

By the time he broke it off, her head was spinning. Her knees felt weak. Her body burned and throbbed.

"Lisa."

He was holding her so tightly against him that she was left in no doubt at all about the strength of his desire. Dizzy with need, she clung to him and tilted her head back and opened her eyes to meet his gaze.

"Hmm?"

"If you want me to leave, now would be a good time to tell me."

She looked at him, at the hard, handsome face, at the sensuous curve of his mouth, at the sky-blue eyes that smoldered now with wanting her, and shook her head.

"You know I don't want you to leave." Her voice was unsteady, but she didn't care. "When have I ever wanted you to leave?"

His eyes blazed at her. She felt his chest expand against her breasts as he took a deep breath. Then his mouth was on hers again, hard and hot and demanding, and he was kissing her with a fierce passion that sent fire shooting clear down to her toes. When one hand came up to brush the long fall of her hair back from her face, then cup her jaw, then stroke down over the soft smoothness of her throat, she thought her bones would melt. He pulled his mouth away from hers to nuzzle her ear, her jaw, her neck, and she let her head fall back against his shoulder to grant him better access. The touch of his lips, the rasp of his chin that was bristly now with five-o'clock shadow, the wet heat of his mouth on her skin, was so deliciously disorienting that she closed her eyes and clung to him as if to the only stable thing in the room.

His hand found her breast and flattened over it. Through the thin layers of her dress and bra, Lisa felt the size of his palm, the length of his fingers, the latent strength in his grip, with a shiver of delight. Her nipple instantly turned pebble-hard, jutting into his palm. His hand moved then, molding her, caressing her, and she arched her back to deepen the contact and murmured her pleasure against the warm, salt-tinged column of his neck. When his hand slid away from her breast, she nipped his earlobe in protest, then was rewarded when he made a sound halfway between a growl and a groan and kissed her mouth again with a naked hunger that made her go up in flames.

She never even realized he was lowering

the long zipper that fastened her dress until the snug-fitting silk loosened around her breasts and she felt the cool breath of the air-conditioning on her back. A warm hand slid down the long vee of skin he had bared, tracing the curve of her spine. Lisa trembled, but not from the cold.

His hold on her tightened, and then he was turning with her, pressing her up against the wall, one hand hard on her breast as he kissed her so hotly that her blood sizzled and her heart pounded as if she'd been running for miles. The wall was cool against the overheated skin bared by her open zipper. She could feel the heat radiating from him as he leaned into her, the tension in his long muscles, the size and weight of him, all along her body. The solid hardness that was the proof of his passion was unmistakable, and feeling it swelling against her made her knees threaten to sag. She was suddenly grateful for the support of the wall at her back.

"I want you so damn much." His voice was low and rough, nothing like his usual cool tones. She opened her eyes to find that his hair was ruffled and his jaw was set and hard and his eyes gleamed at her.

"Scott." She loved saying his name in this context, she realized. When she was a teenager, he had been the embodiment of every sexual fantasy she had ever had. Now that she was an adult, she still counted him as the sexiest man around. She had wanted him so much, for so long, that just the thought that it was finally going to happen, that she was finally going to sleep with him, was enough to make her go all hot and liquid inside. As her hands slid down from around his neck to find the knot of his tie he pressed quick, deep kisses to her mouth. The heavy silk felt cool and supple in her hands, but she was so distracted by his kisses that she barely remembered what she was doing. Senses reeling, she nevertheless eventually managed to pull the knot free so that the tie hung loose around his neck.

"You taste like sugar," he murmured against her lips.

"Lip gloss," she told him, determined to try to sound lucid no matter how drugged with passion she was feeling.

He ran his tongue over the soft fullness of her lower lip, then bit it very gently.

Forget lucid. She burned for him. Wrapping her arms around his neck, she pressed her lips to his.

Then he was kissing her again, really kissing her with a thoroughness that made her woozy. His hand slid inside her loosened neckline, caressing her breast through the barely there barrier of her bra. His hand felt big and warm against her bare skin; his fingers glided over the slick surface of her bra. He cupped her breast, then rubbed his thumb over her nipple through the thin layer of nylon and lace, and the resulting sensation was so mind-blowing that it swept away her half-formed intention of unbuttoning his shirt next, swept away her plan to go aggressor on him, swept away everything except the way he was making her feel. He handled her like someone who knew his way around women, knew what turned them on, and she was reminded that he wasn't the boy she had known almost all her life any longer but a man. An experienced man who'd made love to a woman before, undoubtedly many times, undoubtedly to many different women.

She stiffened a little, because she didn't like the thought.

"What?" He must have felt her resistance, because he lifted his mouth from hers. Her eyes flickered open to find that a high flush rode his cheekbones and his eyes were heavy-lidded and blazing at her.

"You're good at this."

He looked at her closely. "Why do I get the feeling that that isn't a compliment?"

She was being ridiculous and she knew it. Jealous, she'd called him. Well, it turned out she was jealous, too. To compensate, she closed her eyes and kissed him again, pressing her lips to his, licking into his mouth, touching his tongue with hers, enticing him as she had wanted to do forever. He made an inarticulate sound under his breath and wrapped his arms around her, clamping her against him, kissing her with a fierceness that drove everything else out of her mind.

She was still lost in the blazing sexual attraction that raged between them when he reached up to catch her arms and pull them down from around his neck, breaking off the kiss. As she grudgingly resurfaced and opened her eyes with the intention of protesting, he forestalled her by saying, "I've wanted to take your clothes off for years."

His voice was thick.

"Have you?" Her reply was no more than a soft breath of sound as he put his hands on her shoulders under the loosened straps.

"Since way before you were legal, believe me." He slid his hands sensuously down her arms, their warm sweep raising goose bumps as he pushed the straps of her dress down with them until they fell past her fingertips, leaving her arms free. With nothing to support it, the dress dropped with a slither of silk to puddle around her feet.

Lisa sucked in air as she was left standing in the strapless black bra and matching tiny panties that were all she wore under the dress. Her eyes flew to his, but he didn't meet them. Instead his eyes were all over her, scorching her, sliding from the round, high swell of her breasts in the lacy demi-cups, over her narrow waist and flat abdomen and slender hips, to the black lace and satiny nylon triangle that barely concealed her sex, to her long, tanned legs. It was only as she saw him taking them in that she remembered she was still wearing Nola's lipstick-red high heels.

Just watching him look at her brought its own fiery thrill.

He must have felt her gaze, because he met it then. Naked lust gleamed in his eyes. "Sexy," he said, in a voice that didn't sound like Scott's at all.

Lisa realized that she was just standing there in practically nothing at all, her lips parted, her heart pounding, feeling ridiculously shy and at the same time so turned on she could scarcely breathe.

"Your turn." Mustering her resources, she reached for him, hands stroking over his chest, sliding beneath his jacket, feeling the warmth of his skin and the firmness of his muscles through his shirt. She pushed his jacket from his shoulders and he shrugged out of it so that it fell to join her dress on the floor.

He was, she saw, breathing hard.

"Lisa," he said, then took a deep breath as she reached for his shirt buttons. Even as she flicked him a sultry glance and curled her fingers around the top button just below his open collar he leaned into her, kissing her, a blistering kiss that made the hot quickening inside her start to spiral out of control. She was kissing him back, clutching his shirt front because she had forgotten all about his buttons, when she felt him unhooking her bra. Just as quickly and dexterously as that, it was done: Her bra fell by the wayside, and she was naked except for her panties and shoes, with her bare breasts pressed up hard against his chest. She felt the heat of his skin and the taut wall of his chest, with only the fine cotton of his shirt separating his flesh from hers. Lisa's heart gave a great shuddering leap as her nipples instantly tightened into hard points. Pressing against him, clinging like she would never let him go, she arched her back to deepen the contact and felt the world start to spin out. Then his hands flattened on the bare warmth of her outer thighs. She shuddered as he slid them upward, slowly, seductively. They felt warm and utterly masculine and faintly abrasive, a working man's hands still. She thrilled to their touch. When he hooked her panties and began to tug them down, she moaned into his mouth. Her knees, which had been weak before, threatened to give way entirely. When he bent to pull her panties all the way down her legs, she had no choice unless she wanted to slide like melted butter to the floor: She leaned back against the wall and pressed her palms flat against the cool plaster for support — and felt her bones dissolve.

When, at his urging, she stepped out of her panties, she was burning inside with excitement. Heart thudding, breathing way too fast, expecting him to rise and take up where they had left off, Lisa was surprised when he didn't, when he stayed crouched in front of her. The sight of him, of *Scott,* of the thick brown hair; blunt, masculine features; and broad-shouldered form that had been the stuff of her dreams for years, still fully clothed, crouched in such intimate proximity to her nakedness, was the most erotic thing she had ever seen in her life. Heat raced through her like a flash fire. She felt her loins clench. Shivery with arousal, she must have moved then, or made some small sound, because he gripped her hip bones as though to hold her still and pressed her back against the wall. Then, to her shock, he put his mouth on the cleft between her legs and kissed her there, using his mouth and tongue to ignite a wildfire inside her until she was clutching at his hair and writhing with helpless pleasure.

Finally she cried out, then cried out again as she experienced an explosion of passion so fierce and primitive that her insides turned to steam. She would have slid down the wall then, because she was spent, because her knees had absolutely given way, but she didn't get the chance. He pulled her down to him, wrapping his arms around her and kissing her mouth and laying her on her back on the carpet and stripping off his clothes in a frenzy before coming down on top of her.

He didn't say a word, just came inside her so fiercely that she cried out again. Then he was kissing her mouth and kissing her breasts and taking her (taking was the only word that would do), hard and furiously, with such carnality that all she could do was hold on and, in the end, call out his name as she came with an intensity that she had never even begun to imagine she was capable of.

Then he drove into her one final time and found his own release as he held himself shuddering inside her.

She was still floating back to earth when he rolled off her.

Her eyes flickered open. For a moment she found herself looking up at the ceiling, white and smooth, unremarkable, a plain generic hotel room. The foot of the nearest bed loomed beside her. A little more fore-sight, a little less heat, and they'd have made love on a presumably comfy mattress instead of the floor. She'd lost the shoes sometime during the previous fifteen minutes, so she was completely nude. Various sensations fought for her attention: the prickle of the inexpensive-feeling carpet against her back, the rattle of the window unit as it pumped out air that felt too cold blowing across her sweat-dampened skin, a faint piney scent that she thought might be room freshener. Then she turned her head to find Scott. He was lying flat on his back beside her, close but not touching. He was stark naked, one brawny arm flung over his eyes, presumably to shield them from the soft glow of the lamp that stood on the table between the two beds and not the sight of her. Of their own volition, her eyes slid down his body.

She hadn't had much of a chance to look at him earlier — after he'd gotten naked, everything had happened fast — so she was interested. She had known that he was built like an athlete, had known he was muscular, had known about the wedge of dark brown hair on his chest that narrowed down to a trail that led over flat abs. She'd even known how long and powerful his legs were, and the size and shape of his bare feet. What she hadn't known was that even at half-mast, as he was now, he was as well endowed as the stud muffin Nola had once called him.

Looking at him, remembering what they had done together, she felt a warm glow start to build inside her. But then she frowned, and her gaze moved up his supine form to stop on that protective arm over his eyes. She'd never had sex with Scott before, of course, but she knew him well in other ways.

And she was willing to bet almost anything she possessed that this was not the typical way he expressed postcoital bliss.

Something was up.

Grimacing, she sat up and, casting a quick glance around at the various items of clothing strewn nearby, selected his shirt. As far as she was concerned, being naked when she was not lost in the throes of lust was just embarrassing, especially when she meant to have a meaningful conversation with the object of that lust in the very near future. She was just pulling the shirt on when his arm moved, dropping away from his face. Then he opened his eyes and looked at her.

Warily.

25

It was without a glimmer of a doubt the best sex he had ever had in his life. That was the good news. The bad news was, it was with Lisa.

He'd wanted her for years. Fantasized about her forever. Lusted after her with a constancy that was one of the ongoing themes of his life.

Now he'd had her, and the net result was that he was in trouble, just as he'd known he would be if he was ever such a fool as to succumb to that particular temptation.

The things we regret most in life are the things we don't do.

Somebody had said that to him once, and those words had come back to haunt him while they were dancing. He'd been absolutely intoxicated by the feel of her in his arms, by the soft scent of her hair under his nose, by the proximity of her mouth to his when she'd reared her head back to talk to him, by the way she had looked at him, by her smile. The thought that she was with Peyton, not him, was driving him around the bend. They were just dancing, just like he'd danced with a dozen other women that same night, but with Lisa there was chemistry, passion, smoldering desire so intense that he could almost feel the flames licking at his body every time she moved. By the end of that dance, he had wanted her so much that he would have walked barefoot over hot coals to get her, and he had absolutely no doubt that she wanted him, too.

If he let her walk away from him again, if he turned his back on this window of opportunity now that they were both adults and both single and both eager to see what things would be like between them in bed, he might never get another chance. And he would kick himself forever, he knew.

That was the conviction that had sent him after her to the hospital, where he'd hoped against hope she would be. That was the thought that had caused him to reverse the hands-off-Lisa policy of a lifetime.

That was the reasoning that had brought them here to this hotel room and seduced him into the quagmire he found himself in now.

But what was done was done, there was

no taking it back, and even if he could take it back he wouldn't do it, not in a hundred million years.

So, all that was left to do was deal.

She was sitting cross-legged beside him, buttoning up his shirt, which she had put on to cover a body that had been everything he had ever dreamed it might be and more, her long black hair spilling over one shoulder, her slim, tanned legs bare. Her cheeks were flushed, her lips were rosy and slightly swollen, and there was a mark on the left side of her neck that he thought might well darken into a hickey by morning. She looked as though she had just been thoroughly fucked, which was the truth. Very thoroughly, in fact.

She was the most beautiful thing he had ever seen in his life, just looking at her provided the kind of rush he'd never expected to feel this side of illegal substances, and she was scaring the shit out of him.

She was also frowning at him. Not the reaction he was looking for, considering that he knew for damn certain he'd just rocked her world into next week.

"Hey," he said, and sat up.

"Hey, yourself."

Her steady gaze was unnerving him. They knew each other so well, and he was afraid she could read something in his eyes that he really didn't want her to know. Not yet, anyway. Maybe not ever.

So, better start acting normal. How would he behave if he'd just had sex with, say, Nola? A great time, with no emotional minefield attached?

"You're beautiful," he said, and leaned over to kiss her. Her lips were warm and luscious, and she kissed him back, sliding one of those slim, cool hands behind his neck, no hesitation whatsoever. Which made him start to get hard again, and not coincidentally showed him the best way forward.

He could sleep with her. They could have red-hot sex until the cows came home. They could even have a relationship, a steamy, no-holds-barred, let's-do-it-till-we're-tired-of-each-other-or-the-lady-runs-off-to-Boston affair.

What he couldn't do, at least not if he was smart, was fall in love with her.

Only he was afraid it was already too late for that.

As soon as he pulled back from the kiss, she was fixing him with that unnerving look again.

Damn.

"So, what's up with you?" she asked. Those gorgeous golden eyes were unblinking on his face.

"What do you mean what's up with me?"

In sheer self-defense, he got to his feet, and then held a hand down to her to help her up. She took it, and he pulled her up, pulled her tight against him so that he could feel every warm, curvaceous, silky-skinned inch of her, which, plastered against his nakedness, felt erotic as hell. Even the sensation of his own shirt rubbing against him was sexy, because she was inside it. Wrapping his arms around her, he kissed her again, partly to end the conversation but also because he really, really wanted to kiss her. She slid her arms around his neck and kissed him back, hot and sweet, a long, lingering kiss that sent his libido — and everything else — skyrocketing. He was naked, she was almost naked, and when she pulled her mouth away to frown at him again, undeterred, he was pretty sure she could now, at the very least, tell definitively just what was up.

She said, "You're wary. You're defensive. You're acting funny. So, what gives?"

"I'm horny," he clarified, trying not to sound defensive, which answer was absolutely not a lie even if it was not the answer to the question she was asking. "This is how I act when I'm horny." He let her go, took her hand, pulled her toward the nearest bed. "Come to bed."

"You're staying the night?"

"Of course I'm staying the night. You think I'd leave you alone in a hotel room at this hour with this whole cold-case thing still up in the air?"

"You can't think I'm going to come to any harm in here."

"I don't think you're going to come to any harm in here. But I think, if I were to leave, you'd be scared. You'll never admit it, but I know you: Your imagination will go into overdrive, and you'll be awake the rest of the night."

She didn't say anything, just narrowed her eyes at him, which he knew meant he was dead-on, and pulled her hand from his. The nettled look she gave him was so typically Lisa to him that it underscored the whole punched-in-the-stomach feeling that was making him as antsy as a perp in a lineup.

"If, having had your wicked way with me, you're ready to kick me out, you're shit out of luck. You don't want to sleep with me, I'll sleep in the other bed." They were standing in the narrow space between the two beds by then, and in an effort to avoid more eye contact than was absolutely necessary, he was pulling back the covers as he spoke.

He just happened to glance at the bedside clock. Jesus, it was three a.m.

"You know I want to sleep with you." Her tone was almost sulky, and he had to smile a little. She hadn't liked being called out on the scared-to-go-to-sleep thing. "But just for the record, you weren't worried about me sleeping here alone before this."

"You've spent every night since the fire with your mother at the hospital. Think I don't know that?" He'd done what he could with the bed, and they were facing each other now. He couldn't help it: His eyes slid over her. His shirt had never looked so good. As his eyes rose to meet hers she smiled at him, a beautiful, sexy smile that told him she was no slouch in the mind-reading department, either, and made his heart skip a beat and had his eyes lingering on her face despite his best intentions. The bottom line was, he decided, he wanted her, she wanted him. That relegated everything else — such as the endangered state of his heart — to a problem to be dealt with later. "You planning to sleep in my shirt?"

"Not necessarily."

She was already reaching for the three or so buttons she'd fastened earlier as she spoke. Brushing her hands aside, undoing the buttons for her, he then flicked the sides of the shirt apart preparatory to sliding it off her shoulders, and felt his pulse go into turbo-charge mode as he was treated to a view of as sexy a pair of breasts as he'd ever seen. Round and firm and creamy-skinned, they curved out from her chest in silent invitation. Her nipples jutted toward him, dark pink, fully erect. He couldn't resist. He bent his head and drew one into his mouth, just sampling but in the process making her gasp and clutch at his shoulders, and somewhere about then he lost his grip on every bit of rational thought remaining to him.

By the time he tumbled her naked to the mattress, her arms were wrapped around his neck and her legs were wrapped around his waist and he was already thrusting inside her. He didn't quit until steam was rising around them like heat shimmers in the summertime and she was panting and sobbing out his name and coming hard beneath him. Then he came himself, in a fierce explosive release that ranked right up there with the best he'd ever felt.

Afterward, spent, sated, and so tired that it required an effort to lift his arm, he finally managed to turn off the damned bedside lamp. As the room plunged into darkness, he pulled the covers over Lisa, who was curled against his chest and already asleep, and tucked them in around the pair of them.

Settling down to sleep himself, he tightened his hold on her and dropped a kiss on the tumbled, sweet-smelling softness of her hair.

You're never going to put your heart on the line enough to fall in love.

Ryan's words replayed themselves in his mind as sleep closed in on him.

He hadn't meant to put his heart on the line, that was for sure.

But the fact remained that however it had happened, however the thing had snuck up on him, he now found himself deeply, crazily, stupidly in love with the woman sleeping in his arms.

With Lisa.

And that wasn't good.

Lisa's eyes popped open. For a moment she lay there, disoriented, trying to figure out where she was.

In bed. In a dark room. Not alone.

Not alone?

Scott. Remembering, she felt a jolt of pure happiness.

I'm sleeping with Scott.

Her heart beat faster at the thought. A warm glow began to pulse inside her. They were lying in spoon fashion, so that she could feel the tickle of his chest hair against her back. His arm was around her waist, one big hand cupped her breast, and his leg was thrown over hers. He radiated body heat, his arm and leg were heavy as wet cement, and he snored.

Or at least, he had snored. Now he had stopped.

She was just registering that when he moved, nuzzling her hair — or, alternatively, freeing his face from it, as she rather suspected — and tightening his arm around her waist and his hand around her breast.

Her nipple hardened, and her body quickened in instant response.

"Is that your phone?" His voice was a sleepy-sounding growl in her ear.

Oh my God, that muffled sound — Beethoven's Fifth.

"Let me go. I need to answer it. It might be about my mother."

He complied, although not without a last lingering fondle of her breast. It sent a shaft of fire shooting through her that under the circumstances she had no choice but to ignore. As she scrambled out of bed in search of her errant phone, he flopped onto his back. Feeling his eyes on her, which made her suddenly acutely conscious that she was naked, she glanced back — sure enough, he was looking — and yanked the bedspread off and wrapped it around herself. Even after everything they had done together, the mere memory of which was enough to make her tingle and burn and blush, she still wasn't comfortable with swanning around naked under his interested gaze.

The phone was in her purse, she knew that, but it was locating her purse that was the trick. The room was dark, with only a few glimmers of light beaming in around the edges of the heavy curtains to tell her that it was daylight outside and to lighten the gloom. Behind her she heard a creak, and she glanced over her shoulder to see Scott rolling out of bed. She looked — *God, he was built* — but the insistent phone demanded her attention. Forcing herself to turn away, she hunted frantically for her purse. The sound told her that it was near, in the same general area as their discarded clothes. Behind her, there was a rustling as Scott pulled the cord to open the curtains. Bright daylight poured in, making her flinch a little but aiding in her search. She didn't even remember dropping her purse, but she must have, probably when Scott had first kissed her. Eyes skimming over the scarlet puddle of her dress, her bra that was laid out like a small black banner on the beige carpet with her panties nearby, her kicked-off shoes, his discarded pants with the belt still in the loops, his fallen jacket striped with the blue of his tie, his navy boxers and black socks and shoes, she looked for the small black evening bag that contained her phone.

There it was, beside the closet. For the first time since encountering Scott in the hospital last night she remembered Katrina, tucked away behind the sliding door, but she didn't have time to dwell on the doll right then. Snatching up her purse, she grabbed her phone out of it and answered it without checking the caller ID.

"Lise?" It was Joel. Conscious of Scott behind her, knowing that he could hear every word she said whether he wanted to or not, she grimaced inwardly and didn't turn around. "Can I take you to lunch? I think we were both maybe too hasty last night."

"There's no point," she said. "I meant what I said."

She heard the sound of footsteps padding across the carpet. Out of the corner of her eye she saw Scott walk into the bathroom, giving her an excellent view of his broad back and small, tight rear. He closed the door while she was still reflexively admiring it, and she turned her attention back to Joel.

"It's that damned guy, isn't it?" His tone was accusing. "You've got a thing for him."

She wasn't going to talk about Scott, not to Joel. "You and I weren't going anywhere. You know it as well as I do. We're better off as friends."

From the bathroom came the muffled sound of the toilet flushing. Then a rattle — the shower curtain — and the water being turned on.

Scott was taking a shower. Just the thought made her heart beat faster.

"Friends," Joel said bitterly. "That's what women always say when they find somebody else. Fine, don't worry, I know when I'm being dumped. Give me a call if you change your mind."

"Bye, Joel." He was already hanging up in her ear. She grimaced, disconnected herself, and checked the time: eight twenty-seven a.m. She almost groaned: They'd gotten maybe four hours of sleep, if that. And she needed to call her mother — soon. But first she had to shower, which presented a whole range of interesting possibilities. She could, of course, wait until Scott was finished. Or — not.

"Not" got her vote. Losing the bedspread,

she went into the bathroom, which was typical hotel-issue, nothing fancy.

Steam was already starting to fill the air. The mirror was fogging over. The shower sounded like a waterfall. The tub was small, with a plain white shower curtain drawn across it, and behind that shower curtain was Scott. She could just see the top of his head and hear the sounds of him soaping up. Quickly she made use of the facilities, then flushed. He yelped as apparently the cold water cut out.

That made her smile. She was still smiling as she stepped into the shower.

By the time she got around to calling her mother, and learned she was fine, and Robin assured her that she had nowhere more important to be and Lisa should take all the time she wanted before coming into the hospital, it was getting on toward ten. She and Scott had rolled out of bed for the second time not long before. Having brushed her hair back into a sleek ponytail and applied minimal makeup, she had dressed in a yellow T-shirt and navy shorts, all under Scott's interested gaze. Scott was wearing his suit from the night before, slightly crumpled now, with his tie crammed into his pocket. With scruff darkening his cheeks and chin, and his eyes heavy-lidded from lack of sleep, he looked so impossibly sexy that practically every time she glanced his way Lisa felt her heart skip a beat. At the moment he was holding Katrina upside down as he stared at the mark on her foot. Lisa had already told him all about the doll, including her resemblance to Marisa Garcia's picture and Barty's extreme reaction to seeing her.

"Just so you know, the doll looks like *you.*" Scott handed Katrina back to her. "Maybe your father's reaction was because looking at her is like seeing a miniature *you* all scorched and beat up."

Lisa snorted as she put Katrina carefully back in the closet. "I don't think so."

Scott opened the door and held it for her to precede him into the hall. She was headed for the hospital, and he was headed for his apartment to change and then to the office to do some work, but they had agreed to grab breakfast first. Probably somewhere like IHOP, where they had a reasonable hope of not running into anyone either of them knew.

"You ever think about trying to work on your relationship with your father?" From the look he gave her, Lisa knew he knew she wouldn't welcome the suggestion. They weren't holding hands or anything, but their arms brushed occasionally as they walked down the hall. They were being cautious with each other, both of them, as if neither of them quite knew what to do with this new romance, but Lisa felt enormously happy just being with him, and for now that was good enough.

"No," she said baldly.

"Maybe you should." They were at the elevators by that time, waiting for one to show up.

"Are *you* really talking to *me* about my relationship with my father?" Her eyes touched on the injury to his face as the elevator arrived. They got in, and Scott punched the button to go down. "What about you and your father?"

"I'm working on it, okay? Probably so should you." The elevator stopped, and they stepped out into the lobby. To Lisa's surprise and dismay, it was full of people clad in their Sunday best, apparently intent on enjoying the lavish brunch spread out on long tables at the far end of the room. Lisa saw multiple interested looks thrown their way as Scott took her arm and steered her toward the door.

"Back in college, we called what I'm doing here the walk of shame," he muttered for her ears alone, and she grinned.

Just as they made it safely out into the steamy heat of the parking lot, Lisa's phone rang again. This time she looked at the caller ID: Rinko.

Why he would be calling her on a Sunday morning she couldn't fathom, but it was unusual enough that she answered.

"You got to come out to the Garcias' house," he told her without preamble. "We found something here that you're going to want to see."

26

"You can't come with me." Lisa stopped behind her car to frown at him. Scott stopped, too, his pants leg just brushing the Jag's back bumper, which was gleaming in the sun. With the bright daylight that was pouring down around them leaving nothing to the imagination, he looked like a man who had been up most of the night doing scandalous things. Which he had been, of course, but no need to advertise it to the people who worked for him.

"I'm sure as hell not letting you go alone. For one thing, there's an awful lot of empty countryside between here and there. For another, in case you've forgotten, somebody knocked you unconscious last time you were out there."

She'd seen that look on his face before. *Determined* was a nice way to put it.

"It's broad daylight. And Rinko's there."

"No offense to your basement buddy, but

I don't find that all that reassuring. Anyway, you actually think I'd get anything done worrying about you?"

"You think Rinko isn't going to notice that we're together on a Sunday morning? And for your information, you look like the morning after the night before. Sexy but a dead giveaway about how you spent your Saturday night."

"I'm glad you think I'm sexy. And if we're talking about dead giveaways . . ." Leaning forward, he pressed a hot, wet kiss to the side of her neck. The feel of his lips on her skin made her go all soft and buttery inside, but concern that they might be seen more than made up for it. They were in the Marriott parking lot with no one in particular to notice but lots of potential for public exposure, and she cast a swift glance around even as he straightened. "You have a hickey on your neck. Right there."

Her eyes widened with horror. "I do not!" She clamped a hand to the spot he had kissed. "Do I?"

He nodded and grinned. She punched him in the arm, punishment for that grin, then reached up to pull the coated elastic from her hair. Thick and heavy, it fell around her shoulders, as effective as a turtleneck for throat concealment. Unfortunately, it was just about as hot.

"A hickey is so juvenile. We're not teenagers."

"I know. I'm sorry. I got carried away."

Just remembering how carried away he'd gotten, how carried away they'd both gotten, was enough to make her stomach flutter. He must have seen something of what she was feeling in her eyes, because his darkened. But unlike her, he hadn't lost sight of the original item of contention.

"You go on to your mother in the hospital, and I'll go see what Rinko's found."

"Not a chance." Keys in hand, having beeped open the lock, she curtailed the argument by walking around to the driver's-side door. "You go do whatever it is *you* need to do, and I'll go see what Rinko's found."

"Not a chance." Not entirely to her surprise — she hadn't thought he would just give up — he moved to the passenger door and looked at her over the roof of the car. "If you go, I go."

"Fine. Just be aware that the office is gossip central, and *everybody's* interested in the boss's sex life."

"Nice. Uh, how about I drive?"

"My car, I drive."

"I love it when you go all controlling on me."

She gave him a hard look. "Keep it up and I really will leave you."

Double-beeping the key so that his door unlocked, too, she got into the car, which was hotter than the inside of an oven. The seat baked through her shorts and seared the bare backs of her thighs where the shorts ended. Jiggling her legs in an effort to minimize the impact of the hot leather, she turned on the ignition and started rolling down the windows while the air conditioner blasted out hot air. Taking a quick peek in the rearview mirror, she confirmed that she did indeed have a tiny love bite on the side of her neck, and in consequence scowled at Scott, minus his jacket now in clear deference to the heat, as he slid in beside her.

"Told you," he said, tossing his jacket into the backseat as she shook her hair down over the telltale mark, and she made a face at him.

She put on her seat belt and backed out of the space, glad to be in motion because it provided a modicum of a breeze. Out of the corner of her eye, she saw that he was fastening his seat belt, too, and rolling up his sleeves.

As she pulled out of the parking lot, she closed the windows when the air conditioner finally started to kick out cold air, and turned right toward the light. There was some traffic but nothing too bad. Church and early restaurant-goers, mostly.

"I'll tell Rinko that I called you and picked you up on the way," she said.

"That'll fool him."

"You know this is going to make things awkward for both of us, if it gets out."

"Thus my rule about not dating women who work for me."

"I hate to be the one to point this out, but you done broke that rule, pardner."

"I'm aware, believe me." He gestured toward the McDonald's up ahead. "Want to grab some drive-thru coffee?"

"Good idea." Turning into the parking lot, she ordered — she knew he liked his coffee the same way she did, black — then paid with the five-dollar bill he handed over and passed him his cup, along with the change.

As they got under way again she looked at him with the slightest of frowns. "You know, we could just file last night away under the great one-night-stand category and move on. It would make things a lot easier at work."

He took a sip of his coffee. "I don't want

to do that."

Her suggestion had been in the nature of an experiment, and she felt a tiny little frisson of relief at his response. Of course, she hadn't really expected him to agree. The attraction between them was too potent for either of them just to easily walk away. It had some burning out to do first.

"Then we need to be very discreet." Swallowing some of her own coffee, she cast a reproving look at him. "Which you coming with me out to the Garcia house on a Sunday morning does not fall under the heading of, by the way."

"*Discreet*'s a relative thing. As long as you don't start jumping my bones at the office, we should be okay." At the indignant look she shot him he grinned, then changed the subject before she could reply. "What did Peyton want this morning?"

"Nosy, aren't you?" They were out of the city now. She discovered that she was really, really glad of his company after all as she turned down the first of several narrow country roads that led to their destination and traffic became nonexistent.

"Yeah. Are you going to tell me?"

"He wanted to take me to lunch today."

A beat passed. A sideways glance at his face revealed exactly nothing.

"You planning to keep seeing him?" There it was: The careful neutrality of his tone told her all she needed to know.

She shook her head. Making Scott jealous had turned out to be more fun than she ever would have imagined, but it wasn't a game she ordinarily played. Straightforward was more her style. And this thing between them — it was too new for her to even characterize it as a relationship, exactly — deserved better.

"Not as anything other than a friend." She cast him another sideways glance. "I never slept with him, you know. Not once."

"Oh, yeah?"

"Yeah."

"Good to know," he said, and smiled at her.

"What about you?"

"If you're asking me if I'm sleeping with anybody else, the answer's no."

"I heard you were seeing some woman who works in a bank."

He looked surprised, then shook his head. "The gossip network's out of date. That's been over for a while."

Good hovered on her lips, but she didn't say it. Instead she said, "We're here," because they had just crested a rise that brought the Garcias' house into view.

He followed her gaze, studying the property with a slight frown as they drew close. Rinko's van was parked at the end of the long drive, Lisa saw as she pulled in. Everything else, from the For Sale sign to the overgrown grass to the fortresslike woods crowding the property on either side to the small brick ranch house itself, looked exactly the same as it had when she had been there before.

Lisa shivered.

Scott gulped the last of his coffee as she parked behind the van and put the empty cup back in the cup holder between them. Her own coffee was only about half finished, but she suddenly didn't want it anymore. Feeling more nervous than she cared to admit, she looked around, but Rinko was nowhere in sight.

"Stay close to me, hear?" Typical high-handed Scott, his tone made it a command rather than a question, but under the circumstances Lisa discovered she had no fault to find with the sentiment thus expressed. She nodded, and they got out of the car.

Elsewhere in the area, it was a typical sunny, blazing-hot July day. But here, in the shadow of the tall trees, it was measurably cooler, and darker, and quieter. An insistent cicada chorus was the only sound. The isolation was palpable. It did not, Lisa thought, give off the feeling of a happy place, and she was doubly grateful that Scott had insisted on coming with her. She would never in a million years have admitted it, but right about now, on her own, she would have been scared to death.

So maybe she *was* overimaginative.

She had already whipped out her phone and was dialing Rinko as Scott joined her on her side of the car.

"We're here," she told Rinko when he answered. Then, with a glance at Scott, who was frowning at the house as they walked toward it, she added in a quieter voice, "Um, I brought Buchanan with me."

Scott flicked her a derisive look.

"Shit." Rinko's consternation was obvious. "What'd you go and do that for? He's going to be pissed. He told me to leave this case alone."

"Sorry, I had no idea." She glanced at Scott. He didn't look pissed. Actually, he was looking pretty mellow. She had a shrewd idea why that was, and Rinko could thank her anytime. She spoke to Rinko again. "Where are you?"

But even as she asked the question it was answered. Three teens emerged from the woods on the far side of the house. Although she was initially surprised to see them, she realized that she shouldn't have been. Of course Rinko would have brought his protégés, and she was willing to bet dollars to doughnuts that Jantzen was somewhere around, too. One of them, the blond girl, Ashley, waved at her. The other girl — Sarah — and the tall boy with the spiky black hair — Matt — just stood there looking her and Scott over with obvious interest. The girls wore shorts, the boy jeans.

"Never mind, I see the kids," she told Rinko, then waved back at Ashley and disconnected.

"Great." Scott had seen the teens, too.

"It's the wayward lambs," Lisa reminded him.

"Yeah, I got that. This just keeps getting better and better. If they're here, my nephew is probably here, and he's been under the impression that you're my girlfriend since the night Grayson Springs burned. He also thinks you're a babe, by the way."

"You and your nephew talked about me?" The idea of Scott exchanging confidences with a fifteen-year-old was mildly mind-boggling. They were heading across the yard toward the kids now, and Lisa stole uneasy glances at the house. It was suddenly impossible to forget that someone hiding inside had attacked her last time she'd been here. Her skin crawled. Lisa had to remind herself not to walk too close to Scott, or take hold of his arm, or slip her hand into his. *Professional* was going to be her byword, she was determined, even if she was feeling decidedly spooked.

"He's the one who told me you got knocked unconscious last time you were here, remember? The rest were just comments made in passing."

"Did you correct him? I *wasn't* your girlfriend." Lisa noticed she used the past tense only after the words left her mouth.

"No, you weren't," he agreed.

It didn't escape her notice that he used the past tense, too, and her heart gave a funny little flutter at the thought that now, maybe, she was. But at the moment she had other, more pressing, concerns, and so she pushed the whole rather charming concept to the back of her mind to be examined more carefully later.

"Just so you know, you've got Rinko worried. He says you told him to leave this case alone."

"I did."

His tone had gone surprisingly grim, which boded ill for Rinko.

"Why?"

"I don't want to get all kinds of other people involved until I've got a better idea of what we're dealing with here."

"What do you think we're dealing with?"

He shook his head. "I don't know. So far, all I've come up with is a lot of coincidences. But they're funny coincidences, and I don't mean the ha-ha kind. I mean the kind that makes me think I need to look into them further."

"*You* need to look into them? I thought you'd passed the grunt work off to somebody."

"I decided to do it myself, just in case whatever turned up ends up being about you."

That touched her so much that she stopped walking. When he turned to look at her, she smiled at him. "That's really sweet," she said.

He looked mildly revolted. "Just for the record, Princess, I don't do sweet."

Despite that "Princess," what she wanted to do was walk into his arms, wrap her arms around his neck, and kiss him until they were both breathless. Because they had an audience, she made a face at him instead and resumed walking.

"Yes, you do. Sometimes. Be nice to Rinko. He's a good guy. And he's only trying to help."

Falling in beside her, Scott grunted.

The kids were already fading back into the woods when they reached it, with Ashley beckoning excitedly at them to follow. There was a path, Lisa saw, as she and Scott ducked into the woods after them, a narrow path that ran between rough-barked trees crowded in so closely together that no matter which way you looked, more trees were all you could see. Branches wove a canopy overhead that almost completely blocked out the sun, with only a few stray beams of light managing to pierce the foliage. It was gloomy and cool, and quiet except for the cicadas. The carpet of fallen leaves underfoot deadened their footsteps. Vines climbed tree trunks, and scrub bushes and brambles tangled together on the ground. The air smelled of earth and was so still that not even a leaf moved.

Scott stayed so close behind her that he practically stepped on the heels of her Keds.

"You're not going to believe this." Ashley was waiting for them at the edge of a clearing about the size of a small bedroom. She pointed toward where Rinko stood by a knee-high leaf pile that had obviously been raked up by Chase — obviously because he was leaning on a rake. Beside Chase, Noah held what it took Lisa a second to determine was a vacuum cleaner–sized silver metal detector. Austin, dirty gardening trowel in hand, stood beside Rinko. Sarah and Matt stood next to them. Jantzen, who held a digital camera, appeared to have been taking pictures. They were grouped around what appeared to be a shallow hole, freshly dug, no doubt by Austin and his trowel.

All eyes turned toward Lisa and Scott as they headed toward the assemblage.

"We've been going over this whole property with a metal detector, inch by tedious inch," Rinko told them as they reached the group. "Just to see if anything interesting turned up. Look what did."

Eyes glowing with pride, he handed something to Scott, who frowned as he looked down at the object in his hand. Lisa looked at it and frowned, too.

It was the approximate size and shape of a coaster, dark gray now though, from a few specks of color remaining around the raised edge, it had once been gold. A frayed and dirty bit of blue ribbon was still attached to one end.

Lisa realized that what she was seeing was a medal of the type sometimes awarded in athletic competitions that was meant to be worn around the neck.

"See, it's got a book engraved on the front." Rinko was clearly too eager to show off his find to let any nervousness about Scott's presence deter him. "And look on the back." He flipped the medal over in Scott's hand, and pointed. "It says, *Marisa Garcia.* What do you think about that?"

27

"Hello? Hell-o-o? Where is everybody?" A hearty male voice calling from the direction of the Garcias' house cut through the sudden silence. "Owners of the van and the Jaguar? Hello?"

Having glanced in the direction of the voice like everyone else, Lisa returned her attention to Scott as he ignored the distraction to say to the others, "I suppose everybody's had their hands on this?"

Rinko immediately looked self-conscious.

"We dug it up and passed it around before the Rink and Emily caught up with us," Chase said. It was clear to Lisa from his slightly truculent tone that he thought he was standing up for Rinko.

"I guess I should've told 'em if they found anything not to touch it, but I didn't think about it." Rinko was now slightly shamefaced. Lisa felt a spurt of sympathy for him. Admitting to a screwup with Scott's eyes on him, and Jantzen and the kids watching, couldn't be easy. "My bad, huh?"

Scott's lips twisted. Lisa was glad when he didn't reply.

"If it hadn't been for you, it wouldn't have been found." Jantzen's chin was up, she was shooting Scott a challenging look, and she moved loyally closer to Rinko, who gave her a quick, grateful smile. Unlike the other guys, who all wore jeans, Rinko was wearing rumpled khaki shorts and a madras shirt, and his hair was curling wildly in the heat, and his glasses were slipping down his nose. Beside him, Jantzen, with her hair in braids and wearing a pink sundress, looked cool and pretty. They made an unlikely couple, but Lisa considered Jantzen's presence in the buggy, steamy woods on a Sunday morning, to say nothing of the alacrity with which she came to Rinko's defense, to be a good sign. "The metal detector was your idea. You get the credit."

"Or the blame," Noah said under his breath, his eyes on Scott's face.

Ashley frowned at Scott. "That thing we found is important, right? I mean, it belonged to one of the missing people."

"You know how many hours we've spent doing this?" Matt sounded exasperated. "We've gone over every inch of this property, practically. We've been coming out here for days. I've got so many bug bites, my bug bites have bug bites."

"It'll pay off," Ashley assured him. "Wait till you start putting on your college applications that you helped solve cold cases for the prosecutor's office."

"Hey, brainiac, guess what? Some of us don't care about that," Austin said. "I'm out here because it's better than being at home." He cast a dark look at Scott. "Or going to juvie hall."

"Or church with your grandparents," Sarah put in.

"You're out here because you like Sarah," Matt said to Austin.

Casting a self-conscious look at Sarah, who looked surprised, Austin reddened. "Well, you like Ashley."

It was Matt's turn to redden as Ashley's eyes shot to his.

"You absolutely did good." Lisa stepped into the breach before the discussion could deteriorate further. Scott might have his reasons for not applauding the search effort, but they'd worked hard, and she didn't see any point in raining on their parade now. "All of you should be proud."

If there had been any way to conceal what she was doing, she would have elbowed

Scott in the ribs.

"Hell-o-o? If you're interested in the property, I'd be happy to show it to you. Who's there?" The hearty voice sounded closer now. Everybody flicked glances in its direction, but no one replied.

"You get any pictures of this before it was moved?" Scott asked Jantzen, indicating the medal.

She shook her head. "But I got some shots of the site after."

"That's something, at any rate." Scott's hand closed around the medal, and he slipped it into his pocket. The action surprised Lisa. She would have expected him to be calling for a tech unit, or at the very least wrapping the thing and transporting it with care until it could be handed over to the police lab. While she wondered, Scott's eyes swept the group. His expression softened. "Okay, I got to hand it to you: This is quite a find, and it wouldn't have happened without you guys. Good work, all of you." Everyone looked gratified, except maybe for Rinko, who was looking at Scott a little mistrustfully. Lisa didn't blame him. She had a feeling Rinko hadn't heard the end of the matter. Scott added in an affable tone that even Lisa couldn't hear anything amiss in, "Come on, let's go see what that guy out there is yelling about."

When they emerged from the woods it was to find a portly, balding man in maybe his mid-fifties standing on the house's small front stoop. He saw them immediately, waved, and started walking across the yard toward them.

When he was close enough he introduced himself as Jim Gage, the real estate agent for the property. On Sundays, he told them, he liked to drive around and check on his listings. He'd seen their vehicles, stopped, and was glad to answer any questions they might have about the house.

It had been empty for about a year. And no, he didn't know anything about a family who had lived there thirty years before that had gone missing. But he was also glad to show them the house, if they cared to see it, which they did. He took them in via the front door, then let them wander through on their own.

It didn't take long. The house was small, just three bedrooms, a single bath, the living room, and the kitchen. The decor didn't look like it had been updated much from the eighties, including brown shag carpet in the living room. Lisa found the atmosphere oppressive, and not just because there was no air-conditioning and it was stiflingly hot inside. Whether or not it was because she knew that this was the last place the Garcias had ever been known to be, Lisa thought she could sense enduring vibrations of distress. When whatever happened happened, the police had thought Angela was in the midst of giving Marisa a bath: That was the image that flashed into Lisa's mind as she stepped into the small, green-tiled bathroom. Bathtub, sink, and toilet were obviously original to the house. Looking at the tub, Lisa pictured it filled with water in which a child's toys floated, and had to turn away. She lingered longest in the kitchen. The fittings had been inexpensive to begin with, and over the years had been allowed to run down. The cabinets were plain varnished wood, and the only appliance that remained — because it was worthless, Lisa was sure — was an old Sears dishwasher. No refrigerator, no stove. The linoleum floor was in a red-brick pattern, and clearly far less than thirty years old, which meant it couldn't be harboring any of the blood that had been spilled on the night the Garcias had disappeared. In fact, the floor from that time had probably been pulled up to remove any traces of blood, and replaced many times since. From the windows over the sink, she saw, it would have been easy for anyone standing inside to observe her approaching the back door.

Scott, who had stayed with her like an extra appendage throughout, asked Gage who else had access to the house.

"Any real estate agent can call up and get a key. Then there's the owners. And I guess anyone who had a key — like the renters who used to live here — can still get back in. As far as I know, the locks haven't been changed."

"I already checked to see who had access to the house that day," Lisa told Scott when they were back in the car again, heading for Lexington. Rinko and the others were in the van ahead of them, with, she was amused to see, Jantzen driving. They were heading for Waffle House, where Lisa and Scott had respectfully declined to join them. "According to the secretary at the real estate company, no one was scheduled to be there. And both the owners and previous renters have moved out of state."

Scott settled more comfortably in his seat and folded his arms over his chest. He looked tired. She knew how he felt. Last night's lack of sleep was beginning to catch up to both of them.

"Efficient, aren't you?"

"Very." She shot him a censorious look.

"By the way, did you have to ruin Rinko's day?"

"I don't know what you're talking about."

"I heard you tell him to be in your office at nine a.m. tomorrow."

Scott smiled. "It won't hurt him to sweat it overnight."

"You're not going to fire him or anything, are you?"

He shook his head. "I'm just going to make sure he understands that when I tell him to leave a case alone, I mean it. Nothing for you to worry about."

"I thought that was pretty good work they did, actually, finding that medal like that."

"And then digging it up and passing it all around so that any evidence that might have remained on it after all these years was almost certainly lost." His voice was dry.

She threw him a troubled glance. "Why didn't you call a forensics unit out to the scene? Or at least try to preserve what evidence might have been left on the medal?"

He looked at her for a long moment without saying anything. The stretch of backcountry road they were on seemed extraordinarily dark all of a sudden, and she saw that thunderclouds were starting to pile up overhead.

"I didn't call for a forensics unit because I don't want to stir things up. That case has been off the official radar for a long time, and for now it's probably best that it stays that way. As for the medal, I plan to have it checked out privately."

Her chest suddenly felt tight. "You think there's a reason why I look like Angela Garcia, don't you?"

"There's always a reason for everything."

"Scott . . ."

"Baby, before we go any further with this, you need to ask yourself: Do you really want to know the truth? Because sometimes the truth can change everything. Sometimes it's better to just leave certain questions unanswered."

The uncomfortable feeling in her chest intensified. "Okay, spill. What do you know that I don't?"

He shrugged.

"Scott. Tell me."

"Michael Garcia broke into your parents' house in Maryland. He was arrested, but the charges were subsequently dropped. Just a couple of weeks later he and his family moved to Lexington."

Lisa drew a breath. "That's quite a coincidence."

"Yeah."

"You know Angela Garcia used to work at the hospital where I was born, right? Although the dates didn't overlap. She and her family were living in Lexington by then."

"I know all that."

"There's a connection there, isn't there? Something real. This isn't my overactive imagination."

"I'm pretty confident there's something there. Something that's big enough for somebody to set fire to Grayson Springs in an effort to conceal it. Something that made somebody go back to the Garcias' house for some reason, and when they saw you there, hit you over the head to prevent you from seeing them."

"Like what?" Lisa's mind raced over the possibilities. She had considered them so often and discarded so many that only a few remained. "I saw pictures of myself being born, so I clearly wasn't adopted. Maybe I'm a test-tube baby. Maybe Angela Garcia donated her eggs, or sold them, and my mother used one. Or maybe it was a whole embryo. Or maybe that's not it, and the Garcias are related to us in some other way I don't know about. Or maybe it's just the most amazing coincidence."

"The thing to keep in mind here is that the Garcia family disappeared. I've been checking into financial records, and as far as I can tell there was absolutely no financial activity by any of them after that night. They never contacted anybody, not employers, not friends, not family. Social Security has no record that the adults ever worked again. That leads me to conclude that they're probably dead. It may well be that their disappearance and probable death have nothing to do with the fact that you bear a striking resemblance to the females of the family. Nothing to do with you at all."

"But?" She heard the reservation in his voice. They had reached town by now, and there was traffic to contend with. Up ahead, the van pulled into the far left lane and then, with a farewell honk, turned. A few fat drops of rain splattered on the windshield, and from the look of the clouds, a downpour wasn't far behind.

"But it may be that it does. And if it does, whatever happened to them may well involve someone in your life."

Lisa let that sink in for a minute, then reacted with dawning horror. "Are you saying that you think someone in my life killed them? Who? And why?"

"I don't know. And I'm just saying that it's a possibility you need to consider. The thing is, whatever happened to the Garcias happened a long time ago. It's over. We can't help them, whatever we do. But if we keep digging, if we find out the truth and it's anything like where the facts are pointing right now, the person who I'm afraid is going to be hurt the most is you."

Lisa felt suddenly light-headed. "Are you saying you think I should back off?"

"I think you should definitely think about where we're going with this before we take it so far it's irretrievable. You have a good life, a secure and happy life, a career that's going to take you places. You have people you love, people who love you. You got to ask yourself, is digging up the past worth jeopardizing what you have? Or would it be better to simply leave things as they are and move on?"

Lisa's hands tightened on the wheel as Scott's words seeped into the furthest reaches of her mind and heart.

"You're a prosecutor, for God's sake," she burst out. "We may be talking about murder here. Multiple murders. Shouldn't you be grabbing this evidence we've uncovered and vowing to pursue the truth to the furthest reaches of the law, no matter what?"

"That would make it easier, wouldn't it?" The ghost of a smile just touched his lips. "Baby, one thing you can count on is that I have your best interests at heart. I'm not going to do anything that I think might ultimately be harmful to you."

"I appreciate that." Lisa took a deep, steadying breath. "You've been great through this, by the way. I don't think I could have gotten through it without you." She saw the Marriott sign up ahead, and pulled into the turning lane. "The thing is, though, I feel as if I owe it to them — the Garcias — to find out what happened. I don't think I'll ever feel at peace otherwise. I might wish I'd never seen that picture, and that file, but now that I have I can't just turn my back and walk away."

As she turned into the parking lot, she could feel him looking at her. His expression was a funny mix of tender, rueful, resigned. She was suddenly fiercely glad that he was in this with her, that whatever was uncovered, she would not have to face it alone. Scott was a rock that she could grab on to if she needed to, and the knowledge was beyond comforting.

"You want to go ahead and damn the torpedoes, *hmm?*"

She laughed, although the sound was a little shaky. "Yes. That's what I want."

"Fair enough. I've already sent for medical records from the early eighties for everybody involved: your parents, the Garcias, you. I'm hoping to get them early this week. I'm also having a background check run on everyone who was around when the Garcias disappeared, as well as on everyone who might even possibly have had access to the house on the night it burned. Age-enhanced pictures for all of the Garcias as they might look today are ready to go out on the BOLO network."

As she pulled in beside his Jeep and parked, he was still looking at her with an expression she couldn't decipher.

"What?" She shot him a quick frown.

"You probably want to have a DNA test done. Depending on what the results are, that could rule a lot of things out right there."

Or rule them in. But she didn't say it.

"That was one of the first things I thought of, but —" She wet her lips. It was raining now, the drops coming fast and thick so that they sounded like a continuous drumroll as they hit the car. Steam rose from the pavement all around them. Even with the air conditioner going, the smell of rain was strong. "I can't tell my mother anything about what I'm doing, not the way she is, and I hate to do something as sneaky as grab a glass she's drunk out of and rush it off to the lab. Then there's Barty, who's a whole other problem, as you know. And . . . and . . . what if it does turn out that I'm not their biological child?" She swallowed. "I guess some part of me just doesn't really want to know after all."

"Lisa . . ."

"No, I do want to know. I *have* to know. But . . . my mother . . . This is the last bit of time we'll ever have together. And I hate to spend any of it on this." All of a sudden she couldn't talk anymore because her throat was closing up. Not that she needed to say anything else: She knew Scott understood. Even as she looked at him with mute anguish, he unfastened his seat belt and leaned toward her, sliding a hand behind the back of her neck. Then he kissed her.

Lisa closed her eyes and kissed him back. In a moment the kiss that had started out as something gentle and tender turned torrid enough to make the windows fog over. He was just undoing her seat belt to pull her more fully into his arms when her cell phone rang.

28

Lisa let it go to voice mail, but it broke the kiss up nonetheless.

"Want to get lunch before we go our separate ways?" Scott had let her go and was back in his seat. His voice was husky. His eyes were hot.

Shaking her head regretfully at him, she was at the same time listening to the message that had been left. Robin said: *Just wanted to let you know, Dr. Spencer is coming at two. He wants to talk to you.*

"I have to go to the hospital." She told him what Robin had said.

"Do you want me to come with you?"

"I thought you had work to do."

"If you need me, it can wait."

She smiled at him but shook her head. "I don't need you. Go do your work."

He looked at her for a moment without saying anything, then nodded. "Okay. I'll stop by the hospital later."

Then he snagged his jacket from the backseat and got out of the car, seemingly oblivious to the raindrops pelting him.

He followed her to the hospital, gave her a ride through the now pouring rain from the parking space she found to the front door, then drove away.

Preoccupied as she was, Lisa had almost reached her mother's room before it registered that he hadn't kissed her good-bye.

Again, she'd never been in a relationship with Scott before, so she couldn't be certain, but she was willing to bet quite a bit that he was the kind of guy who made a habit of kissing the woman he was sleeping with good-bye.

Something's up with him, she thought for the second time in less than twenty-four hours.

But then Mrs. Dalmain and Mrs. Henderson, two of her mother's friends, came out of the room, and she put the matter out of her mind as she greeted them. From there, she was drawn into the social vortex that was her mother's room on a Sunday afternoon until Dr. Spencer arrived promptly at two.

Her mother would be released soon, probably on Tuesday. That was the good news. The bad news was that he recommended that she move to a nursing home that provided around-the-clock medical care. The worse news was that tests showed her ALS was progressing to its final stage.

"She hates the idea of a nursing home," Lisa, shaken, told Dr. Spencer. Knowing, rather than suspecting, that her mother's time was measured in weeks now was making her feel light-headed and nauseated. "Our house is unlivable just at present, but I can find something to rent, or . . ."

Dr. Spencer shook his head and thrust a hand into the pocket of his white lab coat to come up with a folded sheet of paper. He was a short, thin, gray-haired man of about Martha's own age with a brisk manner that concealed a real dedication to his patients. Martha trusted him completely, and Lisa saw no reason to question her mother's judgment. It was just that what he was saying was very hard to accept.

"She's going to need around-the-clock skilled care in the very near future." He handed the folded paper to her. "I've already made arrangements with the Worley Center for her to take the bed they have available starting Tuesday." He nodded at the piece of paper. "That's the name of the new patient coordinator there. If you'll give her a call, she'll answer all your questions. Of course, if you object, you're welcome to make alternative arrangements or get a second opinion. But I feel this is what is best for Mrs. Grant."

Lisa was heartsick over it, but in the end she reluctantly agreed. Dr. Spencer had her mother's best interests at heart, she knew. But she also knew her mother would be upset, and for that reason she decided to put off telling her until Monday.

Fortunately, Martha had so much company throughout the afternoon and evening that Lisa's lack of sparkle went unnoticed. By pleading work, turning to her laptop, and relying on the steady stream of visitors to entertain Martha, she was able to stay out of her mother's direct orbit until her feelings were once again under control. The last thing she wanted was for Martha to sense that something was wrong.

Scott came by later to visit briefly with Martha and the ladies in her room before he and Lisa slipped off to the hospital cafeteria for a quick supper. As soon as she saw him, the news practically burst out of her. It was a relief to tell him everything. His calm good sense steadied her, and she was grateful for his strength. When he left she badly wanted to go with him, to spend the night with him, but at this point there was no way she could leave her mother even if he had suggested it, which he didn't. But this time at least he kissed her good-bye, a quick, hard kiss when she walked him to the elevator, dropped on her mouth in the teeth of the interested gazes of several of her mother's friends who were leaving at the same time.

She felt a ridiculous sense of loss when the elevator doors closed on him. For the first time it occurred to her that she was starting to rely on him a lot. Too much? Maybe, but the thought of not having him to turn to was bleak indeed.

When she went back to her mother's room, she settled down with her laptop to finalize some work while her mother chatted with the last of the visitors. Finally she finished everything that was urgent, only to look up and discover that the visitors were gone and her mother had fallen asleep while watching TV.

For a moment Lisa looked at the slight figure in the bed and listened to her labored breathing. Love and a sense of utter helplessness in the face of her mother's illness filled her with an indescribable sadness. But there was, simply, nothing she could do but stay at her mother's side as the clock ticked inexorably down. With a lump in her throat, she turned off the TV, then thought about going to sleep herself. It was already after eleven, and she had to be at work at eight. But sleep was beyond her for the moment, and instead she turned her laptop back on and wound up Googling the mark she had discovered on Katrina's foot: MBF, surrounded by a heart.

To her surprise, it was as simple as that.

The symbol was the trademark of the My Best Friend dolls, a line of expensive, limited-edition dolls that were custom-made for each lucky customer. Only a few thousand were created each year, from 1978 to 1985, when the company was sold to a larger toy manufacturer. The customer specified hair color and style, eye color, and skin tone, and chose the doll's clothing. The object was for the finished doll to look as much like its intended little-girl owner as possible. It was suggested that a picture of the child be sent in along with the order. If that wasn't possible, the company would do its best with the information provided.

Other than a telephone number and address for the new, larger toy company and a number to be called for doll repair, there was no more information to be gleaned from the website. With the fixed intention of calling the company in the morning to find out anything else she could, Lisa logged off the laptop.

Then she sat staring into space for a moment as it occurred to her that whoever had ordered Katrina had made a mistake. Unlike her own, the doll's eyes were blue.

Work the next morning was hectic. ADAs Pratchett and Ellis were in court as the defense in the Gaylin grandmother-killer case argued for a competency hearing for their client. It had been Lisa's job to document all the defendant's previous mental health issues, and she was there with the prosecution team to walk them through what she had uncovered. As soon as she got back to the office, she had to rush back to court with copies of cell phone records for a vehicular homicide case. Kane was the prosecutor in that one. There was no mistaking the dislike in the woman's eyes as she practically snatched the papers from Lisa's hand. Knowing the cause, Lisa was fairly sanguine about it. Other than handing Scott over to Kane, which she wasn't about to do, there weren't a lot of options. After that she stopped by police headquarters to go over some crime scene photos with the detective who had taken them. While she was there, she made a trip down to the evidence room in the basement to check out some items that would be needed in court the next day.

By the time she finally made it back to her desk, it was after three o'clock. Rain had fallen in sheets all day, and despite the umbrella she had strategically provided herself with, she was damp all over and her feet were soaked. By way of a late lunch, she opened the Diet Coke and package of peanut-butter crackers she'd picked up at a vending machine on the way back in, and dialed the number for the toy company that was listed on the My Best Friend doll website.

She was on the phone waiting for her call to be transferred to the correct department when Scott, all business in a navy suit with his briefcase in his hand, walked into her line of vision. She hadn't set eyes on him all day, and she was surprised at how glad she was to see him now, especially when he wasn't doing anything any more exciting than striding toward his office, flanked by two ADAs and talking on his cell phone. He didn't as much as glance her way, but her eyes tracked him automatically. Her heart speeded up, and that "Hey, I'm really glad to see you" tingle was out in full force. She watched him until he was inside his office and the door closed, blocking her view, then recollected her surroundings and glanced self-consciously around to see if anyone else had noticed her interest. Fortunately, everyone else seemed to be too busy working.

"Can I help you?" a voice spoke in her ear, distracting her. Lisa explained that she was trying to track down the purchaser of a My Best Friend doll that was sold in the early 1980s.

"We've maintained the records of all our sales for that particular doll, so I should be able to help you. Do you have a serial number?"

"Serial number?"

"The dolls all came with certificates of authenticity that included serial numbers. If you have the doll, the number is also stamped on her lower back."

Lisa hadn't thought to look for a serial number. Of course, it would be a simple thing to check tonight and call back with the information in the morning, but she would rather not take the extra time unless she had to. "I don't have the serial number."

"Do you have the purchaser's name and state?"

"Grant," Lisa tried. "In either Kentucky or Maryland."

"Hold on." A moment later the woman was back. "Yes, we do have a My Best

Friend doll that was sold to a C. B. Grant of Lexington, Kentucky, on January twelfth, 1981."

Barty. The date was before her own birth. Lisa frowned. Had he ordered the doll in anticipation?

"That date — was that when the doll was picked up or ordered?"

"All our dolls were delivered rather than picked up, which is why we retain a registry of states. That would be the date when the order was placed. Payment in full was required at the time of the initial order, and so the records would indicate that was when the sale took place."

"When was the doll actually delivered?"

"Just a minute." She came back on. "I don't see the date in the file. The orders usually took about four months to fill."

That would make it April 1981, which made sense: It was her birth month.

Except Barty would have had no way of knowing what she was going to look like when the order had been placed. She had still been inside her mother's womb.

If he'd guessed, it had been a really outstanding example of precognition — except for the color of the eyes.

Then something the woman had said finally registered.

"Did you say you have a file there? For this particular order?"

"Yes, I do."

Lisa swallowed hard. "Is there a picture? Of the child?"

"No. If there was a picture, it would have been sent back along with the doll when the delivery was made."

Lisa thanked her and hung up. The urge to run to Scott and tell him what she had just learned was strong, but a quick look around discouraged her. There were too many eyes to see and tongues to wag if she did something so unprecedented as to head for his office. For herself, she didn't really care, but for Scott she did. He had carved out a brilliant career for himself, and she refused to provide fodder for gossip that might embarrass him or, worse, subject him to the kind of "creating a hostile environment in the workplace" drama that knowledge of their relationship might subject him to.

But there *was* something she could do. She could get her answers directly from the horse's mouth.

Picking up the phone, she called Barty.

And got his voice mail, which wasn't a shock. He had caller ID on his phone, and she figured that the chances that he wanted to talk to her were probably about nil. She left a message asking him to call her, and hung up.

The thought she couldn't get out of her mind was that maybe Katrina wasn't her doll at all. Maybe Katrina had been created for Marisa Garcia.

Why Barty would have bought a doll for Marisa she didn't know. How such a doll could have come into her own possession she didn't know. What she did know was that the doll resembled Marisa more closely than it did herself, especially if Marisa's eyes were blue. And the clothes Marisa had been wearing in the picture in the cold-case file looked to be almost identical to the clothes Katrina was wearing.

So, what did that tell her?

Maybe Barty had used Marisa as a model for a doll to be made for his unborn daughter, who would turn out to be herself. Maybe he suspected that they would look alike because he knew they were related. Presumably if some sort of egg or embryo transfer had been involved, he would know about it. Maybe the fact that Michael Garcia had broken into the Grants' house in Maryland was because he was angry about his wife's egg or their embryo being used for another couple's fertility treatment.

Maybe . . . well, she didn't know what, but somehow it all had to tie together. All those disparate facts had to combine to make a cohesive whole. The problem was that she wasn't yet quite sure how.

It occurred to her then that Barty might have been involved in the Garcias' disappearance. *No,* she corrected herself fiercely as the idea took terrible root, *in their murder.* Scott was reluctant to investigate the case further because he was afraid of implicating someone in her life, someone close to her. She didn't know why the other shoe hadn't dropped before, but now she saw it: The person Scott was afraid was involved had to be Barty.

Lisa felt as though a giant hand was slowly squeezing her insides.

Picking up her phone, she sent a text to Scott: *I need to talk to you. Are you coming by the hospital later?*

She spent the next couple of minutes tightly clutching her phone as she waited for his reply to come through. Instead the door to his office opened, and Scott emerged. He was alone, and she surmised she must have missed the exit of the two ADAs. She watched in growing surprise as he said something to Sally Adams, then headed her way.

"Hey," he said when he reached her. His eyes took on a glint of appreciation as they moved over her, not that there was anything very special to see. Her hair was pulled back in a simple ponytail, and she was wearing a short-sleeved black blouse tucked into white slacks, along with tall black pumps. Her black jacket hung over the back of her chair. "You wanted to see me?"

Lisa didn't say anything for a moment. Given the circumstances, what reply could she possibly make to that? Standing there in the entrance of her cubicle, he looked big and tough and so handsome he stole her breath. She hadn't spoken to him all day, hadn't seen him except for that brief glimpse just a little while earlier, and her heartbeat speeded up just because he was there. Her first impulse was to stand up and walk into his arms. Which she didn't do, of course. She was too conscious of the listening eyes and ears of her pretending-to-be-oblivious colleagues.

The speaking look she gave him was meant to remind him of their presence.

"It's after five," he said without bothering to even so much as lower his voice. "I'm going to have to come back and finish up some things, but I need a break. What do you say we go get a quick dinner?"

29

"I thought we were going to try to be discreet about this?" Lisa's protest came as they ran through the pouring rain for the Jaguar and she pressed the remote button to unlock its doors. Scott had an arm around her to keep her close as he held her umbrella over both their heads. Their feet splashed in the inches of running water that sluiced over the pavement. The plan was that they would go in her car to Joe Bologna's, a casual Italian restaurant not far from the office. Then he would ride with her to the hospital and catch a lift back to the office from Andy, who was watching over Martha and would be leaving when she arrived.

"To hell with it." Scott practically had to yell to be heard over the roar of the rain. The sky was overcast and dark, and thunder rumbled in the distance. "It is what it is, and I'm not planning to tie myself in knots trying to hide it. Like I said, as long as you don't go jumping my bones at the office we should be fine."

Lisa was sliding in out of the rain by that time. It was only after he closed the door behind her that she realized she was in the passenger seat of her own car. A slight smile touched her lips as she watched him run around the hood toward the driver's side. She'd known he wasn't the kind of man who liked being driven. He just happened to be smart enough not to push the point when he couldn't win.

"Remember the whole 'my car, I drive' thing?" she asked drily as he got behind the wheel and tossed the umbrella into the backseat.

Blue eyes met brown ones. "You want to drive?"

There he had her. "No."

He held out his hand for the keys, which she handed over. "Anytime you want to, you just let me know. I'm happy to be a passenger, baby."

"You are such a liar." Fastening her seat belt, she settled back in the seat as he started the car and headed out of the lot.

He grinned at her. "Only when I need to be."

They reached the street, and he braked to

wait for the light to change. Then he leaned over to kiss her. It was a quick kiss, a nothing kiss, really, just another kind of hello, but still heat shot clear down to her toes.

The light changed and he straightened, pulling out into traffic that was moving slowly because of the rain.

"So, what did you need to talk to me about?" he asked.

Lisa took a deep breath. All the warmth his presence and that kiss had engendered in her fled. She was wet and cold, and felt about as gloomy as the day.

"It's Barty, isn't it? He's responsible for what happened to the Garcias. You figured it out, and that's why you started backpedaling and telling me that maybe I should just leave the whole thing alone."

Scott didn't say anything for a moment. He just drove, frowning out at the rain splashing down on cars and buildings and pavement, letting the steady swish of the windshield wipers and the hum of the defroster fill the silence while she watched him and waited.

"I won't deny that the evidence seems to be pointing that way," he said finally. "But I don't know that he's involved for sure. Except for the break-in, I have no proof of a link between him and the Garcias. I certainly don't have enough to even think about charging him at this point."

"But you think you can get it, which is why you were hesitating about going any further." Lisa thought about Katrina. The link to Marisa Garcia was not clear. As Scott had pointed out, the doll resembled her, too. Except that she hadn't been born when it was ordered. And she didn't have blue eyes. Nor did she have, at least as far as she knew, a childhood outfit that exactly matched the doll's.

She had a terrible feeling that if Katrina's origins were probed as thoroughly as they probably needed to be, Scott might have the evidence of a link that he needed.

By then they had reached the restaurant. He parked, killed the ignition, and looked at her.

"He's your father."

Lisa felt that terrible internal squeezing sensation again. "I know."

Scott reached in back for the umbrella. "Sit there. I'll come around for you."

Lisa nodded. Then, as he got out of the car and walked through the downpour toward the passenger door, she opened it, ready to get out as he reached it. She did, and they rushed through the rain into the restaurant.

Usually Lisa loved Joe Bologna's, with its homey decor and robust Italian smells, but today she was barely aware of their surroundings as the hostess led them to a table. With the waitress coming and going with menus and drinks and salads and breadsticks, the conversation stayed light and general. Then, when the waitress left them to eat their salads in peace, Scott looked at Lisa steadily.

"Some of the medical records I sent for came today. Your father's, Miss Martha's, and yours. I'm still going through them, but I already found something you should probably know about."

Lisa hated to ask. In fact, she hated to ask so much that she put down the breadstick she'd been about to bite into before it even touched her mouth. And she loved Joe Bologna's breadsticks. "Like what?"

"Eat your salad." He made sure she obeyed before continuing. "To begin with, you have the same blood type as your father. That's nothing definitive, but it means that we can't rule out that you are your parents' biological child."

"Okay." She waited, watching him eat. Knowing Scott as well as she did, she knew there was more.

"Apparently, you were one sick little girl

when you were born."

Lisa frowned. "I was?"

"You didn't know?"

She shook her head. "No one's ever said anything to me about it."

"You were premature — a seven-month baby. Barely five pounds."

"I knew that." She remembered the pictures she had seen of her tiny, wizened-looking newborn self being cradled by Martha and, yes, Barty in the hospital immediately after her birth.

"And according to your medical records, you were born with ARPKD — autosomal recessive polycystic kidney disease." He recited the name as though he'd spent some time memorizing it.

"I take it that's bad."

He nodded. "Seventy-five percent of babies born with it die before their first birthday."

"Really." Lisa quit eating to frown at him. "I've always been perfectly healthy. At least, as far back as I can remember."

The waitress came to replace the salads with their entrées. Lisa inhaled the aroma of the lasagna she'd ordered and knew she wasn't going to be able to eat much of it. There was a knot in her stomach.

"You must be one of the lucky twenty-five

percent." Scott tucked into his own spaghetti and meatballs with no difficulty that she could see. He'd clearly been hungry, and despite the tension she was feeling, she smiled at the rate at which his meal was disappearing.

"I've never heard of — what did you call it?"

"It's called ARPKD. Eat your lasagna."

"I'm not really hungry." But because he was watching her instead of eating himself, she took a bite. "They must have gotten it taken care of when I was little, because I don't remember ever being treated for anything like that. In fact, the only time I remember being sick is when I had chicken pox when I was six."

"A lot of the children who survive have lingering symptoms."

Lisa shook her head, and with his eyes on her ate some more. "I've always been perfectly healthy."

"Yeah, I know. At least, I thought so."

"I'll ask my mother."

"You do that. I'll be interested to hear what she has to say."

Lisa hesitated. He must have sensed something, because he looked at her questioningly. "I found out what the mark on my doll meant." Until the words came out of her mouth, she hadn't been sure she meant to tell him. She continued almost reluctantly. "You know, the MBF surrounded by a heart."

When she paused again his eyes narrowed at her. "You going to tell me the rest, or am I supposed to guess?"

Again she hesitated, because she now saw the information as one more step on the slippery slope she was no longer so certain she wished to tread. But in the end she did tell him, and by the time she had finished they were on their way out of the restaurant. The rain had stopped, she was glad to see, but clouds hung ominously low and dark overhead. Puddles lay everywhere, sparkling in the streetlights that were already coming on. The heat was so thick that it was like walking through a steam room. It was only about six-thirty, early for a summer night, but it seemed more like full twilight.

"I don't want to do this," she said as he got into the car beside her. He was driving again, an automatic thing on his part, it seemed, and one she wasn't in the mood to dispute. He didn't reply, just started the car and pulled out onto the street while she stared blindly at the oncoming traffic.

"Did you hear me?" She turned her head to look at him. "I don't want to do this.

Continue with the investigation, I mean. I want to stop it right now. I want to walk away."

"I heard you." Most of the cars had their headlights on, and bright yellow beams slashed across the front seat. He was looking grim. "All in all, I think it's probably a wise choice."

Lisa didn't say anything more for a moment as an image of the Garcias took center stage in her mind's eye. It was the picture, of course, the one from the file, the one in which Angela Garcia looked enough like her to be her double. Her heart ached for them. Her conscience smote her. Her need to know what had become of them would live inside her forever, she knew. But there were other ties, closer ties, ultimately unbreakable ties, to consider, and those, she knew without a shadow of a doubt, had to take precedence.

"It's Barty," she burst out, clasping her hands tightly together. "I can't do it. He's my father."

The words sounded as though they had been wrenched out of her.

"I know." Scott's voice was quiet. She knew he *did* know, and the knowledge provided some small degree of solace.

"I despise him. He deserted my mother

and me. He's ignored me practically all my life." She laughed, a tremulous, angry sound with nothing of amusement in it. "I called him this afternoon to ask about the doll. He didn't pick up. He didn't call back. Where I'm concerned, he just doesn't want to know." She took a deep breath. "But I can't stand the thought that he might be arrested for murder, much less tried and convicted. Even if he got off, the scandal would ruin him, professionally and probably financially. Then there's his family — his *other* family. I don't know why I care that it would tear them apart, but I do." The look she shot him was full of naked anguish. "How stupid is that?"

"It isn't stupid. It's human. Hell, I'm still telling myself that somewhere deep inside, my father is a decent human being." His twisted smile spoke volumes. Her eyes just touched on the scrape on his cheek before meeting his. "Truth is, families are a bitch."

They had reached the hospital now, and he was parking not too far from the entrance. "I had a feeling you were going to react this way, once you figured out where this thing was headed."

"It's wrong. I know it's wrong to just turn our backs on this. What happened to the Garcias needs to be uncovered. They deserve justice." She broke off, took a deep breath. "But he's my damned *father.*"

She could feel the unwelcome sting of tears, and angrily blinked them back.

He turned off the ignition, then unbuckled his seat belt and her own.

"I know," he said again. Then he leaned over and kissed her. And she wrapped her arms around his neck and kissed him back and clung to him like he was the only solid thing in her world.

Later, when she was in her mother's hospital room and Scott had left with Andy, her mother smiled at her.

"So, Annalisa, when were you going to tell me — about Scott?"

Lisa looked at her mother in surprise. Martha was sitting in her wheelchair — the nurses now made it a point to keep her out of bed for a good portion of the day — and Lisa was curled in the chair beside her, feeding Martha her evening meal, which rested on the small table between them. In her opinion, Martha looked better than she had since arriving in the hospital. All the tubes and monitors had been removed, and she used oxygen only at night, as she had for months. She was dressed, she had a hint of color in her cheeks, and her eyes were bright. It was difficult to accept that she was actually getting worse. Lisa felt her stomach churn at the thought and tried to banish it. Along with the knowledge that soon, probably as soon as her mother had finished her supper, she was going to have to tell her about tomorrow's planned move to a nursing home.

"What about Scott?" she asked.

"You and he . . ." Her mother's voice trailed off, but her expression left Lisa in no doubt about her meaning. Then she remembered that quick kiss in front of the elevators the previous night with Martha's friends as witnesses, and had little doubt that her mother's phone had been ringing with the news as soon as the women had awakened.

Busted, she thought, but she didn't really care.

"Okay, so I'm dating Scott," she admitted, although "dating" didn't quite cover it. No way was she getting any more graphic with her mother, however. "It's not that big of a deal, and I was going to tell you one of these days. Maybe. If it lasted long enough to talk about."

No need to let her mother start thinking this was some deathless romance. Not until she herself had had time to get over the surprise of it, and the heat that sizzled between them whenever they were in each other's company had died down to a manageable level, and she had caught her breath to the point where she could see the way ahead a little more clearly. At some point her plan had always been to head back to Boston. . . .

"When did — this start?" Although her mother was clearly trying to be low-key, she was looking at her as though Lisa had just given her the best present possible. If ever delight had shined from someone's face, it was shining now from Martha's.

"Fourth of July. We were at the country club and we just — clicked." The PG version was all her mother was going to get, and it was clearly enough for her. She beamed.

"I'm so — glad. I've always — liked him. Ever since you — came back — I've been thinking — he's perfect for you. You should . . ."

A nurse tapped on the open door then, interrupting, and walked into the room as Martha broke off. Lisa looked a question at the nurse.

"Dr. Spencer asked me to tell you that he's made arrangements for an ambulance to take Mrs. Grant to the Worley Center at ten. They'll be expecting her."

Martha had been looking at the nurse. Now she frowned and turned bewildered eyes on Lisa, who abruptly put down the spoonful of applesauce she'd been holding.

"The Worley Center?" Martha asked. "What's this?"

Martha knew what the Worley Center was. They had even talked about the possibility that she might have to be placed there one day, when the ALS drew near to its inevitable end. But she had always wanted to die at home, and Lisa had promised to do her utmost to keep her there. Now, however, it just wasn't possible.

"Thank you," Lisa said to the nurse, who nodded and left the room. Then she looked at her mother.

"You're being released tomorrow." Drawing on her reserves of inner strength, she summoned a cheerful tone, as if she was giving her mother good news. "Since we can't go back to Grayson Springs just yet, Dr. Spencer suggested the Worley Center."

Martha wasn't fooled. "It's getting — worse, isn't it?"

Lisa knew she meant the ALS. With every fiber of her being she wanted to lie, wanted to deny what Dr. Spencer and the tests had said, wanted to allay the fear she saw in her mother's eyes.

But what felt like a long time ago now, when she had first come back home, she had promised her mother that where her illness was concerned, she would tell her nothing but the truth.

"Yes," she said.

The color leached from Martha's face like someone had pulled a plug, allowing it to drain away.

"Ah." Martha's fingers curled around the arms of her chair.

"You wouldn't be going there tomorrow if Grayson Springs hadn't burned," Lisa said swiftly, moving to crouch in front of her mother's chair. "The disease hasn't progressed to the point that you really need that kind of care yet. It's just that you can't go home, and . . ."

"The end's coming," Martha finished for her. She was looking down at Lisa. Her fingers had relaxed, and her expression was quite calm now. "That's all right. I'm all right. I've known it — somewhere inside — for a while, I think. I'm not afraid, and — I don't want you to worry about me. It's just that — Annalisa, could you — take me home? Tonight? Just for a little while? I'm afraid I'll — go into that place — and never come — out again."

"Mother . . ."
"Please, Annalisa."
"It's raining."
"Please."

30

"This is — fun." Color had crept back into Martha's cheeks, and her face was more animated than Lisa had seen it in a long time. "I've never — run away — from a hospital before."

Lisa knew that her mother's outward gaiety was largely assumed for her benefit. Her own heart was heavy, but still she managed a smile. They were in the Jaguar, with her mother strapped into the passenger seat beside her and her wheelchair folded into the trunk. If Martha hadn't weighed about as much as a sack full of nothing, Lisa would never have managed getting her into the car on her own. But Martha was so tiny now that it hadn't been hard, like lifting a child, and with the seat back upright and the seat belt locked in place, she was as secure in the passenger seat as she would have been in her wheelchair. Lisa had a great many reservations about this, but she wasn't proof against her mother's pleas — her mother never asked for anything for herself — or the yearning she saw in her eyes.

Plus she had a terrible suspicion that Martha was right: Once she was established in the Worley Center, she would probably never come out again.

Her heart ached at the thought.

So she drove through the gathering darkness toward Grayson Springs, listening to the intermittent hiccup of the windshield wipers that she had turned on to combat the drizzle, watching the neon glow of passing strip malls and the gleam of headlights hitting shiny, wet streets, pretending to a lightheartedness she did not feel.

"Dr. Spencer's going to yell at me if he finds out." Lisa glanced mock-reproachfully at her mother.

Her mother chuckled. "I'll take the blame." Her head turned as she looked out at her surroundings. "It's so good to be — out of that hospital. Could you — roll down the window? I want to — smell the rain."

Lisa obligingly rolled her window down about halfway. She chose her window rather than the passenger one because she didn't want the full force of the wind blowing in on her mother. The warm, damp air with its earthy smell rushed into the car, ruffling her mother's hair, lifting tendrils of her own, the bulk of which was confined in a ponytail, to whip around her face. She tucked them behind her ears with one hand.

Martha inhaled.

"I used to love — rainy nights. You were born — on a rainy night."

"Was I?"

"*Mm-hmm.* I remember — your daddy rushing me to the hospital — through the rain. Of course — that night — I had other things on my mind. Like having you. You came — early, you know. I was — so scared. But excited. So excited to be — a mother."

"Was I sick when I was born?" The question had been burning in her mind ever since Scott had told her about the medical records, but she hadn't liked to just abruptly spring it on her mother. With such an opening, though, she couldn't resist. "With something called ARPKD, or whatever?"

Martha glanced at her in surprise. "How did you know? You were — indeed. When you were born — you seemed fine. You were small — but you were early — and I thought that was — all it was. Everybody did. Then — the next day — they told me — you had a very serious disorder. It was something — to do with your — kidneys. ARPKD. I'd never — heard of it. But they said — you might not live. They said most babies — who had it — died." She went quiet for a moment. Glancing at her, Lisa saw that her face had gone almost gray.

"Mother —" she said sharply, fearing that something was wrong.

"I'm all right." Martha looked at her. "I was just — remembering. It was — the worst moment — of my life. I was so — afraid. If you had died — I would have died, too."

"But I didn't. I got well."

Martha smiled. "Yes. Thank God. I prayed, you know. I got down on my knees — by your little bassinet — and I begged God to — leave me my daughter. The doctors said — there was no way to know — if you were one of the ones who would live — or not. Three quarters died — within months. They wanted — to keep you there — but I took you home. To Grayson Springs. It was — the right decision. Mama and Daddy — took care of us both. I never left your side. I held you, and I cried, and I prayed. I prayed day and night. And you got better. You were fine. You *are* fine. It was a miracle, Annalisa. A miracle — for us both."

"You never told me."

"I hated remembering. It was — a terrible

time. And you had — gotten well. I was — afraid to jinx it. Afraid that if — I thought about it — or talked about it — the thoughts or words would go out into — the universe, I guess — and you would get sick again." She smiled. "That sounds stupid, doesn't it? But I was — so afraid. And you've been so — healthy. Except for the chicken pox — you've hardly been sick."

They were out of the city now, driving along the two-lane road that led to Woodford County. Here beyond the reach of any streetlights it was dark as pitch, and Lisa switched to her high beams. In her rearview mirror, she could see the lights of maybe two other cars, one close, one farther away. The rain was picking up, and a fat drop blew in to splatter on her shoulder. She would have closed the window if she had been alone. But her mother liked the smell.

"The chicken pox was bad, though." Lisa tried to lighten the mood. "I remember feeling like my skin was on fire, it itched so much."

"And you always wanted — to scratch. I had to put you in — baking-soda baths."

"That just made me itch more!"

Martha laughed. "It was supposed to — bring all the pox out — so that you recovered faster."

Lisa laughed, too. "That was torture, Mother. Of your own child, too. You should be ashamed."

They were nearing thc bridge that marked the boundary with Woodford County. She could just see its low stone walls, denser than the night as they arched against the dark sky. Below it, the river rolled past black as oil, and Lisa realized that the water had risen almost to the top of the banks. Very much more rain and it would flood.

"I'm glad about — you and Scott," her mother said. "The thing I've hated — most — is the idca that you'll be — all alone when I'm gone."

Lisa cast her a quick frowning look. "You're not going anywhere for a while yet. And as for Scott and me, well, we'll just have to see where it goes."

"I wish I . . ." Her mother began, only to have her words cut off abruptly as something slammed hard into the car from behind. Lisa screamed as the Jag was catapulted forward. The shriek of metal crunching metal rent the night.

The jolt snapped Lisa's head back into the headrest. Her eyes went wide. Her heart leaped. Her hands clenched the wheel. Instinctively she slammed on the brakes. The tires shuddered and screeched as they fought for purchase to no avail. The back end started to fishtail on the wet pavement. The smell of burning rubber reached her through the open window.

"Annalisa," her mother cried.

Galvanized with fear, Lisa jerked the wheel to the right, toward the center of the road, and might possibly even have regained control if the rear wheels hadn't left the pavement and taken the front pinwheeling after it. The car bumped and rocked and skidded over grass that felt slippery as ice. The tall trees edging the road loomed terrifyingly close. Her foot was to the floor, jammed down on the brake. Horror flooded her as she felt something in the brake assembly snap, and suddenly there was no resistance at all beneath her foot. The pedal went flat against the floor.

The brakes are gone.

Disbelief suspended her every faculty for an instant. Time slowed down, stretched out. Her heart hammered. Her pulse pounded. Her mouth went dry. Foot straining against the now useless brake pedal, fighting the wheel as if she might actually be able to alter their course, Lisa realized that she was helpless. The car was out of control. The edge of the bridge flashed past the windshield as they spun. Another vehicle streaked through her line of vision, lights blazing, at right angles to the Jag. Then they were flying backward, shooting out into nothingness. Gasping with horror, Lisa found herself looking back the way they had come: at trees and fields and oncoming headlights silhouetted against a black sky.

The Jaguar tilted with its trunk downward and dropped like a stone. Heart thundering, stomach plummeting along with the car, she heard screams that she only dimly recognized were her own and her mother's. Frozen with horror, she realized that they were plunging into the river only an instant before they hit with a tremendous splash.

Something smacked her hard in the face, violent as a punch. She saw stars, but a wave of lukewarm water surging through the open window sent a life-saving rush of adrenaline rocketing into her veins that restored her to her senses almost instantly. What had hit her was the air bag; it was already deflating. They were in the river. Water was filling the car. It was sinking, back end first, the headlights slicing up toward the low-hanging night sky. She glimpsed the silver sparkle of raindrops falling through their beams. Inside the car, it was dark and claustrophobic and terrifying. As she shoved the limp air bag out of her way, she saw that the backseat was already almost submerged. The Jag was slipping beneath the surface fast.

A jolt of icy panic shot down her spine.

"Mother!" she cried, her eyes slewing toward Martha as she fought to free herself of her seat belt. Her mother was a shadowy pale figure lying limp as a rag doll in her seat. For one heart-stopping second Lisa thought she was unconscious, or even dead, but then Martha's head turned in her direction, her eyes gleaming through the darkness, and Lisa felt a quiver of relief. They had at best only a few minutes, Lisa judged. She hit the horn, in sharp, hard blasts in hopes that someone might hear and realize that they had gone into the river. There had been cars behind them; the vehicle that had hit them — where was it? Where were its occupants? They had to be nearby. She screamed out the window for help even as she struggled with her seat belt. Her hands shook, her fingers were clumsy, the seat belt clasp wouldn't release. Water sloshed between the front seats, licking at the console, getting her wet, rising fast as it worked to swallow the car. Black and swirling, it gurgled as it tried to suck them down.

"Annalisa." Her mother's eyes were fastened on Lisa's face. The air bag hung down in front of her, limp now, like a tired ghost. Her fingers twitched frantically in her lap.

"I'm going to get you out." Fighting to stay calm, Lisa got her seat belt off and grabbed for her mother's, fumbled with it, yanked. The car was sinking fast. Water covered the console now. They were awash to the waist. Time was running out.

"No." Martha's voice was a hoarse, almost unrecognizable rasp. Her eyes, Lisa saw as she glanced up to meet them, were black with terror. "We're going to — go under any second. Leave me. I'm dying anyway. Annalisa . . ."

"I'm not leaving you." Lisa's voice was fierce. Her hands were underwater now as she struggled with the seat belt. "Damn it, why won't this thing . . . ?"

Turning her head for the window, she screamed for help again.

The seat belt unlocked. Water was reaching chest height, starting to pour in through the open window. Lisa could feel the rush of it hitting her back like a waterfall. Time was, she feared, down to seconds only. Already she thought she could feel a gathering suction, a sense of increasing pull.

Oh my God, if we don't get out of here we're going to drown.

In the distance she thought she could hear sirens.

The water swirled toward her shoulders, lapped at her mother's chin. Martha was gasping like a landed fish, her face ghastly white in the gloom. The harsh sound of her breathing filled the small space. Frantic with fear, screaming for help at the top of her lungs, Lisa grabbed her mother's arm and hauled her over the console with a strength born of desperation, closing her ears to the panicked sounds Martha made, to her jerky pleas for Lisa to leave her and go.

We have to get out.

If there were indeed sirens, she could no longer hear them. She couldn't hear anything above the sound of her own pulse thundering in her ears. The water was rising fast. It was warm, like a living creature, as it swirled and eddied around them. Only Lisa's head was above the surface now. Freed of the seat belt, her mother floated with her face turned up toward the ceiling. Paradoxically, it made moving her easier, as the water took her weight. Panting with terror, Lisa grabbed the edge of the open window and pulled herself and her mother toward it. She felt that there might be no more than a few heartbeats' worth of time left. The sensation that the car was sliding backward into the depths was suddenly pronounced.

"Help! We're in the water!" she screamed into the night.

It's too late. The car's going down.

She knew it instinctively. There was no time left to think or scream or do anything but get out of that car as the river surged up toward the roof. Swallowing what seemed like gallons of dirty-tasting river water, choking as it went up her nose and down her throat with as much thrust as if it was being shot from a fire hose, half blinded by the onslaught of it against her face, she forced herself through the incoming torrent. She slithered head and shoulders first out the window, pushing herself through the opening in the teeth of the rushing water that poured in now with terrifying force, gripping the top of the window frame with one hand as she thrust up with her feet against the seat until her head was completely above the surface. Gulping air, determined not to let go even to save herself, she held on to her mother's wrist for dear life. A desperate glance down at the scant inches of space remaining between the top of the window and the river told her nothing: She couldn't see her mother at all. All she could see was the black water pouring into the car and the gleam of the Jaguar's roof floating like a turtle's shell on the surface. But she could feel, and what she felt told her that Martha wasn't moving, not her head, not her hands or fingers. She wasn't even trying to grasp Lisa's hand anymore. She was as limp as — as a corpse. That dreadful thought made Lisa go cold with fright.

"Mother!" she cried, but of course Martha didn't answer, and she could only pray that her mother was still in a position where she could get air. Lisa was all the way out now; she was through the window, clinging to the window frame, kicking frantically to stay afloat. Heart pounding with fear and exertion, using the car for ballast and calling on every bit of strength and will she possessed, she finally managed to pull her mother out, too, dragging her through the torrent that gushed in the window, fighting against the water until her mother's head was above water. But Martha's eyes were closed. Her lips were slack. Her head lolled back so that only the pale oval of her face was visible above the blackness. Her limbs floated, limp as wet ribbons, bobbing in the current.

"Mother!" Lisa called to her, terrified, but Martha remained unresponsive. It took all

Lisa's strength to keep her from sinking again. Behind her she was vaguely aware of splashing sounds, of spurts of white water kicked up against the blackness, of flashing blue lights and shrieking sirens heading her way, but she was so focused on her mother that she registered those things only peripherally.

With one part of her mind she knew that people were coming, but she was afraid to the depths of her soul that they were too late.

There was a loud gurgle, and the car went down. Just like that. It happened so fast that she was still holding on to the edge of the window and had to let go. Hampered by her mother's weight, she made a convulsive effort to kick away, to swim. But the suction caught her, pulling her down, dragging her beneath the surface, grabbing at her mother as if she was engaged with the river in some life-or-death tug-of-war for her.

Sucked down in the Jaguar's wake, Lisa found herself caught in a vortex of choking wet blackness that rendered her blind and helpless. It whirled her downward with such strength and unexpectedness that her mother's wrist was wrenched out of her hold.

No!

Frantically she snatched at the water in

every direction, trying to find her mother again, opening her eyes and enduring the sting of it but unable to see anything at all. Lungs full to bursting, knowing that she was just seconds from drowning herself, she had to give up. Clawing for the surface, she fought instinctively to reach air, while inside her head Lisa screamed and screamed and screamed.

31

It was hours before her mother's body was recovered. Lisa stood on the riverbank all that time, wrapped in a blanket that someone had draped over her shoulders, shaking until her body passed beyond that stage, crying until there were no more tears, adamantly refusing to leave. As she talked to the police, telling them about the accident, learning from them that it was a hit-and-run, that the other vehicle involved hadn't even stopped but had, instead, fled the scene, Scott arrived. Summoned at her request by the police, who had asked her if there was anyone she wanted them to call, he appeared within fifteen minutes of the time she was pulled from the water by a cop who'd tied a rope around a tree and come in after her at considerable risk to his own life.

As soon as she had seen Scott, she'd melted into his arms. He'd stayed with her ever since, holding her when she cried, conferring with the rescue teams in low-voiced conferences that she wasn't meant to overhear, acting as a buffer with the police, keeping the media away from her.

The rain had stopped, but the night stayed dark and overcast and a light wind blew. It carried the smell of the river on it, a smell that now made her nearly catatonic with horror and fear. She couldn't take her eyes from it, or tear her thoughts away from the terrible picture of her mother lost in its depths. Police cars and rescue vehicles lined the road, their flashing lights bright as colored sparklers in the dark. TV trucks crowded in beside the official vehicles. Their spotlights shone out over the river, illuminating the scene for their viewers who were watching the rescue efforts live at home. Lisa knew they were on TV because Nola arrived, breathless and stunned at what had happened, to tell her so and to be with her. Joel came, too, with his father, as did Robin and Andy and Lynn and, it seemed, practically everyone she or her mother knew until a crowd had gathered to stand vigil. Kept back from the water's edge by hastily erected barricades, they huddled on the wet bank in an amorphous, murmuring group that watched in dread as patrol boats swept the river with searchlights and helicopters circled overhead, turning their beams on the racing water, too, so that it was crisscrossed with light and churning with activity.

It was Scott on whom she leaned during that terrible time, Scott into whose arms she turned when one of the boats searching the river radioed back that they had found her, Scott who supported her when her mother was brought to shore and pronounced dead and taken away.

It was Scott who took her home with him, although Nola as well as a weeping Robin and Andy wanted to step in, wanted her to go with them. She just shook her head at them and went with him, leaning on his strength, instinctively seeking comfort from the person whose presence most comforted her. It was Scott who put her in a hot shower, summoned a doctor, got her some sedatives, and put her to bed, lying down with her and holding her close and letting her cry in his arms until at last exhaustion claimed her and she fell asleep. It was Scott who was there when she woke up, who fixed her scrambled eggs and toast and made sure that she ate some of it, who went with her to the funeral home to make arrangements, who took care of her in a thousand and one ways in the first terrible days after her mother's death.

If it hadn't been for Scott, she couldn't have gotten through it.

He was a rock, as she had always suspected he would be in times of trouble.

After the first two days, when he barely left her side, he had to return to work, but he made sure she was never alone, although that meant his apartment — a big, airy, loft-style space on the top floor of a newly converted former downtown warehouse — always had people in it. Nola was there with her for hours at a time. In fact, it was because of Nola that she made a slightly unsettling discovery. Nola brought over some photo albums, and in looking through them in search of pictures of her mother to display at the funeral home, she found pictures of herself, at maybe two or three years old, sitting on the front steps of Grayson Springs while a dog lay panting at her feet. The dog was big and black, a dead ringer, she thought, for the dog in the picture with the Garcias, and the caption, written neatly in her mother's hand beneath the picture, read *Annalisa and Lucy.*

So, there had been a dog named Lucy after all, although it had apparently belonged to her family and not to the Garcias.

It was one more troubling coincidence, but almost as soon as she stumbled across it, she let it slide from her mind. All her energy had to go toward simply making it through the next few days.

Nola was not the only one to keep her company. Robin and Andy, nearly as riven with grief as she was, practically haunted the place, and paradoxically in attempting to comfort them she found some comfort for herself. Joel came, and for her sake he and Scott were perfectly civil. Barty stopped in with Jill and the boys, and stayed for the obligatory half-hour condolence call. For the first time ever Lisa was thankful for the existence of his second family, because their presence kept her from having to talk much to Barty, which she could hardly bring herself to do, given the terrible thing she was now pretty sure she knew about him. Not that he seemed to want to talk to her, either: Jill and her sons were left to carry the conversational load, while the few words she and Barty exchanged were as stilted and uncomfortable on his part as they were on hers.

Other friends visited, bearing flowers and cards and various other tokens of sympathy. Chase was in and out. So were the other kids, and Rinko and Jantzen. Scott's brother, Ryan, who Lisa only vaguely remembered, came over several times. Martha's friends were there in force, bringing with them full meals, soups, desserts, breads, so many that Scott soon ran out of room in his refrigerator, and every night devolved into an impromptu dinner party for whoever was over at that time. Most of the prosecutor's office dropped by, which meant that any hope of keeping her and Scott's relationship private had pretty much flown out the window by the end of the week. Not that she cared. She was too grief-stricken to care about much of anything, and Scott gave no indication that having everyone who worked for him know that they were a couple bothered him.

If it was going to be a problem, it was a problem that could be dealt with later. After the funeral, after the media hoopla had died down, after the police had found and charged the hit-and-run driver. What they were going to charge him with was still up in the air. The obligatory autopsy (which Lisa could hardly bear to think about) had revealed that Martha had not drowned, as Lisa had feared. Her heart had simply given out under the stress of the accident. Given Martha's physical condition, the charge was more likely to be manslaughter than murder.

Unless . . .

"What if it wasn't an accident?"

The suspicion had been in her head almost since the moment the Jaguar had been struck, but it had taken days — until this moment, in fact — before Lisa felt strong enough to voice it. It was Sunday night, almost eleven-thirty, and the funeral was scheduled for the next day, Monday at five. She had spent most of the day at the funeral home, where Martha lay closed inside the beautiful bronze casket that Scott had helped her choose, where the line of people who had come to offer her a few words of condolence had stretched out the door and around the corner without letup for hours. At ten, Scott had taken her out of there despite the fact that some people still lingered, and she was now curled in a corner of his couch flipping channels as she sought anything to watch but the news, which featured regular updates on the accident that had claimed the life of the owner of the fabled Grayson Springs farm. The couch, like the matching chairs at either end, was black leather. The TV was a forty-two-inch plasma affixed to one of the exposed brick walls that was a feature of the combined living/dining/kitchen area. A number of steel-framed floor-to-ceiling windows, shades still open to the night because the height made it impossible for anyone to see in, looked out over Lexington's sparkling skyline. Highly polished oak floors and chrome-and-glass tables added to the clean, contemporary look. There were two bedrooms, a master with a king-size bed, which she and Scott now shared, and another, which he had turned into a home office, and two and a half baths. It was all very sleek and modern, the perfect bachelor pad. To Lisa, it now felt like home.

"The crash?" Scott came out of the open galley kitchen where he'd been feeding the remains of their take-out dinner down the garbage disposal. They had both showered (separately, because sex, even phenomenal sex with Scott, was the last thing on Lisa's mind these days, and he seemed to appreciate how she felt, and thus had made no moves even though she slept in his arms every night) and changed clothes since arriving back from the funeral home. He was wearing ratty gray sweatpants and a white tee that hugged his broad shoulders and clung to the muscles of his wide chest, while she had on a thin cotton summer nightgown covered up by his big blue terry-cloth robe, which she had borrowed and wore belted snugly around her waist. Her hair was loose;

her legs and feet were bare. "It's possible. But I checked, and your father was at a fund-raiser that night. A hundred people saw him there."

His answer told her that he'd been suspicious, too, and acknowledged the fact that if the accident wasn't in fact an accident, if the death of her mother was the result of a deliberate act, then the most likely reason would be because of Lisa's connection to the Garcia case, which would make the most likely perpetrator their prime suspect, her father.

The thought tore at Lisa's soul.

She could feel her heart start to thump with agitation. "I wouldn't expect him to do something like that himself."

"No, probably not."

"If he was involved — he killed my mother." Her voice shook. "If he did it — if he had someone do it — I want to go after him. For the Garcias and everything. I don't care if he is my damned father."

"If he did anything that led to Miss Martha's death, all bets are off," he agreed, stopping beside the couch to look down at her. "I'm already having that angle checked out, okay? You trust me to do that, don't you?"

She nodded. The truth was, she would

trust him with anything.

"Then stop worrying about it. I'll let you know what comes up." Scott dropped down on the couch beside her and took the remote out of her hand. "You want to watch a movie?"

She looked at him. One arm draped casually behind her, his legs sprawled out in front of him, and he was clicking through the On Demand listings. His hair was tousled, his jaw was unshaven, and he looked really tired. *No wonder,* she thought. He had a couple of big trials under way, plus the usual stuff that came through the DA's office on a regular basis, and over the last week he'd been staying up half the night with her because without the sedatives, which she was no longer taking, she couldn't sleep. When she did, she woke up screaming as the accident replayed itself in her mind.

Watching movies together late at night had become something they did.

Shifting positions, she curled against his side and rested her head on the now familiar pillow of his shoulder. Glancing down at her, he slid his arm around her and then smiled at her as their eyes met.

"You are so good to me," she told him. "Thank you."

"No thanks required." His voice was a

little dry. He looked back at the TV. "How about *Independence Day?*"

"Sounds good." She'd already learned that he had a penchant for action movies. Settling in comfortably, she prepared to pass the next two and a half hours in a state of near-mindless numbness that was preferable to the alternative.

By the time the final credits rolled, they were both stretched out at full length on the couch, and Lisa had fallen asleep.

She only became aware of it when she felt herself being picked up. Her eyes snapped open, she saw nothing but a whole lot of dark, and she stiffened in sudden panic.

"It's okay. The movie's over, you fell asleep, and I'm taking you to bed." Scott's voice provided instant reassurance. He was carrying her. She could see him as her eyes grew accustomed to the dark, and she relaxed against him, curling her arms around his neck. No harm could come to her if Scott was there: That was the thought that flitted through her mind as a week's worth of exhaustion finally overcame her and she fell asleep again before he had even put her down on the bed.

Only to dream, terribly, of her mother's white-faced body floating in the black depths of the river.

She woke up and sat bolt upright, shaking and gasping for air.

"Lisa?" Scott sounded sleepy. She glanced around at him. There was enough light coming through the windows to allow her to see, she discovered, although the bedside clock said it was three twenty-two a.m. and the room was dark. She had been sleeping in his arms, and he had rolled onto his back when she sat up. Now he lay there, his head on his pillow, the covers twisted around his waist — he slept in his boxers, so his chest was bare — blinking at her. Hands clenching, she fought to keep the hysteria that clutched at her out of her voice. There was no need for them both to pass sleepless nights.

"I'm fine. Go back to sleep." She was proud of how steady her voice was.

He made a sound that was part snort, part unamused laugh, and caught her arm, tugging her down beside him. Craving the comfort he offered, she didn't resist, letting him pull her against him, wrapping her own arm around his waist as his arms came around her. He felt warm and solid and wonderfully safe against her, and she gave up the fight to suffer alone and snuggled close.

"Bad dream?" he asked.

She nodded. Then she took a deep breath.

"I miss her." She couldn't help it. Her voice was wobbly. "All my life — she was there. She was the only real family I have."

"Nah," Scott said. "You've got me."

Lisa closed her eyes. "She loved you."

"She asked me to take care of you, you know. In her hospital room, one night when you were busy talking to Loverboy out there in the hall. I promised her I would." He paused, and she felt him tense a little. "She knew I was in love with you almost before I figured it out myself, I think."

Lisa's eyes opened. For a moment she forgot to breathe. She stared at him, wishing there was more light so that she could see something of his expression instead of just the shadowy outline of his face and the gleam of his eyes.

"What did you just say?" she asked faintly.

"You heard me: I'm in love with you."

"You're in love with me." Her tone made it a statement rather than a question. She was surprised — and yet she wasn't. The connection between them that had always been there, the chemistry, even the friction and baiting and occasional bouts of intense dislike: What else could it add up to? "Oh my God, Scott."

His body still felt tense against hers. " 'Oh

my God, Scott'? What the hell does that mean?"

Lisa sucked in air.

"It means I'm in love with you, too," she said, the words very clear, very sure. Then she slid an arm around his neck and slithered up his body and kissed him.

"I love you." This time he said it against her mouth, in a husky murmur as she pressed her lips to his, and when she replied in kind, he kissed her back and his arms came hard around her and he rolled with her. Then they went up in flames, the two of them, their bodies coming together in a kind of spontaneous combustion that burned away everything else with its heat.

Afterward, for the first time since her mother's death, Lisa slept dreamlessly, wrapped in his arms.

The funeral was every bit as bad as she had imagined it would be. The only thing that kept her from breaking down completely was Scott's stalwart presence at her side. The church was filled to overflowing, and local media was out in force. At the grave site, the police had to set up a barricade to keep the television crews at bay. Then, later, they went to the country club for the expected after-burial reception that was traditionally held at the home of the deceased, which unfortunately everyone understood was not possible in this case. Lisa was standing there in the main dining room in her sleeveless black funeral sheath and black pumps, red-eyed and pink-nosed but tearless now, as she was all cried out. She was trying to make polite conversation with one of her mother's many friends while hardly knowing what she was saying when Scott came up to her.

"Excuse us a minute, would you please?" he said to the old lady, who gave him an admiring smile. Which didn't surprise Lisa, because in his black suit and tie he was looking very hot. He took her arm and steered her out to a back hallway, where, except for a few of the wait-staff, they were alone.

"What is it?" It had taken her a moment to notice how grim he was looking, but now that she did she felt a stirring of alarm.

"Detective Watson just called. He wants us to head out to Grayson Springs as soon as we can." He hesitated, his hand sliding restlessly up and down her bare arm. "They've found a baby's skeleton buried in the garden."

32

By the time they reached Grayson Springs, a crowd had gathered. Lisa was almost glad of it, because being surprised at the sheer number of people she could see behind the house and the variety of vehicles parked in the driveway and on the lawn served to lessen the ache that seeing the house caused her. The house was such a potent reminder of her mother that she felt a wave of grief just looking at it.

Suck it up, she ordered herself fiercely as she felt the sting of tears at the back of her eyes. The last thing she wanted to do was cry in front of strangers — or TV cameras.

Besides a number of police cars, of course, and an ambulance and the Woodford County coroner's van and another official van that she thought belonged to the forensics unit, trucks from three different TV stations were present. There were other work truck–type vehicles she suspected must belong to the construction workers who were still on the scene, although their work almost certainly had been stopped by the grisly discovery. A large number of other random cars apparently belonged to the small crowd of neighbors and curiosity seekers that was bunched not far beyond the porte cochere, craning their necks in the direction of the walled gardens.

Scott pulled into the grass and drove around the massed vehicles to the side of the house, getting as close to the scene as he could before parking the Jeep. Then they walked the rest of the way to where maybe a dozen official-looking types bustled in and around the back garden. Obviously having been barred from coming any closer, camera crews were filming from the periphery, and one TV reporter recognized Lisa and called to her, inviting her over for an interview. Lisa shook her head and kept walking. Crime scene tape cordoned off the gardens, but Scott lifted it for Lisa to duck under and followed suit himself. Near the back porch, a knot of construction workers, hard hats in hand, stood talking to a uniformed police officer who was taking notes. The foreman, Bill Bruin, whom Lisa had talked to several times, waved at her, and she waved back. A yellow bulldozer had been abandoned near the Baby's Garden, and as they drew closer, Lisa saw that part of the brick wall surrounding it had been knocked down and the fountain itself had toppled over. A woman in the blue jumpsuit of the Woodford County forensics unit was taking pictures of the area where the fountain had stood, and two men in blue jumpsuits knelt beside the hole that had been left when the fountain had fallen over. The surrounding roses were in full, colorful bloom, but their scent was even stronger than it should have been, which, Lisa discovered as she and Scott reached the entrance to the garden and started walking down the brick path toward the fountain, was because a number of the bushes had been crushed.

Detective Watson had been staring down at the hole where the fountain had been. He glanced up as they neared him, then headed toward them. The three of them met just a few feet from where the forensics team now worked with such care.

"Miss Grant. Buchanan." He nodded at her and shook Scott's hand, his expression grave. "First, let me say how sorry I am for the loss of your mother, Miss Grant."

"Thank you."

"What've you got?" Scott asked, his tone brusque.

"Like I told you on the phone: the skeleton of a baby. It was found buried back here under the fountain. Dozer driver lost control; the dozer backed over the brick wall and knocked into the fountain. When he moved his machine, he saw the skeleton." His eyes moved back to Lisa. "You ever heard of any baby being buried in your garden, Miss Grant?"

Lisa shook her head as a terrible coldness began to steal through her veins. If there was a baby buried in the garden, the question that had to be asked was: Whose baby? The property had belonged to her mother's family for generations.

"No."

Scott's hand curled around her arm. She could feel the steely strength in his fingers.

"How long has it been there?" He was talking to Detective Watson.

"Forensics will have to tell us that. Miss Grant, the question I want to ask you is, how long has that fountain been there?"

She couldn't ever remember the backyard without the Baby's Garden and its tinkling fountain.

"As long as I can remember." She took a deep breath. It had been a long, difficult day, and she was so tired she was beginning to feel light-headed. "You should ask Robin.

Or Andy. Mrs. Baker and Mr. Frye."

"I will. They live back there in the manager's house, don't they? Nobody seems to be home right now. I tried giving each of them a call on their cell phones, but they didn't answer."

Lisa had lost her phone along with her purse and other belongings in the accident. Without it, she had no way to check the time, but she knew it had to be around nine. Robin and Andy could be anywhere, of course, but in the days before the house had burned, they'd almost always been home at that time. Andy especially tended to go to bed early.

"They were at the funeral earlier." She was proud to be able to say that without so much as a tremor. "They must have stopped somewhere on the way home."

"When you say *baby,* what age child are we talking about?" Scott asked.

Detective Watson looked at him. "It was an infant, and my people say it was born alive. It wasn't a stillbirth or a late-term miscarriage. Other than that, we're going to have to wait until they can do some testing at the lab."

"How did" — Lisa couldn't bring herself to follow Scott's and Detective Watson's example and say "it" — "the baby die?"

Detective Watson shrugged. "That's another question for the lab."

"Boy or girl?" Scott was looking past Detective Watson toward the hole. Following his gaze, Lisa could see that they were lifting out a tiny skull. She suddenly felt faint.

"Girl."

"Scott." Lisa's knees were threatening to give way. "I'm going to go sit down on the wall for a minute. I'll be right here."

He glanced at her and nodded, his expression faintly distracted. His hand dropped away from her arm, and she turned thankfully away from the terrible sight and walked toward the lowest part of the wall, which was near the entrance. Dusk was moving on toward full night now, and the sun had set, although pink and orange streamers still shimmered just above the western horizon. It was hot and steamy, and mosquitoes and lightning bugs alike were out in force. A few stars had already popped into view, looking like diamonds glittering in a purple velvet sky. Reaching her destination, Lisa sat on the warm brick, took in the familiar, beloved surroundings, and wanted to drop her head into her lap and weep.

Mother.

She clenched her fists and firmed her lips

and concentrated on the here and now. On the baby in the garden, which was a terrible alternative but at least kept her from collapsing with grief. She was dizzy and sick. Her stomach heaved, and her head was starting to pound. Glancing back at Scott, she saw that he and Detective Watson had moved. They were now looking down at the open box the skeleton was being placed in, piece by careful piece, and appeared deep in conversation.

Lisa, shuddering, looked back toward the house.

And saw Robin through the kitchen window. Her red hair was unmistakable.

Lisa glanced around again, with the intention of alerting Detective Watson to Robin's presence. But he was still talking to Scott, and instead she decided that the thing to do would be to go tell Robin that Detective Watson wanted to talk to her.

She got up and headed toward the house, waving at the construction workers who were apparently giving statements one at a time to the cop, glancing to the left as she felt someone watching her, only to discover a TV camera turned her way. She hurried then, up the steps and across the porch and into the kitchen. Opening the back door and walking inside the house felt wholly familiar and at the same time almost obscene.

Her mother wasn't there.

If there'd been any kind of food inside her at all, she would have been in danger of throwing up.

You just have to keep going.

"Robin?" Lisa called, walking determinedly across the kitchen as a glance made it obvious that Robin had left the room. "Robin?"

Inside, the house was gloomy and still, as if it, too, mourned its mistress. Lisa went through the dining room — no Robin — and headed for the TV room, both of which were still relatively intact. Fortunately the curtains were open, so a good amount of light was available. Glancing around, Lisa was sad to see a layer of dust on every surface. And the smell — the house was starting to smell musty.

As if it, too, was dead.

She was just closing her eyes against the sudden onslaught of another wave of grief when she heard a sound behind her and opened them again.

"Robin?" Forcing a smile, she started to turn around — and then was knocked back into nothingness as something crashed with brutal force into the back of her head.

33

"Lisa?" Scott's voice was sharp with anxiety as, holding a flashlight he'd borrowed from a construction worker, he walked quickly through the parts of the house that were still accessible. It was dark in there, not so dark that he couldn't see, but shadowy and gray as the last vestiges of daylight faded away outside. A dozen or more people had seen her go in, they'd told him so when he'd turned around in the garden to discover that she was gone, but nobody had seen her come out. He'd followed her as soon as he'd realized where she was. Not more than ten minutes could have elapsed from the time he'd last seen her.

But he couldn't find her.

"Lisa!" He was yelling now, his voice echoing through the empty rooms, shouting for her with real panic as the flashlight beam darted into every last nook and cranny with no luck. "Lisa!"

Something was wrong. He could sense it, and a terrible fear seized him. His gut clenched, and cold sweat popped out on his brow. The house was silent. Too silent. If she'd been inside it, and able to hear and respond, she would have heard him by now and answered.

"Lisa!"

Heart pounding, he turned and sprinted out of the house, bellowing for Watson.

Lisa's head hurt so much she was woozy with it. She was also hot and cramped — suffocating, almost. Whatever she was on, or in, lurched and rattled. The surface beneath her was hard. There was no pillow, no support for her head: It bobbed painfully with every jolt. She was wedged in the most uncomfortable position imaginable, and when she tried to move, tried to stretch out her legs, she couldn't. There wasn't room even for her to turn onto her back. She drew in a shuddering breath of stale, dusty air and opened her eyes.

It was dark. Pitch-black. She could see absolutely nothing. She was lying down, on her left side, with her knees wedged tight against her chest and her arms drawn behind her back. She couldn't open her mouth — she tried — because something was plastered over it. Her wrists were strapped tightly together. So, she discovered, were her ankles.

Her heart began to slam in her chest.

Where am I? What's happened?

A series of quick impressions made her think she was in a box of some sort. A metal box, barely large enough to hold her folded body. She could feel its lid against her right shoulder; her bound hands were tight against its back, and her knees and shins strained against its front; her head was touching metal, and so were her — bare, she realized — feet.

Her blood ran cold. A scream gathered in the back of her throat as the truth burst upon her: *I've been kidnapped.*

The sheriff's department cordoned off the area, as everyone who was present was blocked from leaving. They searched the house from top to bottom, doing what they could to go into the sections of the house the fire had rendered inaccessible or even downright dangerous. They searched every vehicle on the property. They searched the barns, the grounds, the outbuildings. Within half an hour the place was crawling with sheriff's deputies and state police and even some of the Lexington cops who were

Scott's friends. They searched everywhere, and they found nothing.

Ten p.m. Ten-thirty. No trace of Lisa.

Scott was sweating bullets.

Watson had suggested that maybe she had simply gotten tired of waiting for him and caught a ride home. Scott had roared his rejection of that, but as a result he'd called his apartment so many times that his answering machine was now full. Ryan, who had gone by to check Scott's apartment at his request, just to make sure Lisa wasn't in there and for some reason not answering the phone, called back with a negative and then showed up in person, Chase in tow, to help in the search. Nola and Joel came after Scott called them both to check if Lisa could possibly be with either, only to get the answer he had expected: no. They were working the phones, going down the list of practically everyone Lisa knew. No one had seen her. No one had a clue where she could be. A number of the people they called came rushing to Grayson Springs. Outside the house, the atmosphere, despite the deadly desperation of the situation, gradually took on the air of a macabre carnival. The TV stations, cameras still in place, were having a field day. Not only was there a dead baby but a missing woman who was young, beautiful, the heiress to one of the world's most famous horse farms, and the recent survivor of a terrible accident that had killed her socialite mother. Breaking news, live at eleven!

Scott was going quietly insane. His blood had turned to ice in his veins and his pulse hammered relentlessly at his temples. It was all he could do not to pant with fear. Wherever she was, she was in trouble. Bad trouble. He knew it, with a gut-churning certainty that was tearing him apart. It required a tremendous effort of will to stay focused, to try to think. But he had to ride herd on his panic, for Lisa's sake.

There were only two real possibilities, as far as he could see. Either she was trapped somewhere in the house or someone had taken her.

He was putting his money down on taken.

That being the case, he had a pretty damned good idea about who had done it.

Whatever she was in — a truck, Lisa thought, a metal box in the back of a pickup truck — stopped. Her heart lurched as she heard the grinding of gears, the muffled slam of a door. *One door. One assailant.* She made the assessment automatically, with the part of her mind that had gone into ice-cold survivor mode. Which was how it had to be, if she was going to make it. Because the object of what was happening to her was for her to die. She harbored no illusions about that.

She'd been hit over the head and snatched from the TV room. Bound quickly with duct tape — because that was what, she had concluded by dint of rubbing her tongue around the sticky stuff covering her lips and straining against the bonds confining her wrists and ankles, had been used on her — and thrust into this horrible box. Driven away from Grayson Springs, and Scott, and any possibility of help. Now she guessed — feared — they had reached somewhere sufficiently remote for her to be killed.

Oh, God, will I vanish like the Garcias? Suddenly I'm just gone and nobody ever sees me again?

Terror washed over her at the thought. Her heartbeat went ragged. Her breathing became scarcely more than a shudder in her chest. Her hands and feet were numb, cold, dead — just like she would be dead soon if she didn't do something to save herself. Feverishly, using her nails, she clawed at the slick layers of tape around her wrists. Her shoes with their stiletto heels were in the box with her, although unfortunately not within reach of her hands. If she could just manipulate one of them into the right position, maybe she could use the heel to punch a hole in the tape around her ankles.

A loud rattle from the direction of her feet was followed by a pronounced bouncing of the truck.

Someone just jumped into the truck bed.

The knowledge galvanized her. Her heart slammed against her breastbone. Her body turned clammy with sweat. Nails scrabbling at the tape around her wrists, she shifted her legs as best she could, trying with savage intensity to loosen the tape that bound her ankles.

Too late, too late, too late . . .

A clanging blow to the box she was in made her jump. Her stomach cramped. Her heart stopped. She froze, not even daring to breathe. Not the right response but the instinctive one, like a scared rabbit staring into the teeth of a fox.

The lid opened with a loud creak. Sick with terror, Lisa found herself looking up at a dark, faceless figure that loomed over the box, blocking out the night.

Nostrils flaring, she drew in air through her nose.

Then she nearly jumped out of her skin as something came hurtling down at her, a fist holding something, a weapon, shiny silver metal in the moonlight. . . .

Heart thundering, cringing, trying uselessly to move or duck or somehow get out of the way, she felt a whoosh of air and then the blow fell, slamming hard into her skull.

She saw stars and then, for a while, a short while, she thought, nothing.

She thought the time that had passed was short because when she came to she was hanging, head down, over a man's shoulder. He was carrying her like that, in a fireman's carry, and for a moment she imagined that it must be the night Grayson Springs had burned. It took her a second to remember that it was not, to fully grasp what was happening, because she was dizzy and sick and disoriented, and her head hurt so much she wanted to cry out with pain, only she couldn't, there was still tape on her mouth, and on her wrists and ankles, too.

It was the presence of that tape that snapped her back into the present.

Bound and gagged, she was being carried through a dense woods by a man who was at any minute probably going to put her down and kill her.

At the realization, she was suddenly so terrified that her brain refused to function. Her heart went into frantic mode. She could taste the fear in her mouth, salty and acidic. Her instinct was to struggle, scream, try to escape. But she managed to clamp down on it in time.

If he knew she was awake, he would hit her again. She didn't think she could survive another blow like the last one. Her skull felt like it was broken now.

Think.

Oh my God, is this Barty? was the question that came to her.

The pain that thought caused her was almost worse than the pain in her head. How could he do this? Whatever else he was, he was her father.

He had to feel something for her, didn't he? Somewhere deep inside? So, maybe if she could get him to look at her, get him to listen, and she begged . . .

Then she didn't have any more time to think or do anything else but scream, raw, terrified screams that tore through her throat only to be muffled by the damned tape, because just as casually as if she was a sack of feed, he heaved her off his shoulder and tossed her down — what? She didn't know. All she knew was that she was helpless to save herself and she was falling a long, long way.

■ ■ ■ ■

Bart Grant had been in town for the funeral but had since gone home. Having been informed that his daughter was missing, he was on his way back to Lexington again. When Scott had inquired as to Grant's whereabouts, that's what Sanford Peyton, who'd rushed to Grayson Springs not long after his son and was presently ensconced in the kitchen making calls on his cell phone, had told him, adding that Grant was at that moment about twenty minutes out. Not wanting to give away his hand to this thuggish multimillionaire who seemed to have a finger in everything Grant did dating all the way back to before Lisa's birth, Scott had greeted the news with outward equanimity. On the way out of the kitchen, he'd even grabbed one of the sandwiches Mrs. Baker was busying herself with slapping together, in an attempt to feed the gathered troops, from supplies somebody had brought in, and spent a minute or so listening to her babble on about how devastated Miss Martha would be if she knew. She and Frye, who had finally gotten home after having, as they told Watson, gone for a long drive to clear their heads in the aftermath of the funeral, were reacting to this new calamity with abject horror. Trembling and pale, they were both more hindrance than help, in Scott's opinion. Having soothed Mrs. Baker to the best of his ability, Scott then had left Watson in charge of the search, tossed the sandwich away uneaten on his way out the door, and gone to wait in his Jeep at the end of the lane that led down to the house for Grant to show up. He meant to confront Grant himself, in private, before Grant had a chance to talk to anyone else. He didn't want to have Watson or any other law enforcement type going after Grant, because as soon as he told them what he knew, it lost its power. Once Grant found himself caught up in the legal system, he would make like a lawyer and shut up. If Grant had Lisa, if he knew where Lisa was, that could be fatal.

The thought sent a fresh burst of fear through him.

It was twelve minutes after Scott got in place before Grant showed up, his big white Lexus unmistakable even in the dark. Those were some of the longest minutes of Scott's life. He wasn't a religious man, but all that time — and it seemed like a lifetime — he was praying that it wasn't already too late.

Because if Grant was on his way to Grayson Springs, where the hell was Lisa?

"You sure about this? Dude's a judge, man." Ryan was riding shotgun as Scott pulled the Jeep across the end of the lane, blocking Grant's path. He'd asked Ryan to come with him because, when the shit hit the fan, as it was about to do, his brother was about the only one he could trust to help him do whatever illegal thing he might have to do and keep his mouth shut about it. His plan was to ask Grant nicely first, explaining what sort of information was going to come out if he didn't get Lisa back alive and well, and then if that didn't work, beat the bastard to a pulp until her whereabouts came oozing out of him.

Also, his always-ready-for-trouble big brother kept a highly illegal loaded gun in his glove compartment. Black and deadly, it was now in Scott's possession. He didn't mean to shoot Grant — at least, not unless he found out the bastard had harmed Lisa — but it would hurry things along.

Instead of answering, Scott rolled out of the Jeep and sprinted to waylay the Lexus as it braked at his makeshift roadblock.

"Shit," he heard Ryan say, but when he reached the Lexus's window — fool had already rolled it down, probably to ask what was up with the Jeep blocking his path —

and shoved the pistol in Grant's face, his brother, jiggling uneasily but there, was at his back.

"What the . . . ?" Grant gasped, gaping at him in disbelief even as Scott barked, "Get out of the car."

"Buchanan? Is that you? My God, have you lost your mind?"

"Get the fuck out of the car."

Because Grant was sputtering, not moving fast enough, Scott reached in, grabbed a handful of the slimy bastard's jacket, and practically yanked him out. Then he shoved him into the Lexus's backseat and got in with him, making sure he could see the gun, making sure Grant knew he had trouble. Ryan, having already been briefed on his part in the plan, got behind the wheel and did a one-eighty, pulling into the driveway of their dad's deserted house.

Then Ryan turned off the headlights and got out of the car. As dark as it was, the Lexus would be practically invisible.

"Stay put," Scott told Grant when the older man made a move to get out, too. "I want to talk to you."

"This is kidnapping, Buchanan." Grant's voice wavered between outrage and fear. Scott wished for the advantage of light — it would help if he could read what was going on in Grant's eyes — but light would draw attention, so he was going to have to do without it.

"Where's Lisa?" Scott's voice was very quiet. Deadly quiet.

"What? Do you think I know?"

Clenching his teeth, trying to control his impulse to slam his fist into Grant's mouth before repeating the question, Scott looked at him steadily. The moon was high enough now so that it cast sufficient light to allow him to see, if not the nuances of Grant's expression, at least the broad strokes. The man was looking at him as if he was a live grenade.

God, Lisa's been missing for more than two hours; please let her be alive. Let her be safe.

The thought filled him with a cold rage that it was all he could do to keep under control.

"Before we go any further with this, let me tell you what I know. I know your daughter was born with a potentially fatal kidney disease. I know the skeleton of a baby has been recovered that was buried under a fountain in Grayson Springs's backyard. I got some medical records a couple of days ago pertaining to a woman named Angela Garcia" — Grant started, and Scott gave him a wolfish smile — "yeah,

I can see you've heard of her. I know from those records that she was a little over eight months pregnant when she and her family disappeared. I know you were making regular payments over a period of some five years prior to her disappearance to Angela Garcia through a dummy corporation. Just so we're clear, I've got copies of the checks with your signature on them. I know the family moved here just a few months before they disappeared, and I know the husband was bragging to a few people that he was getting ready to come into a large sum of money." He paused to look hard at Grant and was satisfied with what he saw. The man had shrunk back against the door. His eyes were wide and scared, and unless Scott's nose was misleading him, he was sweating like a pig. "Now let me tell you what I can prove if I have to. The baby buried under that fountain had ARPKD. So did yours and Miss Martha's newborn daughter. Lisa doesn't have, and never has had, ARPKD. She's your daughter, all right, but not with Miss Martha. She's your daughter with Angela Garcia."

He broke off as Grant started to make gasping noises. He looked as though he'd seen a ghost.

"You fathered Angela's older daughter,

too, didn't you? You bought that older girl a doll for her fifth birthday right before she disappeared. Oh, yes, I can prove that, too, if you make me. As you know, Lisa has the doll, and the company kept the names of the purchasers of all the My Best Friend dolls sold." As Grant's hand rose to cover his mouth Scott pressed on relentlessly. "You were having an affair with Angela all those years you were in Washington, right under the noses of your wife and her husband. You even had a relationship of sorts with the older girl, Marisa. What, did she know you as uncle something? Those checks you wrote Angela were for child support, weren't they? And then she got pregnant again. This time the husband found out what was up. This time you two got caught. He was pissed, wasn't he? He wanted big money to keep his mouth shut, didn't he? When you didn't cough up big enough or fast enough, he moved his family here, practically right next door to your rich wife with her rich daddy who was funding your political career, and threatened to tell all. And you had a problem, because you knew that no matter what you did, no matter how much you paid, you weren't going to be able to keep the husband quiet forever. So, you dealt with it. You either killed them or hired somebody to do it. All except for your little baby, who was in your girlfriend's womb when the murders went down. Somehow she was born. Somehow she was spared. That baby is Lisa. For whatever reason, you switched your wife's dying child for Lisa. And now you're afraid it's all going to come out, that you're looking at multiple charges of murder one that will put you in prison for the rest of your life, if you don't get the death penalty, and you decided to get rid of the one absolutely irrefutable piece of evidence of the crimes you committed: Lisa."

"No, no, no!" Grant's hand had fallen away from his mouth, and his breathing was so loud and harsh that it sounded as though he was dying. Scott didn't give a shit, as long as he told him where Lisa was first. "You've got it all wrong! I —"

"Shut the fuck up," he growled, lunging toward Grant and pinning him to the door with one hand around his neck while Grant flapped and fussed like a chicken whose neck was about to be wrung. Smiling grimly, he positioned the gun maybe six inches from Grant's forehead, and the man went still. "You're going to tell me where Lisa is."

"I don't have her! I wouldn't hurt my own daughter!" Grant wheezed with panic. His eyes were practically starting from his head. "What do you take me for?"

"Here's the deal," Scott said, speaking through his teeth as he tried not to panic in the face of Grant's continued denials and the amount of time that was passing. "If you tell me where Lisa is, if I get her back alive and in one piece, I'll forget I know any of this. The Garcia thing is in the past. As far as I'm concerned, you can work it out with God or whoever. But I want Lisa. So, I'm going to ask you one last time: Where the hell is she?"

That last was a muted roar.

"I don't know. I swear to you, I don't know." Scott's hand tightened around his neck and he must have looked as murderous as he felt because Grant held up both hands in surrender even as he choked and coughed and squirmed. "Jesus, Buchanan, listen to me a minute. I tell you you've got it wrong!"

"How?" Fixing him with a murderous glare, Scott eased his hold on Grant's neck enough so that the man could talk easily. "You've got about one minute to convince me."

Grant took a great, rasping breath.

"All right. All right. I admit, Lisa is my daughter with Angie Garcia. You're right about that. I know it's true, although I don't have any proof other than the way she looks. I did have an affair with her mother. Her other daughter — Marisa — was my daughter, too. And you're right that that violent animal of a husband of Angie's found out and threatened us. Me. He was going to kill her and expose me if I didn't pay him a million dollars to keep quiet. But I didn't have a million dollars. All the money I had came from Martha's family. I told him that, and the bastard moved the family down here practically right next door to my wife's and told me he was going to go to her father for the money if I didn't pay up. But I never did anything to any of them. My God, I loved Angie, and Marisa, my little girl, and even her boy, Tony. I never knew what happened to them." The sudden anguish in Grant's eyes made Scott's eyes narrow. "I never knew. They just disappeared. But then, as Lisa started to grow up, I noticed how much she looked like Angie, and I began to suspect."

He broke off, licking his lips. Blood pounded in Scott's temples as he faced the terrifying realization that he might indeed have gotten this wrong. Jesus God, if he was wrong, where did he go next? Where was Lisa? Breathing hard, he let his hand drop from around Grant's neck, and lowered the gun.

"You began to suspect what?" Scott's voicc was hoarse.

"It was the old man. Martha's father. He did something to them. He and that damned Frye."

She was alive. Hurt and sick and scared to death but alive. She'd fallen a long way, maybe twenty feet, but because she'd landed in water, the fall hadn't killed her. She'd been dropped into a well, she thought, an old, abandoned well with standing water in the bottom. It was capped, which meant that down where she was, way at the bottom of the shaft, it was absolutely pitch-black. She wouldn't have been able to see her hand in front of her face even if she'd managed to free her wrists from the duct tape and hold one up there. There was no sound, cither, except for the sounds created by her movements: sloshing water, squelching mud. The smell of mold and stagnant water was strong. The fall, plus the sounds, plus her sense of touch and smell, had given her a general picture of where she was. The well had curving walls that, from the feel of them, were made of brick. Slimy brick. She had to lean against the wall to keep her balance because, bound as she was, staying on her feet was difficult. Everything she could feel above the waterline was covered with slime. The water was armpit-deep and cool but not cold, with a thick layer of leaves and mud and who knew what else at the bottom that her bare feet kept sinking into. She'd plunged beneath the surface when she'd landed, and for a minute or so, bound as she was, she had feared she might drown. Without the use of her hands, she'd writhed and fought to get to the surface as terrible flashbacks of the car accident had spun through her mind. Then her feet had touched bottom, and in a spasm of blinding terror she'd launched herself upward. And then she had discovered that the water was shallow enough so that she could stand upright in it and breathe.

At first, that discovery had seemed like cause for elation.

But gradually it had borne in on her that the only way she was going to survive was if she could continue standing upright. If she could not, if her legs grew tired and gave out, if exhaustion overwhelmed her and she had to sleep, she would sink down into the water and drown.

And then as more time passed, minutes stretching into hours stretching into what felt like eternity, and she got cold and her muscles weakened and her breathing grew more and more labored, it wasn't so much if she was going to sink down into the water and drown. It was when.

Frye wouldn't talk. Not a word, not a syllable. Nothing more than a contemptuous *"You're crazy,"* even after Scott's hands closed around his neck. Hampered by the fact that Frye was in the house surrounded by people when he caught up with him, and Ryan had taken back his gun before they got inside, Scott was pulled off before he could choke or beat or do whatever he had to do to get the truth out of him, which was what he fully intended to do. Held by two deputies, he could only watch as Watson, having been told the whole story but still threatening to arrest Scott, too, if he didn't back off, had Frye carted off to jail.

"He knows where Lisa is. You've got to let me get it out of him," Scott pleaded, practically on his knees.

Watson was obdurate: There would be no abuse of suspects on his watch. But Frye's demeanor convinced Scott that what Grant had long suspected was the truth: Frye and Martha's father were responsible for the disappearance of the Garcias. And Frye alone was responsible for whatever had happened to Lisa.

Which left Scott more terrified than he had ever been in his life. He was bleeding inside, shaking inside, a basket case, as he realized that Frye was going to be given refuge in the legal system and Lisa still hadn't been found.

On the verge of an explosion fueled by sheer panic, he caught himself: Giving in to emotion was the worst thing he could do.

Lisa, where are you? The thought morphed into a prayer. *Please, God, let her be found. Let her be alive.*

Then he remembered Mrs. Baker.

Lisa had no idea how long it had been: days, months, years. Her strength was fading, and in order to stay upright she had to brace her back against the wall and dig her feet down deep in the silt. The good news was that the water had eroded the duct tape's adhesive until she'd been able to get it off. Her arms and legs were free, and she could scream. She'd tried that, screaming for what felt like hours, screaming until her throat ached and her voice went and she just couldn't scream anymore. No one had come, and she suspected that if the sound could be heard beyond the shaft at all, it wouldn't carry very far.

But she wasn't going to give up. Just as soon as her throat had recovered enough she was going to start screaming again.

That, and praying, was all she could do.

She had already prayed so much that the words ran in a never-ending loop through her mind.

Dear God, please help me. Please don't let me die.

But she was afraid she was going to. She had made a grisly discovery, down there all alone in the dark. That had been when she had still been trying to find a way out. She'd been feeling around on the bottom to see if the hard things she kept bumping her toes into and stepping on might be rocks or something she could use to dig hand and footholds with in the slippery brick, maybe by prying out some of the old mortar that held them in place. What she'd found, when she had maneuvered one to the surface, was that she was holding a skull. Oh, it had taken her a few minutes to realize, because of course she couldn't see a thing. The curving shape of the head and then the unmistakable spacing of the eye sockets and nasal cavity were what had clued her in.

She had screamed and dropped the thing.

Now she knew there were at least three of

them in there with her. At least three skeletons scattered at the bottom of the well. Actually, there should be one more.

Because she was pretty sure she had found the Garcias. And she was pretty sure she knew who had dumped them in this horrible, stinking, wet hell to die.

Down there in the dark she had nothing but time, and she had used some of it to review every minute detail of what had happened to her. She took the shadowy glimpses she'd caught of the man who had brought her here, added in his height and build, which she had absorbed while being carried over his shoulder, considered the truck and the metal box that she'd been confined in, and came to a conclusion: The man who was probably going to turn out to be her murderer wasn't Barty at all. It was somebody she liked a whole lot better: Andy Frye.

Taken to the Woodford County jail and threatened with capital murder charges, Mrs. Baker crumbled. She cried and shook, wailing that she'd never meant for any harm to come to anyone. At Scott's urgent request, Janice Bernard, the no-nonsense, twenty-year veteran Woodford County DA, offered Mrs. Baker a deal: tell everything she knew, cooperate with the prosecution in every way she was asked to, and the worst she would face would be several counts of accessory after the fact. She'd probably be out of prison in less than five years.

Her court-appointed attorney advised her to take the deal. She did.

Scott, meanwhile, who had no jurisdiction in Woodford County, could only chew his nails and watch from behind the one-way mirror that formed a window on the interrogation room as this negotiation took place. A glance at his watch told him that it was already after eight a.m. — full daylight now. Lisa had been missing for more than eleven hours.

Oh, God, where was she? What were the chances that she was even still alive?

Please, God, please, God, please.

The first question Mrs. Baker was asked was: Where is Lisa Grant?

Snug in the protection of her new deal, Mrs. Baker said she didn't know.

Spewing curses, Scott tore out of the viewing room, determined to shake the truth out of the damned woman if need be. Stymied by the presence of two armed deputies ranged outside the door, he was just about to go ballistic on them when his cell phone rang.

A glance at it told him that it was Chase.

His heart skipped a beat. His nephew would be calling him at a time like this only if there was news.

"Yeah?" he barked by way of answering it.

"Hey, Scott, guess what?" The excitement in Chase's voice made Scott take a couple of steps back until he could lean against the wall. "We found her. We used Noah's metal detector. She's in a well on the Garcias' property."

It was all Scott could do not to slide down the painted concrete blocks.

"Is she alive?" His voice was hoarse.

"What, you think I'd call you if she was dead?" Chase sounded indignant. "I'd leave that for Rinko. Or Dad. Of course she's alive."

Scott closed his eyes.

34

By the time Scott got to her, Lisa had already been pulled out of the well, which was at the very edge of the woods where the kids had discovered Marisa's medal. According to Chase, they'd found the well — actually, what they'd found was its metal cap — while they'd been searching the woods that Sunday. Sometime after Lisa went missing, it had struck Rinko that since everything bad that had happened to Lisa had happened after she had started looking into the Garcia case, the answer to her disappearance might be found on their property. So he and Jantzen and the kids had started searching it at dawn, and one of them — they couldn't agree on whom — had remembered the capped well. Having decided to check it out, they couldn't locate it again amid all the undergrowth until Noah had gone home and come back with his metal detector. After that, according to them, it had been a snap.

The TV trucks were pulling up even as Scott jumped out of his Jeep at the top of the driveway. Cop cars were all over the place, blocking him from driving any closer to the place where the assembled crowd told him Lisa had to be. A forensics team van — a Fayette County forensics team van, because now they were back in his bailiwick — was parked near the woods on the far side of the house. The actual team members were probably off in the trees. He knew they were there to check out the skeletons that had been found in the well with Lisa.

Everyone was assuming they had once been the Garcias. Scott was almost a hundred percent certain they were right.

An ambulance was over there, too, next to the forensics van. It was idling with its rear doors open, and as he got closer he saw that paramedics were doing something to Lisa's left arm. Chase and his friends — God bless that kid with the metal detector — were standing around, looking proud of themselves. Rinko and Jantzen were there, too, talking to a pair of cops. Rinko, to whom he'd given a pretty good dressing-down for continuing to investigate the Garcia case against his express orders a little more than a week ago, looked slightly nervous as he watched Scott's approach. Scott barely glanced at any of them. All his attention was for Lisa. She must have heard his approach, because she looked his way. She was pale and haunted-looking, her long black hair dripping water as it trailed toward the ground. Lying barefoot on a stretcher in the torn black rag that had once been the chic dress she'd worn to her mother's funeral, soaking-wet and covered with mud, she was the most beautiful thing he had ever seen in his life.

"Hey." His throat was so tight that that was all he could manage as he reached her. *Pretty eloquent, huh?* But it was the best he could do. He took her right hand, careful to be gentle. Her fingers twined with his.

"Scott." She looked exhausted, but she smiled at him as she clung tightly to his hand. Looking down at her, he realized that that beautiful face with those big caramel-colored eyes was seared forever on his heart. Ryan's theory about him never falling in love had officially been blown to smithereens. Whether she knew it or not, he was hers for life. "I was afraid I wasn't ever going to see you again."

He nodded, not trusting himself to speak.

"It wasn't my father."

"I know."

"It was Andy."

"I know. He's in jail. It's looking like he killed the Garcias, too."

"Mr. Buchanan?" One of the paramedics wrapped a blanket around Lisa as he spoke. Scott knew him, but he sought for and failed to remember his name. Probably it would come back to him sometime. When he hadn't just been through the scare of a lifetime. "Could you stand back, please? We've got to load her up."

Lisa's hand tightened on his. Her eyes sought his and clung, a touch of panic in their depths. "Don't leave me."

Scott shook his head. "Not in this life." He looked at the paramedic. "I'm going in the ambulance with her."

The paramedic met his gaze and nodded.

After they got Lisa inside, Scott climbed in, too. He rode beside her, holding her hand all the way to the hospital.

By late that afternoon, after the hospital staff had checked her out and patched her up — she had a concussion, a badly bruised left arm, and other assorted small injuries but nothing serious enough to require her to stay overnight — they waited in the curtained-off room in the ER where she'd been treated for her to be discharged. She'd been allowed to shower, and she was dressed in a yellow T-shirt, a pair of white jeans, and some sandals, all of which Nola had brought with her when she had rushed to the hospital on getting word that Lisa had been found. There had been so many visitors after that that a nurse joked that instead of a curtain their room needed a revolving door. Even Grant had come. Scott and Lisa's father had shaken hands, all animosity from their last encounter put aside in the light of Lisa's safe recovery, but Grant hadn't been able to have a private word with his daughter because there had been too many people around. Still, Scott thought Lisa had been pleased that her father had come. Finally there'd been so many people in the room that the staff had shooed everyone out except him, and that was only because he'd made it clear that he wasn't going anywhere, and Lisa had made it clear that she didn't want him to. At the moment she was propped up in the hospital bed while he sat in a chair beside her. Scott had just gotten off the phone with Watson, who had called to tell him that the baby whose skeleton they found beneath the fountain had definitely suffered from ARPKD. It would be a few weeks before the actual DNA tests came back, but as far as Scott was concerned, that made the baby's identity definitive.

Something else he still had to tell Lisa. Tomorrow, maybe, when they weren't both half dead from exhaustion and still shaken from the previous night's trauma.

"What did he say?" Lisa was looking at him with a frown. Scott sighed. Since her mother's death, he'd been keeping a lot of things from her that he thought might add to her distress. Chief among which was the fact that Angela Garcia had been more than eight months pregnant with Grant's baby when she died, and that Lisa was, in fact, that child.

"How about we talk about it when we get home?" he asked. He had a feeling the conversation might get emotional, which could very well call for more privacy than a curtained-off cubicle in a busy hospital ER afforded.

She seemed to get that he didn't feel this was the place to talk about it, because instead of arguing she nodded agreement. Then she smiled at him a little wryly. "Speaking of home, I guess I better start to think about getting my own place."

He looked at her for a moment without saying anything.

"What?" she asked, wrinkling her brow at him.

"You're welcome to stay with me for as

long as you want." The next bit was the part that bothered him, but he'd be damned if he would let it show. Just to make sure it didn't, he kept his tone carefully casual. "It would be kind of a waste to rent something if you're thinking about moving back to Boston anytime soon."

It was what she had always meant to do after her mother died, he knew.

"I'm not sure about moving back to Boston now." She looked at him steadily. "What I do next kind of depends."

His pulse started pumping a little faster. He knew his girl inside and out, and that was a statement designed to lead to a question with an answer he could see coming a mile away.

He asked the question. "On what?"

She smiled at him, a heart-stoppingly beautiful smile that blinded him to everything except her.

"You."

There it was, the answer he'd been expecting. Was that a lead-in or what? Or maybe it wasn't meant as such, and he was about to get burned. Whatever, he was going for it. All or nothing, that was how he felt about her. How he had always felt about her.

"You could stay here," he said. "And marry me."

She looked at him with widening eyes. "You're proposing."

"Yep."

"I don't believe it."

He stood up, suddenly restless under her fascinated regard. "Is that an answer?"

"No."

His eyes narrowed at her.

"No, it isn't an answer," she clarified. Then she grinned at him, his own beautiful Lisa with a lifetime's worth of mischief in her eyes. "My *answer* is yes."

Scott took a deep breath. Then he stood up and took the two steps required to bring him to her bedside. She was already reaching out for him when he got there, and the gentle, tender kiss he'd meant to give her was turning into something a whole lot hotter when the curtain behind them slid back with a rattle.

Giving him a disapproving look, the nurse who'd been taking care of Lisa all day walked into the room. "Here are your discharge papers, Ms. Grant."

Later, when they got back home, he did it up right: went down on one knee, told her that he loved her more than anybody or anything in his life. He said all the mushy stuff he never thought in a million years he'd ever say, and he meant every word of it.

Then he kissed her and took her to bed. Where, too exhausted to make love, they immediately fell asleep.

They made love the next morning. And after that, while they were still in bed and she was still curled up warm and soft in his arms, Scott bit the bullet and told her the truth about her parentage.

"That means — my mother isn't my real mother. All those years — all my life — she loved me so much. And I loved her. And all of it — everything, my whole life — it was all a lie."

There was so much heartbreak in her voice that Scott felt her pain like a knife to his chest. Then he realized: From then on, for the rest of his life, whatever hurt Lisa was going to hurt him more.

A love like that was a scary thing. But he was in it now, head over heels, so all that was left to do was deal.

He gathered her close and plunged in. "The love wasn't a lie. She loved you more than anything in her life. You were her shining star, her reason for getting up in the morning. And you loved her like any devoted daughter loves her mother. That makes her your real mother, and you her real daughter. That bond is as enduring as it gets."

Then he kissed her. And made love to her. And after that, just to make sure she got the message, he made love to her again.

35

By that afternoon, Lisa was feeling recovered enough to drive out to the Woodford County jail and watch through a big one-way mirror as the county DA, a dynamic, sixtyish woman with chin-length gray hair and a nice taste in pastel suits named Janice Bernard, along with Detective Watson, interviewed Robin. Yesterday's interview had been postponed, Detective Watson said, after she'd been found and the bodies had been discovered. Scott was with her, of course. The way she was feeling right now, they were joined at the hip for the rest of their lives. She was crazy in love with him; he'd proposed marriage; he was hers. Her amazing lover, her soon-to-be husband, her family now. He was showing no propensity to let her out of his sight, either. Probably it was going to take them both a little while to recover from the trauma of the night she had disappeared. But tomorrow, Scott had told her mock-sternly, life started getting back to normal. To begin with, they both had to go back to work.

Which was fine with her. She was suddenly craving normal. And normal with Scott? That could be fun. Things were never going to be the same. Her mother — yes, her mother, no matter what the biology was, which, as Scott had pointed out, didn't make one iota of difference to love, anyway — was gone. Many changes were coming. But normal life — the new normal life — was looking bright.

Barty was there with them in the viewing room. He'd asked to be present, not so much for his concern over what had happened to her and her mother as because of his connection to the Garcias, Lisa suspected, and because of his position, they'd bent over backward to accommodate him. Lisa still had mixed emotions about her father. It was good to know that he wasn't a murderer, but that still left him with much — her whole life, in fact — to atone for.

Looking through the glass, Lisa saw Robin seated in the small, beige, windowless room on one side of a long conference table with the prosecutor and Detective Watson sitting opposite her, and felt sick. Her mother had loved this woman and trusted her.

Lisa had, too.

Ms. Bernard started off. "All right, Mrs. Baker, the first thing I want to do is tell you that we have proof, by means of certain items found with the remains, including a set of military dog tags with Andrew Frye's name on them, that your brother was the shooter in the Garcia family murder. I have no doubt that the DNA evidence that was recovered, when it comes back from the lab, will provide further confirmation. What this means is that we no longer need your testimony to get a conviction, which makes your position precarious. If you lie to us, if you are caught in a lie, that will be grounds to withdraw the very lenient plea agreement which we entered into with you in an attempt to locate Lisa Grant. In fact, I've been informed that you've already lied to us in that, when you were asked where Ms. Grant had been taken, you claimed you did not know. Suppose you explain that."

Robin looked frightened. "I — I didn't know. Not for sure. Andy put her in his truck, in his gun box in the back. And I got in the cab with him, and he dropped me off at the grocery store because we knew we had to go back to the house, knew there'd be this big to-do when that Buchanan boy discovered she was gone, and Andy thought that if we came back with groceries that would give us an alibi. He thought that would be enough."

"Come on, you may not have known for sure, but you had a pretty good idea where he was taking her. You knew he was going to kill her. Of course he was going to put her in the place where the Garcias' bodies had stayed so well hidden all these years." Detective Watson's gaze was blistering. Lisa, watching through the glass, had never thought she was going to like the man, but she was starting to.

Robin's hands, square and blunt-fingered and oh, so familiar, rested palms down on the wooden table. They came together as she suddenly clasped them in front of her. She looked at Ms. Bernard. "We never wanted to kill her. Not Lisa. This is all just one big mess! If Lisa hadn't come back home, if she hadn't started working for that damned boy in that damned office, if she hadn't found that picture and started nosing into what happened to those people, everything would have gone along just like it was doing, just fine. I thought Andy was going to die when she came home one day and started asking about those Garcias. Then I saw that file from where they disappeared in her bedroom, and I told him, and we knew we had to do something to get rid of it and get her mind on something else. If we just took the file, that would just make her more interested in it, we thought, because she'd wonder why someone had taken it. Anyway, there was only us and Lynn in the house, so it would have been obvious it was us, wouldn't it? So Andy started a little fire, just a little fire right down the hallway from Lisa's bedroom. We thought that in all the confusion, what with fire trucks coming and everything, she probably wouldn't miss it later, and if she did she would probably think that it got thrown out in the cleanup or something, because we were going to get in there and grab it as soon as she ran out."

"So, Andrew Frye — Andy — set the fire." Ms. Bernard's expression was impassive. Unlike Detective Watson, whom Lisa was beginning to realize showed everything he was thinking on his face, she was hard to read.

"Yes. But we didn't mean to hurt Lisa, or Miss Martha, or anybody else. We just wanted to get that file away from her. Only Andy forgot about Miss Martha's spare oxygen tanks, which were stored in her old bedroom right up there by Lisa's. That's what did it. The fire got to them and the whole place just went up. That we never expected."

Lisa remembered the fire and shuddered. If it hadn't been for Scott, she might have died that night. He was standing beside her, between her and Barty, acting as kind of a buffer. He must have felt her shudder, because he put an arm around her. She leaned against his side.

"You didn't mean to hurt anybody." That was Detective Watson, his voice heavy with sarcasm. Ms. Bernard shot him a quelling look.

"No! We never did! Andy never did. But Lisa wouldn't leave it alone. It was because she looked so much like them. If we'd realized she was going to look like that, we never would've . . . well. Anyway, after the fire we really started getting scared. Those dog tags you were talking about. Andy always wore them around his neck, from the time he got out of the service, and he knew he had lost them. He thought the chain had broken in the kitchen of that house the Garcias were renting, that night — well, that night. He knew if the dog tags were found, people would start looking at him. He'd searched for them before, but everything had died down over the years so he'd almost forgotten about them. But when

Lisa started stirring things up, he went back to look one more time. He started thinking they might have fallen down the heating vent or something. He was in the house when there she was, poking around outside. When she started to come in, he couldn't let her see him, so he had to do what he did. But he hated to do it, and he wouldn't have done it if she'd just let things alone. Which she never did do."

"So, it was all her fault." Detective Watson had at least succeeded in tamping down on the sarcasm. Still, Ms. Bernard shot him another of those warning glances.

"It was! It really was. You'd think, after Andy had to hit her over the head, she would have left it alone. But she didn't. Lisa's like that, you know. Real stubborn when she sets her mind to something. Miss Martha was always saying she didn't know where that had come from."

On Scott's other side, Barty made a restive movement. Lisa wondered, then, if Angela Garcia — impossible to think of her as her mother — had been stubborn. Of course Barty had known her well. Been in love with her, even. Lisa found she didn't much like the idea of that. Her loyalty to her mother was still strong.

"So, from there Andy decided to kill Mrs.

Martha Grant by staging the car accident in which she drowned." Ms. Bernard's voice was as calm as if she was discussing what to have for lunch. Her hands clenching around the smooth wooden bar that kept them a few inches back from the glass, Lisa began to shiver. Scott, shooting her a concerned look, tightened his arm around her.

"You don't have to listen to this, you know," he said in her ear. "You can wait outside."

Lisa shook her head. "I'm staying." Then she gritted her teeth, willed the tremors racking her to stop, and turned her attention back to the room on the other side of the glass.

". . . never meant for Miss Martha to die!" Robin was leaning forward earnestly, talking to Ms. Bernard. "Andy didn't even know she was in the car. 'What was she doing in there?' was what he asked afterwards. She never rode in Lisa's car; it was too hard getting her in and out. And Andy was there in his truck across the street from the hospital parking lot when Lisa left, so you'd think he would have seen. But he didn't. It was just that he had to stay way back, out of the way, because that Buchanan boy" — Robin said that with real venom this time — "had somebody following Lisa, keeping an eye on her, sometimes. Andy had been following her real close, just to see if he couldn't get a chance to maybe cause her to have a little fender bender, or do something else to scare her, just to give her thoughts another direction, you know, than those Garcias, until he figured out that somebody else was following her, too, then figured out who. But that night, Andy saw nobody was following her and he saw the chance to make her wreck her car. He wasn't really trying to kill her. He thought she'd survive, maybe have to go to the hospital. But maybe she'd be thinking about something besides those people, after that."

Lisa realized that she had never really felt anger before. Real anger was a hot, primitive tide that made you want to kill. She felt it now, looking at Robin, thinking of how scared her mother had been that night, of how she had died. She let out her breath in a little hiss, and felt Scott look at her with concern. But she kept her attention on Robin.

"But Mrs. Grant did die." Ms. Bernard stated it baldly, as the stark fact that it was, and Lisa barely managed not to flinch. The hard truth was that nothing could change what had happened. "Is that when Andy made up his mind to kill Lisa?"

Robin shook her head. "After Miss Martha died, we thought — Andy thought — Lisa would be so upset she'd forget all about those Garcias. And she might have, too. But then they found the baby. The baby's bones."

Robin abruptly hung her head. Lisa leaned a little forward, suddenly intent.

"Why did that make a difference?" Ms. Bernard was doing all the questioning now, and Lisa wondered if maybe she'd kicked Detective Watson under the table or something.

"Andy knew they'd do one of those DNA test things on that baby's bones. He knew it would show that she was Miss Martha's and Mr. Bart's baby. Then they'd look at Lisa. Probably take her DNA. If they did, that would be the connection to the Garcias, don't you see? There wasn't ever any connection between us and the Garcias, none nobody ever looked for, no reason to, but there would be with Lisa. And then when they found that, the whole thing would start to unravel, and they would know what we did. Andy and I were inside the house, watching while they were bringing out that baby from underneath the fountain, and we knew sooner or later we were going to be cooked. And then Lisa came in the house, looking for me." Robin licked her lips and unclasped her hands, spreading them wide. "We didn't want to hurt her, Andy didn't want to hurt her, but getting her out of the way was the only thing we could think of to do."

Lisa was glad for Scott's solid presence at her side. She leaned against him and held on to the rail, and breathed very consciously in and out, as she watched this woman she had considered almost as an aunt talk so casually about deciding to kill her.

"You never wanted to hurt anybody, did you?" The sarcasm was back in Detective Watson's voice. "I bet you didn't want to hurt that little baby we found under the fountain, either. But one of you suffocated her."

Robin gasped. Her lips trembled. The color drained out of her face. Folding her arms over her chest, she hunched her shoulders and seemed almost to shrink.

"We have evidence the baby was suffocated, Mrs. Baker." In contrast to Detective Watson's, Ms. Bernard's voice was almost gentle.

"It wasn't me. Andy did it. Old Mr. Carmody — Miss Martha's father — told him to do it, but Andy did it. I didn't even know. I wouldn't have agreed to that. She was so sick, but she was the sweetest little baby. Miss Martha loved her so. I did, too. We took care of her, Miss Martha and I. The doctors all said she was going to die. But we didn't think so. Miss Martha prayed and prayed and prayed over her. And we thought she was getting better. Then, that night, that night all these terrible things happened, it was maybe one in the morning and Miss Martha had gone to lie down in her bed for a little bit. I — I had come back in, all shaken up, you know, and I was rocking that little baby in my arms, just rocking her so we could both feel better. She was a little bitty thing, wouldn't hardly eat, but I'd gotten her to go to sleep by rocking her, and then Mr. Carmody came in and took her. Just took her away from me. And I didn't know a thing that was happening until Andy came back carrying the baby, all wrapped in the blanket she'd been wrapped in when Mr. Carmody took her, all dressed in the same clothes, but not the same baby. I knew she was not the same baby. I knew what baby she was, because I'd watched her being born in the kitchen of that cursed house just a few hours before. Then Andy told me what they'd done, what Mr. Carmody had told him to do. He'd told him to smother my little baby, because the doctors had said she was going to die anyway, and if her baby died it would kill Miss Martha. So Mr. Carmody was going to save his daughter, save Miss Martha, whom he loved like nothing you've ever seen, by giving her a healthy baby who would live to grow up. He was going to give her that Garcia woman's baby. There wasn't anything I could do."

Detective Watson made a sound, but something — Lisa suspected something Ms. Bernard had done, such as kick him under the table — stopped him. Instead, Ms. Bernard spoke, her voice still very gentle.

"Mrs. Grant — Miss Martha — didn't realize that it was a different baby?"

Robin shook her head. "Mr. Carmody, he made sure of that. He went and got Miss Martha up out of her bed that very night and took her off to a sanitarium — I guess you'd call it a psychiatric hospital now — and told them she was having a nervous breakdown because of her baby's health. He had a lot of money and a lot of influence, Mr. Carmody, and he knew a lot of people. They kept her for a month, and by the time she got back we'd all settled down and the baby — the new baby — was thriving, and Miss Martha never noticed any difference. She only knew that her baby was well and she was so happy. You couldn't help but be happy for her, happy it had worked out so that she didn't lose her baby. After a while, we all, Andy and I, and Mr. Carmody, just kind of forgot what had happened. Just moved on, you know."

Just moved on. The words echoed through Lisa's mind. Just moved on, after having murdered an entire family and a helpless infant and wrenched her out of the life she had been born into and given her someone else's life.

She couldn't bear to think about it too much. If she did, it seemed as though she could feel the earth starting to shake under her feet. Everything she knew seemed to shimmy and shift. She must have made some kind of movement or sound that was indicative of distress, because Scott's arm tightened around her.

"You okay?" he whispered.

She nodded, grateful for his strength. He was the rock she would lean on until she got her equilibrium back, the lifeline to which she would cling with both hands until the storm eased.

"I love you." It was the merest breath in her ear, but she heard it and nodded. Then she rested her head on his shoulder, knowing that he knew that she loved him back.

"Okay, Mrs. Baker, let's move on to the

night the Garcia family died. You want to tell us what happened?" Detective Watson was looking at Robin without any sympathy whatsoever.

Robin sighed. Her arms dropped so that her hands were once again resting palm down on the table. She looked at him, then at Ms. Bernard, who gave her a small, encouraging smile.

"I wasn't there, you know. At least, not at first. Not at their house. Where I was was at Grayson Springs. Miss Martha was with the baby, and I was down in the kitchen fixing supper, because it was suppertime and everybody has to eat, no matter what happens. This man came banging on the back door. I opened it. Wasn't any reason not to, far as I knew then. He said he was Michael Garcia and he'd come to see Mr. Carmody about a matter that had to do with his daughter. He was real loud, real rude. Well, Mr. Carmody must've heard him, because he came into the kitchen. He seemed to know who he was, and he took him back outside to talk. We were being real careful not to let anything disturb Miss Martha in those days, because she was so sick about her baby. Andy told me later that Mr. Carmody did know who he was, that he'd had a private detective checking into Mr. Grant because he thought he was being unfaithful to Miss Martha while they were up there in Washington, and he'd found this guy and his family, and knew all about the bad things Mr. Grant was doing, about the second family that he had. Mr. Carmody hadn't said a word because he didn't want Miss Martha to know, but he knew everything, knew about Mr. Grant's girlfriend moving her family right down here near us, knew the whole thing. Andy knew, too, because Mr. Carmody had sent Andy over to kind of check them out and report back. Andy had been there several times. He told me he always hid in the woods there by the house, and they were so thick and overgrown nobody ever knew he was there." She paused to take a breath, and Detective Watson made an impatient gesture.

"So, what happened after Mr. Garcia and Mr. Carmody went outside?"

"A few minutes later Mr. Carmody came back in. Only he was white, and he looked real mad. He didn't say anything, just went on back to whatever he was doing, but a few minutes later Andy came in. He said Mr. Carmody wanted to see him. A few minutes later Andy and Mr. Carmody left together. Andy had this look on his face — he's my brother, I know that look, and every time I've ever seen it, Andy's getting ready to get himself in trouble. I didn't like to ask him anything in front of Mr. Carmody, but then I was looking out the kitchen window and I saw Andy putting his rifle in his truck before he got in and drove off after Mr. Carmody, who was in his Mercedes. That's when I decided to follow them. By the time I got there, Mr. Carmody's car wasn't anywhere in sight, and neither was he, but Andy's truck was there, parked right up behind the house, so anybody passing wouldn't be able to see it from the road. The back door was open, so I went inside. There were already three people shot in that house. That Michael Garcia was lying right by the door, and a woman was lying in the hall. She wasn't dead, but she was bleeding real bad, blood coming out everywhere, and that's when I realized she was pregnant and having a baby right there and then. She could talk. She said, 'My babies,' and kind of jerked her hand toward the next room. I went in there, and I saw a boy. Just a little boy, and he'd been shot, and he was dead. The door was standing open, so I went outside and I saw a flashlight moving around over in the woods, and then Andy came out of the woods. I said, 'What have you done?' That kind of thing, and he told me he'd only done what Mr. Carmody told him to do. Then he said I had to help him, that the little girl had run out of the house and was hiding in the woods. He was supposed to find her and kill her, too."

Lisa heard a sharp in-drawing of breath, and realized that it was Barty. Glancing past Scott, she saw that he was pale. Of course, that little girl, that woman, they would have been his family, too.

"So, did you find the little girl?" Ms. Bernard asked the question.

Robin nodded. "We did. She was all huddled down under a bush. We might not have found her, but she had a dog with her, a big black dog, and when we got close the dog started barking, and so we found her. When Andy turned his flashlight on her, she had her arms wrapped tight around this doll, and she wouldn't open her eyes and look at us for nothing."

Barty made a choked sound and grabbed hold of the rail. Scott leaned over to say something to him. Barty shook his head, which Lisa took to mean he was all right.

"So, Andy killed her." That was Detective Watson, his voice flat and hard.

Robin shook her head. "No, he did not. I wouldn't let him. I couldn't do nothing about what had already been done, but I wasn't letting him kill a helpless little girl. I would have stopped the other if I could."

"He didn't kill the little girl?" Ms. Bernard gave her a surprised look. "Then what happened to her?"

"I made him take her out of there, her and her doll and that dog, because we didn't want to leave anything that might give what Andy had done away. It was just a plain old black dog, the only thing that might identify it was that it was wearing a blue collar that had its name, which was Lucy, and an address, which was up in Maryland someplace, on it. We took the collar off, and we kept that dog at Grayson Springs for many a year after that, and not even Mr. Carmody knew it was the same dog."

"What happened to the little girl?" Detective Watson's voice was sharp.

Robin looked at him. "I made Andy take her up to our sister Judy in Montana. We changed her clothes, cut her hair, made her leave her doll behind because we were afraid somebody might be able to trace it. Lisa found it down in the basement one day, when she was about three or four, and since Miss Martha was with her there wasn't much I could do but let her have it. So much time had passed by then I didn't see what harm a doll could do. Anyway, Judy and her husband couldn't ever have kids, and she wanted one so much. I told Judy that her dad had killed her mom and himself and there was no other family and it was a terrible mess, but she could have the little girl if she would keep her mouth shut about where she came from. I told her nobody else wanted her, and down here they'd put her in a home if she didn't take her. Judy was just as excited as could be."

Barty was clinging to the rail, leaning toward the glass, biting his lip. Lisa watched as Scott put a comforting hand on his shoulder.

"Are you saying Marisa Garcia is alive?" It was Ms. Bernard who was sounding sharp now.

Robin nodded. "She's living up in Montana still. She's a nurse. She's Mary Frye now."

Everything seemed to stop as they all, Ms. Bernard and Detective Watson in the interrogation room, Lisa and Scott and Barty behind the glass, stared at Robin.

Robin continued, "So I took the little girl away with me and left Andy to clean up the mess. He told me later when he got back in the house the woman had died but her baby had been born and was alive. He'd had some paramedic training in the military, so he knew how to take care of it, and that's what he did. After he got finished getting rid of the bodies, he brought it to Mr. Carmody." She took a deep breath. "And that's what happened."

36

A little more than two weeks later, on a bright, sunny Saturday afternoon, Lisa stood just past the security checkpoint in Lexington's small airport, waiting for her sister to deplane. The very fact that she had a sister was something she didn't fully have her mind wrapped around yet, but it was true, and she was looking forward to seeing what could be made of the relationship. Scott was with her, and so was Barty. Unlike herself and Scott, who were casually dressed, Barty was in full judge mode, wearing an expensive suit and tie that were clearly designed to impress. He was nervous, Lisa could tell, and excited, too.

She and Barty were on better terms than they had been for years. They'd talked, last Sunday afternoon in Scott's apartment when Barty had stopped by, and he had apologized for practically disappearing from her life. Now that she knew the truth, he said, he was finally free to explain.

"I was devastated when Angie and the children disappeared like that, but I didn't know what to do. At first I thought — hoped — that somehow she'd persuaded that thug husband of hers to just move them somewhere else, somewhere away from Martha and her family. For a long time I kept expecting Angie to get in touch. When she didn't, I . . . I, well, I just decided to leave it alone, for everyone's sake. No, for my own sake. That's the truth. I was trying to stick it out with Martha — we weren't compatible at all, and if I'm being honest, which I'm trying to be, I had really just married her for her money and her family's connections, anyway. But then you started to grow up, you were a little girl and not a baby anymore, and you started to look just like Angie. Just like Marisa. At first I couldn't believe it. But as the resemblance grew more marked, I knew there wasn't any way it was just coincidence, and I knew who you had to be. It scared me to death. I didn't know what had happened, not for sure, but I suspected Mr. Carmody had a hand in it. He was a ruthless old bastard, if you'll forgive my French. I was scared, and I wanted to get away from him and Grayson Springs and everything and everybody associated with it, and that meant getting away from you. I should have told somebody, I know, should have gone to the authorities with what I suspected, but if I had, I would have ruined myself, too. So, I just kept quiet, and went away, and made a new life." They were sitting on the couch, and he took her hand, and she didn't pull it away. It felt as though they were in some way the sole survivors of a terrible accident. For better or worse, they were connected for life now. "That makes me a coward, doesn't it? I apologize, Lisa. I see now how unfair it was to you."

"I forgive you," she said, and she did. They even hugged, a little awkwardly, but hey, they were trying. Some rifts take a while to fully mend.

After that Scott had come out of his office, where he'd gone ostensibly to get some work done but really to afford them some privacy, and talk had turned to their upcoming wedding.

And Lisa had surprised herself by asking her father to give her away.

So, now they stood there together, father and daughter, waiting anxiously for their last remaining family member to arrive.

Then all of a sudden she was in view, walking toward them, smiling and beautiful.

Lisa clutched Scott's arm. There was no mistaking who she was: The resemblance to Angela Garcia and herself was too marked.

The first thing Lisa noticed about Marisa as she drew near was that she had the most gorgeous bright blue eyes.

ABOUT THE AUTHOR

Karen Robards is the author of thirty-five novels, most recently the *New York Times* bestseller *Pursuit.* She lives in Louisville, Kentucky.

The employees of Thorndike Press hope you have enjoyed this Large Print book. All our Thorndike, Wheeler, and Kennebec Large Print titles are designed for easy reading, and all our books are made to last. Other Thorndike Press Large Print books are available at your library, through selected bookstores, or directly from us.

For information about titles, please call:
(800) 223-1244

or visit our Web site at:
http://gale.cengage.com/thorndike

To share your comments, please write:
Publisher
Thorndike Press
295 Kennedy Memorial Drive
Waterville, ME 04901